THE
RING

THE ✠
RING

THE LAST KNIGHT TEMPLAR'S INHERITANCE

JORGE MOLIST

ATRIA BOOKS

NEW YORK LONDON TORONTO SYDNEY

ATRIA BOOKS

A Division of Simon & Schuster, Inc.
1230 Avenue of the Americas
New York, NY 10020

First Atria Books trade paperback edition May 2008

ATRIA BOOKS and colophon are trademarks
of Simon & Schuster, Inc.

For information about special discounts for bulk
purchases, please contact Simon & Schuster Special Sales
at 1-800-456-6798 or business@simonandschuster.com.

Designed by Suet Y. Chong

Manufactured in the United States of America

10 9 8 7 6 5 4 3 2 1

Library of Congress Cataloging-in-Publication Data
Molist, Jorge.
   [*Anillo*. English]
   The ring : the last knight templar's inheritance/by Jorge Molist.
      p. cm.
   I. Title.
PQ6663.O39A6513 2007
863'.7—dc22   2007025063

ISBN-13: 978-0-7432-9751-6
ISBN-10:   0-7432-9751-2

To Jordi, David, and Gloria
In memoriam Enric Caum

Hidden in his papal ring, there lives a demon.

—Accusation against Pope Boniface VIII
made by Philip IV of France, the executioner of the Templars

CHAPTER 1

It's not often that a woman receives two engagement rings in one day. That's what made my twenty-seventh birthday so special.

The first ring was a stunning diamond solitaire from Mike, the man I'd been going out with for over a year. A real coup.

Mike's the perfect guy, the kind every girl dreams of. Or at least should be dreaming of, and if she's not, her mom definitely is. Any mother would be thrilled to marry her daughter off to someone like Mike. He's not just a stockbroker, but also the son of the company's owner, with a future beyond promising. You could say that he was born with a silver bond in his mouth.

The other ring was a surprise. It also demanded a commitment from me, but it had nothing to do with wedding vows. Or did it? That second ring would engage me not to a man, but to an adventure, an unusual adventure.

Of course, when it arrived I didn't know that. I didn't even have a clue as to who could have sent it to me. And if someone had told me who it was, I wouldn't have believed it. The second engagement ring was a gift from a dead man.

* * *

Neither did I know at the time that the two rings, or I should say, the two commitments, were incompatible. But I kept them both and started getting used to the idea of a wedding and changing my last name to Harding, although I was very intrigued by the other strange ring. I'm a very curious person, so mysteries really get to me. But I suppose I should just tell you how it all happened . . .

The party was in full swing when there was a knock on the door. My friend Jennifer, in her long dress with its plunging neckline, and Susan, in tight, low-slung pants, had started to dance, flirting with the men. The guys, some of whom already had a few drinks under their belts, followed them with their eyes. Those girls really loved to tease! Then a couple of clowns joined them, drinks in hand, and that got the dancing started all around.

I didn't mind that those two booty-shaking women were making the guys drool. I was an engaged woman and Mike, my gorgeous fiancé, held me by the waist. We kissed. We laughed. We sipped our drinks. I was flashing on my hand an awesome engagement ring with a hefty multicarat diamond. Mike had given it to me a few hours earlier, in the elegant French restaurant, near my apartment on the east side of Manhattan, where he had taken me out to lunch for my birthday.

"Let me choose the dessert today," he'd said.

The waiter brought me a magnificent chocolate soufflé. I'm crazy about chocolate, so I dove in, but after the third or fourth mouthful, my spoon hit something hard.

"Life is like a chocolate soufflé," Mike said in his best Tom Hanks-as-Forrest Gump imitation. "You never know what you'll find inside." I think he was trying to warn me. The way I was wolfing down the soufflé I might have swallowed whatever was in there.

As I pushed aside the soufflé, I got a glimpse of a sparkle inside the luscious dark chocolate. I'd been expecting that one of these days my stock-market genius would present me with a small fortune in the form of a diamond ring, wrapped in promises of eternal love.

"Happy birthday, Cristina," he said very seriously.

"But this is a . . . !" I screamed, sucking the chocolate off the ring.

"Will you marry me?" He was down on bended knee.

How romantic! I thought to myself.

The waiters and patrons at nearby tables, whose attention had been drawn by my shriek, were watching us with curiosity. I became thoughtful and, enjoying the show, looked around—the Persian rug, the lavish crystal chandelier hanging from the ceiling, the drapes. I acted as if I was mulling it over. Mike watched me anxiously.

"Of course I will!" I said when the suspense had reached its climax.

I jumped up from my chair and kissed him. He smiled, and the elegant audience gave us an enthusiastic round of applause.

But let's get back to the party . . .

Amid the sound of clinking glasses, the music, and the simultaneous conversations, I didn't hear the buzzer, but John and Linda did and opened the door. Instead of calling me, they decided the visitor was so interesting that everyone should get a look at him. So they asked him to come in. I found myself facing a very tall man decked out in black motorcycle gear, who hadn't even deigned to take off his helmet when he entered the apartment.

"Miss Cristina Wilson?" he asked.

I felt a chill run down my spine. There was something sinister about the man. It suddenly felt as if he'd brought in all the darkness of the night outside. Someone had lowered the music and everyone was listening attentively.

"That's me," I replied. Then, a moment later, I smiled.

Of course, that guy was going to sing "Happy Birthday" and do a striptease. A little surprise gift from one of my girlfriends, probably Linda or Jennifer. It would be fun. He paused and unzipped his jacket. Just as I thought he was about to take it off to reveal his buff triceps, he pulled out a small package from an inside pocket. The guests gathered around us, exhilarated.

"This is for you," he said, handing it to me.

I took the package, but kept looking at him expectantly, waiting for the show to begin. But instead of bumping and grinding, he unzipped another pocket and took out a pen and a piece of paper.

"Can I see some ID?" he asked curtly.

That seemed a bit much, but I had to go along with the joke. So I searched for my driver's license and showed it to him. He calmly jotted down the information. He was a consummate actor; we were all glued to his words and slightest movements. Was he about to start singing?

"Sign here."

"Okay, are you going to get on with it or what?" I said once he had my signature; all this intro was too much.

He gave me a strange look, tore off a copy of the document, handed it to me, and with a "See you later," he left.

I wasn't expecting that, and I shot Mike a puzzled look. He shrugged his shoulders. I looked at the paper the messenger had given me; the copy was almost illegible and I could make out only my name. There was no sender.

"Wait!" I shouted and ran out after him.

I couldn't find him in the hallway; he had taken the elevator.

I went back inside, where Mike still had a puzzled look on his face. So he wasn't a birthday surprise; he was a real messenger. I was intrigued. Who could have sent me that package?

"Are you going to open the present or not?" asked Ruth.

"We want to see what it is," said a man's voice.

I realized that I still had the package in my hands. I had forgotten about it because I'd been focused on the man dressed in black.

I sat down on the sofa and rested it on the glass coffee table. I tried unsuccessfully to remove the cord tying the wrapping. Everyone crowded around me, asking what it could be and who had sent it. Someone brought me the cake knife, and when I got it open I found a small box of dark wood with a metal clasp. I could tell that it was very old.

And inside, nestled in a green velvet cushion, was a gold ring inset with a deep red stone. It looked antique.

"A ring!" I exclaimed.

I tried it on and it fit loosely on my middle finger. I left it there, next to the diamond that sparkled on my ring finger.

Everyone wanted to see it, and there was a round of oohs and aahs.

"It's a ruby," said Ruth.

She is an expert in antique jewelry at Sotheby's and knows a lot about gemology.

"It's strange looking," said Mike.

"That's because centuries ago they didn't cut stones the way they do now," replied Ruth. "The cutting was rudimentary and the gems were polished into round shapes, like this ruby."

"How mysterious!" exclaimed Jennifer, before losing interest in the whole affair.

The music was turned back up and she started dancing. The party revived to the beat of her shaking booty.

While Mike mixed some drinks, I took a closer look at the box and the ring. And the delivery slip. There it was, on the coffee table. I had trouble reading it because the carbon had barely left an impression on the paper, but I finally made out: Barcelona, Spain.

My heart skipped a beat.

"Barcelona!"

That city certainly brought back a lot of memories.

CHAPTER 2

With a spine-chilling roar, the burning tower collapsed onto the poor souls below. People fled. A cloud of dust and ashes, like a desert wind loaded with sand, moved through the streets, covering everything with a grayish blanket.

I rolled over in bed. My God, what a horrible feeling. The memory of that fateful morning when the tallest towers fell came flooding back to me . . .

It's okay, I said to myself. That happened months ago; I'm in my own bed now. After my birthday party, Mike had stayed over and I could feel the pleasant warmth of his body next to mine, breathing slowly, contented. I caressed his wide, strong back. Holding him calmed me. Our bodies rested naked under the sheets. Although our lovemaking had been passionate, he'd had enough energy left to tell me that he loved me. He whispered sweet nothings in my ear before falling into a deep sleep. I was worn out by such an intense day, and I fell into a gentle sleep, until those distressing images came to me.

I looked at the alarm clock. It was four thirty in the morning on a Sunday; I still had plenty of time for sleeping.

I closed my eyes, finally calm, but I once again found myself with the tragic vision of the collapse, the rubble, the panicking people.

But the dream had changed. It wasn't New York anymore. It wasn't the twin towers collapsing. It was something different, and as the images and sounds came to me I was unable to stop them.

People screamed. The collapse of the towers had opened a breach in the wall and men clad in mail and iron helmets rushed through the cloud of dust, toward the opening, waving their swords, lances, and crossbows. They sank into the filthy mist, the deafening clatter, and never returned. Soon thereafter, the fog heaved out a horde of howling Muslim warriors brandishing bloody scimitars. My sword was still in my belt. I couldn't fight. I felt my strength flowing out with the blood oozing from my open wounds. I couldn't brandish a weapon; I couldn't even lift my arm, and I struggled to find shelter. I looked at my hand and there, in that dream, was the deep red glow of my ruby ring.

Women, children, and the elderly, loaded down with bundles, some pulling horses, others, goats and sheep, ran toward the sea. The terrified little ones cried, their tears leaving meandering tracks down their dust-covered faces. The older ones followed their mothers, who pulled the smaller ones by the hand or carried them in their arms. When the attackers charged, stabbing the runaways, panic set in. The mob screamed, some abandoned their belongings, some even their children. They just wanted to escape, but didn't know where to go. It was terrible. I felt great sadness, but couldn't do anything to help them. What would happen to the motherless children? Perhaps some would survive and be sold as slaves. Enormous metal-reinforced wooden doors began to close. There was salvation behind them, but the troops, swords drawn, kept a tight rein on the crowd, letting only some through. Those crowded together outside began to plead loudly. There was pushing, weeping, begging, swearing. The gatekeepers shouted for them to move aside, to leave, to head out toward the port. And when the crowd tried to force its way in, the gatekeepers began to slash at those closest to them. Poor wretches, how they howled with pain and fear. The crowd opened up and I saw that the doors were about to close. I was bleeding and feared that I would die right there, among the desperate multitude. Stumbling, I launched myself toward the soldiers' swords. I had to get through that door.

I sat up in bed with a start. I was short of breath and my eyes were filled with tears. It was agony. I felt even worse than I had when the twin towers were attacked. The dream even seemed more real to me than what had happened on September 11. I don't expect anyone to understand that, since I still don't entirely understand it myself.

A final image was etched on my mind. The man who had ordered the guards to attack the desperate people at the gate was dressed in white and on his chest was the same red cross that was painted on the wall of the fortress. That cross . . . it was somehow familiar.

I turned toward Mike, in search of comfort. He was now lying faceup and still sleeping like a baby, a faint smile on his angelic face. He obviously wasn't having the same dream I was. I couldn't share his peacefulness. I could not stop thinking about the ring. Not the one he'd given me, but the other one.

I was wearing both rings. I didn't usually sleep with jewelry on, but when I went to bed that night I hadn't taken off the diamond ring, the pure symbol of our love, of my promise, of my new life. I still don't know why I lay in bed with the other ring on.

* * *

I wanted to get a better look at it, so I took it off and held it under the lamp on my bedside table.

That was when it first happened, and I was so shocked that my mouth was literally hanging open in surprise.

The stone was set in such a way that the metal held it only on the sides, and the light that fell on the ring projected a red cross on the white sheets.

It was lovely, but unsettling. It was a very unique cross; it had four equal arms, but they widened at the ends, opening up at each extreme to create two small arches.

Suddenly I realized that it was the exact same cross I had seen in my dream—on the soldiers' uniforms.

I closed my eyes and took a deep breath. It couldn't be . . . was I still dreaming? I tried to calm myself by turning off the light and curling up beside Mike. He was still sleeping and had turned onto his side. I hugged him. This relaxed me somewhat, but my thoughts continued to race.

Everything about that ring was mysterious. The way it had arrived, the fact that it had shown up in my dream, then seeing that cross and finding it again in the ring . . .

That piece of jewelry had a story to tell. It was no ordinary gift; it had a secret.

I started to feel even more curious. And more afraid. Something told me that this unexpected gift hadn't arrived just by chance. But rather that fate was challenging me and that a life parallel to the one I was living, like a secret door, was suddenly revealing itself, opening up to me and tempting me to cross its dark threshold.

I sensed that this ring would disrupt the comfortable, predictable life, filled with the promise of happiness; that I had begun to live. It was a threat and a temptation. Damn that ring. It had just come into my life and now I couldn't sleep.

I switched on the light again and focused my attention on the red stone. It had a strange, inner glow shaped like a six-pointed star that seemed to move beneath the surface as I turned the ring, so that the bright star was always facing me.

I examined the inside of the ring. Ivory was inlaid at the base, carved so that it made an inverted design on the back of the ruby. The ivory design was what caused the light passing through the gem to project that beautiful blood red cross through the back.

Okay, I had managed to figure out how that little trick worked. But my curiosity about where it had come from, and why, was growing by the minute.

Suddenly, my eyes opened as wide as saucers as a thought dawned on me. The ring with the red ruby, I had seen it before.

It was as if an image had returned from the mists of my childhood memories. I was sure, absolutely certain. I could see it in some place in my past, someone wore it on his hand.

I turned restlessly in bed. I was sure that the memory was from when I was a girl, in Barcelona. But who had worn the ring?

I concentrated but couldn't remember.

I was convinced that it was from my childhood, and maybe from a much more distant past. But who had sent it to me? And why?

And then it came to me, again, that question I had always wanted to ask my mother but never managed to voice out loud. It was one of those questions you never give much importance to but that keep buzzing around softly in some part of your brain and suddenly, one day, have become a big mystery.

Why was it that we had never gone back to the city where I was born?

We moved to New York from Barcelona when I was thirteen years old. My father is from Michigan and was, for many years, the head of the Spanish subsidiary of an American company. My mother is the only child of a "good" family, the old-school Catalan bourgeoisie. My maternal grandparents were dead. All my relatives in Spain were distant ones, and we weren't in touch with them.

It was in Barcelona that my parents met, fell in love, married, and I was born.

My father has always spoken to me in English. I've always called him Daddy, instead of Papá, and he calls María del Mar, my mother, Mary. Anyway, I tried to ask Mary why we never went back, but she shied away from the subject.

Daddy fit in pretty well with my mother's group of friends, and he loves Spain. It seems that it was she who insisted we move to the United States. And finally her insistence won out; they gave my father a job in the corporate headquarters on Long Island. And we moved. María del Mar left her family, her friends, and her city, and she came to America happily. We never went back, not even for a visit.

I rolled over in bed and looked at the alarm clock again. It was early Sunday morning, and that day we were going to visit my parents at their house on Long Island to celebrate my birthday. My mother and I would have a lot to talk about, I thought. That is, if she wanted to, of course.

CHAPTER 3

I love you," Mike said to me, taking his eyes off the road for a moment as he caressed my knee.

"I love you, my darling," I replied, kissing his hand.

It was a lovely winter morning and Mike was relaxed and happy as he drove. The sun made the bare trees gleam, and then disappeared among the evergreens. The clear, bright day was deceptive; from inside the car no one would have guessed how cold it was outside.

"We have to choose a date," he said.

"A date?"

"Yeah, of course. A date for the wedding." He looked at me as if surprised by my absentmindedness.

"Yes, of course," I said. Where was my head? Once you get engaged, you have to get married. And Mike had given me a ring because he wanted to get married. And I'd said yes because I wanted to as well.

I should have been anxious to plan the wedding. My brain cells should have been fully engaged in making decisions about my white dress, my bridesmaids, the cake, and all the details of the happiest day of my life. Instead, Mike had caught me thinking about the ring. And not exactly the one he had given me. I had been thinking about the other one, the mysterious one. But, obviously, I wasn't going to tell him that.

"And once we decide on the date," I added, "we'll have to plan the invitations, the wedding gown, the tux, the reception, the church . . ."

"Of course."

"That's so great," I said cheerfully. What a mess, I said to myself. How did I get into this situation? And then I remembered the day it had all started . . .

In the morning the birds of death arrived. With their fire they cut short thousands of lives, destroyed the symbols of our city, and made our hearts mourn.

They came from the dark night, a thousand years away, where only a bloody half-moon illuminates the fanatics. And now we are hurting. Those collapsed towers hurt, the way they say an amputated limb can hurt. All that remains is the pain.

The huge hole is there, and at night ghosts seem to wander the surrounding streets. The city is not the same, and it will never again be the same. But it's still New York. It will always be New York.

That day and the night that followed it changed my city, changed the world. It also changed me, and my whole life.

That morning I should have gone to court for a complicated divorce case. As I crossed the lobby of my law firm, I felt something. An echo, a minor jolt. Strange, I remember thinking. There are no earthquakes in New York. I went up to our floor, and I had just said hello and walked into my office when I heard the news. A secretary screamed, "Oh my God!" into the telephone, and a circle of shocked people formed around her.

We went up to the roof of the building to see what had happened. As from so many other roofs in New York, we could see the towers in the distance. We saw the smoke and we shouted in horror as another plane crashed into the second tower then burst into flames. From that moment on, it was chaos. It wasn't an accident, it was an attack, and now it seemed anything was possible. At first the news reports were confusing, then tragic. Then came the order to leave the building and the suggestion to get out of Manhattan. The gentle buzz of the helicopters' blades slicing the sky above the streets contrasted with the wail of the sirens from the fire trucks, police cars, and ambulances below, running every which way, like ants in an overturned anthill, not knowing where to go or what to do.

I considered leaving Manhattan on foot over one of the bridges and taking a cab to my parents' house on Long Island. But I finally decided to go back to my apartment on the Upper East Side and watch what was happening on television.

I had a horrible panicky feeling. I started calling people I knew who worked in or near the World Trade Center. I got a lot of busy signals. It was almost impossible to get in touch with anybody. When I finally reached Mike, he sounded sad and depressed. Since he works on Wall Street, he had a lot of friends in the towers and had spent the morning trying to locate them, without much success. Mike and I had met a few months earlier and I knew he liked me. A lot. I thought he was a nice guy and good looking too, but that was as far as it went. The ingredients were there, but a catalytic agent to make them come together wasn't. He wanted us to see more of each other, to get to know each other better, but I had put on the brakes.

"You're too picky about men," my mother always said. "You find fault with every single one," she insisted. "Let's see if you can find one you can stand for more than six months . . . ," and on and on. Sometimes the woman really gets on my nerves . . .

"Take it easy, Mary," Daddy would interject. "One of these

days the perfect man will appear. Cristina doesn't have to settle for the first one who comes along. Right?" And he would give me a conspiratorial wink.

My mother was right. I enjoyed the company of men, but I got panicky when they tried to put limits on me, asking for more and more; then I'd get tired of them and we'd break up. Luckily I made friends easily, and my father was right: I still hadn't found the man for me. Or if I had, I wasn't aware of it.

I don't know what I felt that morning talking to Mike, maybe it was that I sensed in him the same anguish that was weighing on my heart, but I told him to come over for dinner and we'd share whatever we found in the fridge. I knew he'd accept.

I greeted him with an open bottle of California cabernet sauvignon. As he came in he told me that his best friend worked on one of the floors of the second tower, above the impact. He was missing. We sat in front of the television set drinking wine and whispering to each other, incredulous. That day, with no commercial interruptions, television stations repeated, sometimes with new takes, the same images over and over—people jumping out the windows, doctors and nurses waiting for the wounded who never came, the towers collapsing . . . the unbelievable tragedy of it all. We were hypnotized; we couldn't take our eyes off the television screen.

Suddenly, watching those terrifying images, Mike started to cry. I felt relieved. I'd been wanting to cry myself and so I joined him. And crying, I caressed his cheek and he caressed mine. And then he kissed me. Softly, right on the lips. I kissed him back, deeply. It was the first time we had gone that far. I don't know if you've ever done that with someone in the middle of a good cry. It's kind of a gross, slobbery affair. But in his arms I needed to forget everything. Sometimes I tell myself with a certain regret that perhaps, at that moment, I'd have done it with anyone. But that awful day, I needed a man's protection. Maybe I would have accepted it from a woman as well. I don't know. And he needed protection too. He put his hand under my blouse and found my bare breast. I opened some of the buttons on his shirt and slid my hand down his torso. When I'd decided to go farther, I could tell he was turned on. Between sighs and moans, he kissed my nipples. We made love desperately on the sofa, like junkies looking for a drug to make the world disappear. We didn't take the time to turn off the television, and our sexual murmurs blended with the cries of shock and terror emanating from the screen. He was reaching climax when I opened my eyes and saw some poor people throwing themselves into the void. I shut them immediately and began to pray.

We moved to the bedroom and made love again, without those apocalyptic sounds and images in the background. Afterward, passion gave way to a burst of affection within me. I was grateful to Mike. When he had arrived at my apartment, my heart was sunk so deep inside my chest that it hurt. Our lovemaking had brought it back from the depths.

That horrible night, I felt as if New York was filled with thousands of souls searching, confused, terrified, and desperate, for a path in the darkness, while the living mourned the absence of strangers as their own. Mike and I spent that night clinging to each other on my bed, comforted by that sense of happiness that comes when one stops being very unhappy. The darkness, the horror, was outside, and far away. And I thought that it could be that way forever.

When Mike left the next morning, he asked if we could get together that evening and I said yes. We then began seeing each other seriously. And, obviously, my life as a single woman would never be the same.

CHAPTER 4

My parents' house is in Long Beach, a wealthy part of Long Island. It's not one of those superexpensive mansions right on the beach, but it is a nicely built British colonial–style house, with two stories and a large garden.

As we drove the car into the gravel driveway of the main entrance, I honked the horn. I love it when they come out to greet me.

It was Daddy, with the Sunday paper in his hands, who first showed up.

"Happy birthday, Cristina!" he said, hugging me as we kissed each other on both cheeks. Just then Mom appeared. We must have surprised her in the middle of preparing one of her stews, for she was still wearing an apron.

My mother is a great cook and for a while dreamed of opening a Mediterranean restaurant in Manhattan. She almost never lets the maid cook and, judging by the smell, she was making one of her delicious fish stews, which she called *suquet de l'Empordà*.

After the greetings and the kisses, Mike and my father went to the living room and I accompanied her back to the kitchen. I hadn't told my parents about my engagement. I wanted to give them the news in person, and relished telling my mother first, in private.

"An engagement ring!" she cried out when she saw it, clapping her hands, delighted. "It's beautiful. Congratulations!" she said and gave me another kiss and a big hug. You could tell she was thrilled. She thought Mike was the perfect guy. "Wonderful! Have you set a date?"

"We haven't decided yet, Mom," I replied, a little annoyed by the pressure. "The truth is, I'm in no rush. We have a great life, my work is going really well, and right now I don't want to have kids. Maybe I'll suggest we live together first."

"But you should set a date for the wedding!"

"We'll see." She was starting to get on my nerves. It was good to have a rich, handsome boyfriend. Maybe it was even better to be engaged to him. I was sure he'd be just as good as a husband, but I didn't need to rush things. I wanted to divert attention from the wedding before it turned into an argument.

"But did you see how big the diamond is?" I brought my hand close to her face. She was a bit shortsighted these days. She looked carefully at my hand. Then I noticed that she shuddered. It almost seemed as if she took a step backward. She looked at me, frightened.

"What's wrong?"

"Nothing," she lied.

"You seem surprised."

"I love the ring Mike gave you. It's beautiful," she said after a brief pause. "But that other one? I never saw you wear that before."

"It arrived in the most mysterious way," I replied enthusiastically. "But I'll save that story to tell at lunch with Daddy."

I paused and added, "But I've got a strange feeling about it, as if I've seen it before. Does it look familiar to you?"

"No, I don't recognize it," she answered pensively. But I

knew her well enough to know that she wasn't telling the truth. She was hiding something. My curiosity increased.

During lunch my parents had the good taste to hide how happy the very expensive diamond made them, although my mother would have dieted for a whole week just to know how much it had cost. When, after many compliments, the conversation about the engagement ring flagged, the topic of the other ring came up.

Mike began to tell the story of the appearance of the mysterious biker at my birthday party. He loves to exaggerate and spice up stories. Now the messenger was six feet six and the New York version of Darth Vader, dressed in black, down to his helmet.

The only thing missing from his embellished version of the story was music and special effects. My parents listened intently.

"How mysterious," exclaimed my father, who seemed very into the story. "And you don't think it's some kind of joke?"

"Well, if it's a joke it's a very expensive one," I said. "One of my friends is an expert in gems who works for Sotheby's. She says that by the way it's been polished, it could be hundreds of years old."

"Let me see," asked Daddy, intrigued. While I took off the ring I watched my mother. She hadn't said a word. She was playing it cool, but she seemed to be listening to a story she already knew.

"The strange thing is that the delivery slip says the package comes from Barcelona."

"Barcelona!" said my father excitedly, looking at the ring with renewed interest. "I've seen this ring before. Of course, it must have been in Barcelona."

"I had the same feeling," I replied. "Didn't you too, Mamá?" She looked a little flustered as she answered.

"Maybe, but I don't remember." I was sure that she knew

exactly where that ring came from. Why was she denying it?

"I know," exclaimed my father. He had me on tenterhooks. "Of course I remember."

"Well, tell us," I said impatiently.

"This ring was Enric's. Do you remember, Mary?" he said.

"Maybe . . . it's possible," replied my mother doubtfully.

Yeah, right, I thought. She knows more.

"Which Enric?" I asked. "My godfather?"

"Yes."

"But he's dead."

"Yes, he is dead," confirmed my father.

"How can a dead person send a present?" interjected Mike, who was getting more interested by the second. He must have been imagining the fabulous story he'd be able to tell his Wall Street buddies.

"Enric was my godfather. I've told you about him before. He died in a car accident the year we came to New York, right?" I asked my parents.

They exchanged a strange look before my mother began to answer the question.

"Yes, he died . . . ," she said. And then I knew for sure that they were covering up something about Enric. That's how María del Mar is, for her the ends justify the means, in this case a lie. Because it's socially correct, because she's afraid of offending someone, or maybe because she hates direct confrontation and does all she can to avoid it.

"You guys are hiding something from me," I declared. And suddenly it came to me. "Of course. He's not dead, he must be alive somewhere, that's why he sent me his ring."

Daddy looked at my mother and said, "Cristina's an adult now." His expression was very serious. "We should tell her the truth." And she nodded.

I looked at them, intrigued, and then I looked at Mike, who was as expectant as I was, if not more so.

"Enric is dead." My father looked at me sadly. "There is no doubt about that, but he didn't die in a car accident, like we told you. He committed suicide. He put a gun to his mouth and pulled the trigger."

I was stunned. As a girl, in Barcelona, I had adored Enric. He was like my uncle, more than that, really. After my parents, he was the adult I most loved. I always remember him as friendly, affectionate, and smiling. He used to make up games for the three of us, his son Oriol, his nephew Luis, and me, and it was so much fun.

I remember his enthusiastic laugh, and how he made us laugh too . . . I never would have imagined that someone so full of life could kill himself.

"No, it can't be," I said.

"Yes. That's how it happened, we're sure," said my mother. She looked at me serenely. She no longer had that guilty air I had noticed in the kitchen. "We knew that his suicide would be very painful for you. That's why we kept it a secret."

"But, I just can't believe it," I murmured. My mother was right. Even after so many years it was incredibly painful and made me very sad. "I can't believe he'd do that. Not him."

They watched me in silence, saying nothing but obviously upset.

"But why?" I asked, opening my arms in a gesture of grief. "Why did he kill himself?"

"We don't know," my mother responded. "His family didn't tell me. I didn't want to ask too many questions. Let's remember him as he was: full of life, refined, positive. I still pray for his soul." She seemed sad, very sad. She had loved him like a brother.

I placed my knife and fork on my plate. I had lost my appetite. I wasn't even interested in the birthday cake. It would be better to leave it for a midafternoon snack.

Silence had descended upon the table and everyone was looking at me.

"But, what about the ring?" I inquired after a pause. "What's up with the ring? Why did someone send it to me now, as a birthday present?"

I looked at my mother, I looked at Daddy, and they both shrugged. When my gaze fell on Mike, he shrugged too, confused, as if the question had been directed at him.

"Enric always wore that ring, ever since he got it. He never took it off," my mother said finally.

I wanted to say, "You've been pretending since you saw it in the kitchen," but I kept quiet. I'd save the reproaches and questions for sometime when we were alone. Right now she'd deny it all.

"I never saw him wear any other ring," she continued. "I'm convinced he was wearing it when he died."

I couldn't help shuddering at the thought of that.

"Aren't people usually buried with their most beloved jewelry?" I regretted the question before I had even gotten it out of my mouth.

All three of them stared at me, but no one answered. I looked at the ring. The stone reflected its star-shaped reddish glow. Blood red, I thought.

I was confused. I tried to think clearly and sort out the mysteries that had come with that ring. Why had someone who loved life as much as my godfather committed suicide? Who had sent me his favorite ring? Why? Why wasn't Enric buried with it? For a moment it crossed my mind that maybe he was. That idea made the hair on the back of my neck stand on end.

The others kept staring at me.

"Quite the mystery, don't you think?" I said with a forced smile. I was trying to be positive. And I looked at them one by one. Mike gave me a wide smile; he was thrilled. Daddy made a strange face, as if to say, "What a mess," but my mother was very serious. And she seemed frightened.

She's still hiding something, I thought to myself, and that ring worries her. Worse: it scares her.

We were just about to leave when I remembered the painting.

"Have you ever noticed that picture?" I asked Mike.

It had always hung on a wall in the dining room, but it hadn't caught Mike's eye on his previous visits. We approached it to have a closer look. It's a small tempera-on-wood painting, about twelve inches wide and sixteen high. Insects have eaten the wood on the unplastered sides. Yet the painted surface is almost intact.

It shows a seated Madonna with a child on her lap. The Virgin's head is covered with a wimple and she looks ahead in a still, majestic position. Her face is sweet, but serious. A beautiful golden halo with carved floral drawings surrounds her head. The child, perhaps two years old, is seated on his mother's right thigh, leaning back slightly. He seems to be blessing the viewer and wears a smaller, less elaborate halo and the trace of a smile on his lips.

The contrast between the mother's stillness and the child's movement always surprised me. I didn't know it then, but the child, representing a new generation, had that vibrancy associated with the Gothic style, in contrast to the mother's serenity, closer to the Roman style.

In the upper part of the painting there are two superimposed pointed arches, etched in relief, which are golden, like the painting's background. They appear to enclose the images inside an old chapel. On the lower part, at the Virgin's feet, there is a Latin inscription: *Mater*.

I said before that the painting was always there, but that's not entirely true. When we arrived in New York in January 1988,

mater

we lived in a hotel for a few months until my parents found this house. After some renovations, we moved in in March. On Easter Monday, on the dot, the painting arrived, addressed to me, a gift from my godfather. Since we didn't have many paintings, we hung it up right away. I'd been expecting Enric's present. He had never missed his obligation. But, of course, from so far away he couldn't send me the traditional Easter cake as he had always done before. Instead he sent me that lovely painting.

A few weeks later I received the news of his death.

For me it was a tragedy, and I understand why my parents lied, hiding the suicide from me.

"It's a pretty picture," commented Mike, bringing me back to the moment. "It looks really old."

"Enric gave it to me shortly before he died."

"Did you notice?" he said. "The Virgin's wearing your ring."

"What?" I looked at the Virgin's left hand, the one that held the infant. Sure enough, there was a ring painted on her middle finger. It had a red stone. It was my ring!

I was overcome by a terrible feeling.

Oh my God, I thought to myself. Everything's connected. The ring, the painting, Enric's suicide.

CHAPTER 5

In spite of the shock of suddenly discovering that the ring I had seen so many times in the painting was Enric's; and even though I was convinced that the jewel hid some strange past, I continued wearing it next to the diamond solitaire. Both on the same hand, right next to each other. I developed a strange attachment to those rings; I never took them off, not even when I went to bed.

But I couldn't help being struck by questions, in the most unexpected moments, when I should have been thinking about other things. Even at work, sometimes in the middle of a trial, I would notice a strange feeling in my hand. I'd look at that stone with its bloody hidden gleam and the thought would come to me, Why was I sent this ring? Why did Enric shoot himself?

As a lawyer I'm used to paying a lot of attention to every detail of the case I'm working on. One has to be constantly thinking about all the twists and possible implications of the case, checking on precedents, being a step ahead of the opposing attorney. Definitely, in my profession it's not a good idea to have your mind distracted by Gothic mysteries.

But I couldn't help it.

I thought about calling someone in Barcelona, like my childhood friends Oriol and Luis, but I had lost touch with them since we left Spain. When I asked my mother to help me contact the Bonaplata and Casajoana cousins, she said that she had lost her old address book, and that she'd had no contact with those families since Enric's death and didn't know how to find them.

I didn't believe her. But I also didn't want to pressure her. Something told me she wanted to keep the past hidden and wanted to forget all about it.

One day I called information in Spain. But I couldn't find either Oriol or Luis in Barcelona.

I decided to relax and wait. If somebody had gone to the trouble of finding my whereabouts to send me the ring, then that someone would eventually make himself, or herself, known. At least, that's what I was hoping.

I remember that summer long ago, the Mediterranean storm and my first kiss.

I remember the tempestuous sea and the heavy sand, the rocks, the rain, and the wind.

And I remember him, his warmth, his reserve, the waves and the taste of salt in his mouth.

I didn't forget my first love. I haven't forgotten anything. I remember him. Oriol.

Discovering my ring in the painting had a profound effect on me. I caught myself thinking about Oriol, the young boy who was my first love, and about my childhood. I also thought about Enric, and about questions I had never paid much attention to before.

Why hadn't we ever gone back to Spain? Why didn't we

ever visit anyone in Barcelona? These questions, and others, hounded me insistently, weighing me down. I had asked my mother many times to go, but there was always a "This isn't the time, we'll go next year; Daddy and I have decided that we're vacationing in Hawaii, Mexico, or the Florida Keys." But never Spain.

Not even for the Olympics in 1992. I was about to turn seventeen, and that time my mother said it wasn't right to be celebrating when our friends in Barcelona were still in mourning for Enric's death from that "car accident." It had already been four years since he'd died, and my friend Sharon's family had invited me to go to the Olympics with them. My mother blanched when I told her, and began to come up with excuses. Finally she managed to convince me. A driver's license and a car. And I took the bribe.

But I could see now that she wove a web to keep me from crossing the ocean and going back to Barcelona. María del Mar is an only child, like me. My grandfather died in the seventies, and my grandmother when I was ten. So she wasn't in any rush to return.

"You should adapt to your father's country," she said. "This is your home now and there's no room for nostalgia."

I began to encapsulate my memories and store them in that library of longing that our minds can sometimes be. Memories of my grandmother, my friends, my godfather, Enric, and the many memories of my first love, Oriol. They were perfect memories of a beautiful world. I used them to create imaginary adventures when I lay down in bed, until sleep came. In my dreams he'd come to me, along with the sea, the sun, the storm, the salt, his mouth, and the kiss.

Daddy always spoke to me in English. Classes at my school in Barcelona were taught in four languages, and, of course, I was the first in my class in English. Besides, I'm convinced that, on average, women are better than men at verbal expression. I had no problems making the switch.

I adapted well to New York. Each year I was more popular in school and had more friends. My longing to return to Barcelona began to fade and I accepted my mother's game of postponing the trip for some point in the future. I finished college, then law school, and started my career which, I must admit, is going very well. At least for the moment.

Meanwhile, I had friends, boyfriends, lovers . . . while my memories of Catalonia remained on the shelves of my library of longing, from which they would escape with increasingly less frequency.

But that blood-red ring shook everything up and raised a dust storm in my memories. Those images would now come to me, images of the late-summer storm and Oriol's smile, somewhere between shy and sardonic, and then my friends at school on Mount Collserola, and many other faces and moments from the past.

That ring was a call to return. Yes, definitely, whether Mamá liked it or not, my next vacation would be in Barcelona.

Like a shock wave, the desire to go back ran through my body. And it became more urgent by the day.

It was one of the last afternoons in August or early September. Families had begun to return to the big city and it was a string of good-byes. "See you next summer!" the optimists said. "We have to get together in Barcelona."

We usually stayed until the end, returning with just enough time to get everything ready for the start of school. Those last days had a bittersweet flavor. We had that feeling of something lovely coming to an end and were overwhelmed by the premature nostalgia of something that hadn't yet come to a close.

Our summerhouse, like many of our friends', was on the Costa Brava. The town is beautiful, with a wide beach, practically a small bay, framed on both sides by mountains, covered with pine trees, that descend into rocks and ragged edges before plunging into the sea. On one end of the beach, walls marked by solid round towers rise from the rocks, built to protect the ancient Christian village from the attacks of the Saracen pirates and the occasional local looters, out to pillage and enslave young women.

The rocky outcrops on which the fortress sits are steep, but farther south they open onto a small cove of sand and rocks that's really beautiful. There the green pine trees, the gray rocks, the bright blue summer sky, and the greens, indigos, and whites of the water offer an idyllic, postcard-perfect image.

For us it was paradise, and we almost always went to that cove with Oriol, his cousin Luis, and a group of the same friends from previous summers. With just a snorkeling mask and plastic sandals to protect our feet, we explored underwater and played mostly innocent games. I say mostly because, thinking back, we girls must have been twelve or thirteen that last summer, and the boys fourteen and fifteen. But even though they were older, we were definitely more mischievous.

That day our mothers were busy preparing to close the houses for the winter and pack for the trip back. Our fathers had already returned to Barcelona; their vacations had ended a while ago and they came to the village only on the weekends. That afternoon was muggy and hot and sticky, a sure sign of what was to come.

We were out swimming, chasing fish among the rocks, when the sea turned dark, the wind pushed toward the coast harder and harder, and the sound of thunderclaps became louder than the sound of the waves beating against the rocks. In the span of a few minutes, leaden clouds covered the sky. The water took on a sinister patina and raindrops began to fall.

"Let's go, quick," said Oriol. I could see the nanny on the beach shouting for us all to get out of the water immediately. Luis and the others were already reaching the towels, and they gathered them up as quickly as they could, then ran up the stairs toward the wall and shelter in the town.

"Wait for me, don't leave me!" I begged. We all knew why we had to rush to the beach. We'd heard that a bolt of lightning on the sea would kill all living things around it for some distance.

I was afraid, but something told me not to rush, so I pretended to be having trouble swimming. Oriol came to my aid, and when we got to the shore, the clouds emptied in a fury. There was no one left on the beach. The others had collected all the clothes and in the confusion hadn't even realized we weren't with them. Curtains of rain blocked our vision beyond about ten feet in front of us.

I was exhausted and headed toward a small open shelter among the rocks. We were wet and the tiny space forced us to sit very close together.

I was asking for it. I had always liked Oriol, but in the last few weeks I had been crazy for him.

But he wouldn't make the first move. Maybe because he was shy, maybe because he thought I was too young for him, or maybe because he wasn't into me . . . Or maybe simply because he wasn't mature enough, and those sorts of ideas hadn't yet crossed his mind.

"I'm cold," I murmured, curling up against him.

He opened his arms to receive me. I curled into his shivering embrace. We could feel each other's heat through our bathing suits and our wet skin. If at that moment the world had ended around us, all my senses could only have focused on him. I turned to see his eyes, so blue in spite of the gray light, and that's when it happened. His mouth, the kiss, the embrace. The taste of his saliva and the salt. The sea roared, the sky cracked with thunder, the rain rattled down . . . I still tremble when I think of it.

I remember my last summer in Spain, the tempestuous sea, the sand, the rocks, the rain, the wind, and my first real kiss.

I haven't forgotten anything. I remember him.

CHAPTER 6

And the weeks passed. I still wore both rings, but the strange ring with its blood red stone seemed to hold my attention a lot more than my engagement ring. I liked to project the red cross on paper, napkins, sheets. Every time I looked at it I saw images of my childhood: my godfather Enric; his son, Oriol; Luis. So many of the little details stored in my memory, which I had ignored for so long, came back to me.

I knew that something else would come, that the ring was just the beginning, but I was growing impatient. My curiosity was getting the better of me. And what I was expecting and had sensed had to happen, happened.

"Miss Wilson." It was the doorman of my building calling me on the intercom. "A certified letter came for you this morning."

It must be some documents related to one of my cases, I thought.

"Would you like me to bring it up now?" continued the doorman. "It's from Spain."

"Yes, Mr. Lee, please." My chest tightened with sudden emotion. Here it was! This had to be it.

He was at my door in a New York minute. My hands trembled as I took the letter. I brusquely said good-bye to Mr. Lee, who, as usual, was trying to bring me up to speed about the goings-on in the building.

The sender was a notary in Barcelona. Eagerly, I tore open the envelope.

Miss Cristina Wilson

Dear Madam:

I have the honor of inviting you to the reading of the second will and testament of Mr. Enric Bonaplata, of which you are one of the beneficiaries.

The reading will take place in our office at 12 noon on Saturday, June 1, 2002. Please confirm your attendance.

And it was signed Juan Marimón, Notary Public.

"That's right," I said to myself. "This time my mother won't be able to hold me back. I'm going to Barcelona."

I told her about it at the dinner table the next night when I went to her house on Sunday with Mike. She didn't say anything, but my father looked surprised. Will? It should have been read and distributed shortly after Enric's death. He had left two wills? And the second one to be opened fourteen years after the first? That was strange.

Yeah, it was strange. It was all very strange. Creepy.

"Don't go, Cristina," my mother said when she could talk to me in private. "This whole thing gives me a bad feeling. There's something weird about it, something sinister."

"But why? Why shouldn't I go?"

"I don't know, Cristina. This second-will thing is absurd. Somebody has a reason for bringing you to Barcelona."

"Mamá, you're hiding something from me. What is it? Where does this fear come from? How come we never went back, not even to visit? How come you haven't kept in touch with your friends?"

"I don't know. It's a feeling, an impression I have. But something bad is waiting for you there."

"Well, I'm going."

"Don't go, Cristina." There was distress in her voice. "Forget about all this. Don't go. Please."

The waves beat furiously against a pebble beach at the foot of a cliff. They dragged stones that, returning with the swell, made a deep noise, as if bones were colliding with each other. The sky was festooned with small, fast-moving clouds that projected light and shadows on a terrible scene.

On the beach, a group of ragged, foul-smelling men, chained together to a plank of wood, were shouting, struggling to escape or to defend themselves. Others prayed, waiting their turn passively as their companions' throats were slit. There was blood on the rocks, on the ground, on the bodies that lay there, on those who were still desperately debating . . . and on my hands. The sun came up, illuminating the lethal glimmer of steel, then hid behind the clouds, leaving a trail of death whose shadow hung over the earth, on the corpses littering the beach. I felt my heart shrink with grief, although I was with those dressed in gray tunics who, quickly and expertly, pulled victims' heads back by the hair and cut their throats. More blood. One of my companions, the youngest, cried as he killed. One of the executioners wore a dark tunic with that red cross embroidered on its right side, the same one etched on my ring. The man with the ring was there, ordering the slaughter. Everything that I saw was through his eyes, also filled with tears. The screams died down and the movement stopped. As the last prisoner died, that man fell on his knees to pray, and I felt his pain. I began to cry inconsolably. It was a bottomless pain that came from deep inside my chest.

I woke to find myself sitting up in bed. The crying was real, and so was the pain. So real that I couldn't get back to sleep. Luckily, it was only about half an hour before I had to get up. I spent it awake, thinking about my nightmare. What was happening to me? Had the posthumous gift from Enric affected me that much? Did that ring have something to do with these ancient pain-filled visions? As I looked at my hand, with both rings on it, it seemed the ruby that represented blood shone much more brightly than the diamond representing love. When the alarm finally went off, I felt incredibly relieved. I just wanted to get back to reality.

CHAPTER 7

I didn't realize until the morning's hearing ended that my cell phone and my keys were missing from my bag. My wallet and everything else were there.

How could I have lost them? It didn't make sense. Suddenly I had an idea.

"Ray," I said to a colleague, "let me borrow your phone." I called my doorman.

"Mr. Lee, my keys are missing. I'm just calling to let you know."

His response was surprised silence. I became alarmed.

"What's happening?" I asked.

"But you loaned your keys to the repairmen who came this morning."

"What repairmen?" My voice went up a few decibels.

"The ones who came to fix your stereo."

"What are you talking about?"

"Miss Wilson," he replied with surprise, "don't you remember? You called this morning to let me know that some repairmen were coming to fix your stereo equipment. You said you had left them your keys."

I felt a chill.

"I didn't call you this morning."

"You said that if anything came up, I should call you on your cell. I did, when the men left, and you said, great, thanks."

"That wasn't me. They stole my phone too."

Bob Lee kept a copy of my keys. He accompanied me to check my apartment. They had gone through the closets and moved mirrors and paintings in search of a possible safe. But nothing was missing. What did they want?

I reconstructed the events. This had been carefully planned. Someone knew that I would be in court all morning. The someone who'd stolen my phone and keys from my bag. Then they'd tricked Bob by imitating my voice. According to Bob, two men went to my apartment. One carried a suitcase, which had surprised Bob, but since he thought I was on top of things, he hadn't suspected anything.

All that complicated plotting and they didn't *take* anything? Obviously, they didn't find whatever it was they wanted. What were they looking for?

My life was changing. Quickly.

I'm not a fearful person, sometimes I'm even reckless, maybe because I've been lucky and nothing bad has ever happened to me. But having my house broken into, the fact that someone could get in so easily, and be near me and rob me, then imitate my voice . . . it all had me spooked. I felt uneasy, with a fear I had never known before. I suddenly realized I was very vulnerable. It was a repetition, on a more personal scale, of that feeling of danger after September 11.

But at the same time, I found it all intriguing, and exciting.

* * *

I'd come out of the shower and was drying myself with a towel when the phone rang. Who was calling at seven thirty in the morning?

"Cristina?"

"*Sí. Soy yo.*" I automatically answered in Spanish. My name hadn't been pronounced in English. It's surprising how our minds choose languages. Sometimes you don't even realize when you are speaking one language or another. But I could immediately place that voice as being on the other side of the ocean.

"Hi, Cristina! It's Luis. Luis Casajoana. Remember me?"

Luis. My library of memories spun into action and I instantly drew up the image of a chubby kid with puffy cheeks and a big smile, as if I were videoconferencing with the past.

"Luis! Of course I remember you!" I was happy to hear his voice. "What a surprise. How'd you get my number? I'm so pleased. Are you in New York?"

"No. I'm calling from Barcelona. Forgive me for calling so early, but I wanted to be sure to reach you before you left for work."

"Well, here I am."

"The notary sent you a letter asking you to come to the reading of my uncle's will, right?"

"Yeah. What a surprise."

"You'll come, I hope."

"Yes."

"Fabulous. Tell me when you arrive. I'll pick you up at the airport."

"Thanks, that's so sweet, Luis. And how's Oriol? I've been thinking a lot about you both since I got the letter from the notary."

"Oriol's fine. I'll tell you more later. But I called to warn you about something."

"What is it?" I was alarmed.

"Did Enric send you a painting before he died?"

"Yes."

"Well, put it in a safe place. There are people who are very interested in it."

"Really?"

"Yes. That painting has something to do with Enric's will."

"What?"

"For the moment it's just speculation, a suspicion of mine. I'll know for sure at the reading of the will."

"You're killing me! Tell me something."

"I think that painting is somehow tied to the inheritance. That's all."

I fell silent. They were looking for the painting. The guys who broke into my apartment had been looking for the painting! And they'd known it would fit in a suitcase.

"But that's what you already told me. What's all this about?"

"I don't know. Come to Barcelona and hopefully we'll know everything on June first." I remained silent, thinking. Then Luis spoke again.

"Did you know? People say . . ."

"No, I don't know anything. How could I know if I'm here?"

"They say that my uncle was searching for a treasure before he died." Luis had lowered his voice to a whisper.

"A treasure?" I couldn't believe it. It sounded like one of those stories that Enric used to tell us when we were children. He even organized treasure-hunting adventures for the three of us . . . with clues and maps. They had us excitedly running around his big house on Tibidabo Avenue. I remember my godfather as a marvelously creative person.

"Yes, a treasure. But this one was for real," he declared with

conviction. He was speaking so softly that I could hardly understand him. "But we won't know anything else until June first."

I thought for a few seconds, matching the caller with the file
I had saved in my memory of him, I immediately rejected the
treasure story. He was always a gullible kid who made things
up. But I realized that he hadn't given me the answer to something that really intrigued me.

"Luis?"

"What?" His voice had gone back to normal.

"How'd you get my phone number?"

"Easy," he replied, laughing. "Mr. Marimón, the notary, is
a friend of the family. He hired a detective to find you in New
York. It seemed like the Wilson family had been swallowed up
by the earth . . ."

As soon as I hung up, I called my father.

"Daddy, I'm sorry to wake you up . . . yes, the painting
that Enric sent me as an Easter present. Yes, the Gothic Virgin.
Please, first thing this morning . . . Take it to the bank. Put it in a
safe-deposit box . . ."

A treasure, I thought, standing by the telephone, still naked.
Wow. Then I shook my head in disbelief. We're grown-ups
now . . . although it seemed as if Luis hadn't changed much.
He'd always been immature for his age. It must just be nonsense.

We were both decked out in sportswear. Mike and I had been
running for more than half an hour and I was having trouble
keeping up with his pace. I either had to ask him to slow down
or I was going to get left behind. He liked to show that he was
stronger than I was, sticking out his chest and looking at me as
if he was superior. I liked to remind myself that I was smarter,
so once in a while I'd amuse myself by spoiling his show of
strength and putting on my own show.

The twisted ankle is a classic. I make a pained face and he gets worried. I cry out, he turns around as if to say "Again?" but comes to my aid. He massages my ankle while I lean on him. Sometimes I can't help laughing while he's kneading my ankle and can't see my face.

"Does it hurt?" he asks, worried, not knowing that it's just poorly contained laughter.

"Yeah, a little bit," I respond in a pitiful voice. "But you're making me feel much better. You're incredible."

If an actual laugh gets out, then I say that he's tickling me. Sometimes when I catch my breath, I take off like a shot and it's him who gets left behind.

Then he accuses me of tricking him, but I deny everything. Other times I fake that my heart is racing or that I'm having trouble breathing.

That day was different.

"Mike," I shouted at him when he, inconsiderately, was quite far ahead of me. His excuse was that he needed to go at a faster pace.

"What?" he replied without stopping.

"I'm going."

"What do you mean you're going?" Now he did stop to wait for me. He looked at his watch. "But we've only been running for a little over half an hour. I'm barely warmed up."

"I'm going to Barcelona."

"Sure, Barcelona," he replied. "We're going to Barcelona, but not for a few weeks yet."

"No, Mike. *I* am going to Barcelona. Alone."

"Alone?" He was shocked. "We agreed that I'd go with you!"

"I changed my mind."

"But we have everything prepared to go together. It was going to be like an extra, early honeymoon."

"Listen," I begged. "You have to understand. I've given this a lot of thought. It's a journey to my past, to reconnect with my-

self. I have to do it alone. There are things I don't understand:
my mother's attitude, how my godfather died. I might find
some unpleasant surprises."

"Another reason for my going with you."

"No, definitely not, I need to deal with this myself," I said,
cutting him off firmly. "I've been thinking about it a lot and I've
made my decision." But I quickly turned sweet again. "Listen,
Mike, it's so great being together and normally there's nothing I'd like more, but for our love to work forever, we have to
respect each other's moments of privacy. There are times when
we'll need to be by ourselves."

"I don't understand you." He frowned and crossed his arms,
his body rising before me like a wall. "I can't get you to pick a
date for our wedding. And now, all of a sudden, you tell me
that you want to go to Barcelona alone, when we had already
discussed it and decided to go together. What's going on with
you? Do you still love me?"

"Of course I do, my darling. Don't be silly," I threw my arms
around his neck to give him a kiss. He was tense, he hadn't
liked my news. "Love you? I adore you! But I need to make this
trip on my own." I kissed him again. I could tell that he was
beginning to soften up. "I promise that the day I get back, we'll
pick a date. Okay?"

He grumbled sulkily and I knew that, once again, I'd get my
way.

CHAPTER 8

I t's a beautiful ring, miss," he said in Spanish. That was how the man sitting next to me in business class started the conversation. "It looks very old."

I had noticed him already. He was an attractive guy, at least thirty-five. His hands were free of rings, a sign that he wasn't married, or that he wanted to hide the fact that he was. His open-necked white shirt sported some discreet gold cuff links and he wore a classic watch. A curious combination of austerity and luxury.

I'd realized that he was waiting for the right moment to strike up a conversation and I didn't want to make it too easy for him. First I looked out the window and then I concentrated on my magazine. I was betting that he'd start to speak during dinner and I was right. I decided to finish eating slowly, swallowing what I had in my mouth before responding, seriously and in English.

"Excuse me?" I said, although I had understood him perfectly.

"*¿Habla usted español?*" insisted the man.

I had to admit that I did.

"I said that you are wearing two beautiful rings." I noticed that he had slightly changed the sentence. "And that the ruby one seems to be very old."

"Thank you. Yes, it's an antique."

"Medieval," he stated.

"How do you know?" Suddenly my curiosity won out over my desire to display the indifference befitting an engaged woman, just as my diamond ring attested.

The man flashed a lovely smile.

"It's my job, ma'am. I'm an antiques dealer and an expert in jewelry."

"This ring came to me in a very strange way." My barriers had collapsed. "So you think that it's really quite old?"

The man looked in an elegant leather briefcase that he had at his feet and pulled a magnifying glass, like the ones watchmakers use, out of a small box.

"Do you mind?" He extended his hand. I quickly took off the ring to give it to him. He looked it over very carefully, from every angle, and began to murmur, as if to himself. He had me in total suspense. Then he held the ring up against the light and it projected its red cross on the seat in front of us.

"Amazing," he finally said, absorbed in staring at the image. "This is a unique piece."

"It is?"

"I'm sure that this piece of jewelry is truly antique, I'd say at least seven hundred years old. It could be worth a fortune. If you were able to reconstruct its history, its value would increase manyfold."

"I don't know the history of this ring, but maybe I'll know more when I get to Barcelona." I remembered the painting and the ring on the Virgin's hand, but a sudden cautiousness made me leave out that detail.

"Do you know what makes this ring unique?"

"What?" I asked, suspecting that I knew the answer.

"The cross that it projects through the ruby."

"It's a pretty effect, huh?"

"It is much more than that. It's a flared cross."

"What?"

"I said a flared cross." He smiled and stared at me. He was handsome, and I realized that this was the second or third time I had asked him to repeat something. He must have been starting to think that I was either hard of hearing or not too bright.

"It's the Templar cross."

"The Templar cross, of course," I said while racing through my mental archives, frantically searching for a clue about what "Templar" meant. I was sure I had heard that word before . . . Images of *Ivanhoe* and Robert Taylor, or was it Errol Flynn? and childhood memories of Barcelona and Enric's treasure-hunt games came to mind. That was all. But I was hesitant to admit further ignorance.

"As you'll remember, the Knights Templar were warrior monks who appeared at the beginning of the twelfth century, during the Crusades to the Holy Land, and they died out in the early fourteenth century due to a horrible state conspiracy."

"Yeah, I know a bit about them," I said, hiding my cluelessness. "But I don't remember very much. Tell me more about the Templars."

"They appeared after the First Crusade successfully conquered Jerusalem. King Baldwin gave them part of the ancient temple of Solomon as their headquarters, which is why they are called the Knights of the Temple. They preferred to call themselves, at least in the beginning, the Poor Knights of Christ. Their mission was to protect the pilgrims who visited Jerusalem. The Templars become an impressive military machine, the richest and most disciplined of their time. The Eastern Christian kingdoms relied on them in the face of the relentless advance of the Saracens and Turks. Initially they were popular, and kings, nobles, and villains gave them large donations for their lofty mission and in an attempt to buy a place in heaven. That enthusiasm grew to such a point that the king of Aragon bequeathed his kingdom to the Templars and two other military orders: the Knights of the Holy Sepulcher and the Hospitallers. And only after long, hard negotiations did the legitimate successor to the throne manage to recover it.

"So those monks who had taken vows of poverty, chastity, obedience, and to fight to the death to defend the Holy Land became the largest European economic power of their time, enjoying a prestige that no banker could equal. They invented the bill of exchange, becoming a financial organization in charge of kings' treasures, and lending them money when they needed to spend more than they had on luxuries and wars. Which they tended to do. All that economic strength was needed to defray the Christian presence in the East. They built large fortresses and a vast fleet that transported horses, weapons, warriors, and money through the Mediterranean; they hired thousands of Turcomans, Muslim mercenaries who fought against their own religious kind. They were poor individually, because of their vows, but very wealthy as an organization. This ring must have belonged to someone high up in the Templar hierarchy. A simple monk, even if he were a sergeant, a chaplain, or a knight, would never have worn jewelry."

He again projected the cross onto the surface before us. He took another fascinated look at the ring, then gave it back to me.

"Congratulations, miss, that ring is one of a kind."

I slid it back on my finger while I absorbed his story.

"My name is Cristina Wilson," I said, smiling and holding out my hand.

"Artur Boix," he replied, taking my hand. "Pleased to meet you." His skin was warm and pleasant to the touch. "Did you say you were going to Barcelona?"

"Yes."

"That's where I live. What brings you to my city?"

I explained the story of the unexpected inheritance to him.

"How mysterious," he said when I had finished. "But if that ring is a taste of what that inheritance holds, I think I could be very helpful to you." He gave me a card. "My partners and I have businesses both in the U.S. and in Europe. We not only deal in antiques and jewelry but we are primarily dealers in ancient art. And here there is a big difference. The value of a piece of jewelry can be assessed in three ways: first, by the value of its components, such as gold or precious stones; second, by its craftsmanship and artistic quality; and third, by its historical context. The difference between one assessment level and the next can multiply the price enormously. In other words, a piece of jewelry that in Spain you could normally sell for a thousand dollars, I can get a hundred thousand for in the United States. Don't hesitate to call me, it would be my pleasure to help you. It doesn't matter if you don't want to sell the jewels, I can authenticate them and assess their value." He lowered his voice and his gaze became more intense. "But if you want to take some piece of art out of the country that's cataloged or needs authorization and you want to save yourself the formalities, I can guarantee its safe delivery to New York."

I was surprised to learn that they might be able to stop me from going home with my inheritance from Enric. The truth is that it hadn't occurred to me that the bequest could be works of art. Now I realized that it was most probably the case. Up until that point I had only been thinking about the adventure part of the story, but Artur Boix was making me see that perhaps there was quite a bit of money at stake.

"In any case, for anything you might need, even if it's only a consultation or just to tell me how things are going, call me."

When I heard how open his offer was, I looked at him more carefully. Too friendly. Hadn't he seen my engagement ring? The man smiled. But when I thought about it, it never hurts to have a friend in a place where you don't know what you're going to find. And if he's good-looking, elegant, and pleasant company, well, then even better.

"Thank you," I replied, smiling back at him. "I'll keep that in mind. But tell me what happened in the end to the Templars. You said that they disappeared because of a vile conspiracy. And that they were very rich, right?"

"Yes," replied Boix. "And that was the root of their downfall."

I kept quiet, waiting for him to continue his story.

"In the year 1291, the sultan of Egypt took the last Christian stronghold in the Holy Land. Many Templars died in that offensive, among them their highest authority, the master general, but the worst part of it for the Poor Knights of Christ was abandoning the front, the first line of battle against the Muslims. Somehow, when the town of Saint John de Arce, also known as Acre, fell, their reason for being disappeared. They were needed only in the Iberian kingdoms, where the fight against the Moors continued. But even so, their presence was no longer essential, as it had been two hundred years earlier, when the Christian territories were constantly in danger. In the fourteenth century, Aragon, Castile, and Portugal were powerful monarchies that had the advantage in their war against the Arabs, making frequent incursions into northern Africa, while on the peninsula there was only the Nazari Muslim kingdom in Granada, which was so weakened that it had to pay taxes to the Christians.

"The Templars' dream was to return to the Holy Land, but the spirit of the Crusades had died and the Christian kings weren't up to it. Philip IV of France, 'the Fair,' was always low on money. So after capturing, torturing, and fleecing the Lombard merchants and then the Jews in his kingdom, he set his sights on the Poor Knights of Christ, who at that point were very wealthy.

"It's quite a long story, but the end result is that he jailed the Templars, falsely accusing them of many crimes, which he made them confess to by using torture, and appropriated most of their riches in France. And to top it all off, he burned the highest leaders of the order at the stake, as if they were heretics. The pope, who was also French, was practically a hostage of 'the Fair' king. He tried weakly to resist, but was intimidated and ended up allowing the monarch to do what he wanted. The other European kings were less brutal, but in the face of the pontiff's insistence, they supported the suppression of the order. And of course, in exchange for their assistance, they all more or less helped themselves to some of the Templar assets. But they weren't able to take all that they wanted . . . because they never found it."

"They never found what?" I asked.

"The huge treasures that the Poor Knights of Christ outside France were able to hide."

"Ahh!"

"That's one of the legends about the Templars. Another says that their master general, in the flames at the stake, called the Fair king and the cowardly pope before God's justice. It is a fact that they both died before the year was out."

"Really?"

"Really. But there are other things that people say about the Templars that have no basis in history and are much more dubious."

"Like what?"

"That they were searching for the ark of the covenant that God had ordered Moses to build, that they were in possession of the holy grail, that they were protecting mankind from the gates of hell, and other things like that."

"And what do you think?"

"I don't put stock in any of that," he replied with conviction.

Maybe I didn't know much about the Templars, but I did

know something about people and I thought I could guess what the antiques dealer was thinking.

"But you do believe that they hid their treasures. Right?"

"Without a doubt."

"And you would love to find some of them, right?"

Artur Boix looked at me with interest.

"Most definitely," he said gravely. "There's nothing that would please me more. My work, besides being a way to earn a very good living, is my life's calling. I enjoy it. I would give years of my life to find a Templar treasure. Besides, who better than I? I would know how to value it artistically, I would know how to place it in its historical context, and, if necessary, I'd know how to get the best price for the pieces being sold. If at any point you come across something like that, for example, in your inheritance, please, count on me for whatever help you need. Even if it's only to show me the pieces, so that I can have the pleasure of seeing them." His hand rested on mine. The contact was warm and pleasurable. "Please, Cristina, count on me. Will you?"

I have to admit that his appeal impressed me and I responded politely, "Yes, of course."

We changed planes in Madrid and were seated next to each other again. I was dozing until Artur Boix shook my arm to wake me up and show me the view. Still half asleep, I looked below. The airplane had turned above the sea to enter the airport, offering a splendid view of the city. It was a crystal-clear morning.

"There she is," he said, pointing. "Barcelona's like a grande dame. Forever young, forever regal, nestled between the mountains and the sea, bursting with energy. She's full of art, full of life."

I could see the port and the old city, with its churches jutting out, and a wide avenue snaking through it.

"The Ramblas," said Artur.

And farther on there were blocks of streets, uniform in size, but all different, cut by boulevards and tree-lined avenues. The sun floated above the sea and headed toward its peak, highlighting the southern side of the city and creating shadows toward the north.

"That's the Ensanche, a living museum of art nouveau," he said. "Old lady Barcelona is more than two thousand years old. She seems to nap peacefully under the warmth of the sun, oblivious to the comings and goings of her inhabitants, comfortably nestled between the past and the present. But, actually, her center is swarming and seething."

He made a wide wave of his hand, as if introducing us.

"Barcelona, this is Miss Cristina Wilson. Cristina, Barcelona at your feet. I wish you a good stay—enjoy her."

Well, I thought, the man is a poet too.

I lost Artur at passport control, and we met again waiting for our luggage. One of my suitcases was slow in coming and he courteously said that he'd wait with me.

"Thanks, but I won't have any trouble," I assured him. "I'm a lawyer and I speak Spanish and Catalan perfectly. So if they lost my suitcase, I'll know just how to deal with them."

He laughed and said good-bye, insisting that I call him for anything at all that I might need.

At the time, I was thinking I wouldn't mind seeing charming Artur again, not knowing that the moment would come when I'd wish I'd never met him.

CHAPTER 9

I hate checking my luggage, especially when it arrives late or gets banged up or lost. But sometimes I have no choice and, after a few more minutes, my last suitcase appeared on the conveyor belt. I loaded it onto my cart and made my way toward the door.

"Cristina Wilson," read the hand-lettered sign. It was exciting to see my name written there among the people waiting, so far from home. I looked up at the face. It took me a few seconds to recognize him. It was Luis Casajoana Bonaplata. His features had lengthened, and although stocky, he was no longer the chubby red-faced boy I remembered. When our eyes met, I recognized his smile.

"Cristina!" he shouted. I don't know if he was able to recognize me after fourteen years, or if it was the expression on my face that tipped him off.

He hugged me, gave me a kiss on each cheek, and took my cart.

"You've grown so much!" he said on our way to the exit, shooting me an appreciative look. "You're gorgeous."

"Thanks." I remembered him as kind of clingy and I wanted

to nip his excessive enthusiasm in the bud. "I see you're not so chubby anymore."

He gave a snort and then a laugh.

"And you're as blunt as ever."

Yeah, maybe, I thought, but I hope I lowered his expectations. Honestly, I didn't want to have him all over me during my trip.

Then, as we were leaving the building, I saw that strange man again. He was brazen; he hadn't taken his eyes off me. I had noticed him earlier among the other waiting people. I had been struck by his eyes just as the automatic door opened, a second before I saw Luis and his sign. The man's appearance had caught my attention, but I hadn't paid it any mind. But that second time, when I caught him watching me, I stared back, challenging his audacity. But he continued to stare until I felt uncomfortable and turned my eyes away.

That man gave me a chill, a warning. He was an old guy who had shaved his head about a month before, so his white hair and beard were both less than a quarter of an inch long. He wore a black jacket over his dark clothing, creating a contrast with his hair. But the most striking detail was his eyes—they were dull blue, scrutinizing, cold, and aggressive.

That guy sure looks like he's off his rocker, I thought. I shouldn't have challenged him. As I said before, I'm not easily scared, but that old man was definitely not someone I'd want to run into in a dark alley.

Meanwhile, Luis was cross-examining me about my trip. Was I tired? Did I get any sleep? When we got to the car, a sleek, sporty, silver BMW convertible, he'd gone on to asking about my family and he informed me that his parents had left the city and moved to a charming little village in the northern part of the Costa Brava.

On the way to the hotel, he asked about my personal life.

"Ah! You have a boyfriend."

"No. A fiancé," I clarified.

"Well, I graduated with a degree in business, and got an M.B.A. in marketing, and now I'm a businessman."

"You've been busy," I commented sarcastically.

"Yup. I'm divorced too."

"Sure, sure," I said, laughing, "that I can imagine."

He started to laugh too. Luis was still very good-natured.

"You are naughty," he said.

"You told me that already, fourteen years ago."

He laughed again.

"I was chubby, but wise."

When Luis started to talk about himself it could go on indefinitely, so I changed the topic.

"And what's up with Oriol?"

"Oriol?" The question seemed to make him uncomfortable and I noticed that he was unconsciously accelerating his BMW.

"Yeah, Oriol. You remember? Your cousin?"

"Yes, I remember," he replied with a frown. "And don't pressure me, bossy-boots."

That made me laugh again. It was the tone of his voice and that word I hadn't heard in fourteen years. He had called me that all the time.

"Well," he continued, "the well-endowed one in the family . . . I mean with brains, of course; in other respects, I'm the well-endowed one . . ." He looked at me, smiling smugly.

"Okay, cut it out."

"Yes, bossy-boots."

I shut up and waited for him to speak. When he saw that I wasn't responding to his provocation, he continued.

"Well, the genius of the family became a hippy, an anarchist, and a squatter."

"What?" I was totally shocked. Oriol, brilliant Oriol, the horse everyone had bet on to win, was a misfit?

"Well, you see, he ended up living on the margins of society."

"He didn't finish college?" I was flabbergasted.

"Oh yeah, he finished college. Plus he got three or four doctorates. He's something of a brainiac."

"And what does he do for a living?"

"He teaches history at the university. And along with some other kooks who have tight pants and dreadlocks, he sets up cultural centers for the people and does social work in old abandoned buildings. Until the police come and kick them out."

"It's hard for me to imagine."

"Well . . . He's been in a lot of scuffles. Of course, you wouldn't have heard about the police storming the Princesa theater, right? It was quite a scene. And my little cousin was there."

"Did something happen to him?"

"He spent a night in jail. Our family still has connections in this city, and he's not one of the violent ones." Luis made an ambiguous gesture with his hand.

We had reached to the hotel, and a smiling young doorman held the door for me. Another attended to my suitcases while Luis handed the car keys to a third.

What had he meant by that gesture? It had left me wondering. What in the hell was Luis insinuating about Oriol?

"Come on, the reception desk is on the first floor," he said, and led me by the elbow toward the elevator.

"I reserved a room with southern exposure for you on the eighteenth floor. An incredible view. And I should tell you that normally they don't take reservations for the upper floors. I know that for New York this isn't a tall building, but here it's something special."

Sure enough, the concierge had given me a room on the eighteenth floor.

"I'll go up with you for a minute to see the view and make sure everything's okay."

"No thanks," I said, smiling. "I know you. You always spied on us girls when we changed into our swimsuits."

"Yeah, okay, fine," he replied with a naughty expression. "But I've changed. And you have too . . . now you're much more to look at," he said and shot a glance at my chest.

Normally, if it had been anyone else, I would have been offended. But I just laughed.

"Good-bye. Thanks for picking me up."

"Come on, let me just check that everything's okay," he said, leering at me.

"Everything's fine. Just fine," I assured him. "Believe me. And good-bye," I said, raising my voice. The sound spread through the large room, which was between the elevators and the glass wall. Some of the people seated at the wicker tables, near the large glass window, turned to look at me.

"All right. At least give me a good-bye kiss . . . bossy-boots," he said, bargaining.

Luis was right. The room faced the south and the view was fantastic. To the left, the sea and the beaches stretched to the city's old port, which was now a walking mall. I could see the slips of the sailboats at the marina, a wide area with stores and bars and restaurants. Farther off I saw several large ships that looked like ocean liners waiting to take tourists on a pleasure cruise.

In the distance rose Montjuïc, with its castle at the edge of the cliff overlooking the sea and its wooded gardens along the rest of the elongated summit. On the other side, there was the Palacio Nacional, a cluster of grandiose buildings. The promenade at the shoreline and the statue of Columbus marked the start of a metropolis that extended toward green mountains.

Barcelona, city of my birth. I looked toward the neighborhood of Bonanova, where we'd lived, but I couldn't make it out. I wasn't sure of its exact location in the vast expanse of rooftops that, despite the chaos of so many shapes and sizes, was a thing of beauty.

But a thought kept coming back to me. What was Luis insinuating about Oriol?

The bellboy brought up my luggage and I started unpacking while I thought about it. Well, I decided, I'll have to spend some more time with Luis. I had many questions and I was hoping that he had the answers. But who I really wanted to see was Oriol, my first love.

Today is Wednesday, I said to myself, I'll have some dinner and get some rest. I'll definitely see Oriol on Saturday at the reading of the will. But could I hold out until then without trying to find him? I was hoping he'd get in touch with me. What was Luis trying to say about Oriol? Did Oriol know I was in the city? And what if I called him? I didn't have his number. Could I get it here even though I couldn't from New York? I should have asked Luis for it.

I called my parents and Mike to let them know that I had arrived safely. Even though I was tired, I browsed through some books, with large photographs of the city, that I found on a little table. I didn't want to go to bed before ten so my body could adjust to the new schedule.

Later I ordered a light dinner and ate it while I watched night fall over the city. A curious feeling came over me as the darkness advanced. I sensed that among those buildings, crammed together there below in the distance, were the answers to my questions. What was this strange inheritance? Why did Enric commit suicide? Why didn't my mother want to come back to Barcelona? What secret was she keeping from me? What enigma was buried in that red ring? I looked at the ruby with its six-pointed star inside the stone. I had the feeling that it glowed more intensely here in this city. It seemed even more puzzling. Too many questions. I was dying of curiosity and I longed to know what Luis could tell me.

I dialed his number and got his machine.

"Luis," I said, "it's Cristina. Can you have lunch with me tomorrow? My treat."

I changed into my pajamas and turned off the lights. I decided not to close the curtains. The city lights barely reached up that high, and only the ones on the outside of the building softly illuminated the room. I didn't ask for a wake-up call because the sun would be my alarm clock.

I stretched out in bed and let my thoughts wander . . . being in Barcelona, after so long . . . what a strange feeling.

Suddenly the phone rang.

"Cristina!"

"Hi, Luis."

"I knew you couldn't live without me."

I was about to change my mind and just hang up. I felt that he was hounding me.

"I'll take you out for lunch tomorrow," I said, ignoring his nonsense.

"No. I'll take you out for dinner."

"Oh no," I replied sharply. "Sorry. I don't have dinner alone with any man who's not my fiancé. Not even for work; it's a matter of principle."

He made a weird sound, something like Nooch! . . . Nooch! . . . Nooch! . . . It sounded like his comical way of refusing.

"Okay. How about—" he said.

"It's lunch or nothing," I said firmly.

"I have a meeting tomorrow at noon with the shareholders of one of my companies."

"Well, tough luck," I said in a resigned tone of voice. "We'll see each other at the reading of the will. Thanks for calling."

I was bluffing. I didn't buy his story and I was trusting that he'd give in. If not, my curiosity about all those unanswered questions would force me to accept his dinner invitation.

"I'll take you out for dinner," he repeated, refusing to give up.

"I said no!" I shouted into the telephone.

There was silence on the other end of the line.

"Okay, you win," he finally said. "To hell with the shareholders. The company is bankrupt anyway. I'll tell them that I fled to Brazil with the money. I'll pick you up at the hotel at two."

"So late?"

"This is Spain, remember, bossy-boots?"

CHAPTER 10

"There was always plenty of secrecy in my family about Enric." Luis stuffed his mouth with lobster salad and watched me calmly while he chewed. He knew I was hanging on his words and he enjoyed keeping me in suspense. Given the mystery in which he had shrouded the conversation, I had the feeling that he was going to reveal something surprising, but I wasn't about to give him the upper hand. So I played along. I had a spoonful of my cold almond soup and admired the high ceilings, the art nouveau furniture, and the decoration of the restaurant, located in a hundred-year-old building on the Diagonal.

"The fact that Enric was gay was hard for the Bonaplatas to accept."

I stared at him with my mouth open. Enric, gay? He observed the effect of his revelation with obvious pleasure.

"My mother knew," he continued. "But he always hid it from the rest of the family. He did a good job, he had no obvious affectations. Unless he wanted to, of course."

"Gay?" I exclaimed. "How could Enric have been gay? He was married to Alicia. And he's Oriol's father!"

"Duh. They don't show Almodovar films in New York, or what? Wake up, girl, life's not just black and white." Luis smiled smugly. "The cowboy's not always the good guy. And the good guys only win once in a while.

"Enric and Alicia were never married, at least not in the eyes of the church. Even though our parents made an effort to make us kids believe that they were. Socially, they were a couple when it was in their interests. But they both had lovers of their same sex. What I don't know is if they also had some fun together when they shared the same bed."

Luis's eyes lit up and a salacious smile played across his lips.

"Maybe they had orgies, can you imagine?" He paused.

I imagined. Not one of those supposed orgies, but rather, Luis as a mythological faun, with little horns and a goatee. I laughed at the expression on his face. Then I immediately regretted it.

"No, I can't imagine it," I said decorously.

"Come on . . . Yes you can, you can imagine it . . ."

"No."

"Come on, Ally McBeal, you know you can."

I hate it when people call me Ally McBeal. It's such a facile joke, calling a young successful female lawyer that.

"Not very original, Luis. Calling me Ally McBeal is so tired."

I saw his smile and it reminded me of how we'd fought as kids. He always liked to get me worked up. He'd start by pulling on my braids or some other small physical or verbal attack.

I had always had a large vocabulary, so I would usually let loose with "repulsive fat slob" or "sack of blubber and shit," or some other equally astute and subtle observation about his appearance. He wouldn't get upset, he'd just stick a finger in his nose and puff out his cheeks to make himself look more like a pig. At that point, it was usually me who started laughing. And it's very hard to stay angry with someone who's making you laugh.

"Why are you smiling?"

"Nothing. I was remembering how we fought when we were kids. You haven't changed very much."

"Neither have you. I can still get your goat."

Man, I thought, the fat slob is still just as confrontational. Even though he's lost weight. All of a sudden I remembered the start of our conversation and I got serious again.

"Poor Oriol," I said. "It must be hard."

"Are you talking about his sexual preferences?" He was no longer smiling. "Well . . . his leanings . . . you know, he grew up surrounded by women who took the masculine role. What do you expect? It's normal. Besides, genetically . . . since both his parents were, well . . ."

"What?" I asked, filled with curiosity and a tinge of alarm. I had been thinking about his family situation, but Luis was talking about Oriol. "What are you insinuating? I don't know anything. Tell me what you have to say."

"Just that. That my cousin's case isn't exactly clear either."

"But why? What do you base that on? Has he told you something?"

"No. He doesn't tell me his secrets. But you can see these things. He has no girlfriend that we know of. And a bizarre lifestyle . . ."

I scrutinized my friend. There was no trace of joking in his eyes. He seemed to be speaking seriously. That Alicia was gay didn't surprise me, and I didn't really care. That Enric was did surprise me, but the idea that Oriol was homosexual felt like an unexpected slap in the face.

My teenage fantasies, those beautiful memories of the sea, the storm, and the kiss, were completely shattered. I had imagined Oriol as my boyfriend, my lover, my husband.

I thought back to those days, and the truth is that I was

always the one who made the first move; it was never Oriol. He went with the flow and I had attributed it to his shyness. When vacation was over we'd see each other at our elite school, located on the Collserola hillside, looking down on the city at its feet. It was there that the progressive, free-thinking, upper-middle class sent their little ones to be schooled in the Catalan style with a European flavor. Oriol was one grade ahead of me, so we hardly saw each other. I started sending him little notes.

We were also both at the get-togethers that our parents' friends would sometimes organize on the weekends. I remember the last one, before we left for New York. Oriol seemed sad, and I was devastated. They had prepared a going-away party at Enric and Alicia's mansion on Avenida Tibidabo. It was hard to get away from Luis so that we could be alone, but the garden was large and we managed to get a few minutes of privacy. We kissed again. I cried and his eyes got red. I'd always thought that he cried too.

"Do you want us to be boyfriend and girlfriend?" I had asked him.

"Okay," said Oriol.

I made him promise that he'd never forget me, that he'd write to me and that we'd see each other as soon as we could.

But he never wrote, and he never replied to my letters. I never heard from him again.

I realized that Luis was still talking to me and that I hadn't been listening. I tried to pay attention to what he was saying.

"Oriol doesn't have his own apartment, he lives with his mom. Of course, in Spain that doesn't mean that you're a loser, like it does in the States. Oftentimes, though, he stays over with his squatter friends in one of those houses that belong to other people. And when he feels like it, he sleeps in the big house on the Tibidabo. His room is kept clean, they feed him well, they wash his clothes, and it makes his mom happy."

"Well, there are girl squatters too, right? . . . I mean, he could have girlfriends."

"Sure, of course there are girl squatters too." He smiled. "Well, well, it looks like you're worried about who my cousin's sleeping with."

"What you're saying is only based on supposition, circumstantial evidence. You have no solid proof that shows Oriol's gay."

"This isn't one of your trials," said Luis, smiling. "There's nothing to prove; I'm just giving you a heads-up."

I thought that what Luis was doing was worse than judging. He was convicting Oriol on the basis of malicious insinuations. I decided it was time to change the subject.

"What do you think is going to happen this Saturday?" I asked. "What's this mysterious inheritance all about? It's not every day they read a man's will fourteen years after his death."

"Well, when Enric's will was read shortly after his death, Oriol and Alicia were the main heirs. This is something else."

"Something else?" I was getting annoyed with the way Luis was doling out information. He was enjoying keeping me on tenterhooks.

"Yes. Something else."

I decided to keep quiet and wait for him to continue the story and not prod him with more questions.

"It's a treasure," he said after a few minutes of silence. "I'm convinced that it's a fabulous Templar treasure."

I had been expecting this ever since he had called me in New York. I remembered the conversation I'd had with Artur Boix the day before, on the plane.

"Do you know who the Knights Templar were?" he continued.

"Of course I do." Now it was Luis who seemed to be shocked.

"I didn't think they taught much about medieval history in the United States."

"Stereotypes. Well, now you see that we do know about the Middle Ages," I replied with satisfaction.

"Well, then you know that most of the European sovereigns, even though they had strong suspicions that what was happening in France was unjust, followed the pope's orders. At the same time, they took advantage of the situation to line their own pockets as much as possible.

"However, they say that in the court of Aragon, where action against them was deferred for a while, the Templars were able to hide part of their wealth, including large quantities of gold, silver, and precious stones." Luis's eyes shone. I thought I could see in him again the chubby face he'd had fourteen years ago when Enric would suggest one of those treasure-hunting games in his large house on Avenida Tibidabo. "Can you imagine how much a huge batch of gold and silver items from the twelfth and thirteenth centuries could fetch on the black market? Gold, silver, and enameled crucifixes with inlaid sapphires, rubies, and turquoise stones. Chests of carved ivory, chalices covered with precious stones, royal crowns and tiaras . . . ceremonial swords . . ."

He closed his eyes as if blinded by all that gold's glitter.

"So you think that this Saturday we are going to get a treasure?" I asked incredulously.

"Not a treasure, no. But I think we're going to get the clues to find it, like Enric used to do when we played as kids. But this time for real."

"And how do you know all this?" I suspected that Luis was living out one of his fantasies, but I didn't have anything to gain by questioning his assumptions and starting an argument.

"Well, some comments within the family. It seems that that was what he was up to when he died."

"And how does my Gothic painting fit into this story?"

"I still don't know. But during the same period, around the time Enric shot himself, he was trying to acquire some Gothic paintings. If my information is correct, the one you have is from the Templar era, thirteenth or early fourteenth century."

He looked at me for a while without saying a word. He seemed quite convinced.

"And . . . why did he kill himself?" I finally asked.

"I don't know. The police think it was related to settling the score among art traffickers. But they couldn't prove anything. That's all I know."

"Then why did you call to warn me?"

"Because apparently that painting has clues to finding the treasure."

I was dumbstruck.

"Did you know they tried to steal it?" I asked.

Luis shook his head no and I told him the story.

"Where did Enric commit suicide?" I asked when I realized I couldn't get any more information out of him.

"In his apartment on Paseo de Gracia."

"And what does Alicia say about all this? She's supposedly his wife."

"I don't trust anything she might say."

"Why?"

"I don't like that woman. She's always hiding something. She wants to control everything, and everyone. Be careful with her. Very careful. I think she belongs to a sect."

I wondered if it was a coincidence that my mother had warned me in almost those exact words about Alicia before I left. She'd asked me to keep away from her.

Which made me even more anxious to see her.

CHAPTER 11

I decided that the local police station would be a good place to start my investigation into Enric's death. I went back to my hotel to change my clothes. I put on a pair of low-slung pants. Showing a little belly button would be my best calling card if, as I was imagining, most of the cops were men. It wasn't about flirting. It was strategy.

"I'm a detective now, not a lawyer," I said to myself.

I noticed the message light blinking on the telephone.

"Mrs. Alicia Núñez called," said the operator. "She asks that you get in touch with her as soon as possible."

Well, I thought, there she is, the woman who frightens my mother and spooks my chubby friend.

My curiosity was piqued. I tried to picture Oriol's mother. Both mother and son had the same deep blue, slightly almond-shaped eyes. Those eyes I was so crazy about as a teenager.

Alicia hadn't spent much time with our summer group. Actually, Oriol spent summers at his grandparents' house, on the Bonaplata side, with Luis's mother, his aunt. Enric would come some weekends, and he'd spend about two weeks out of each summer there, but he and Alicia were rarely there at the same time. When she wasn't traveling abroad or busy with tasks that were, in those days, not considered appropriate for women, she'd visit Oriol on weekdays but never spent the night in the town. Even at a very young age, I sensed that Alicia was not a typical "mamá" like the others.

But I had never thought about it again until now.

What did Alicia want from me?

I told myself that there was no rush to call her back. At least not for the moment.

At the police station I told the truth, that I was visiting after fourteen years and wanted to know what had happened to my godfather.

No one there remembered the incident, a suicide on the Paseo de Gracia. Perhaps it was my smile, perhaps it was my emigrant-in-search-of-her- roots story. Or maybe it was my belly dancer's belly button. But the officers were very friendly. One said that López should remember, he'd been around at the time of the incident. He was out patrolling, so they called him on the radio.

"Yeah, I remember a case like that." They turned up the volume on the receiver so I could hear. "But the one who worked the case was Castillo. A guy called, and while they were talking on the phone the guy blew his brains out."

"Castillo doesn't work here anymore," the policeman told me. "He got promoted to captain and they assigned him to another precinct. You should go see him there."

When I arrived at the captain's new location, they told me he wouldn't be in until the following morning. I recovered quickly from the setback and told myself that at least I would enjoy the walk. Holding tightly to my purse, as Luis had suggested, I went back to the Ramblas, immersing myself in the river of humanity that flowed through the city's main artery.

The word *rambla* also means riverbed, and that's what the Ramblas are in Barcelona. People flow where water once did. Except this flow, even when it thins out at dawn, never runs dry, unlike the stream that once ran parallel to the ancient medieval walls. How can that boulevard maintain its charm, its spirit, when the human fauna is constantly changing? How can a mosaic maintain its design when the tiles keep moving? It must be that we take in the whole, its essence rather than each separate element. Some places have a soul so large that they absorb our energy and turn it into a part of something bigger. That's what the Ramblas are like.

There goes a lady in her long evening gown, her escort in his tuxedo, on their way to the opera at the Gran Teatro del Liceo; farther on there's a transvestite in full makeup, competing with the prostitutes for uniformed sailors of every color and nationality. There are blond tourists, brown immigrants, pimps, cops, beautiful women, old winos, and curious folks who look at everything but don't see anything.

That's how I remembered the Ramblas, more from what I had heard than what I had seen as a little girl, and that's how I found them that radiant spring afternoon. Wandering among the flower stands, I felt that with each breath I took, I absorbed the explosion of color, beauty, and fragrance swirling around me.

I joined small groups of spectators watching street performers: musicians; jugglers; living statues powdered in white or glitter, princesses and warriors who stood stock-still, then made a sudden movement to thank the onlookers for their coins.

I saw a young man, waiting, leaning on the thick, lumpy trunk of a hundred-year-old plane tree. And a young woman, with a wide, mischievous smile, stealthily approach him from behind and give him a rose. I saw his surprise and her happiness, which culminated in an embrace and a kiss. I felt longing, envy.

I looked for comfort in the diamond ring, proof of my own love, sparkling on my hand. But beside it, intruding with its red gleam, the mysterious ruby glowed mockingly. It must have been my imagination, but that strange ring seemed to have a life of its own, and in that moment I felt that it was trying to tell me something. I shook my head to banish such nonsense and watched the young lovers, hand in hand, disappear into the crowd.

And then I thought I saw him again. The man I had now dubbed Barbablanca. The man from the airport, the old guy with the white hair and dark clothes. He was standing at a nearby newsstand. He pretended to be flipping through a magazine, but he was watching me. When our eyes met, he glanced back at the magazine and, leaving it on the pile, headed off. I was startled. I abruptly continued my walk, wondering if it were really the same person.

CHAPTER 12

O f course I remember that case." Alberto Castillo was about thirty-five years old and had a pleasant smile. "It made quite an impression on me. I'll certainly never forget it."

"What happened?"

"A man called to say that he was going to kill himself." The police captain became serious. "I was a rookie then, and had never before been in a situation like that. I tried to convince him otherwise, to calm him down. But he seemed calmer than I was. I don't remember what I could have said to him, but it was of no use. He talked to me for a bit and then put a gun in his mouth and blew his brains out. It sounded like 'boom-bah!' I jumped out of my chair when I heard the shot. It was only then that I was convinced he was serious.

"When we finally found him, he was sitting on a sofa, his feet up on a little table, the balcony doors open over the Paseo de Gracia. He had been sipping one of those very expensive French cognacs and smoking a fancy cigar. He was wearing an impeccable suit and tie. The bullet had exited through the crown of his head. It was an old, luxurious house, with high ceilings, and all the way up there, next to some lovely friezes of flowers and leaves, I saw that blood, and even part of his head, had stuck there. He had one of those old record players, and on the turntable was a record by Jacques Brel. I realized that that was the music I had heard while we were talking on the phone. Before that he had listened to 'Viatge a Itaca' by Lluís Llach."

I closed my eyes. I didn't want to imagine the scene. It was horrible.

I remembered Enric, on Easter Monday, arriving at our house with Oriol and an enormous *mona*, the typical Catalan cakes that godfathers give to their godchildren on that day, with a dark-chocolate figurine in the center. Once he'd brought a cake that had a chocolate castle on it, with a princess and all. It was huge, and I wouldn't let anyone touch it. I wanted to save the castle, as if it were a dollhouse. He enjoyed it as much as we did. I can still see his excited smile. I loved Enric almost as much as my own father.

There was a lump in my throat and my eyes were teary.

"But why?" I stammered. "Why did he kill himself?"

Castillo shrugged his shoulders. We were seated in a typically austere police office. That day I had a different strategy. I wore a short skirt and I had my legs crossed, one over the other. The man's eyes strayed every once in a while, but I pretended not to notice.

On top of a filing cabinet he had a framed picture of a smiling family. Wife, son, and daughter. I could tell that the captain was enjoying my company and was going to tell me everything.

"I don't know why he killed himself, but I have a theory."

"What's that?" I asked.

"As you can imagine, at twenty-something, it made a big impression on me. So I asked to participate in the investigation. I remembered that in our conversation he said he had killed someone. A few weeks earlier someone had murdered four people in a big house in Sarriá. We couldn't prove it, but I was sure it was him."

"That he killed four people?" I couldn't imagine Enric, who was always so friendly and easygoing, killing anybody.

"Yes. They were people involved in the antiques business, like he was. Except two of them had priors for theft and the illegal trafficking of works of art. And the other two were just thugs, some kind of bodyguards. Dangerous types. But your godfather's business dealings, when we went through them, seemed to be on the up and up. What's more, he had inherited so much money that even if he threw it away on all kinds of extravagant living and partying, he would still have had plenty; he could have kept that pace up until he burst."

"How do you know that he was acting alone?"

"Because he killed them all with the same gun."

"That doesn't mean he didn't have help."

"Well, I think he did it alone. And I'll tell you why, young lady. That house was like a bunker, and those people were a gang of criminals. They had security systems with alarms and video cameras that were all connected to a central unit. That's starting to be common now, but it wasn't in those days. Unfortunately, they were only around the outside of the house, and they weren't hooked up for recording. He must have tricked them somehow. Him alone. They never would have let two people in there at once, and they never would have let themselves get caught off guard if they suspected anything. He came in through the door, so they must have let him in. And before he went into the room where the bosses were, they definitely would have frisked him. They were professionals, and the two younger men were armed, although they didn't have time to shoot back. We found one of them with his revolver in his hand. Also, the older guy tried to use another gun that he must have kept in one of his desk drawers. There was a ton of bills scattered on the desk, proving that the murderer wasn't interested in money, which fits with Bonaplata. His motive was revenge."

"How could one guy kill four men, three of whom were armed? Where did he get the gun? He wasn't the aggressive type."

"I don't know where he got it or where he stashed it afterward."

"Didn't he shoot himself? Didn't you find a gun by the body?"

"Yeah, of course."

"So?"

"It was a different one. Ballistics checked, and the bullets that killed the dealers didn't come from that gun."

"Then he's not the killer."

"Yes, he was." He looked into my eyes, convinced. "I'd bet anything that it was him."

"Why would he have gone to the trouble of hiding the gun and killing himself with a different one? It's absurd."

"No, it's not. Enric Bonaplata was a smart guy. If he'd killed himself with the same gun, we would have had the evidence to charge him with the murders."

I started to laugh. That was ridiculous.

"How would being charged mattered to him, if he was already dead?" I asked sarcastically.

"His inheritance. He had thought of everything. His heirs would have had to pay compensation to the heirs of the victims."

Well, that shut me up. The captain was right. That was a good motive.

Castillo had been looking at me with a half smile beneath his mustache. He seemed like a nice guy. He checked out my legs again rather brazenly and then just spit it out, addressing me unofficially, "Did you know your godfather was a fairy?"

"A fairy?"

"No, not a fairy. More like a full-blown faggot."

I looked at him, pretending to be shocked.

"What are you talking about?" Even though Luis had warned me the day before, I decided to take advantage of Castillo's loose lips to get everything I could out of him.

"Just what I said." He paused and, seeing my reaction, searched for a more tactful word. "He was a homosexual."

"You know he has a son . . ."

"That doesn't mean anything."

"What makes you say that?" I posed the question very seriously, as if I were interrogating a witness at trial.

"When he called on the phone, after telling me that he was going to kill himself, he started asking me how old I was and what color my eyes were. Like he was hitting on me. Can you believe it? From a guy who's decided he's going to blow his brains out?"

"That's strange for someone about to kill himself," I replied thoughtfully. "No matter how homosexual he may be. Don't you think?"

"Not for him," stated Castillo emphatically. "Yeah, he was a fag, but he had balls."

Deep down I was grateful to the captain, in spite of his choice of words, for conferring upon Enric what must have been his highest praise. There was a tone of admiration in his voice.

I waited in silence for him to continue his story.

"I reconstructed the events," continued Castillo. "I calculate that he killed the dealers between six and seven in the evening. At eight thirty the wife of the oldest one called us, very upset, to report the crime. She had just arrived home.

"I'm convinced that Bonaplata had it all planned and had decided to exit the world in high style. We lost his trail for a few weeks while he traveled around, and he didn't seem to care that my colleagues on the case interrogated him several times here in Barcelona. They were collecting evidence to charge him.

"But he knew it and got away, for good. One day he went, as he often did, to eat at his favorite restaurant. Alone. He stuffed himself with his favorite dishes and downed a whole bottle of the most expensive wine in the house. He had a cordial and a cigar after the meal.

"Then he went to his apartment on the Paseo de Gracia, put on some music, chose another cigar and a cognac and, like the good citizen he was, decided to inform the police. And, of course, at that point he couldn't help hitting on a young guy like me. After pretending his whole life that he wasn't a fag because of all that stuff like 'What will they say and what will my family think,' why hold back at the last minute? He liked young men. You know?"

"Are you saying he was a pedophile?" I said in disbelief.

"No," Castillo replied smiling at my upset tone. "We have no evidence that he was interested in little boys, just young men, ones who were over eighteen but still ten or twenty years younger than he was."

I was relieved and took a moment to think before starting to interrogate the captain again.

"But why did he kill himself?" I was hoping to avoid hearing more about the details of Enric's sex life. "From what you've told me, he didn't seem to be depressed and he was enjoying life to the fullest. Besides, if he had done everything so well, and you couldn't prove his guilt, you'd never have been able to catch him."

"We were about to nab him. If the questioning continued he'd have had a lot to explain. But we never got the chance because he bought a first-class ticket to the other side." Castillo seemed to have a heavy heart as he spoke, as if he had never been able to understand Enric's final decision. "It might have been tied to the death a few weeks earlier of a young man who was about twenty years old," he added after a pause. "It seems they were a couple."

"Really?"

"Yeah. The boy was the manager of the antiques store that Bonaplata ran in the Old City."

"This all seems a bit far-fetched, don't you think?"

"No, I don't. I think this is how it happened: Bonaplata and the dealers were having a dispute over something. Something that must have been very valuable. They beat up the kid to make him talk, but they went too far and killed him. That must have really hurt Bonaplata. He set a trap for them, managed to sneak in a gun, and when they least expected it . . . Bim! Bam! Boom! With balls of steel, he sent all four to the cemetery. They killed his guy, and he got revenge. It's that simple."

"But that doesn't fit with the man I knew—he loved life, he was a wonderful person." Remembering him, I could feel the tears welling up again. "It's hard for me to believe that he was a homosexual, but it doesn't matter, it doesn't change who he was. But I refuse to believe that he'd commit suicide to escape justice. And killing those people? I don't see him murdering in cold blood either. He was such a gentle person. And how could he have done it?" I realized that I had been raising my voice with each question. "How could he trick them when they must have known he hated them? Didn't you say they were professional criminals?"

"I don't know. I don't know everything," protested Castillo, a look of despair darkening his face. He opened his arms, the palms of his hands turned toward the ceiling. "I've been thinking about it for fourteen years and I still don't know. That's my theory. It's still got gaps in it, but I'm sure it was him. He killed them. And he did it alone."

CHAPTER 13

I needed to sort out my thoughts. In the taxi I kept turning over in my head what Castillo had told me. When I arrived at the hotel, I decided to take a walk around the garden and pool area. That was where I was headed when I saw him. Again.

He was sitting at one of the tables near the large plate-glass window and he was watching me. Now I was sure—it was the guy from the airport. The same hair, the same white beard, dressed in dark clothes that might even have been the same ones. And those threatening blue eyes. He was watching me like he had in the airport, and, startled, I immediately looked away this time.

What was Barbablanca doing in my hotel? I changed my mind about the walk, turned around, and headed toward the elevators located in the opposite direction, past the reception desk. In the hallway I looked back. There was no way I was going to let him follow me. I was horrified by the idea of finding myself alone with him in the elevator. As I walked, I thought it out. It was too much of a coincidence to bump into him again and again considering Barcelona's size. Besides, he did not look like a hotel guest, not in the least.

I rode up in the elevator with a reassuring older American couple.

I tried to think of a logical explanation. It wasn't so improbable, after all, that I'd run into the man again. He must have been waiting for someone at the airport who'd arrived on my flight. Maybe he was a driver for a car service and had been waiting for a client. And he was doing the same thing now, in the hotel. Sure, that must be it . . . But what was he doing on the Ramblas? Showing some tourist around?

Whoever Barbablanca was, once I was in my room, with the door locked, I felt much better. It was his intense gaze that made me uncomfortable. There was no other reason, I said to myself.

I went straight to the window to see the city again from that privileged panoramic vantage point. There below, to the right of the wide sea, Grande Dame Barcelona lay spread out, napping beneath the afternoon sun. I found the end of the Ramblas at the foot of Columbus's statue, and with my eyes I retraced my walk from the day before. It was hard to follow the route since, from that distance and height, the buildings hid the streets, and I could only guess the avenues, based on the shapes of the buildings. Still, my eyes wandered, a bird's-eye view, over the most unique street in Barcelona.

As I turned around I noticed the phone. The red message light was blinking. One was from Luis, at four in the afternoon. He insisted on taking me out to dinner. And that I should call him either way. He was curious about my discoveries and wanted to chat. The second message was a woman's voice I didn't recognize at first.

"Hello, Cristina," she said. "Welcome to Barcelona. I hope you remember me. It's Alicia. Call me. We have a lot to talk about and, as your godmother, you are my guest while you're in the city." She sounded warm, unhurried, sure of herself. Then she repeated a phone number twice. I jotted it down on a notepad that sat on the nightstand. "I'll be waiting for your call, sweetheart."

Wow, I said to myself, here's my mother's nightmare, the woman she seems to fear so much. The monster did have a deep voice, but it was velvety and pleasant. I was considering calling her back, but I wanted to think a little first. What would seeing her entail? Upsetting my mother, that was clear. But I had done that many times before. It wasn't a decisive factor in my equation. Luis had also warned me about her. But that wasn't really all that important to me either. And Alicia must know a lot of things that would be helpful to me with my investigation into Enric's death. That is, if she was willing to tell me.

I had to admit that my curiosity was piqued. Oriol's mother. Why did she sound so affectionate toward me? I had been expecting him to call me, not his mother. Did he still cherish the sweet memory of that last summer years ago? Why hadn't he called me? Maybe for the same reason that he hadn't responded to any of my letters, maybe because of what Luis had told me about him. Was he really gay?

Alicia had said she was my godmother. That wasn't true, although it's not wrong to call the wife of your godfather your godmother. Actually, I didn't remember who my real godmother was; it must have been one of my mother's friends or relatives. But it wasn't Alicia.

She had sometimes come to visit with Oriol and Enric, but they almost always showed up alone. As a girl, it always seemed to me that Enric and Alicia made a strange pair. They had separate houses. Oriol lived with his mother in the house on Avenida Tibidabo. Sometimes Enric slept there and other times he stayed at his own apartment on Paseo de Gracia.

My relationship to them was through my mother's family, the Colls. My maternal grandfather and Oriol's paternal grandfather (Enric's father) were like brothers. Their fathers, our great-grandfathers, became close friends at the turn of the twentieth century, when Barcelona brazenly tried to compete with Paris as the world's art capital. They frequented a restaurant called Els Quatre Gats, rubbing elbows with the likes of Isidre Nonell, Picasso, Santiago Rusiñol, and Ramon Casas.

Our great-grandfathers were children of upper-middle-class Catalan families, but they had turned out rebellious, and before they signed up devotedly for season tickets to the Liceo opera house, as befit tradition and their families, they frequented the artistic circles of the period. There they briefly came to know almost all the *isms* of the new century, including anarchism, communism, cubism, existentialism. They had a more lasting relationship with "brothelism" on Calle Aviñó and Calle Robador, where artists short on cash but rich in talent and libido, like that young man Picasso, were welcome.

The art collections of many of my great-grandparents' contemporaries come from that time. They bought paintings for next to nothing to help their needy artist friends. These collections, handed down to their offspring, were worth a fortune now.

I went back to the window to contemplate that city whose spirit continued to vibrate with creativity. Why did my mother leave behind all her past, all that legendary history? Why did she end up marrying an American and practically fleeing the city? Of course, she had fallen in love with my father. The heir to past fortunes from textile mills and shipping companies, enlightened by the avant-garde art movement her family had helped support financially, had fallen in love with a simple American engineer.

It must have been love . . . that's what it was. Love. But there was something else in that story. Something I sensed was there, hidden.

The telephone rang.

"Hello," I answered.

"Hi, Cristina!" I identified the speaker immediately. "It's Alicia, your godmother."

"Hi, Alicia! How are you?"

"Great, darling. I left two messages for you to call me." There was a hint of reproach in her warm, deep voice.

"I was going to, Alicia. But I just got in," I looked at the clock and saw that that wasn't true; I had been in the hotel for over an hour.

"Well, fine. I beat you to it," she concluded. "I'm here, waiting for you in the lobby."

"Here?" I asked stupidly.

"Yes, darling. In the hotel."

In the hotel? What was Alicia doing in my hotel?

"Come on, don't make me wait. Come on down," she concluded in the face of my silence.

"Okay, I'll be there in a sec," I replied obediently.

"See you soon, sweetheart."

"See you soon."

So I finally meet up with Alicia, I thought.

I recognized her immediately. Alicia must have been over sixty, but the woman who stood up with a smile from one of the tables in the bar near the reception desk seemed much younger.

She was stocky. I remembered her as being wide hipped and somewhat matronly, and that had grown with time.

"Darling—what a pleasure it is to see you!" she exclaimed in her deep voice, spreading out her arms. She embraced me, squeezing me tightly, and gave me two loud kisses. Her perfume was pungent and her gold bracelets jingly.

"Hello, Alicia!" Somehow the woman's personality and charisma made me feel like a thirteen-year-old girl again. And her eyes. Those deep blue doe eyes, just like her son Oriol's. Seeing them again made me quiver.

"You look fantastic!" she exclaimed, stepping back to see me better. "You've turned into a fabulous woman. I can't wait to see Oriol's face when he sees you again."

She watched my expression when she mentioned her son. I held on to my smile and didn't say anything.

"But have a seat," she urged, ignoring my silence. "Tell me about your family. How's it going for you in the United States?"

I obeyed, but first I checked the place where that strange man had been shortly before. I didn't see him and felt relieved.

Alicia was a great conversationalist and we had a nice time chatting about this and that. I had a lot of things I wanted to ask her, but I didn't know how to slip them into the conversation. I felt that we didn't yet have enough trust between us. Suddenly she said, "I came to get you so you'd come to my house."

"What?"

"You should come home with me."

"But . . ."

"There are no buts here, darling," she said in an even deeper voice. "I have a huge house with several guest rooms. I'm not going to let my goddaughter stay in a hotel by herself."

"I couldn't do that," I said, resisting, while I thought quickly. Alicia, the woman my mother feared, the dangerous witch Luis had warned me about, Cruella De Vil in the flesh, was inviting me to stay at her house, the house where Oriol lived. "I don't want to be a bother," I added.

"The bother would be you staying here," she said emphatically. "It would be almost offensive. It's decided; we're going to my house, and tomorrow I'll go along with you and Oriol to the reading of the will."

"But—" She ignored me and headed toward the reception desk, where she began giving instructions. I went to stop her, even though I had the feeling it was useless. Actually, I wanted to go. I watched how she displayed her amazing authority. She spoke in a near whisper and everyone leaned in to hear her better.

"Don't even think about paying my bill."

"It's already done," she said.

"I can't accept."

"You're too late. The hotel manager is a friend of mine and they won't take your money. You're my goddaughter and it's my treat."

In spite of her words, I forcefully advised the clerk at the counter that I'd be paying my own bill. He replied that I was too late. Madam had settled the bill before I had come down from my room.

"I have to get my things," I said finally. I was annoyed with her, not so much because she was paying for my room, but because of the control she seemed to have over everything around her, including me.

"Don't worry about that, darling," she replied with a gesture that said, It doesn't matter. "The maid, and my personal assistant, who's already on her way, will take care of your luggage. In no time you'll have it all set out nicely in your room at my house." And putting her arm through mine, she led me toward the exit.

"What great legs you've got, darling." Alicia's car stopped at one of the stoplights on the Ramblas. Her unexpected appearance at the hotel hadn't given me the chance to change my clothes and, sitting in that low seat, the miniskirt I had used on the police captain had ridden halfway up my thighs. She caressed my knee, setting off my inner alarm. For a moment I regretted having accepted her hospitality.

"Thank you," I replied cautiously.

"I gave instructions at the hotel for them to take a message if you get any calls, just as if you were still their guest." She smiled. "So no one in America needs to know that you're staying with me."

She knows my mother doesn't like her, I said to myself.

We crossed the city on the vertical axis that goes from the

old port to Mount Collserola. We passed the Ramblas, Paseo de Gracia, then Mayor de Gracia, all the way to Avenida Tibidabo, where Alicia still lived in the Bonaplatas' large art nouveau house with its fabulous view. On the way she told stories about the city, and on the Paseo de Gracia she pointed out where friends of our families still lived, telling me juicy bits of gossip about some of them. She used the same complicit tone that girl-friends use to tell each other secrets. Alicia was making me feel a strange camaraderie with her.

CHAPTER 14

The city had changed in many ways, but that house was just as I remembered it. Except for the fact that everything had shrunk. The last time I was there, for our farewell get-together, I must have been a lot shorter. I had memories of the cheerful clattering of the blue tram, the only one that still ran in the city, as it passed by Alicia's house. It was one of the oldest models still in circulation, and it brought visitors from the Catalan Railways to the funicular that left them on the summit near the Sacred Heart Cathedral and the Tibidabo amusement park. The avenue; the tram; the funicular; the old park, which was always old in spite of the renovations, with its marvelous nineteenth-century rides that still wor.'ed; the fake airplane, the labyrinth, and the witch's castle; it all held special magic for me as a child, and it still does today.

"Your hotel is not the only place with panoramic views of Barcelona," said Alicia after showing me the large main staircase, the kitchen, and the living room that opened onto the groomed garden, the site of many memorable childhood adventures. "Come."

We went directly up to the third floor, where she had her

private office. I had never been in that room before. I could see the city from up there in an opposite panoramic view. In the distance was the intense blue of the sea, lit by the sun that arrived from behind us, and Mount Montjuïc, with its castle. And there, in the center, the city stretched herself amid the encroaching evening shadows.

"So it was you who inherited Enric's ring," Alicia said suddenly. Maybe it was the tone of her voice, or the expression on her catlike face, or the sharpness of the question. But it startled me.

Alicia had dinner served in her office on the top floor. In the small pink clouds that floated over the sea, the sky still showed reflections of the sun, already hidden, while below, dusk reigned. The city's lights began to turn on at our feet. I had had time to make sure my belongings, which had arrived incredibly quickly, were arranged in my room to my satisfaction and to take a walk through that much-loved garden.

But to my disappointment, he didn't appear.

The only mention Alicia made of her son was to point out that "this is Oriol's room." It was next to mine, but she didn't show it to me, as if he kept it locked. I held back my questions but, deep down, I was hoping to bump into him on the stairs or in a corner of the garden. I figured he must not be in the house.

We talked about my parents, about how different life is in New York. All of a sudden she focused on my hand.

"Is that an engagement ring?"

"Yes."

"He must be quite a guy," she said, smiling.

"Yes, he is. He's a stockbroker."

"Those Wall Street types are used to getting the best." There was a mischievous sparkle in her blue eyes.

I smiled and didn't respond, which was when she suddenly

let loose with the "So it was you who inherited Enric's ring." I took some time before answering.

"It arrived as a surprise for my last birthday, a couple of months before I received the letter from the notary asking me to come."

"Your godfather loved you very much," she said slowly. Her gaze turned sad, as if she were jealous. "He adored you," she emphasized.

"He was always very sweet to me," I replied. "As if he were my uncle."

"And he also loved your mother very much. Very much."

I didn't know how to respond to that. I didn't like her bringing my mother into the conversation. Was she trying to insinuate something?

"I should have guessed it," she continued. She spoke as though she were thinking, mulling over an old slight. "The ring. It wasn't for me. He wasn't saving it for his son. He had it sent to you as a birthday present."

That woman was making me feel guilty for wearing the ruby ring. It was an uncomfortable situation and I wished I were back at my hotel. Alone. Or even having dinner with Luis. Now I was missing that pain in the neck, thinking about how much fun he was. But it was as if Alicia read my mind, and her wide feline face lit up with a cordial smile.

"But I am so glad that you have it, darling." She ran her hand along the part of the table that wasn't filled with dishes and caressed mine. "Can I have a look at it?"

I removed the ring and held it out to her. She took it in her hands, with respect, and held it up to the light.

"It's beautiful," she said. "A masterpiece of thirteenth-century goldsmithing. Look." She stood up to turn off the electric light and brought the ring close to one of the candles on the table, projecting the image onto the tablecloth. There was the red cross, diffused by the light of the flickering flame. Disconcerting, mysterious. "Isn't it fabulous?"

"It certainly is, " I replied. "It's incredible how they were able to set the ruby, with the base carved in ivory, within a gold ring."

"Ivory? What ivory?"

"Well . . . the ivory in the ring, the base that holds the stone and creates the red cross with its white outline. In ivory . . ."

Alicia let out a little laugh.

"That's not ivory, darling."

"What is it?"

"It's bone."

"Bone?"

"Yup. Human bone."

"What?"

She laughed again.

"Don't be afraid, but the white piece carved into the base of the ring is part of a human bone."

I looked at the ring apprehensively. I wasn't the least bit amused about wearing a piece of a dead person on my finger. I thought maybe Alicia was pulling my leg with old ghost stories, making fun of a gullible American tourist.

"It's a relic," she added. "Haven't you heard about relics before?"

"Well, yeah, some, but I never . . ."

"They are not so popular anymore. But they were very important in the Middle Ages and pretty much up until fairly recently. They are the mortal remains of saints. These holy remains used to be set into sword handles or were housed in fabulous metal containers. To this day, many churches venerate relics. We don't know what saint the relic in the ring came from. Maybe it was a Templar hero, a martyr who died defending the faith."

"A Templar?"

"You haven't heard about the Templars either?" Alicia opened her eyes wide, as if she were surprised. The reflection from the candles gave her an eerie appearance.

"Well, I . . . I have heard some things about them." I realized that with her I couldn't pretend to know more than I did, like I had with Artur Boix and Luis. It would be better to just listen to what she had to say.

"Well, there were monks who, in addition to their vows of obedience, chastity, and poverty, vowed to defend the Christian faith on the battlefield. They were grouped into monastic orders, and each order had various hierarchies and a supreme leader: the grand master. Besides the Order of the Temple, there were the Orders of the Hospitaller, the Holy Sepulcher, the Teutons, and later, when the Templars died out, many, many others rose up. I won't go into any more now because I have a feeling that, in just a few short days, you are going to become an expert on the Templars." She projected the cross once more on the table-cloth. "They say that your ring belonged to the grand master. Owning it is a big responsibility, darling."

"Why?"

"Because you have to be worthy of it. It represents a vast moral authority, and you are the first woman to ever own it."

I stared at her without knowing how to respond. Alicia took my hand and caressed it. I felt a strange mix of attraction and revulsion. Then she tenderly, slowly, placed the ring back on my finger. She caressed my hand again. "If it is yours, it must be because you deserve it." She paused. "You don't know how much I envy you, darling."

That night I had trouble sleeping. It was a pretty room with a large window overlooking the city, decorated with lovely period furniture. I had been enjoying the conversation with my hostess, but I wanted to call it a night. I went to my room and bolted the door. I was glad there was a bolt. Alicia was certainly a strange woman. I felt uneasy. Where was Oriol? I looked at my ring apprehensively. That was quite a story. The stone glimmered weakly in the lamplight, as if it were about to fall asleep.

What would the next day bring? I would see him. In the notary's office. And the inheritance? Enric's last practical joke? I changed into my pajamas, but I was too nervous to go to bed. I turned off the lights and opened the window. A cool, yet pleasant breeze welcomed me. Night. Night and the city again in the distance. Below I heard the hum of a car from a nearby road and the screech of another that was going too fast. Then, silence.

CHAPTER 15

There is no amount of impatience that can make a clock move faster. Sometimes impatience makes the clock seem that it has stopped or is moving backward. When I'm nervous I tend to talk nonstop. I'm learning to control myself, but on a day like that, sitting in the taxi, I couldn't keep my inner voice from compulsively talking to some other part of me who was also chattering incessantly. I don't have the faintest idea of where that voice comes from.

I was so tense because I was finally going to see him.

I didn't get a good night's sleep because I couldn't stop thinking about what Enric must have been feeling in his last hours, or what he could have done in those days that Captain Castillo wasn't able to reconstruct. I was also thinking that Alicia was too warm and friendly. And about the horrific chill I got from knowing there were human remains encrusted in my ring, or about what my mysterious inheritance would be. Or that I was finally going to see Oriol.

And then it would all begin again. I wondered how Oriol

would react when we met, what relationship that inheritance, fourteen years after Enric's death, would have with the murder of those men in Sarriá. I thought perhaps it had been a mistake accepting Alicia's invitation, and then I saw that blood red ruby shine. In dreams, half asleep, I even got to the point of being obsessed with the idea that the stone was trying to warn me about something.

I did manage to sleep a bit, but it's hard to say how much. All I know is that in the morning, I had to use makeup to cover the bags under my eyes.

I arrived at the notary's in a taxi. Alicia had told me: "I'd be happy to go with you, but I don't think they are expecting me." And so, that easily, I got out of the offer she had made the day before.

I was twenty minutes early. I told myself that a lime blossom herbal tea would do me more good than a coffee, but I still went into a bar and ordered an espresso and a croissant. The coffee smelled amazing and the croissant wasn't glazed, instead it had toasted ends. With pleasurable nostalgia, it reminded me of the *granjas*, those uniquely Barcelonan cafés that serve breakfast and afternoon snacks, and thick, bitter hot chocolate.

When it was five minutes before the appointed hour, I went to the office, on the ground floor of the building.

It was one of those old buildings filled with lovely flowers and scrolls carved in stone, and interior walls decorated with plant motifs. The door to the notary's office, made of rich chiseled wood and decorated with a handsome peephole and other polished metal ornaments, was on a par with the rest of the building.

"Mr. Marimón's waiting for you," said the fifty-something secretary who opened the door, which surprised me. Notaries and lawyers almost always make you wait.

The woman took me to a light-filled office, with high ceilings and two large windows overlooking the street. The floors and halfway up the walls were covered in oak paneling.

"Miss Wilson!" A man of about sixty stood up from behind a large desk to greet me. He introduced himself as Juan Marimón and brought my hand to his lips as if to kiss it. Luis was also waiting, seated in front of the desk, and he got up, smiling, to kiss me on both cheeks.

"Have a seat, ma'am," he said, pointing to a chair next to Luis's. "Mr. Oriol Bonaplata will arrive in a few minutes."

"We hope . . . ," added Luis with a smirk.

"Mr. Enric Bonaplata was a good friend," continued the man, ignoring Luis's comment, "and his death affected us all very much."

"Would you mind showing me your passport, Miss Wilson?" he asked. "I have to follow legal procedures. I've known Mr. Bonaplata and Mr. Casajoana for years."

I took out my passport and handed it to him. He jotted down some things and then began to speak about Enric's good qualities. My gaze found Luis's and he took the opportunity to give me a friendly wink. He wore an elegant gray suit, a very pale, almost white, salmon shirt, and a tie. Then I glanced at my watch: it was already two minutes past twelve. My eyes returned to make contact with the notary's, who hadn't stopped talking in a slow, friendly tone since we had sat down. Where the hell was Oriol? Wasn't he coming to the reading of his father's will?

". . . on the very same morning of the day of his death, Mr. Bonaplata was in this office . . ." That phrase pulled me from my thoughts. Suddenly here was the opportunity to reconstruct Enric's final hours. But the man's speech continued in a different direction.

"Did you say that that morning he was here?" I interrupted.

"Yes, that's what I said."

"At what time?"

"I couldn't tell you exactly."

"More or less."

"Mr. Bonaplata called me in the morning and asked for an appointment for that same day. My schedule was full, but since it was him . . . well, my father was his father's notary, and my grandfather was his grandfather's. And our great-grandfathers too. So of course, I couldn't refuse him a favor that he was asking for so insistently—"

"So you gave him an appointment." I couldn't help cutting him off.

He'd stopped talking and was looking at me with a hurt expression. I felt guilty. Mr. Marimón was definitely not operating on New York time. Luis looked at me, an amused smile on his face.

"Yes. I gave him an appointment," he said finally. "I made a space for him in the late morning, almost lunchtime."

"And how was he? Did he seem upset to you?"

"No. I don't remember anything in particular. But I was surprised that he wanted to make a second will without changing the first one."

Just then a few knocks on the door interrupted my thoughts.

"Come in," said the notary.

"Mr. Oriol Bonaplata," announced the secretary. And then he appeared.

The first thing I saw were his almond-shaped blue eyes. The ones I remembered. And his smile, that same warm, wide smile. In spite of the time that had passed I would have recognized him anywhere.

"Cristina!" he cried out as he came toward me. I got up and we kissed on both cheeks. He squeezed me in a hug that left me breathless, not because it was so strong but because of the feelings it stirred up.

"How are you, Oriol?" I replied. But if I had followed my

racing heart, I would have said, "Damnit, why did you break your promise? Why didn't you answer any of my letters?"

He and Luis greeted each other with a hug and then Oriol shook hands with Marimón.

He was no longer that tall boy with a pimply face, skinny and shy, who didn't know what to do with his lanky legs. He was still tall, but he now had an athletic physique and moved with confidence. He sat in the empty chair to my right and in a sweet gesture put his hand on my knee saying, "When did you get here?" Without waiting for a reply he added, "You look stunning."

I almost lost it. The brief touch of his warm hand on my leg felt like a thousand-volt electrical charge.

"Thanks, Oriol," I stammered out. "I arrived on Wednesday."

"And how are your folks?" He paid no mind to the other two; it was as if we were alone in the office. I felt flattered by that. As I took a closer look, I saw that he was quite presentable. Nothing like what I'd feared after Luis's description. He wore narrow-legged pants, a round-collared sweater and a matching dark jacket. His hair was in a ponytail and he had definitely showered and shaved that morning. I was relieved. He didn't smell like anything. I wasn't expecting him to wear cologne, but in terms of smells, no news was good news.

In one of my thoughts during the tumultuous night before, seeing that he hadn't shown up at his mother's house, I had imagined him in a sleeping bag on the floor of an abandoned house, without running water and with dreadlocks in his hair.

"If you don't mind, Mr. Bonaplata," interrupted the notary with a friendly smile, "I'm going to proceed to the reading of your father's will. I'm sure that afterward you two will have plenty of time to chat."

Oriol agreed and Marimón, after putting on a pair of glasses and clearing his throat a bit, began to read in a solemn voice.

He was saying that on the first of June 1988 appeared before him, a notary of the illustrious guild, blah, blah, blah and who considered Enric to be of sound mind and body . . . and after all the usual rhetoric, he said:

" 'To Miss Cristina Wilson, my goddaughter, I bequeath the middle section of a triptych from the late thirteenth or early fourteenth century that shows the Virgin Mary and Son. It is painted in tempera on wood and measures approximately twelve by eighteen inches.' "

I was surprised. So that meant my painting was part of a group of three?

" 'And also a ring from the same time period, a ruby set in a gold band. The painting in question is already in her possession, having been sent to her at Easter of this same year, and the ring I will give now to the notary so that he can send it to Cristina for her twenty-seventh birthday, months before the reading of this will.

" 'To my nephew Luis Casajoana Bonaplata I leave the right-hand side of the triptych, a painting of some six by eighteen inches, which represents Jesus Christ on Calvary in the upper part and Saint George below, and which is in a safe at the bank.

" 'And to my son, Oriol, I leave the left-hand side of said triptych, of the same measurements and showing the holy sepulcher and the Resurrection above, and Saint John the Baptist below.' "

The notary made a digression to state that the following text was a letter that Enric Bonaplata himself had authenticated, and then he continued reading:

My Dearest Ones,

This triptych contains, according to legend, the keys to finding a fabulous fortune. It is the treasure of the Templar Knights of the kingdoms of Aragon, Valencia, and Mallorca that King James II was never able to find. There are those who believe that this treasure contains nothing less than the holy grail, the chalice with the coagulated blood of Christ that Joseph of Arimathea collected at the foot of the cross. If this is true, the spiritual power of that holy chalice is immense.

The legend is confirmed when the three paintings are X-rayed, which will reveal that below the paint appears writing that mentions the treasure. I haven't had much time to study it, but enough to know that something is missing, all the information isn't there. The three of you must find the missing clues since my time is running out and I don't have the energy to continue the search.

I must warn you that you are not the only ones interested in the treasure. I hope that with the passage of time my enemies have lost the trail or given up hope of finding it. If that is not the case, I want you to know that they are very dangerous and although I won a battle against them in the past, the victory is still far off. Be discreet and cautious.

For different reasons, I love you three as my children. Life separates people and my wish is that you will come together as you were in 1988 as teenagers.

The least valuable parts of your inheritance are the paintings and the ring. Even if you include the legendary treasure, which is a king's ransom. The inheritance that I want to give you is the adventure of your lives and the chance to renew, in yourselves, the friendship that united our families for generations. Enjoy your time together, enjoy the adventure. I hope you succeed. I have written a separate letter to each of you. May God give you happiness.

Marimón looked at us fixedly over his glasses, professional and serious. He studied our faces. And then, an almost childlike smile appeared on his face and he said, "It's so exciting, isn't it?"

CHAPTER 16

We asked Mr. Marimón to let us use a space where we could be alone. I was moved. I didn't know what was more exciting, the confirmation of the treasure's existence or my reencounter with Oriol. I was dying to talk to him alone, but it wasn't the right moment. I would have to wait.

"It's true. There's a treasure!" exclaimed Luis as soon as we sat down in the small room Marimón had let us use. "A real one, not like in our childhood games with Enric."

"My mother had warned me," interjected Oriol, calmly, his enthusiasm just barely concealed. "So I'm not surprised." He looked at me, smiling. "What about you, Cristina, what do you think?"

"Despite what Luis told me, I was still taken by surprise. I can't believe it's true."

"Neither can I," agreed Oriol. "But my mother is convinced. How much of this could be real? My father had a pretty wild imagination. But what if this treasure really existed? Wouldn't someone have found it hundreds of years ago? And if it does still exist, would *we* be able to find it?"

"Well, of course it exists," declared Luis. "And I'm going to do whatever it takes to find it. Can you imagine opening chests filled with gold and precious jewels? Wow." Then he became serious and, looking at his cousin, said, "Come on, Oriol, don't rain on our parade. That money would come in very handy for me. And if you don't have any material interest, you can leave the treasure to us poor folk."

Oriol gave in. Of course he'd do what he could to find the treasure. After all, it was his father's final wish, right?

"I want to take part in the search too," I told them. "Whether the treasure exists or not. It's the last of all those games we played with Enric as children. Let's do it in his honor, and for the adventure."

Then I thought about it. I had asked for a week's vacation from the law firm. I had arrived on Wednesday, it was now Saturday, and I was supposed to catch a plane next Tuesday. I had no idea how long it took to find a treasure, but I was sure that three days was not going to cut it.

They must have seen something in my face because the Bonaplata cousins were looking at me quizzically.

"What's going on?" asked Luis.

"I have to go back to New York on Tuesday."

"Oh, no," said Oriol, placing his hand over mine, resting on the chair's arm. "You can stay with us. Until we find whatever it is." His touch, his gaze, his smile brought back the smell of the sea and that summer kiss of long ago. A shiver went up my spine.

"I have to go back to my job," I said.

"Ask for a year's sabbatical," replied Luis. "Just imagine how good it would look on your resumé to say that you found all these medieval riches. 'Brilliant lawyer, expert in wills and treasure hunts.' You'll be a guaranteed success. Every law firm in New York will be fighting over you."

His silliness made me laugh.

"Stay with us," interrupted Oriol, in a deep voice that reminded me of his mother's. He still had his hand on top of mine.

I didn't say yes. I know how to resist pressure. But I wanted to stay with all my heart. We agreed that they would go running to the bank before it closed to get the other two pieces of the triptych. I suggested we meet after for lunch at Luis's apartment; I needed time to think and I wanted to read Enric's letter alone.

I walked toward the port and was soon immersed in the colorful atmosphere of the Ramblas. That diverse crowd, vibrating with life, drew me like a magnet.

I remember one day when Enric had taken the three of us to the Christmas fair and we passed by that fountain crowned with streetlights, Canaletas.

"Did you know," asked Enric, "that if you drink from that fountain, no matter how far you go, you'll always return to Barcelona?"

The three of us drank. For years I told myself that I must not have really swallowed.

A couple of street performers danced the tango energetically, making my feet tap along to the beat of a powerful radio-cassette player. He wore a black suit and hat; she, a tight skirt with a slit on the side revealing her thigh, her hair slicked back. They oozed sexual energy. A circle of onlookers surrounded them, dropping coins into the hat that another lovely tango dancer was passing around. I stopped to watch. They were very good.

I went into a café with wide windows that allowed me to see the people roaming on the street. I ordered something to eat and pulled Enric's letter out of my bag.

I paused to look at the envelope with my name handwritten in careful calligraphy. I felt a reverent fear of the paper that had not been opened in fourteen years and was starting to yellow. My heart was as tight as a fist.

Finally, I used a knife to carefully tear open one side of the envelope.

> My dear. I've always loved you like a daughter. What a shame I won't be able to watch you grow up, you're going so far away."

And there, with my chicken salad and my Diet Coke in front of me, tears sprang to my eyes. I loved him so much.

> If what I think will happen does happen, today you will be living a very different life, far from your childhood friends. You probably won't have seen Oriol or Luis for many years. That's why I wanted you to have the ring, because you're so far away from the others. The ring will force you to come back. That ring can't belong to just anybody—it gives its owner a unique power. But it also requires that you give back, sometimes more than you have. Take it to the bookstore Del Grial, located in the Old City, and show it to the owner. I'm quite sure that that business will still exist fourteen years from now. But if for whatever reason that's not the case, Mr. Marimón has a list of names and addresses, which I entrusted to him in a sealed envelope, of people you should see.
>
> This ring symbolizes your mission. You must hold on to it until you find the treasure. In the end you may succeed in this task, or you may decide to give up. But only in one of these instances should you get rid of it. Then, give it to the person you consider most appropriate. It must be someone very strong in spirit, because that ring has a life and a will of its own. Perhaps you yourself could be that person.

Enjoy this last game with me. Find the treasure that
I couldn't find, or didn't deserve to, or didn't want to
find. Be happy with Luis and Oriol.

I love you very very much, as I have since before you
were even born.

Your godfather,
Enric

Tears rolled down my checks, threatening to fall on the table. I
covered my face with my hands. "Enric, dear Enric." My God, I
loved him so much too. What did it mean that he had loved me
since before I was born? Now I'd never know. Was he referring
to my mother? I noticed my fingers were damp. I pretended to
look at the crowded, colorful street. The glass window returned
my reflection, blurred by pale, impressionistic strokes. A short
blond bob, lips that still had some of the morning's lipstick, eyes
I could hardly see. Was that me? Or just the ghost of the girl
I would have been if I had never left Barcelona? Now I could
never be that woman. I could no longer hold back my tears.

Oh God. My heart ached for my missed childhood. And
the memory of Enric. And the longing for the lanky teenager I
had kissed in the storm, who was definitely not the Oriol I had
greeted today.

My sadness about Enric had turned into self-pity. But my bitter tears had a sweet taste. I felt sad for that girl lost in time, and
for the young woman exhausted by the emotions of the last few
hours, and for those feelings that kept her awake at night.

I called the waiter over and asked for a glass of wine, then I
thought maybe half a bottle would be a better idea. I'm not used
to drinking alcohol at lunch, but I had decided to give myself
the pleasure of a good weepy trip down memory lane. And that
didn't go well with Diet Coke.

CHAPTER 17

Luis lives in a penthouse overlooking the convent that gives the Pedralbes neighborhood its name. The convent is made of a cluster of buildings—the church, cloister, and other fourteenth-century structures, with lovely towers and roofs, all protected by high walls. Pedralbes had been swallowed up by the big city, but Luis told me that when Doña Elisenda de Montcada, wife of King James II, founded it in 1326, it was far from the city. There were many outlaws, and the nuns had to protect themselves, behind walls and armed guards, from unwanted visits.

On the other side, the penthouse has a view toward the city and, in the background, the Mediterranean. The apartment is in Luis's mother's name, God knows why. Maybe it was a protective strategy, like the nuns of the Order of Saint Clare and their walls. Except modern. That's why when I had called information they had no listings for any of the Bonaplata and Casajoana cousins in Barcelona. Both, in one way or another, hid behind their mothers. They must have had their reasons.

I was expecting to find them excited. But that wasn't the case. Luis opened the door with a long face, pointing to his cheek and tracing the track of a tear down it with his finger. I understood him immediately; he was saying that Oriol had cried. Then he made the limp-wrist gesture again, knowing Oriol couldn't see him. I didn't like his little pantomime.

"Hello, Cristina," said Oriol without getting up from his armchair. He looked depressed. The whites of his eyes were reddened. Yes, he had been crying. I understood why. Enric's letter had definitely set me off on a good sob. How many tears would I have shed had Enric been my own father? Oriol's father had disappeared in his childhood. He must have missed him for so long, and now, after fourteen years, he had his father's last thoughts in that posthumous letter. Who wouldn't get emotional?

I'd have given anything to read his letter. But it was personal and I'd not dare ask. At least not now.

"Look at them," said Luis, pointing to the two small paintings on wood that rested on top of a chest of drawers. They measured a bit less than a hand span in width and two in height and together they were about the size of the one I had in my parents' house. They were identical in style and color.

"So these make a triptych with my painting, right?"

"That's right," confirmed Oriol. "The wood, even though it's been treated, is pretty worm-eaten, but you can still see traces of joints on the sides. Luckily the painting was made in tempera over a plaster base, which woodworms can't digest."

"Joints?" I asked.

"Yes, hinges," clarified Oriol. "Based on its size, this triptych was a small portable altar. These two pieces functioned like doors to close on top of yours, the larger one. There must have been some type of handle, and with its small size it was easy to carry. The Templar Knights would have used it for mass in the field."

"The Templar Knights?" asked Luis. "How do you know it belonged to the Templars?"

"From the saints."

"What saints are those?" I asked.

"In Luis's painting, the one below the scene of Christ crucified on Mount Calvary, is Saint George, standing over the legendary dragon."

I looked at the painting to my right, which was the left side
of the triptych. Just as Oriol had said, it was divided into two
paintings. The lower image was that of a warrior standing over
a creature shaped like a small lizard and no larger than a dog.
He wore tights and a short tunic, a cape, a helmet, and a crown,
and held a lance in his hand.

"What a shitty excuse for a dragon," I said.

They both laughed.

"That's true," said Luis. "It's a lame beast. Instead of killing
it he could have just frightened it off with a swift kick."

"Gothic painting, at least in the thirteenth and early fourteenth centuries, wasn't too concerned with proportions or per-
spective," explained Oriol. "What was important was just being
able to identify the saint. If they painted a warrior standing over
some kind of reptile, it was Saint George. Except that this one
has something different."

"What's that?" I inquired.

"Generally he's represented with a red cross, but a long,
thin one, the regular Crusade cross. Not like this one. This
one is a flared cross, the cross of the Knights Templar. This
saint comes from Asia Minor. He was an officer in the Roman
army and he converted to Christianity. He suffered every kind
of torture and eventually got his head chopped off. There are
no historical references to the character, but legend has it that
he rescued a princess from a ferocious dragon. The Crusaders
made him a knight and he became a powerful symbol of the
victory of good over evil. It's said he fought battles in Aragon
and Catalonia, swashbuckling his way to victory over the
Muslims."

"And that's why he's the patron saint of Catalonia and Aragon," added Luis.

"That's true, but he's also the patron saint of England, Russia, and several other countries. He was quite popular in the Middle Ages. Anyway, note that he died by decapitation. In the upper part, within what looks like a chapel, you'll surely recognize the scene of Christ crucified at Calvary. It's a classic. The Virgin looks about to faint and Saint John the Apostle is suffering, with his hand on his cheek in a gesture of dismay. This image was so often repeated in the Gothic period, both in painting and in sculpture, that antiques dealers call him 'the saint with a toothache.'

"And in my painting, which according to the hinge marks goes to the right, or to your left if we face it, shows above, also within a chapel, a triumphant Christ resurrecting, coming out of the holy sepulcher."

I looked at the upper part, crowned with a slightly pointed arch, like my painting of the Virgin, and I realized that that element was different in Luis's painting. His arch had a central foil that divided it in two.

"And in the lower part we have Saint John the Baptist, Christ's precursor," continued Oriol, "the one who baptized him in the River Jordan. He was the patron saint par excellence of the Poor Knights, as the Templars called themselves."

"Yeah, he definitely looks poor," I said. He was a bearded man with long hair and some sort of scroll in his right hand. He wore a sheepskin loincloth.

"He died by decapitation too, like Saint George," explained Oriol.

"Thanks for the info. It's more than I needed," I joked, pretending to be repulsed.

"Salome, King Herod's concubine, asked him to grant her a wish. He agreed. She asked for the head of Saint John the Baptist on a silver platter."

"Gross," said Luis.

"So the Templars liked saints who lost their heads," I concluded, looking at Oriol pointedly.

"They certainly did," he replied, holding my gaze with a slight smile. I wasn't sure if he had gotten the tone of my remark.

"That requires an explanation, Mr. Historian." Now it was Luis who spoke. "The Templar Knights seem to have been a very strange sect."

"It's a long story. It started when the Christian princes, mostly the ones from Burgundy, plus the French, the Teutons, and the English, inspired by the stirring speeches of various monks preaching throughout Europe, fell upon the Holy Land like a plague of locusts. Actually, much worse. Even the Byzantines, and their capital city of Constantinople, who were Christians, but Orthodox ones, suffered from that band of savages. It was an indescribable bloodbath. The Iberian kingdoms sent hardly any contingents. We had our hands full trying to take back our lands from the Moors. We're talking about a century before the battle of Las Navas de Tolosa. At that point the Moors controlled the majority of the peninsula and the Christian kings were under constant threat."

"Okay, what does that have to do with the heads?" I asked impatiently.

"With time and attrition, the Christian momentum in the Holy Land slowed down and the noblemen started to make pacts. So when a knight fell prisoner in battle, they would negotiate a ransom for his freedom. If the prisoner was a plebeian with nothing to pay, he would become a slave. That didn't happen with the Poor Knights of Christ. They had taken vows of poverty and to fight to the death for their faith; they were trained killing machines. So the Moors knew that no matter how high ranking a Templar Knight they captured, and no matter how much treasure the order had, they would never get any ransom for one of them. And they couldn't be used as slaves either; it would be like placing a time bomb in your own house. So, with great respect and admiration, when they managed to capture one of the knights of the flared red cross alive, they slit his throat as soon as possible. That's also why the Templar Knights fought to the death—they never gave up, never asked for a truce or expected mercy."

"I see," said Luis with a bemused smile. "That's why the Templars felt such kinship with the decapitated saints; they had a lot in common."

Oriol nodded.

"Oh," I exclaimed, adding my sarcasm to Luis's, "that explains a lot. Like why they kept pieces of dead people in their rings. What weirdoes."

"Well, what should we do now?" continued Luis. "Here we have the side paintings, of decapitated saints before they lost their heads, and in New York we have the center piece. According to Enric, that triptych contains the secret to a fabulous treasure." He looked at me. "You should have the missing piece sent to us, don't you think?"

"Hold on a minute," interrupted Oriol. "No one is forced to accept an inheritance. Cristina didn't want to give us an answer before, and now she should decide whether she wants to search for that treasure or not. If she decides to do it, she'll be making a life-changing commitment. Starting with spending some time here." He shot a look at my engagement ring. "And I'm sure she has commitments in America."

"What's with you, Oriol?" asked Luis. "Why are you even asking that question? Of course Cristina wants to find the treasure."

"Let her speak for herself. I have conflicting feelings on this matter too. I think that, sometimes, it's better to let sleeping dogs lie."

In his voice there was a sad note that moved me.

"What is that supposed to mean?" Luis was getting mad. "Not that again, Oriol. For God's sake! We're talking about your father's last wish."

"Count me in for the treasure hunt," I said impulsively, nipping their argument in the bud, fully aware of the trouble my decision would cause in New York.

"Me too," said Luis, and we both waited for Oriol's answer.

He looked at the ceiling and seemed to be thinking it over. Then his face lit up with that smile, the one he'd had as a kid, the one I fell in love with. It seemed as if the sun was coming out from behind the clouds.

"I'm not going to let you guys have all the fun." He lifted his chin with playful arrogance. "Besides, you'd never find it without me. Count me in too."

I almost jumped for joy. I looked at Luis and saw that his anger had passed and that he was smiling too. It was like returning to our childhoods, and playing with Enric again. Except, he was no longer with us. Or was he?

"Bravo!" exclaimed Luis, raising his hand to give us each high fives. "Let's go get that treasure!"

Suddenly Oriol's expression darkened as he said, "I don't know, but I have a strange feeling." He swallowed hard. "This might not be such a good idea."

Our smiles vanished. Did Oriol know something that we didn't? Why was he hesitating? What had his father told him in that posthumous letter?

CHAPTER 18

That night, again, I had trouble falling asleep. I kept thinking about this confusing situation. I sat in the dark, gazing at the lights of a Barcelona that, in spite of its being after four in the morning, looked more alert than the previous night. Of course, I realized, it was a Saturday.

The three of us had gone out for dinner and afterward we'd had a few drinks in a popular local spot. Luis kept messing with me, acting as if he was the cock of the walk. And I guess I must have been the hen. He'd compliment me, using double entendres that grew more and more sexual the more he drank. His flattery didn't bother me, it made me laugh. I didn't tell him to stop because I wanted to see Oriol's reaction. He just watched his cousin with amusement. Once in a while he chimed in with a compliment of his own. How was it that the same words sounded so much better when they came out of his mouth? And those blue eyes that shone in the bar's half-light. He wasn't loud like his cousin, so each time he said something I had to move closer to hear him over the racket, and the proximity left me almost breathless. At first I found the little game amusing, but I was left with the impression that if Luis was

playing the role of the rooster, and I was the hen . . . then Oriol
was the capon? That bothered me, so I didn't want to make it a
long night, and anyway, I could still call New York at a reasonable hour.

My mother hit the roof. She had already told me that it was
a trick, that the treasure was just a ruse to keep me in Barcelona. How could I just throw away my law career by taking a
year off? It didn't matter if it was only a month or two. But this
would ruin everything.

Alicia! That witch is behind this. Don't even go near her. And
no. Forget about it. There's no way she'd send me the painting
of the Virgin. I should come home, please, she didn't like any of
this. Oh! And Mike? What about Mike?

I reasoned with her, explaining that it was a fabulous adventure, the kind most people dream of but never experience, that
she should calm down, that Mike would understand, and so
would the people at the firm. And if they didn't accept it, I'd be
able to find a better job when I got back.

"What is it that you don't understand, Cristina?" she said.
"If you stay there now, you'll never come back," she sobbed.

I did what I could to calm her down. In general, my mother
is a very restrained person. Why was she going to such an extreme? What was going on with her?

Mike was much more reasonable.

"It's okay, I'll admit that it sounds like an Indiana Jones adventure," he maintained, "but are you sure everyone's playing
with a full deck? A treasure? That's all very exciting, but finding
treasures doesn't happen every day. Well, maybe in the stock
market or a casino or raising the *Titanic* . . . but that's only for
professionals.

"If you want to stay a few days more, go ahead, but let's
decide how many. What do you want? A couple of weeks, a

month . . . but then it's over. Remember, we're engaged and we haven't even set a date for the wedding."

"Yes, sir." When Mike reasoned things out, there was no refuting his logic. "That makes sense. Deal. As soon as I get back, we'll settle on a date. Okay?"

"Yeah. Okay," he replied cautiously. "But you still haven't told me how long you're staying."

"I can't say yet . . . less than a month. Definitely," I declared emphatically.

"But didn't we just agree to set a specific time period?" It seemed like he was getting mad.

"Yes, of course," I said, rushing to assure him that he was right. "But to know how much time I need, I need time."

The line was silent. I wondered if Mike was having trouble digesting the wordplay (he's very much a numbers guy) or if he was just getting furious.

"Honey?" I inquired after a little time had passed. "Are you there?"

"Yeah, but I don't like this," he grumbled. "I want to know how much goddamn time my fiancée is going to stay on the other side of the ocean. *Capeesh?*" Sometimes Mike tried to say a word or two in Spanish and it came out in Bronx Italian.

That, along with other things, was what I was thinking about at four in the morning as I gazed at the distant light of the city. I could feel that only one wall separated me from Oriol.

I understood why Mike didn't like it that I hadn't given him a date for my return. But I thought I could keep him pretty much under control. On Monday I'd talk to my boss. I'd ask for an extended leave of absence. Maybe they wouldn't guarantee I'd have a job when I returned, but I had a certain reputation and, at my age, finding another job wouldn't be a problem. That wasn't what was worrying me.

María del Mar. Now there was a problem. My mother refused to send me the painting and I knew she wouldn't do it even if the fate of the world depended on it—we are alike in some ways. I would have to go to New York myself to get it. Damn, it was my painting. I wasn't asking her to lend me something of hers.

But it was her attitude that made me nervous. It's not as if she has such a balanced personality. Her strong emotions, even though they're buried, prevent that, but it had been a long time since I'd seen her so upset.

Alicia. There was something very personal between her and Alicia. I didn't even want to imagine how she'd react if she found out that I was staying at Oriol's mother's house. Something must have happened between them, something that my mother had never told me and had no intention of telling me. Of course, that was before, maybe now she'd have no choice but to open up her box of secrets. I would have to find a good argument to get her to send me the painting. Otherwise, I'd go get it, just show up and surprise her, without giving her time to hide it from me. I fell asleep exploring my options.

When I woke up, the sun was seeping into my room through the slits in the blinds behind the curtains.

It took me a while to place where I was. I wasn't in my apartment in New York, or in my parents' house on Long Island. I was in Barcelona, in Oriol's house. It was Sunday, my fifth day in the city, but I felt as if I'd been here a lot longer. Two thoughts hit me at the same time: I was hungry and I wanted to see Oriol again.

My stomach had to wait. I took a shower and fixed myself up a bit. Then I went down to the kitchen hoping to find him there. Instead I found Alicia.

"Good morning, darling," she said with a smile and gave

me a kiss on each cheek. "You guys got in late last night, didn't you?"

She held me by the hands and, as if it were an uncontrollable impulse, searched for the ring with her eyes. I only had the chance to say good morning back before she began talking again, now making eye contact with me.

"Alchemists classified the ruby as a burning stone, an anthrax. Yes, the same name as that biological weapon that has become fashionable in your country lately. Anthrax, as far as gems are concerned, is now in disuse. You won't find it in the dictionary," she purred. "It was used in the occult terminology. It comes from *carbunculus,* which means burning coal and refers to the stone's inner fire."

She took my hand. As she caressed it she got closer to the rings so she could see them better, focusing on the Templar ring, looking for its inner radiance. The stone seemed to fascinate and dazzle her.

"Rubies are ruled by Venus and Mars. Love and war, violence and passion. Blood red. They are named for that color. Did you know that there are male and female rubies?"

I looked at her, taken aback, although I was beginning to get used to these surprises.

"Yes, according to occult knowledge"—she lowered her voice a bit more, as if sharing a secret—"you can tell the difference from their glow. Yours is masculine. Look, it has an inner gleam. Do you see the six-pointed star that moves inside the gem when you turn the ring?"

I nodded.

"Female rubies glow outwardly. Venus rules them. Not yours. Yours is the color of pigeon's blood. It's male and it responds to Mars, the god of war, of violence . . ."

Her blue eyes sought mine again, as if awakening from a trance. She tenderly released my hand and a warm smile spread across her face.

"There's toast for breakfast in the kitchen. But don't eat too much; in a couple of hours we'll have lunch." The chameleon woman had changed again, and now she seemed to be an attentive, sweet mother figure. She was charming, nothing like the witch my mother and Luis had described, or the enchantress I had just sensed a few moments ago. "I invited Luis over for lunch too. Now go on out to the terrace, Oriol is having breakfast there."

That sounded like an excellent idea, so I went there as quickly as I could. I was afraid that Alicia would again become entranced by the ring and make me even more edgy.

CHAPTER 19

Oriol sat at a table in the rose garden, now in full bloom, sipping coffee, the newspaper spread out in front of him. The flowers burst with color against the canvas of bright green leaves. The sun lavished pools of light among the trees' shade. A soft breeze caressed my skin.

I stopped to observe him and his surroundings. It seemed like a scene from one of Santiago Rusiñol's garden paintings that hung on Alicia's walls. In fact, I was sure that one of them was a painting of that very same garden. I took a deep breath and realized that all the anxiety Alicia's story had provoked in me had now disappeared. I focused on Oriol, who continued reading, unaware of my presence. I said to myself that, although he had changed, he was still the same boy I had fallen in love with as a girl.

"Good morning," I said, greeting him with a smile.

"Good morning."

"I'm glad to see you here," I said to feel him out, "glad you didn't spend the night squatting in some building."

He looked at me playfully, gesturing for me to take a seat.

I did and continued prodding him as I nibbled on a piece of toast.

"I've been told that when you aren't teaching at the university, you spend your time squatting in other people's properties."

He shot me that look again, as if to say, You wanna play, huh?

"Abandoned property," he corrected me, taking a sip of coffee. "There are people without homes and poor children who need education and after-school activities. Using a building that's just sitting empty, waiting for speculators to drive up the real estate market, to help others is an act of charity. Not a crime."

"You could bring them here; there's plenty of space."

He started to laugh. He was so charming. He calmly spread butter and orange marmalade on his toast. He wrinkled his brow as if thinking it over, then he began to eat, nodding his head as if to say that I had a point.

"That's not a bad idea. But I don't do it for two reasons."

"Which are?"

"First of all, because my mother would kill me."

I laughed.

"And second, because this place is not unoccupied."

"But there's room for more people. Why don't you put someone up?" I wanted to corner him.

"Come on, little lady lawyer." His blue eyes fixed on mine with an amused look. "Let me be a little inconsistent in my principles. Besides, my mother is already giving refuge to a poor little American girl, right?"

I didn't answer. Smiling, I focused on the taste of the coffee and the pleasure of a sunny morning as I looked over the trees, the blooming rosebushes, and the well-kept lawn. And I admired him, openly. I was enjoying the moment.

"You've grown up, young man," I told him. "No more pimples, and you are very handsome."

He laughed.

"In this country it's usually the man who compliments the woman, not the other way around."

"Well, then go ahead." I raised my chin defiantly. "But please, do it with more style than Luis did last night."

I thought to myself, Cristina, you're flirting. Be careful, it's early. Don't go too far. But I was already in gear and I didn't feel like putting on the brakes.

I got another amused look from him. He took his time with his coffee, and his toast . . . he was making me wait. He knew how to control the moments of silence, he didn't rush, and he avoided attacks well, as he had when I'd questioned his principles. He'd have made a good lawyer.

"You've grown up too, bossy-boots." That was a low blow, I thought to myself. It wasn't a good sign that he was using that not-too-flattering nickname. "You used to have tiny breasts and look what a lovely set you've got now. If they're real, that is."

"They're real," I quickly clarified.

I wasn't expecting that sort of response. He paused again, as if he was gauging my reaction. If I didn't have a high opinion of myself, I would have been very, and I mean very, uncomfortable. I figured he was doing it deliberately, that for some reason he wanted to punish me.

"And your rear end. So nice and round."

"Are you insinuating that it's fat?"

"No, I'd say it's almost perfect. When you sit down, you must make the chair awfully happy."

"I thought that kind of *piropo* went out with chastity belts," I replied. He watched me with obvious amusement. No, I said to myself, he can't be gay, like Luis said. Or the castrated bird I took him for last night. But who knows, maybe he's faking it, and that's why he's being so crude and biting, to keep me at a distance. Maybe I'd been too bold.

"You are very good looking," he concluded.

"Thanks. It took you long enough to say it. Although you haven't learned much since last night." And after exchanging smiles, we returned to our breakfast. In spite of the clumsiness of Oriol's compliments and his sly aggressiveness, I felt happy and I savored the moment. But suddenly what I had been holding in for so long washed over me in a surge of anger.

"How come you never wrote to me?" I accused him. "How come you never answered any of my letters?"

He stared at me, dumbfounded.

"We made a commitment to each other. Don't you remember? We said we'd write." I could feel the old resentment, and pain, and disappointment coming out. "You lied."

He continued looking at me, his blue eyes opened wide in astonishment.

"No, that's not true," he said finally.

"Yes, yes it is!" I insisted.

"No. It's not true," he repeated.

"How can you deny it?" I paused to take a deep breath. I was furious and sad. Oriol was trying to rob me of my best adolescent memories. I was about to tell him, If you're gay and you regret the past, just tell me already. I felt very hurt. That jerk hadn't answered my letters and now he was playing dumb. "I dare you to deny it, if you've got the guts," I insisted.

"I deny that I lied to you. Of course I remember. We kissed and we were boyfriend and girlfriend. Or at least we said we were. And we promised to write." He was serious. "But I never got a letter from you and you never answered any of mine."

I stared at him with my mouth hanging open.

"You wrote to me?"

Just then Luis appeared, smiling. I hated him for interrupting.

He started to chatter and I was left wondering if what Oriol had said was true.

During lunch we discussed the will and the treasure, with Alicia egging us on. She seemed as enthusiastic as we were. It was obvious that it would be difficult to exclude her. I hadn't realized that when I accepted her invitation, this would be the price I had to pay—or at least part of it. And we were too excited to keep quiet or talk about something else. Luis didn't hold back either, despite the warnings he himself had given me about Oriol's mother. I got the impression that Alicia had it all planned. That she'd known about the treasure before we had, and that she knew other things we still didn't know. She didn't talk much; she'd listen long enough to ask the right question and then ponder our reply, watching us carefully. The memory of the trance she had gone into looking at the ring and her references to alchemy made me uneasy.

What did that woman know that she wasn't telling us?

CHAPTER 20

I had forgotten how wide the avenue leading to the cathedral was, and how spacious the open spaces between buildings. But I remembered as a kid going to the Christmas fair to buy trimmings for the tree and figurines for the nativity scene.

It was usually cold and, wrapped in our winter coats, we passed the glowing stands, some decked out with twinkling strings of colored bulbs. In the background, *"El vint-i-cinc de desembre, fum, fum fum"* or some other Christmas carol would be playing. It was a world of fantasy, of sacred history, with little clay figurines set in scenes of moss and cork. Those were magical days that led up to the night when El Tió, the Catalan Christmas log, would poop out its candies and Santa Claus and the Three Kings would compete to bring the best gifts. The aroma of damp moss, spruce trees, eucalyptus, and mistletoe filled our noses. The memory of those scenes full of shepherds and their flocks, angels, *caganers,* houses, mountains, rivers, trees, bridges—everything tiny and innocent—I still cherish as among the treasures of my childhood. And Enric. Enric enjoyed it like one of the children. Most of my memories of those fabled visits to the fair were with him. He always offered to take us. His store was close to the cathedral and he wouldn't take no for an answer, so the three of us, plus him, my mother, and Luis's mother would go to the Christmas fair. Afterward, he'd treat us to a cup of hot chocolate at one of the *granjas* on Calle Petrichol.

"Do you remember our trips to the Christmas fair?" I asked Luis.

"What?" he replied, surprised. He must have been thinking about treasures, gold and precious stones, while I was thinking of treasured memories. It was midmorning when Luis parked in an underground lot near the cathedral. We had decided with Oriol that Luis and I would go to Del Grial, and he, with the help of some restorer friends, would be in charge of X-raying the painting.

"Do you remember when we came here to buy figurines and moss for our nativity scenes?" I repeated.

"Oh yeah. Of course." He smiled. "We always had a great time. The fair is still here at Christmastime, but now this whole area is a pedestrian mall."

As we crossed the avenue I rediscovered the cathedral's magnificent stone facade, carved with delicate filigree.

"I want to go in," I said.

The day before, Alicia had confirmed that the bookstore still existed, and I didn't feel in any rush. I was hopeful about what could happen there, and at the same time anxious and fearful that nothing would happen and the treasure-hunt game would end right there. That it would suddenly slip through my fingers, like when I was a little girl and I'd squeeze a handful of fine sand at the beach. I wanted to delay our arrival by a few minutes.

"You want to do tourism? Now?" complained Luis.

"It'll just be a moment," I replied. "I want to see if it's how I remember it."

He grudgingly agreed.

* * *

Barcelona's cathedral had been built between the thirteenth and fifteenth centuries. When construction started, the Templars were at the height of their power. But by the time the building was actually finished, they had disappeared.

The small wooden vestibule at the entrance gave way to an enormous interior space of carved stone, where pillars rose gracefully, crossing each other to form pointed vaults. At the center of each dome, there was a voussoir, the large keystone that supports everything. The voussoirs are rounded and sculpted with saints, kings, knights, and coats of arms, like gigantic medallions that seem to float in the air. On the sides, above the chapels, multicolored stained-glass windows illuminate the stone surfaces.

The inside of the church lived up to my memories, but it was the cloister that really impressed me. It radiated peace, distance, and isolation from the material world. It was hard for me to believe that I was still in the heart of a hectic, modern city. The central garden is filled with palm trees and magnolias that rise as if they want to escape toward the sky, soaring over the Gothic arches, above a lake with white geese. It seemed as if we were miles away, and hundreds of years in the past.

That was when I saw him again, Barbablanca. Again I felt a chill. It was the man from the airport, the one waiting in the hotel, the same one I thought I saw among the crowd on the Ramblas. The same dark clothes, the same white hair and beard. The same insane look. This time, his cold blue eyes didn't engage mine. He was leaning against one of the pillars, next to the moss-covered fountain on which Saint George rode on horseback. He pretended to be looking at the birds.

"Let's go," I said to Luis, pulling him by his jacket. He followed me, surprised, and we left through one of the doors that opened onto the street, in front of an old palace.

"What's up with you now?" asked Luis. "What's the big rush—"

"It's getting late," I murmured. I didn't want to explain it to him.

We crossed the plaza, headed toward the Del Grial bookstore, located in a nearby alley. I was hoping that our abrupt exit would throw off my pursuer.

Del Grial was a truly old bookstore; it sold very old books and was located in a very old building. The door and the small display windows had wooden baseboards. Looking in from the outside, it seemed as if everything was piled up: windows stuffed with books, old photograph collections, piles of greeting cards, postcards, posters, very, very old calendars, and a layer of venerable dust covering it all. As we went in, a bell rang. There was no one in sight and Luis and I looked at each other, wondering what we should do.

The chaos that the store had promised from the outside was outdone by the reality inside. Along a center aisle, huge bookcases that reached the ceiling were filled with volumes of varying bindings and sizes. In the middle, dividing the passageway into two smaller ones, there were a few tables overflowing with old magazines. The magazine covers had drawings of smiling girls in the style of the 1920s. My eyes were immediately drawn to a collection of paper dolls in full color, with lovely period clothes.

"What a place!" I exclaimed while I looked around. I was tempted to spend hours browsing through those fascinating heaps of old junk. The large illustrated paper dolls, the armies of cutout soldiers, the charts of painted animals. Memories of childhoods lived and left behind perhaps a hundred years ago. But we had come looking for something very specific. After having seen the man in the cathedral, I was feeling uneasy, so I pushed Luis toward the inside of the bookstore.

"Hello!" he shouted, seeing that no one had reacted to the sound of the bell.

Finally, we detected some movement at the end of the passageway. A young man of about twenty was peering at us over his thick glasses. He seemed annoyed by the intruders who had violated his peace as the lone reader in a library. We must have brought him back, at an inopportune moment, from a safe world of ancient fantasies, back to that dangerous, prosaic modern reality from which he had sheltered himself behind barriers of letters, walls of words, trenches of sentences, moats of books.

"What do you want?" he snapped at us.

"Hello," I repeated, moving to Luis's side; I wondered how to tell our strange story to this young man.

"We've come to retrieve something that was left here for us by Mr. Enric Bonaplata," said Luis, getting ahead of me.

The young man made a puzzled face before replying, "I don't know him."

"Because this was many years ago," insisted Luis. "Fourteen."

"I don't know what you're talking about."

Then I showed him my hand with the rings.

"About this," I said.

He looked at me, shocked, as if I were threatening him.

"What is this?" Behind the thick lenses his eyes looked fishlike. He was staring at my long, red nails.

"The ring," I said impatiently. And his eyes moved to the rings on my fingers. He looked at them for a few moments without any reaction.

"This ring!" specified Luis, grabbing it, my finger still inside, and bringing it closer to the guy. He looked at me with a bewildered expression before saying, "The ring!"

"Yes. The ring," reasserted Luis.

The guy turned his back to us and went farther inside the store shouting, "Mr. Andreu! Mr. Andreu!"

To my surprise, the bookstore extended beyond the passageway and from some remote place someone responded, alarmed by the tone of the young man's voice.

"What's going on?"

"The ring."

A thin man, who looked like he had passed the legal retirement age by quite a few years, appeared.

The boring "Ring, what ring?" conversation was repeated and finally I put the Templar signet ring right in front of Mr. Andreu's face.

He moved my hand far enough back for his eyes and eyeglasses to get a look at it, and then he too exclaimed, "The ring." He didn't take his eyes off the jewel even as he asked, "May I see it?"

He examined it from every angle and held it up to the light, then finally pronounced, "It is the ring. No doubt about it!"

Yeah, of course, I thought, that's what we've been saying this whole time. It was then that the frail old man took off his glasses and with his gaze sized me up.

"A woman," he said. Obviously, I thought. A woman and the ring. Do you get it now? All the gesturing and shouting was starting to get on my nerves, but I prudently kept my peace.

"How can a woman have the ring?" His voice was indignant. "So many years of waiting, and a woman shows up! How can this be?"

"Last Saturday, Mr. Enric Bonaplata's will was read," intervened Luis, "and Miss Wilson here, along with his son, Oriol, and myself, are his heirs in regard—"

"I don't care about that," replied the cantankerous old guy, cutting him off. "I'll do what I have to do and that's it."

And grumbling something like, "What was that Bonaplata thinking . . . another woman . . . ," he went back toward his lair, which I imagined to be a labyrinth of old paper that he gnawed at when he was hungry. Judging by his look and his mood, he was having a case of indigestion.

The young guy shrugged his shoulders, as if he wanted to apologize for his grandfather's nasty temper, and I turned to look at Luis, who raised an eyebrow as if to say, What now?

Suddenly my heart leaped. Luis had his back to the door, and as I looked at him I saw someone watching us through the windows. It was the man from the airport. The one I had just seen in the cathedral. I shuddered.

The man held my gaze for an instant, then disappeared. No way was this a coincidence, I thought. Luis turned toward the door when he noticed my fear, but it was too late.

"What's going on?" he asked.

"I just saw that man, the one from the cathedral," I whispered.

"What man?" And then I remembered that I hadn't told him anything about it.

"Here it is." The old man appeared with a sheaf of papers before I could answer Luis. It was tied with ribbons and sealed with red wax. The yellowed outer folder showed handwritten lettering that I couldn't make out. The man put the package in my hands and snorted again, looking at Luis in search of solidarity.

"Another woman," he repeated.

I was tempted to chide the old man for his sexist remarks. But I restrained myself. I gave the large bundle of papers to Luis, thanked the cranky bookseller, and headed for the exit. I stuck my body halfway out the door to have a cautious look around. A couple of elderly women were walking down the alley but there was no sign of the creepy guy.

The man was gone, but I felt uneasy.

CHAPTER 21

We walked through the narrow, almost deserted streets toward the parking lot. A couple of well-dressed young men approached. They didn't look anything like that weird old man, and I felt calmer. But as they passed us, one of them rammed into me, pushing me against a large closed wooden door.

"If you're quiet and do what we say, nothing will happen to you," the guy warned us. I got scared as he waved a knife threateningly in front of my face. Out of the corner of my eye I thought I could see that Luis was in a similar jam.

"What do you want?" Luis asked.

"Gimme that."

"No way," responded Luis.

"Hand it over or I'll slit your throat," growled the one threatening Luis. And the man began to pull on the papers that Luis refused to give up. I imagined my friend dying, stretched out on the ground bleeding, and me trying to help him. Not that file, or the treasure, if it really existed, was worth his dying for. Nothing was worth dying for; that's something I had spent a lot of time thinking about since the twin towers had collapsed.

"Give it to him, Luis!" I shouted.

But Luis continued to struggle with the other thug, who tried to stab him on his hands. Luckily, Luis was pulling on the folder and the guy missed. I had my back against the door. The second thug pricked my neck with his knife and shouted at Luis, "Let go of the papers or I'll kill her!"

Then everything happened all at once. Behind our attackers I saw Barbablanca appear from out of nowhere. His eyes were practically popping out of his head. I was already afraid, but when I saw him, my knees went weak and I almost lost control of my bladder. He swooped down on us, brandishing a wide knife with a sinister gleam. He had his black jacket rolled over his left arm. Luis let out a cry; the mugger's knife had struck the hand that held the sheaf of papers. His scream was followed by a howl of surprise and pain as the old man sank his dagger into the right side of the thug threatening me. He dropped his knife and I let out a sigh of relief. In that moment, the files dropped from Luis's wounded hand. His attacker was too busy fighting the old man to make off with it.

The old guy was angry and surprisingly agile for his age. He fended off the knife with his arm protected by the jacket and immediately returned the attack, going at the thug with his huge blade. The younger guy dodged it by jumping. I still had my back to the large wooden door and saw the wounded mugger run away, limping. The other one tried to slash the old man again, but once more his makeshift shield saved him. The attacker didn't wait for the old man's reaction but ran off after his partner.

I didn't feel it was over, though. The old guy frightened me more than the pair of crooks he'd scared off. He sheathed his dagger, without even bothering to wipe off the blood, in a leather scabbard that hung from his waist. He calmly looked at me and then at Luis with unfocused eyes. He put on his wrinkled jacket. I realized that it hid his weapon perfectly.

What does this lunatic want from us? I wondered. Neither

Luis nor I had moved; we were in a state of shock, looking at our savior suspiciously. Luis covered his wounded hand with a handkerchief. I still had my back against the door.

The old man slowly picked up the sheaf of papers and handed it to me, saying, "Next time be more careful." His voice was hoarse and his eyes were fixed on mine.

He turned around and, without paying any attention to Luis, walked away.

"That guy would have killed us without the slightest hesitation!" exclaimed Luis, waving his bandaged hand through the air. We were back in his apartment in Pedralbes. The sheaf of papers rested on a small table. We sat around it on cushions on the floor.

"Those thugs were lucky to get away," I interjected. "That old guy showed no emotion, he had no mercy in him."

"But he saved you," said Oriol. "How can you explain why he protected you if he seems so evil?"

He smiled slightly, an amused twinkle in his eyes. Our story hadn't made much of an impression on him.

"I don't know," I replied. "I don't understand what's going on. Someone tried to steal that folder from us; we don't know what's in there, but supposedly it's got something to do with the treasure. Then a creepy old man, who's been following me since I got to Barcelona, appears from out of the blue and saves our lives. Those thugs knew what they were looking for. They weren't after money or jewels. They didn't even try to take my purse. They were after what's in that file. They know about the treasure!"

"And what's the old man's role in this story?" cut in Oriol. "Could it be that he was following you to protect you?"

"I don't know," I had to admit. "There are too many mysteries. I have the impression that all of you know more about what's going on than I do. And that you are keeping things from me." I looked at both of them.

Oriol, addressing his cousin, smiled. "What do you say, Luis? Are you hiding things that we should know?"

"No. I don't think so, coz. What about you? What are you hiding?"

"Nothing important," replied Oriol, widening his smile. "But don't worry, if something comes to mind and I think it's relevant, I'll tell you when the time comes."

His ambiguity made me angry.

I yelled, "If you know something, say it. They almost killed us today, damnit."

Oriol looked at me.

"Of course I know more than you do," he said seriously. "And Luis knows more than you do. We all know more than you do. You've been away for fourteen years, remember? In all that time a lot of things happened. You'll find out little by little."

"But there are people out there with knives, and they're using them," I answered, pointing to Luis's bandaged hand. "There are some questions that can't wait. Who are those people?"

"I don't know," he said and shrugged his shoulders. "But I suspect that they could be the same ones who confronted my father when he was looking for that Templar treasure. What do you think, Luis?"

"Yeah, it could be them, and that they're still on the trail of the treasure. But I'm not totally sure."

I remembered how my apartment had been ransacked and I realized that we had rivals and that they were following us very closely. But the old guy wasn't one of them.

"And the crazy old man?" I inquired.

Luis shook his head.

"No idea," he said.

Oriol shrugged, indicating that he didn't know either.

"Okay. That's enough chatting," said Luis impatiently. "Are we going to open the file or what?"

On the stiff cover of the folder could be read with some difficulty the words "Arnau d'Estopinyá." The bundle was tied with faded red ribbons that in turn were held in place by several wax seals. I immediately recognized the flared Templar-cross imprint on the wax—just like the one on my ring. Luis got some scissors and very carefully cut only the ribbons necessary to extract the documents. The pages were yellowed with age, numbered, and written on in royal blue ink in an irregular hand. Luis proceeded to read page one.

CHAPTER 22

I, Arnau d'Estopinyá, Monk Sergeant of the Order of the Temple, feeling my strength fade and knowing I am close to returning my soul to the Lord, herein tell my story, written in the monastery of Poblet on January of the year of Our Lord, thirteen hundred twenty-eight.

" 'Neither the tortures of the Dominican inquisitors, nor the threats of the agents of the King of Aragon, nor any of the other violence and harm inflicted upon me by the greedy wretches who suspected what I knew were able to extract from me the secret that death wants to take away with me.

" 'Until today, I have kept the promise I made to the good Master of the Templars of the Kingdoms of Aragon, Valencia, and Mallorca, Brother Jimeno de Lenda, and to his Lieutenant Brother Ramón Saguardia. But if by dying, my secret dies along with me, my promise will not be fulfilled. It is this concern, and not the desire to relate my life's ups and downs, that has led me to ask Brother Joan Amanuense to write down, under a solemn oath of silence, my story.' "

Luis interrupted his reading, but his gaze continued scrutinizing the page.

"This is a fake," he said after a little while, looking at us with alarm. "It reads too easily to be a medieval text. What do you think, Oriol?"

His cousin, taking one of the pages, looked at in silence. Then he declared, "This wasn't written any earlier than the nineteenth century."

"How do you know?" I asked, disappointed.

"It's written in old Catalan, but not from the thirteenth century or even close. The words are relatively modern. Besides, it was written with an elaborate metal nib and on a type of paper that can't be more than two hundred years old," Oriol explained.

"How can you be so sure?"

"Because I'm a historian and I've read a ton of old documents." He was smiling. "Is that good enough for you?"

"Yes," I replied, disheartened. "And I don't know why you're laughing. What a disappointment."

"I'm not laughing, but I'm not so worried about it either. Reading transcriptions of older texts is pretty normal in my line of work. Just because the document isn't original doesn't mean that the story is false. We have to find out more before we draw any conclusions. And there are also the wax seals with the Templar cross protecting the bundle."

"What about them?" asked Luis.

"The imprint is identical to one left by a seal that I found among my father's things."

"Are you implying that he falsified the files?" I inquired.

"No. It could really be an old document, just not more than two centuries old. And, well, I am sure that he decorated the bundle to make it look more formal."

"I think we're playing one of his games again," declared Luis. "Just like when we were little kids."

"Then is this all just a joke from beyond the grave?"

"No. I think it's very serious," replied Oriol. "I know that he was searching for the treasure with total conviction."

"But is there even a treasure?" I insisted.

"Definitely. Or at least there was. But who knows? Maybe somebody beat us to it. You remember our hunts for the treasures that he hid for us, right?"

We nodded.

"He'd hide chocolate coins covered in gold and silver foil. What was the best part? Looking for the treasure or eating the candy at the end?"

"The search," I said.

"But it's different now," said Luis. "We're not kids anymore and there's a lot of money at stake."

"I think that this is about the search," said Oriol. "My father made it clear in his will: there is a treasure, but the real inheritance is the adventure of finding it. He loved opera and classical music. But do you know what the last thing was that he listened to? It was Jacques Brel's 'Le Moribond,' a song of farewell from someone who is dying but loves life. And before that was 'Viatge a Itaca' by Lluís Llach, inspired by a poem by the Greek Constantin Kavafis. It refers to *The Odyssey*, the story of Ulysses searching for his way back home to Ithaca. Enric believed that life is each person's journey back to his own Ithaca. That life is in the voyage, not the destination. The last port is death. And that spring afternoon fourteen years ago, Enric's ship arrived for the last time to take him to his last Ithaca."

His words left us in a pensive silence, saddened.

"Dear friends," added Oriol after a moment's reflection, "we didn't inherit a treasure. We inherited a search. Like the games we played as kids."

"What should I do?" inquired Luis after a little while. "Keep reading?" I thought that he could care less about the search— Luis wanted the treasure.

* * *

" 'I was born inland, but I was destined to be a mariner,' " Luis continued reading. " 'I am not a nobleman, but my father was a free man and a good Christian. I was not knighted, in spite of my merits, because within the Temple, even with the humility required by our vows, birth rank mattered.

" 'When I was ten years old, there was drought and famine in my father's lands and he sent me to live with one of his brothers, a merchant in Barcelona.

" 'I became fascinated by the sea the moment I saw it. I was also enthralled by the sea of humanity ebbing and flowing through the streets of that great city, always filled with noise and jubilation. The sea trade with Perpignan and the new kingdoms conquered from the Saracens by King James I in Mallorca, Valencia, and Murcia was constant. Catalan ships and merchants traveled over the entire Mediterranean, all the way to Tunis, Sicily, Egypt, Constantinople, and the Holy Land.

" 'But I dreamed of the glory of battle in the service of Christianity, and I loved ships more than trading. I wanted to cross the sea and visit the exotic cities of the Orient. When my uncle sent me to the port on errands, I watched the ships, spellbound. I did everything possible to get the sailors to tell me about their most recent voyages, or how to operate some of the strange artifacts on board.

" 'The docks were a very different world from the inland territory I came from; they were intriguing, fascinating. You could see rich merchants from Genoa and Venice decked out in luxurious apparel, and covered in jewels. You would see very tall, blond Normans arriving from Sicily, and Catalan and Aragonese knights with steeds, weapons, servants, and armed retinues embarking for overseas wars. There were fierce-looking Almogavars dressed in furs, ready to set off to, one day, go fight on the side of our lord King Peter III against the rebel Saracens of Montesa, and the next day, to ship out to North Africa to fight as mercenaries in the employ of the King of Tlemcen. There were also black people from the south, stevedores loading bundles, and Moorish slaves dressed in rags. They spoke strange languages and, at night, around the bonfires and in the guesthouses, one could hear new songs and astounding stories of war and love. The activity was frenetic. Carpenters, both in the shipyards and on the shore, never stopped sawing, hammering, and caulking. They were building a fleet destined to rule the Mediterranean. How I miss those days. I can still smell the aromas of pine, tar, sweat, and roasted sardines at lunchtime.

" 'But it was the monks of the Militia who fascinated me as a boy. They never went to taverns and people stepped aside out of respect. Among them, the Templars stood out. Always austere, with short hair, well fed and well dressed. Their tunics looked hand sewn, they had none of the rags the Franciscans wore, nor clothes that seemed stolen, like the king's soldiers'. The Templar monks, even though rich, never allowed themselves luxuries like other clergy did. Their rules were very strict. The largest vessels in the port belonged to them and their provincial Master presided over the realms of our King Peter and his brother, King James II of Mallorca.

" 'I always tried to converse with the Templars and was always moved by their faith, their strength, and their absolute confidence in the final triumph of Christianity over its enemies. They had an answer for everything, and they were willing to offer their lives in battle at any moment. I also found out that the Templar Knights preferred to fight on their steeds and were rarely in command of ships. This was work for monks of more humble origin. Like me.

" 'Right after I turned fifteen I obtained permission from my father to join the Order. I wanted to be the captain of a warship and fight against Turks and Saracens, and see Constantinople, Jerusalem, and the Holy Land. The noble boys could take their vows at thirteen, but I had no donation to offer, only my faith, my enthusiasm, and my muscle.

" 'My Templar friends from the docks interceded on my behalf before the Commander of Barcelona and he agreed to see me, but in spite of my enthusiasm, the old monk told me to pray a lot and persevere. He made me wait a year in order to test my faith.

" 'That was a very intense year. I continued helping my uncle, whose business was on the rise due to the war preparations. That was when the Aragonese squadron, led by our great King Peter, set out to conquer Tunis. Now there was a great king! May God keep him in his Glory.

" 'Boys my age loved to watch the troops and knights with their steeds embarking. We saw the King, Roger of Lauria, the Admiral of the Fleet, and counts and nobles. It was quite a show and we never tired of following the processions to the docks and shouting ourselves hoarse through the streets.

" 'The Temple Order also sent some vessels and troops to support the monarch's efforts, but out of obligation and without enthusiasm. My Templar friends told me that this upset Brother Pere de Montcada, our provincial master at the time. The Holy Father, who was French, had reserved those kingdoms in North Africa for Charles of Anjou, King of Sicily and brother of the King of France.

" 'So when King Peter, already in Tunis and prepared to begin the conquest, asked Pope Martin IV for support, it was denied. While in North Africa pondering whether to continue the war against the wishes of the Pontiff, a group of Sicilians who had risen up against Charles of Anjou's abuses went to see him. Our monarch, upset by the Pope's attitude, which showed him to be allied with the French, disembarked in Sicily, kicked out the French, and was crowned king. This angered the Pope so much that he ended up excommunicating King Peter.

" 'When the year passed I was finally admitted, as a lay cabin boy, on the ship of Brother Berenguer d'Alió, Captain Sergeant. That year Admiral Roger of Lauria beat the French squadron of Charles of Anjou in Malta and the following year defeated them again in Naples.

"'The Pope, angry with our King because he continued to defeat those the Pope protected, called for a crusade against him, offering King Peter's kingdoms to any Christian prince who could reclaim them. Naturally the candidate chosen was Charles of Valois, son of the King of France and Isabel of Aragon. The French armies crossed the Pyrenees and lay siege to Girona. The Aragonese and Catalan Templars, in spite of owing direct obedience to the Pope through our Grand Master, sought excuses not to intervene and secretly supported our King.

"'The arrival of the Admiral's squadron was the beginning of the end of that disgraceful crusade. Roger of Lauria not only destroyed the French fleet in the Gulf of Leon, but the Almogavar troops he was transporting also attacked the enemy on land so ferociously that they had to flee, suffering great losses. God didn't want the French in Catalonia, nor that wrongheaded Pope.

"'I was eighteen years old, and already a good sailor. The Catalan-Aragonese Admiral was my hero. My dream was to command a galley and take part in great battles, like Roger of Lauria.

"'And what can I tell you? After the good news came the bad. Two years later, Tripoli fell into Saracen hands, and many illustrious Catalan Templar Knights died in its defense, including two of the Montcadas and the sons of the Count of Empúries. It was a sign of the misfortunes to come. It was in that tragic year that I finally took my vows and became a Templar monk.

"'The next big disaster was at Saint John of Acre. I was twenty-four years old and the second in command of the *Na Santa Coloma*, a beautiful galley, the kind they call a bastard galley, with twenty-nine banks of oarsmen and two masts, the fastest of the Catalan Templar fleet. I was still under the orders of Brother Berenguer d'Alió. Our mission was to protect the Templar ships of the Crowns of Aragon, Valencia, and Mallorca, but in spite of having participated in a good number of skirmishes and Berber boardings, I had never seen anything like what happened in Acre.

" 'The *Na Santa Coloma* had never been farther than Sicily, and I was excited. I would finally see the Holy Land. We Templars in the Iberian kingdoms had our Crusades at home, so we rarely fought in the East. But the situation was desperate; the Sultan of Egypt, Al-Ashraf Khalil, was throwing Christians into the sea, after over one hundred and fifty years of Christian presence in the area. Acre was under siege, but luckily our fleet ruled the water, the only way in or out of the city. Upon our arrival we sent a group of crossbowmen to protect the walls in areas under Templar control.

" 'The city was covered in smoke from the fires on the roofs and walls caused by the containers filled with lit naphtha that were constantly being launched by one hundred catapults. The air smelled of burning flesh. Even stones seemed to catch fire, but there weren't enough men to cart water and put out the flames.

" 'Every once in a while a resounding thud was heard, the impact of rocks weighing several tons. They were launched by two gigantic devices that the Sultan had had built. There was no wall, house, or tower that could withstand the impact and they collapsed among clouds of dust.

" 'Everything pointed toward a tragic end, and we decided to take to Cyprus some Christian women, children, and wounded men. But we had to set aside room for them. My orders were to save our Templar brothers first, then the monks of the Holy Sepulcher, the Hospitallers, and the Teutons, and then noted knights and ladies. And finally, if there was room, any other Christians.

" 'One day, we heard a deep rumble, like an earthquake. It

was the sound of one of the highest towers and part of the wall, which had been mined by the Moors and continuously pounded by their projectiles, collapsing. A mist of dust and smoke hid the sun. We heard the howls of the Mamelukes attacking the city and the cries of people fleeing through the streets. Some tried to board the last ship on the dock, others tried to take refuge in our fort that, although located within the city, was protected by walls and had access to its own wharf. But space and resources were limited and we had to leave many behind. It broke my heart having to fend off Christian women, children, and old people with my sword, and leave them in the hands of the bloodthirsty infidels, knowing that they would not find shelter anywhere in that chaotic city . . .' "

"Hold on," I begged, "Just one minute please."

Luis stopped reading and he and Oriol stared at me curiously. I felt a chill, the hairs on my neck were standing on end, and, confused, I covered my face with my hands. My God! That story was the exact same dream I'd had in New York only weeks before. Someone had described my vision hundreds of years before I saw it! The falling tower, the cloud of dust, the fleeing people, the slashing swords of the Templars—as I now knew—to keep the common people from taking shelter in their fortress . . . it was impossible, absurd.

"What's going on?" Oriol inquired, touching my arm.

"Nothing." I sat up. "I have to go to the bathroom."

I sat on the toilet. I was so shocked that my legs couldn't hold me up. I wanted to think, to reason this out. It wasn't something rational, but emotional. What I had felt months earlier and what I was feeling now went beyond any logic. I was scared. I debated whether I should keep it to myself or talk about it. I was afraid they would make fun of me, especially Oriol. Luis definitely would. I don't like being in situations where I can't defend myself. But this whole treasure thing, and the Templars, was beyond weird. Well, let's just say it wasn't the kind of thing that happens every day. I thought it would be best to just accept the surrealism of the story and tell them. The truth was, I was going crazy and I needed to share my feelings.

Luis responded with an incredulous little smirk that reminded me of him as a chubby teenager with the face of a chinchilla, but I didn't say anything. Oriol scratched his head thoughtfully.

"What a strange coincidence," he said.

"Coincidence?" I exclaimed.

"Do you think it could be something more than a coincidence?" He looked at me curiously.

"I don't know what to think." I appreciated the fact that he wasn't taking it as a joke. "It's very weird."

He gestured ambiguously and fell silent.

"If you just tell us your dreams, then we won't have to read this," interjected Luis sarcastically. "Or should I continue?"

"No," I replied firmly. "I'm exhausted. I need to rest." I wanted to know what happened to Arnau d'Estopinyá, but all the emotions of the day had squeezed every ounce of energy out of me.

"Talk to my mother," said Oriol.

"What?" I replied, intrigued.

"Talk to Alicia Nuñez about your dream of Acre."

"Watch out that she doesn't put a spell on you," Luis said jokingly. He had some nerve, I thought. He was crossing the line. It was one thing to secretly call her a witch, but quite another to say it in front of her son.

"Maybe that's it," said Oriol without batting an eyelash. "Maybe her spells, or to put it better, her vision of other dimensions of reality can be of some help to you."

"Thanks, I'll think about it," I said.

CHAPTER 23

Oriol said good-bye at Luis's, claiming he had a meeting with a group that was organizing a charity event for the needy. I would have to take a taxi back to Alicia's. I have to admit I was disappointed. Luis had invited me to dinner, but I didn't want to go. Later, on the way back to Alicia's through that rainy night, I thought that maybe I should have had dinner with him, put up with his insinuations and laughed at his stupid jokes. I felt alone and vulnerable in the city that had suddenly turned dark and hostile.

"Psychometrics."

"What?"

"Psychometrics," repeated Alicia.

I had heard right. But it was the first time I'd heard of it and I hadn't the faintest clue as to what it meant. I waited for her to continue.

"Psychometrics is the ability certain people have to perceive the feelings, emotions, and past events contained in an object."

Alicia had taken my hands in hers and looked me in the eyes. "It happened to you with the ring."

She said it seriously, firmly. She seemed totally convinced.

"Do you mean that . . . ?"

"That your dream about the tower's collapse, about the assault on Acre," she interrupted fervently, "about the wounded warrior who arrived, staggering, to the Templar's fortress, it really happened. The ring absorbs the anguish of the person wearing it at the time. You were able to sense it."

"But how? Do you mean that my dream really happened to someone seven hundred years ago?"

"Yes. That's what I'm saying."

I stared into her eyes. Her large warm hands gave me a strange calmness. Alicia was explaining the unexplainable. It didn't make sense. I wouldn't have believed it myself under normal circumstances, but if something strange has ever happened to you, something that goes beyond logic, you appreciate any argument that justifies it.

"I've never heard of anything like that in my life."

"It's a type of clairvoyance."

"But how can it happen?"

"Honestly, I don't know." There was a sweet smile on her face. "Occultists say that there are records, called the Akashic chronicles, that contain the memory of everything that has ever happened. In certain circumstances we can reach them. That ring seems to be a means of access. The same thing happened to Enric."

"This happened to Enric too?"

"Yes, he mentioned to me that sometimes images of ancient events would appear to him, almost always tragic ones. Events that created very strong emotions in the people who lived through them. He attributed it to the ring; he believed it was a warehouse of experiences."

I looked at the ruby, glowing eerily under the light. I thought about the unusual dreams that had plagued me since it had come into my possession. I could remember only some vaguely, but now I had an explanation for my unusual dreams of the last couple months. But as hard as I tried, except for a few concrete cases in which there were very clear sequences, I was unable to remember anything significant or to distinguish between the few images that I did remember.

Through the wide window I could see the lights of the city, diffused by a mantle of fog.

I distracted myself by observing Alicia's collection of statuettes, ivory bodies dressed in bronze, some covered with precious stones, some in dance poses, others playing instruments, scattered about various pieces of furniture.

A nude ballerina, a life-size art nouveau bronze, standing motionless in a dance step, held a crystal lamp laden with flowers. Under its light, the wine in our glasses sparkled with deep, velvety red tones. We ate dinner again in Alicia's private chamber on the top floor, her secluded vantage point overlooking a magical city. Her company comforted me. She was anxious to find out what had happened that day and I had no reason to hide it from her. When I got to the story of Saint John of Acre she must have sensed my distress and, drawing her chair closer, took my hands in hers.

"This has never happened to me before." I realized that I was moaning, like a little girl who has fallen and scraped her knees.

"It's not you," she assured me. "It's the ring."

Now she caressed the mysterious ruby with its gleaming six-pointed star. Then she stroked my hands. It felt good. It made me a bit sleepy. After all the tension and stress of the day I could feel my body relaxing, letting go. What a day. It had begun with the visit to the Del Grial bookstore. Then came the mugging and the appearance of the old man. Then the shock of reading the manuscript and recognizing my own nightmare in it.

"There is something in that ring; it's not easy being its owner," she said suddenly. "It has powers."

I gave a start. Her remark brought Enric's will to mind. "That ring can't belong to just anybody. It gives its owner a unique power," Enric had said in his letter. He had also said something about my keeping it until I found the treasure. Now those words sounded like a threat. I promised myself that I'd reread his letter as soon as I returned to my room.

"That ring establishes a very particular relationship with its owners, a sort of vampirism," she added after a pause. "It takes your energy to activate what it carries inside and gives it back to you in the form of dreams."

I looked at the ring apprehensively. Now it felt like a leech sucking out my blood, through my finger. If I hadn't felt a commitment to Enric, I'd have taken it off immediately.

There was a particular nuance to her deep voice that made me look into those blue eyes that were so much like her son's. Her words again comforted me and I realized that she was the only person who could understand me. A vague smile danced around her lips as she caressed my hair. Then she kissed my cheek. Her second kiss was near my mouth. That touch disturbed me. And when in the third kiss our lips met, I was shocked. I realized that I was in her arms and I got up with a start.

"Good night, Alicia," I said. "I'm going to go to bed."

"Good night, darling." Her smile had widened. "Sleep well. Let me know if you need anything." She did nothing to keep me from leaving, as if she had expected my reaction and was amused by it.

When I got to my room, I bolted the door.

It had been a day of excessive emotions. I was exhausted but uneasy. I was sleeping lightly when I was again seized by that strange vision. I saw it just as if I were there:

A shriek cut the dense air like a knife and echoed through

the foul basement, bouncing off the large chunks of exposed rock in the walls. The fog seeping through the barred windows mixed itself with the smoke from the embers, where the branding irons turned, red hot, and with the fumes from the torches that lit that hellhole. Brother Roger had held up well for the first hour of torture, but now he was beginning to break down. After the echo of his scream died, you could still hear him whimper, like a wounded animal.

I shivered. Covered by a tattered loincloth, I didn't know whether it was fear or the freezing fog boring into my bones that was making me tremble. My entire body was filled with pain, lying on the rack, hands and feet shackled; I felt that the next turn of the screw would break me. But I had to take it. And I continued my prayer: "Lord Jesus Christ, my God, help me in this time of need. Help Brother Roger, help my brothers, that they may all bear it, so that not one gives in, so that no one lies."

I heard the voice of the Inquisitor interrogating my brother in the faith: "Confess that you worship Bracoforte. That you spit on the cross. That you fornicate with your brothers!"

"No, it's not true," whispered Brother Roger.

Then there was silence. I waited, terrified, for the next scream, which was not long in coming.

The Dominican friar interrogating me had grown silent for a few seconds, perhaps to observe the torture of my brother, but he soon returned to the same questions.

"You renounced Christ, isn't that so?"

"No. I never did such a thing."

"Did you worship that head called Bracoforte?" I opened my eyes, blurred by tears, and looked at the ceiling but could barely make out the beams. I saw the hard features of the inquisitor, partly covered by the cowl of his Dominican habit. "Confess and I will let you go," he said.

"No, it's not true," I replied.

"Give him iron," ordered the torturer. The red-hot branding iron burned the skin of my belly, which was as tense as a drum.

My scream filled the room.

I sat up in bed. The feeling, the pain, was so real that I couldn't fall asleep again that night. At dawn, I finally dropped off, completely exhausted.

CHAPTER 24

It broke my heart having to fend off Christian women, children, and old people with my sword, leaving them in the hands of the bloodthirsty infidels, knowing that they would not find shelter anywhere in that chaotic city.'"

Luis had resumed reading, repeating the last sentences he had read before my interruption the previous day.

"'Our Templar Grand Master, William of Beaujeu, died there from the wounds he received defending the wall as the Mamelukes entered the city in a burst of blood and fire.'"

The sun was gone from Luis's apartment, and now hid behind Mount Collserola. We'd gathered again to continue reading Arnau d'Estopinyá's file. Oriol had been busy at the university that morning, and despite my impatience, I decided to wait until all of us could get together. Luis confessed that he hadn't been able to wait and had already read the whole document several times. Now, all of us seated on large pillows on the lovely Persian carpet, he read it again out loud.

"'We lasted ten more days, although both we and the Saracens knew that in spite of the ten- to thirteen-feet-thick walls, the fortress would fall shortly,'" continued Luis, "'in only the time it would take for the Moors to reposition their largest attack devices. The last day we had to protect the loading of the skiffs with the few crossbowmen we had left. At that moment, it was no longer the infidels who were in danger, but also the people who had taken refuge in the fortress. Seized with panic, they wanted to get to the ship at all costs. They'd pay any price, offering all their belongings. Many men made their fortune off that tragedy. It's said that such was the case of the then Templar Brother Roger de Flor, who afterward abandoned the Order to escape punishment. Later he'd become the great Almogavar captain, scourge of the Moors and the Orthodox, but not before making a large fortune thanks to the refugees' misfortune.

" 'When our ship, loaded with the wounded and infirm, who cried out with each lurch, set off on its way to Cyprus, I could barely make out, among the dust and smoke, the banners of Islam flying over the ruins of Saint John of Acre. I felt a deep sadness. Not only for the loss of the last great Christian bastion in the Holy Land but for the Knights Templar too. I had a premonition that their end was at hand.

" 'Among the wounded were two young and passionate monks, the Knights Jimeno de Lenda and Ramón Saguardia. On the long trip back to Barcelona, I'd become friends with them. Saguardia was with the Master General William of Beaujeu when he fell, fatally wounded, and tried to help him. The Grand Master, as he lay dying, gave him his ruby ring. Miraculously, Saguardia managed to survive by walking, although seriously wounded, all the way to the gates of the Templar fortress at the peak of the Mameluke assault on Saint John of Acre.' "

Saguardia, I thought, he must be the knight wearing the ring in my dream.

" 'Back on Catalonian shores, *Na Santa Coloma* returned to its tasks of protecting ships and participating in raids against the Moors.' "

Luis read with the confidence of someone who knows the text well.

"'A few years later, King James II and the provincial Grand Master Berenguer de Cardona agreed on the barter of the extensive Templar lands near the city of Valencia. His grandfather James I had given us these lands for our help in the conquest of the kingdom. In return we received the city of Peñíscola, its fortress, the port, various nearby castles, forests, and fields. I had been promoted to Sergeant shortly before and it was then that our master saw fit to grant me the command of a *fusta*, a cargo ship that traveled the Barcelona, Valencia, and Mallorca routes.

"'That wasn't what I wanted, but I made the effort, as my vows of obedience required. But those vows didn't forbid my speaking to my superiors and my friends, Brothers Lenda and Saguardia, to try to persuade them that my skills would be put to better use in war than in transportation.

"'After a few years, I was finally given command of a galley with twenty-six banks of oars and one mast. Our Lord granted me victory in various skirmishes and I captured many enemy ships. Everything appeared to be going well, but Brother Jimeno de Lenda was worried. One day he told me that someone named Esquius de Floryan, a former Templar Commander expelled for being a heathen, had gone to see our King James II with atrocious accusations against the Templars. The monarch offered him a large reward if he could provide evidence of his charges. Esquius was unable to provide any and the King forgot about the matter.

"'That year we lost the island of Raud, the last Templar possession in the Holy Land. Brother Jimeno was growing extremely anxious. He said that dark forces plotted our demise, and that unless part of what we'd lost in the Orient was recovered soon, our sacred mission would be sullied and our spirit weakened.

"'Two years later, in 1305, King James II signed the peace treaty in Elche with the Castilians, adding part of Murcia to the Kingdom of Valencia, including all of the coast up to Guardamar. The area to protect was now much larger; it reached farther south and was more vulnerable to Moorish attacks. It was then that my former superior, Berenguer d'Alió, gave up the command of the *Na Santa Coloma* due to his advancing age. I became its Commander.

"'And what can I tell you? The terrible year of 1307 arrived. Brother Jimeno de Lenda became Master of Catalonia, Aragon, Valencia, and the Kingdom of Mallorca. Brother Saguardia became Commander of the main Templar enclave in the Kingdom of Mallorca. Masdeu, in Rosellón, became his Lieutenant. The traitor Philip IV of France enticed our Master General, Jacques de Molay, with honors and trickery, to Paris. On the morning of October the thirteenth the French king's troops launched a surprise attack on the Templar fortress. With no resistance from the Master, he took the fortress, and, later, burned the Master at the stake.

"'At the same time and in the same way, the Templar castles and fiefdoms in all of France were taken. That sacrilegious King, with slander, lies, and despicable accusations, sought and achieved the demise of our Order. Did he do so for the love of justice, for the love of God? No. He only wanted to steal the Templars' riches, used to finance the sacred mission of recovering the Holy Land. Philip IV, "the Fair," knew what the Order had and knew how to get it. It wasn't the first time he had imprisoned, tortured, and killed for money. Years earlier he had persecuted the Lombard bankers to rob them of their assets in France, and later he did the same to the Jews.

"'He not only accused the French monks, but in order to cover up his crime he slandered the entire Order and every Templar Knight individually. The king sent letters to all the Christian Kings, including, as he liked to be called, Count of Barcelona, Our Lord James II, King of Aragon, Valencia, Corsica, and Sardinia. He had added to his titles the islands that the Pope had given him in exchange for going to war against his own younger brother, King Frederick of Sicily. That shows what type of person our monarch was.

"'The news of what had happened in France quickly reached Masdeu's fiefdom. Brother Ramón Saguardia did not delay and, taking two knights and a servant, galloped without rest to our headquarters at Miravet Castle. Ramón didn't trust the Kings. He thought that they were greedy vultures, and therefore carried with him the most valuable possessions of his fiefdom. He sent emissaries to the other Templar holds in Rosellón, Cerdagne Valley, Mallorca, and Montpellier, with instructions to safeguard their possessions by sending them to Miravet. Brother Jimeno de Lenda, upon hearing the news, ordered an emergency chapter meeting of the Order. Among those summoned were the commander of Peñíscola and I myself. It was decided that we'd ask for help and protection from our King James II, although secretly we began to reinforce and supply the fortresses that could best withstand a long siege.

"'Brothers Jimeno and Ramón had reserved a very special honor for me. Now that all the most valuable possessions of each fiefdom had been collected in Miravet, it would be easier to protect them. If the situation got worse, my orders were to head out toward Peñíscola with the treasure, load it onto the *Na Santa Coloma*, a fast ship that no royal galley would be able to catch, and hide it in a safe place until the uncertainty passed. I promised, on my soul's salvation, to never let anyone who wasn't a good Templar get hold of these treasures. Ramón Saguardia gave me his ring, the one with the flared cross etched in the ruby, as a token of my promise and my mission. I was moved by the trust placed in me by the monks. I spent days waiting for the treasure to arrive, fasting and praying to the Lord to make me worthy of such an undertaking.

"'I would give my life, I would give everything, to succeed in my endeavor.'"

CHAPTER 25

That's it," said Luis. "There are no more pages."

"What?" I asked, surprised. "The story's not finished."

"But the document is. That's it."

I looked at Oriol. He was thinking.

"The treasure is not just a legend," he said finally. "At least we know for sure that it existed. Perhaps it's never been found and it's waiting for us."

"And we also know that Cristina's ring is authentic," added Luis. "And that it belonged first to a grand master and then to Ramón Saguardia and then to Arnau d'Estopinyá."

I was still impressed by the coincidence of my dream and the story in the document. I accepted Luis's conclusions without questioning them. Really, at that point I would have believed anything they told me, as crazy as it might have seemed.

It was obvious that, during the fall of Acre, the bearer of the ring was Brother Saguardia. The knight who, although badly injured, managed to arrive at the Templar fortress in the midst of a Mameluke attack. And that was exactly my vision. I saw what Brother Ramón Saguardia saw on the streets of Acre among the people fleeing in search of refuge.

I looked at the ring, its blood-red stone, as always, glowing under the light. How much violence, how much pain did it hold within?

"But there's no mention of the painting," Luis said, continuing his analysis. "It's the only element we can't connect to the story."

"It is related," I interjected. The cousins were silent, waiting for me to continue. "The Virgin on my painting wears a ring on her left hand. The same ring."

They both remained quiet for a little while, looking at me, spellbound, ecstatic.

"Is that true?" asked Oriol finally. I nodded.

"Then everything is tied together," said Luis.

"Yes," said Oriol pensively. "But it's very strange. Are you sure about that?"

"Of course. What's strange about it?" I asked.

"Virgins in Gothic paintings didn't wear rings, much less virgins from the thirteenth or early fourteenth centuries. I know a lot about medieval art and I've seen hundreds of representations of Mary and the child. Ancient depictions of saints didn't flaunt jewels. The Virgin wore a crown only when she was represented as a queen. Bishops and high dignitaries of the church were shown with rings, usually worn over white gloves. The occasional ring began to appear in Flemish and German paintings in the fifteenth and sixteenth centuries. But that was much later than the time our triptych was painted. Really, in the kingdom of Aragon, flaunting jewelry was frowned upon by Catholics of the period."

"Then why does the ring appear in Cristina's painting?" asked Luis.

"It's very strange," replied Oriol. "And not just strange; it would have been a total scandal at the time. In the writings of the period, church authorities warned husbands against buying jewelry and wives against wearing it in public." Then he added, as if he had just remembered, "Well, I do remember seeing a thirteenth-century Virgin wearing a ring. But it was a forgery."

"Do you think that my painting is a fake?" I asked, disappointed. "Do you think your father would have given me a forgery?"

"No," responded Oriol emphatically. "Send you a fake? It's absurd. Sometimes I think he loved you even more than me. Enric had the money to buy any painting he wanted, and he was known for his spending. I'm sure it's real."

"Then why does the Virgin in my painting wear a ring?"

"It must be a sign."

"A sign?" interjected Luis. "What do you mean by a sign? Maybe for you, since you know about ancient art, but for Cristina and me it has no meaning whatsoever. We wouldn't even have noticed."

"Who do you think put that sign in the painting? The original painter or someone else, later?"

"I'm sure it was the same person who hid a message in the paintings."

"So there's really a message in the paintings?" asked Luis.

"Yes. I got the results from the X-rays this morning."

"What did you find?" I asked, dying of curiosity.

"In both paintings, in the lower part, at the feet of the saints—just like my father wrote in his will—there's an inscription that had been covered with paint."

"What does it say?" asked Luis.

"One says 'treasure' and the other says 'underwater cave.'"

"The treasure is in an underwater cave!" I exclaimed.

"Yes. That's what it looks like," conceded Oriol. "And it fits perfectly with d'Estopinyá's story. Lenda and Saguardia entrusted a sailor with hiding the treasure."

"Well, now we have a really important clue," said Luis.

"Yes, it is important," replied his cousin, "but it's not enough.

Who knows how many caves there are along our shores? We'd have to look through the entire western Mediterranean. Even if we limited our search to the areas that were under Master Brother Lenda's charge, we'd still have the Catalan coast, including the French areas of Perpignan and Montpellier, plus the Valencian coast, part of Murcia, and the Balearic Islands. And if we extend that, even leaving out Moorish territories, we'd have Corsica, Sardinia, and Sicily. Without more information we'd spend the rest of our lives searching."

"Well, then we have to find more clues," I said.

"We need your piece of the triptych," Luis reminded me.

"Yes, I must get my mother to send it," I declared, wondering how I was going to do that.

"I'm coming to Barcelona," she said as soon as she heard my voice.

"You?" I burst out. "What for?"

"Look, Cristina, something curious is going on over there," responded María del Mar. "I never find you in the hotel when I call. Even at times when you should be in bed. Do you think I'm stupid? You're not staying at that hotel. They're taking messages for you and you call me later, could be from anywhere."

Wow, I thought, Mamá was a daughter once too.

"I think you're getting yourself into trouble," she continued. "Forget about Enric's inheritance and his silly treasure stories. He always did have a wild imagination. Your life is here, in New York. Come home."

"Mamá, I told you that I want to get to the bottom of this. Whether it's true or not. And you stay home. You haven't been back to Barcelona in fourteen years and now you're in a rush to come here. Let me finish what I'm doing and I'll come back and do whatever makes you happy."

"Ah! So I'd get in your way?"

Now she's upset, I said to myself. Why is our relationship always so difficult?

"You wouldn't get in my way, Mamá." I was trying to be nice. "But this is my business."

"Well, since I wouldn't be getting in your way, I'll be there the day after tomorrow." Her tone was decisive. "Pick me up at the airport."

Oh no. I started to get anxious. I tried to imagine myself with my mother and the cousins discussing the treasure. That would be ridiculous! Or trying to get information out of Captain Castillo with her in tow, both of us showing a bit of leg. What a pair of detectives we'd make. Or with Alicia. It was obvious that the last person she wanted to see was Alicia. Of course, now that I'd had some personal dealings with her, I was beginning to think that maybe my mother had her reasons.

"Well, yes"—it came out suddenly—"to be honest, you'd be getting in the way, Mamá."

The line went silent and I felt guilty. Poor Mamá! I had gone too far.

"You're staying in her house, aren't you?" she spat out.

"What?" I hadn't been expecting that.

"You're staying in Alicia's house. Right?"

"And what if I am? I'm not a little girl anymore, Mamá. I've been making my own decisions for quite a while now."

"I told you not to go near her."

The tone of her voice made me feel like a six-year-old caught in some mischief. But I was twenty-seven and I didn't have to obey her. I kept silent, not really knowing what to say.

"There are things that you don't know." Her tone had changed. It was no longer accusatory, it was pleading. "That woman is dangerous. Get out of there. Please."

I remained silent, disconcerted.

"I'm coming to Barcelona and taking you back to New York with me."

"Not again, Mamá." Her insistence was irritating me.

"Believe me, I know what's best for you."

"Save yourself the trip. You won't be able to take me with you."

She was silent again. And I felt bad for talking to her like that, but I wasn't willing to let her force me to do things her way. Sure, life has its risks and my mother was full of love and had only good intentions for me, but I wasn't going to let María del Mar lock up her little girl in a box filled with pillows to keep her from getting broken. It was a question of weighing her fears and her anger against my freedom. My freedom won.

"I'm sorry, Mamá," I said, trying to be conciliatory. "Don't interfere. I'm going to do what I think I have to." Whoever said it's easy being an only child?

"I'm coming whether you want me to or not."

"You are free to do whatever you feel like and go wherever you want." This is where Mamá starts to play hardball, I said to myself, and I have to keep her from getting too bold. "But don't count on me."

Her response was silence.

"Are you there, Mamá?" I asked after a little while.

"Yes, dear."

"Did you understand me?"

"Look, let's change the subject, you're impossible today," she replied in a tone somewhere between irritated and re- signed. I was surprised that my mother was giving up so easily. But then she said, "By the way, were you calling about some- thing?"

The news of her plan to come to Barcelona had made me forget the reason I was calling: I wanted to convince her to send me the painting. That was when I got it. That was what she had been waiting for.

"Oh! Yeah, Mamá, I forgot," I faked. "I need you to send me the painting."

"It's a valuable object. It would be better if I brought it over personally."

"But, Mamá. Again? We've already discussed that!"

"The painting and I come together. A package deal. " I could sense her triumphant smile.

I fell silent. We both knew that she had won. She was holding all the cards.

"Look, dear," she said, her tone softer now. "You'll be glad I came. There are things you need to know."

That made me see the light. Of course. She had been hiding things about our life in Barcelona. Did she have some clue about the treasure? Or about Enric's death? I definitely had a ton of questions for her. It would be fantastic if I could get her to fess up.

"Okay," I said, accepting. "I'll reserve you two a room."

"Yes, a double. For you and me."

"And Daddy?"

"Your father is staying in New York."

She's coming without my dad, I said to myself. Definitely, she has more to tell me than I thought.

CHAPTER 26

"You want to see the painting I mentioned?" asked Oriol. "The forgery of a Virgin wearing a ring?"

I had woken up pretty groggy. Luckily there was coffee already made in the kitchen. As I'd poured myself a cup, he appeared. He didn't teach at the university that morning and was in a pleasant mood. I accepted, delighted by his invitation to breakfast with him.

"The Virgin can wait, we'll give her a ring when we've finished breakfast." He laughed discreetly, and I realized my comment had probably been more clever than funny.

The house has a large attic that has been used for storage, mostly furniture and other old items belonging to the Bonaplatas, some of them going back several generations. Oriol rummaged through a pile of unframed paintings leaning against the wall, in a corner, and pulled out a small one.

"This is it," he declared. I stared at it in disbelief.

"Oriol, that painting is identical to mine."

"What? Are you sure?" he asked, shocked.

"Positive."

He raised his hand to his chin in a pensive gesture. I

lifted the painting to have a good look at it. The weight was similar, but this one was thicker and the wormholes on the sides seemed to be painted on.

"It's a copy," declared Oriol. "I've inspected it several times, intrigued by the unusual ring the Virgin's wearing. And I've proved that, although it looks good at first glance, it's actually a modern forgery. But the ring's not the only odd thing about it."

"What else do you find odd?"

"The placement of the child. In sculptures and paintings of the period and region, he almost always appears seated on the Virgin's left. Years later, artists started to break the monotony of the composition and the child would appear to be playing with birds, even with the Virgin's crown. But almost always on the left, very rarely on the right."

I was quiet, thinking. It had never occurred to me that somebody could find so many odd things in a painting. I'd always thought the artist was free to do what he wanted.

"It's surprising," he said, looking at the Madonna.

"What's surprising?" I asked, expecting it to be something I would never have thought could be surprising.

"That Enric would have a fake copy. He must have had it made before sending you the original."

"But why would he want an imitation? He liked the painting that much?" I leaned it against an old dressing table and put my ring next to the Virgin's. The only difference was the size, otherwise they were identical. "And if he liked it so much, why didn't he hang it up in one of the many rooms of his house? Why did he hide it?"

"I've always been drawn to antiquities," said Oriol without answering my question. Maybe he hadn't even been listening. He seemed wrapped up in his own thoughts, in the mysteries of the painting. "And as a boy I loved to come up here and get covered in dust rummaging through things. I used to know each and every item by heart. It's family stuff that my father could have sold in his store, but he never wanted to. And now I remember something about the painting that I didn't think was important before. But maybe it is."

"What's that?"

"I discovered it up here right around the time my father died. It hadn't been here before. I remember it perfectly. It was here, in the corner, along with the other paintings, but it didn't have any dust on it."

"Do you think it's related to his death?"

"My mother told me the story of the triptych, of a possible second inheritance and a treasure, but I never thought that this painting could have anything to do with all that." He paused, as if getting his thoughts straight, and then his blue eyes met mine. "But there are too many coincidences. I'm becoming more and more convinced that everything is tied together: the painting, the ring, the treasure, and his death."

I saw that Oriol wanted to talk and suggested we have another cup of coffee, this time at the garden table, under the trees, surrounded by rosebushes in bloom.

"Why did he kill himself?" I asked point-blank, as soon as we sat down.

"I still don't know," he said, his gaze wandering toward the city, which could be made out through some cypress trees on the eastern horizon, below the blue line of the sea. I could tell that he had asked himself that question before, countless times, and that it still hurt. "My mother told me he had problems with some business rivals, members of an international mafia trafficking in art antiquities. Sometimes I want to believe that he didn't commit suicide, that they killed him. It hurts me to think that he chose to give up, to leave, to leave me." His eyes got misty. "I'm sure that whatever his problem, there had to have been a better solution than firing a bullet into his mouth. He left a big hole in my life. It still hurts."

"I'm so sorry," I said, then became silent.

"They say he killed four of those mafiosi," he added after a while. "But they've never been able to prove it."

"Do you think he did it?"

"Yes."

"But why? How could someone so kind be a murderer?"

"I can only tell you what my mother told me. There was a dispute over the paintings. They suspected that they hid a message, a clue to something bigger: the Templar treasure. The writings of Arnau d'Estopinyá, even if they're a copy of an older set or a transcription of an oral history, confirm it. And it's true that there's a message, although it's incomplete, or incomprehensible to us, hidden below the paint. Surely those art dealers knew that such a message existed. They wanted to buy the paintings from my father, he refused, and they resorted to intimidation. My father had a partner, a friend." Oriol paused, significantly here. "Perhaps he was his lover. The other dealers beat him up; I imagine they were trying to scare Enric, but either on purpose or by accident, they killed his friend. My mother says that that was when the threatening phone calls in the middle of the night began. They didn't threaten just him, us too."

"And your father killed them."

"That's what it seems like. He didn't want to give them the paintings. I don't know if he also wanted to protect his family or avenge his friend. Have you ever heard of Epaminondas?"

"Monopoly?" I joked. The name sounded like a Greek hero to me, but I didn't know much more than that.

"Epaminondas, the Theban general," he replied with a smile.

I grabbed my cup of coffee and encouraged him to continue.

"My father was obsessed with that story and its main char-

acter. It was his paradigm; he told it to me many times. Epaminondas was an exceptional military leader and learned man. He
surrounded himself with philosophers, poets, musicians, and
scientists, which is what my father really admired about him. In
the fourth century AD, Sparta ruled Greece. The Spartans were
the best warriors of all antiquity. Neither Athens nor any of the
other city-states dared to challenge them. But Thebes rebelled,
and when the powerful Spartan army fell upon the city, Epaminondas and his holy phalanx beat them time and again."

"What was the holy phalanx?"

"The holy phalanx was the central core of the Theban army,
an elite corps of three hundred young noblemen who were
paired up. Each swore to die before abandoning his partner. It
was that desperate fight for his friend, that intense passion, that
made the holy phalanx invincible."

"Ahh!" I exclaimed. That made things a bit clearer. I knew
that ancient Greece's moral code allowed male homosexuality
and bisexuality.

"The same thing happened with the Templar Knights. When
the situation was crucial, when they were outnumbered, they
fought in pairs and never abandoned their partners—dead or
alive. The Templars didn't give up. One of their seals conveys
this message clearly: two warriors riding on the same steed. It
was a symbolic image. The Templars weren't short of horses,
each knight, according to the order's regulations, had two good
ones . . . The seal was a symbol of that sworn partnership."

"So you think that Enric didn't really kill to defend his family, but rather to avenge his friend's death," I said. I'm sure Oriol
realized that Enric had made a promise to his partner, like the
warriors in the holy phalanx, like the Templars on the seal. But
he didn't say anything.

He let his gaze slide off beyond the cypresses, toward the
sea. I looked in the same direction and let my eyes fill with the
light of that clear morning and the bright blue Mediterranean in

the distance. I took a sip of coffee, which was already cold, and sat observing the boy I had loved so much as a girl. Finally his eyes, glossy with the tears he was holding back, found mine. It was so intense that I felt a tickle on the back of my neck. Then, making a vague gesture, which Luis would probably have described as affected, he said:

"Isn't it beautiful?"

"What?"

"Loving someone so much that you would give your life for that person."

CHAPTER 27

Yes, I said to myself, it was lovely, poetic, moving. "Isn't it beautiful?" he had said. I couldn't stop thinking about his saying it, his eyes damp with emotion.

But behind that tragic romanticism were other feelings that disturbed me. It was obvious that Oriol thought Enric had killed four people and then committed suicide, all for the love of a man. And that he felt abandoned by his father. He admired his heroism, but he couldn't forgive him for knowingly having made him an orphan. Thinking back on my childhood, I remembered Oriol's affection for and adoration of Enric, how he held his head with a proud "That's my dad" look on his face when Enric organized one of his magical games.

And there was also the question of Enric's professed homosexual passion. A boundless, tragic love, which obviously didn't shock Oriol. In fact, he seemed to admire it. Another red flag about Oriol's sexual preference?

That day I speculated again about his sexuality and was scared. Scared of falling in love with him again, like a fool . . . like the girl who'd shed so many tears over him.

That afternoon I had nothing to do and was feeling nervous.

Our search for the treasure was at a standstill, and the excitement of only a few hours earlier had waned. Maybe it was all just Enric's last fantasy, maybe I should have gone back to New York like my mother had asked me to, maybe I was already in the middle of one of those dangerous situations she had predicted. And maybe the biggest danger was Oriol and my feelings for him. So I decided to leave my safe lookout over the city and immerse myself in the swarm of people along the Ramblas. And there, strolling along, I let the colors of the crowd, the sound of the street musicians, and the scent of the flowers for sale flow into me. I wanted to feel and not think.

I crossed the Plaza del Pi almost without realizing it. As I headed toward the cathedral, I became aware of being in front of an antiques shop. This store had belonged to Enric, I was sure of it. My feet had led me back to my childhood. I looked through the window but I didn't dare enter. Even though I knew that they had to be different, the objects in the window seemed the same as the ones I remembered. Several front-loading pistols, a couple of small cryselephantine statues like the ones Alicia collected, a French-style rosewood chest of drawers, some baroque chiaroscuro paintings . . . I felt myself regress to the girl I used to be, my heart pounding in my chest. I waited for Enric to appear from behind the glass. Smiling, with his thinning hair combed back, a bit on the plump side, and with that mischievous look his son now has sometimes. On my right hand I felt his ruby ring pulsating.

But I soon realized that for as long as I waited, for as much I rubbed my memories of the past like a magic lamp, I wouldn't be able to make my godfather's ghost come through that door. I wanted to get out of there quickly, so I hurried off toward the cathedral. As I passed another antiques shop on that same street, I saw the gold letters engraved on a display window: ARTUR BOIX. I knew that name . . . Artur Boix . . . Artur Boix . . . Of course, my travel companion!

Once again I found myself standing spellbound in front of a store window, but this time I wasn't paying attention to any object behind the glass. I don't think I even saw them. I could only stare at the sign: ARTUR BOIX, ANTIQUARIAN.

I don't know if I ran, jogged, or walked like a zombie, but the next thing I remember is being at a pay phone in the plaza of the cathedral, calling Captain Castillo. I was lucky he took my call right away because I felt as if I could die of impatience.

"Captain," I said, trying to make my voice sound normal, "do you remember the last names of the guys my godfather supposedly murdered?"

"How could I not," he replied good-naturedly. "It's my favorite mystery; I keep a copy of the file in my office and another in a suitcase under my bed. Is the young American lady going to help me solve this intrigue worthy of a Marlowe mystery?" he said jokingly. "I only need to know how your godfather was able to take out all four at once . . ."

I promised to help him with whatever he wanted, as long as he gave me the names. He dropped them like someone reciting verses learned as a child. Two of the names didn't mean anything to me, but the other two did: Arturo and Jaime Boix.

I had just confirmed what my instinct told me moments earlier. That attractive man who sat by my side on the trip from New York had always known who I was and why I was going to Spain. He was the son of one of the men my godfather had killed. The mafia of artwork traffickers had survived and, judging by my impression of Artur, it looked to be in good health.

While we made ourselves comfortable at the café table, the conversation revolved around the typical touristy merits of the city, but as soon as the waiter brought the drinks I said point-blank:

"You set up our meeting on the plane, didn't you?"

"It wasn't hard to get a seat next to you." Artur showed his handsome smile. "Just the right tip to the right person. I do it often in my business."

I observed him through my glass of Diet Coke. It hadn't been hard for me to meet up with him either. "It's taken you long enough to get in touch with me," he reproached me, as if our date were personal rather than business. He was a presumptuous guy, but I had to confess that he was also interesting.

"You ransacked my apartment in New York."

He didn't bat an eyelash, or even lose his smile.

"It wasn't me personally. An associate of mine took care of it."

"And you admit it just like that?"

"And why not?" he replied, now completely serious. "I have as much, if not more, right to those paintings, and to the treasure, than the three of you."

He spoke with conviction and I was dumbfounded. On what basis did Artur think he had rights? I waited for him to speak.

"You should know by now that your godfather murdered my father, my uncle, and a couple of their associates."

"Associates? I thought they were bodyguards."

"It doesn't matter what they were. He killed them."

"That hasn't been proved; there's no evidence."

"Evidence?" Now Artur laughed. "What do I need evidence for? I know it was him. I know that they had agreed on a transaction. That your godfather not only didn't hand over the painting of the Virgin, as they had agreed, but instead, after killing them, he stole the other two, the one of Saint George and the one of Saint John the Baptist."

"He stole the smaller paintings?"

"Yes, he stole them." Artur watched me carefully, reading the surprise on my face.

"But how . . . ?"

"Your godfather and my family belonged to a certain secret club. They learned of the treasure at the same time and tracked the paintings to a place near the monastery of Poblet, where it seems they originally came from. All being professionals in the antiques business, they moved quickly to get them, but due to a stupid matter of family inheritances, the central panel had a different owner than the two lateral ones. Someone had divided them up a few generations earlier and it took a while to locate them, with the unfortunate result that while my family found and acquired the small ones, your godfather did the same with the larger one."

"And they couldn't come to an agreement."

"Exactly. Bonaplata and his boyfriend were not reasonable at all, they wanted to buy our paintings and keep the treasure for themselves."

"And your family? Did they want to sell?"

"No. But they were willing to negotiate . . ."

"And what happened to my godfather's partner?"

"Well . . . let's just say that he left the negotiating table before his time was up." A sarcastic spark danced in his eyes.

"You guys killed him."

"It was an accident."

"Or an attempt at intimidation—"

"The fact is that an agreement had been reached—"

"How do you know?"

"My mother told me." I remained silent; I didn't want to question that. "Bonaplata would hand over his painting in exchange for a certain sum. But he didn't do it. Instead, he killed them and stole our pieces."

"It doesn't seem logical to me. How could my godfather manage to trick and kill those professional gunmen?"

"I don't know. But he did." Artur was frowning.

"But you guys started it, by killing the man he loved." Artur might have reasons to hate Enric, but I had to defend him.

"It doesn't matter who started it. He acted like a bastard, like a scoundrel. He broke a pact, he wasn't true to his word."

I pursed my lips and stared at him before responding. "Enric was just protecting his loved ones. You were threatening his family."

I don't think he heard my words. His gaze was lost in the back of the café, as if he were ruminating about something that was hard for him to digest. He took some time to respond and when he did, he fixed his eyes on me and said in a hoarse, low voice:

"Between my family and the Bonaplatas there is blood to pay." And I saw a flash of red in his eyes.

CHAPTER 28

"Enric was my first great love." I stared at my mother. I couldn't believe what I had just heard. She'd said that she wanted to talk to me. And boy did she talk. She almost suffocated for lack of air. I listened, flabbergasted. The secret she'd kept for years was like an invisible dam that had kept us apart. Suddenly the dam had burst and the waters just poured out.

I had obediently gone to the airport to pick her up, and when I saw her luggage I wondered why she was so loaded down. For a moment I was afraid she wanted to stay in Barcelona with me for a long time. Oh no, I said to myself. Then I realized that one of the suitcases held the well-wrapped painting. Even so, there was a lot of luggage. My mother always liked to travel well equipped. She checked into the same hotel I had gone to initially. She had reserved a large duplex room on one of the top floors and she assumed that I would move in there with her.

I watched her cautiously. We had a deal: she'd bring the painting and I'd move out of Alicia's house.

"My mother is arriving today," I told her. "I'm going to the hotel."

"Fine," she murmured, pursing her lips in a near smile.

She knew my mother's opinion of her, even better than I did. "You're welcome back when she leaves."

My mother was talking nonstop about my trip, her trip, how Daddy was when she left him in New York, but she saved the surprise for dinnertime.

When she said, "Enric was my first great love," her eyes sought out mine.

I didn't know what to think, or what to say. My first reaction was disbelief, that it had to be a joke. But her eyes didn't show any amusement, and her mouth wasn't laughing. That face I identify as that of Mamá, with its crow's-feet and wrinkly forehead, looked straight at me, like a defendant awaiting a verdict. I dropped my knife and fork on the table and stammered, "But . . . what about Daddy?"

"Your father came later . . ."

"But Enric, Enric was . . ."

"Homosexual," she stated.

"Yeah, that," I said.

She was quiet for a few seconds, as if catching her breath, then began her story.

"As you know, the Bonaplata family and the Coll family have a history of very close friendship that dates back generations. My grandfather frequented the restaurant Els Quatre Gats with Enric's grandfather in the late nineteenth century and the friendship continued with our parents.

"We played together as children when our families got together, we both went to school at the Liceo Francés, and, as teenagers, we started to go out. We were part of the same group, both in the city and in the summers on the Costa Brava.

"I was always very attracted to Enric. He was smart, congenial, and imaginative. He had a quick, clever answer for everything. I was convinced that he liked me, and when we all started pairing off in that period before college, I saved myself for him and we naturally became a couple. I was madly in love. Our parents were thrilled that we were dating. We'd be the link that would officially unite the two families. It was something that had been looked forward to for generations. When I went out with Enric, my parents never complained if I came home late."

"Did you kiss?" I inquired curiously. I noticed that my mother shifted uncomfortably in her chair.

She was silent for a few moments. It was obviously difficult for María del Mar to have that conversation.

"Yes," she responded finally. "But remember that this was more than forty years ago. In our social environment you married as a virgin. Even when you were engaged and had set the wedding date, you kept the brakes on, although we never got that far. Our kisses and caresses were rather chaste."

"He couldn't have put too much pressure on you," I insisted maliciously. "Right?"

"Yes, that's true. When I thought back on it, I realized that I was the one who always made the first move," she said, sighing. "I thought that it was in my nature to be affectionate, and not in his."

"But how could you not have noticed?"

"I've thought about that a lot too." She sighed again, shaking her head in disbelief. "Nobody knew about his tendencies at the time. But, of course, I was his girlfriend and so I have less of an excuse. He hid it, he didn't want his family to know. In those days, having a son like that would have been a social embarrassment, a humiliation for the Bonaplata family. And since I was in love with him, I became the perfect alibi. I imagine that Enric must have gone through a period of self-definition and that it was useful to have me around as a way to gauge his feelings. I began to notice that he had stopped using the privilege of keeping me out late. He started bringing me home earlier and earlier, and some days he came up with excuses not to see me at all. My first suspicions arose when, several times, I would call him at home hours after he had dropped me off, and he wouldn't yet have arrived. He'd use that time to go to gay bars and meet friends."

"And then what happened? How did you guys break up?"

"Finally, one day, having come to the conclusion that Enric was leading a double life, I questioned him about where he had been the night before. He told me that he loved me very much, but only as a friend. I was stunned. He asked me to please keep his secret, and he confessed his homosexuality to me. He said it had been selfish of him to waste my time. Enric was somewhat older than me, and I must have seemed very innocent because the first thing that occurred to me was, how could he know he was gay when we had never made love. He laughed. Since I was madly in love with him, I told him that I didn't care about wasted time, that I didn't care about anything, but please let's not break up. I begged him. Me! Imagine, me begging! At first he said okay, but then said that I had to get used to the idea that our relationship had to end, and that I should think about finding a nice boy to marry. He said that I should forget about him as a partner, that he couldn't give me what I needed and that our relationship would ruin my life. Then he told me about some of his escapades. Since I didn't want to give him up, I even accompanied him to the gay bars and accepted the caresses of a woman so that I wouldn't look out of place.

"I was desperate, nothing mattered to me anymore. I didn't want a future that didn't include him. I would have accepted his homosexuality, I would have married him and let him continue having sex with men, just so long as he stayed with me. I suggested it to him, and I think that for a while he considered it.

"He gave in to my caresses, but now I think he did it out of obligation and to save me from feeling snubbed. I decided to set a trap for him. I've always regretted that.

"One afternoon, when I was alone in the house, I asked him to come pick me up. I found an excuse to get him into my room. And there, well, we made love."

"You made love?" I exclaimed.

"Yes," she replied, somewhat uncomfortable. "He could perform with a woman if he wanted to."

"Did he resist?"

"Yes, he resisted, but I pulled out all the stops. I wanted to give him pleasure. I was crazy. I wanted to get pregnant. Anything to hold on to him."

"But you told me that you were a virgin, right?"

"Of course I was. I lost my virginity in that desperate attempt."

"What happened next?"

"He didn't want to go out with me anymore." Her tone was sad. "He told me that he was hurting me and that we'd always be friends. That he loved me, but only as a friend or a sister. And I felt horrible; I blamed myself for having violated his trust and I thought I had lost him because of that."

"You made love to the man you loved," I said, trying to console her. "What's wrong with that?"

"No, I shouldn't have done it, I shouldn't have forced him."

"It's silly for you to keep blaming yourself. He couldn't have had such a bad time. But what happened then?"

"The Colls and the Bonaplatas took the news of our breakup very badly, but Enric and I continued to see each other during family gatherings. He was always very sweet to me. Time passed, I went out with friends, trying to get over him, until one day I found out that he was living with a woman."

"Alicia."

"Yes, Alicia. Enric met with me to tell me about it. He said that he and Alicia led similar lives and had come to an arrangement."

"An arrangement?" I was doing a great job of pretending I didn't know any of this.

"Yes. That they would pretend to lead a conventional life together and make their parents happy."

"But they have a son. No pretending there."

"That was part of the deal. They both wanted one. But it hurt me. Everything about it hurt me, our breakup, that he got together with Alicia, that they had a child . . . it was an extremely difficult experience. He comforted me and justified himself by saying that I was a little middle-class girl, that I wasn't prepared for the ambiguous life he could offer me, that I wouldn't have lasted. That I would have been very unhappy. And that Alicia was like him."

"But you met Daddy and you fell in love again," I said, trying to cheer her up.

"Yes."

"And shortly after, you had me."

"Yes, sweetheart. I was able to put my life back together."

"But you continued seeing Enric."

"We maintained our friendship, and to show that I didn't hold a grudge, I asked him to be your godfather. He was very excited, and he always loved you like a daughter."

"But if everything was going so well"—I was taking advantage of the fact that María del Mar was leveling with me to ask her something I had been curious about for some time—"why didn't you ever want to come back to Barcelona?"

She looked at me for a few silent moments. She seemed to be thinking my question over. I looked at her face and thought of the young woman she had been thirty years earlier. She must have been a lot like me. From another generation, with different social concerns, but still a young woman. Like me. She felt, she suffered, she searched for love and love slipped away from her . . .

"Everyone, including Enric, thought that our breakup had

been perfect and that there was no bitterness. But, for me, that was a painful farce. I still had feelings for him and I hated Alicia from the first day I knew she existed. It hurt me to see them together, their stupid fake love; that she was always the dominant one in their relationship, that she seemed so brilliant . . . It made me think that Enric simply preferred her to me. The night that I learned of her pregnancy, I couldn't sleep. Then I met your father and we got married.

"Enric and I still saw each other at family functions. Sometimes, when I was lucky, he showed up with just Oriol, but other times with Alicia too. That contact was painful for me. I tried to withstand it, but as the years passed, it became unbearable. However, there was another much more powerful reason for leaving Barcelona and never coming back."

"What?"

She stared into my eyes before responding. "You."

"Me? Why? What did I do?" I asked in utter confusion.

She took her time. I knew that she had come from New York for this.

"It was early September. You were still almost a girl, and I was packing up the summerhouse, along with the maid, to go back to Barcelona. It was a muggy afternoon. Suddenly a gust of wind rattled the windows. I looked out and saw dark, heavy clouds coming quickly off the sea. A storm was on its way. I knew that you were at the beach and went to look for you with a couple of towels and an umbrella. When I got near the shore, a heavy rain started to fall and I saw the nanny and your friends run toward the town. I couldn't find you, and when I asked them, your friends didn't know where you were. I got frightened and went farther onto the beach. The downpour obscured my vision, but I kept looking and finally, hidden among the rocks, I saw a young couple kissing. It was you and Oriol."

She paused. I was trying to come to grips with the fact that such an intimate memory could be shared with my mother.

If I had known it then, I would have died of embarrassment.

"I was so surprised that I didn't know how to react other than to run home as fast as I could. I was terrified."

"But why?"

"I had been watching Oriol as he grew up. He has his mother's eyes. My God, I hate her so much. But almost everything else he gets from his father. It still hurts me to think about it."

She stopped and her gaze drifted around the restaurant. A tear slid down her cheek. Embarrassed, she hid her face in her hands.

I stroked her arm in a feeble attempt to console her. And I thought that although thirty years ago she might have been like me, I certainly didn't want to end up like her.

"Oriol reminded you of your loss," I said gently.

She didn't respond for a few minutes and I respected her silence.

"Yes. But I was already used to that defeat." She again looked me in the eyes. "It was your defeat that had me terrified. Do you think I hadn't noticed that you liked him before I saw you two on the beach?"

"But what was wrong with us liking each other?"

"I said I noticed that you liked him, not that you liked each other."

"What are you insinuating?"

"Oriol wasn't one of those boys who's always running after a ball, and I told you that he reminded me a lot of his father . . ." She paused and emphatically added, "In that way."

"In what way?" I didn't really want to hear her answer.

"In his sexual orientation."

"That's so unfounded," I said defensively.

"No, it's not," she replied firmly. "He's like his father, and like his mother. They're the same. Don't you see it? He's friendly, he'll love you like a friend, like a sister. Maybe he'll let you have sex with him to avoid hurting your feelings. But in the end he'll leave, and when he does, you'll be left with your heart shattered. It's his nature. Even if he wanted to, he couldn't be otherwise."

"You're wrong."

"No, I'm not wrong. That day at the beach I saw that what had happened to me was going to happen to you. Shortly after that, I began to pressure your father to ask for a transfer to New York. Or to Latin America. I wanted to go far away. I wanted to get you away from him so that you wouldn't suffer like I suffered. And that's why we left and never came back."

"But you had no right—"

"And the letters," she continued excitedly, "and the letters that you wrote him. And the ones he wrote you. I made them disappear . . ."

"Mamá!" I almost jumped out of my chair.

"Yes," she said, looking at me defiantly, "I destroyed them, one by one—until they stopped coming and going."

"How dared you?" I said between my teeth. "You had no right to interfere in my life like that."

"Of course I had a right. Every right in the world. I'm your mother, I had lived through it and it was my duty to protect you . . . Just like I had the right to move to America, to take you with me and in that way radically change your life and your fate. It was my responsibility to keep you from suffering, and it still is."

From there she went into her sermon mode and warned me that I should forget about Oriol, forget about those fanciful treasure stories and go back to New York with her. Enough adventures already, Mike was my future and my treasure, I couldn't ruin that to pursue my godfather's nonsensical games. And on and on and on. I don't know when I stopped listening and just pretended to pay attention.

I tried to picture myself, in thirty years' time, hoping to keep my daughter from making my same mistakes. I was amazed by her story. I wondered where she'd gotten the gumption to force a sexual relationship with Enric. I guess she must have been driven by the same determination with which she was now trying to rescue me from the same potential mistake. I couldn't forgive her for having stolen my letters, but a trickle of happiness was beginning to fill my heart. It was true. I hadn't believed him when he told me, but it was true. Oriol had written to me.

I asked myself whether my mother's leaving Barcelona, leaving behind her past, was really for me or if it was to avoid seeing Enric and Alicia together. We finished the wine and then continued with after-dinner liqueurs until they started to close the restaurant. We then went out for drinks. Suddenly I began to feel a strange camaraderie with her.

"Tell me again," I said to her, after the alcohol had loosened my tongue. "How did you get it on with Enric?"

She, who had drunk as much as I had, giggled and made demure excuses. I wickedly kept pushing her, insisting on details. Out of the blue, she started to cry. I hugged her and started crying too. I cursed her out loud for having stolen my letters from Oriol. Between hiccups, she said she'd steal them again a thousand times, that she wouldn't allow me to suffer like she had, and to please keep away from that man, that he was like the proverbial dog guarding the cabbage patch from which he wouldn't eat himself nor let anybody else eat.

"You really made love with Enric?" I asked again.

I couldn't imagine it. To me she wasn't a woman, she was my mamá, and mamás don't do such things. She ignored my question and went back to her spiel about how fabulous Mike was. We'd have spent the entire night in drunken conversation if I hadn't seen him then.

He was in a corner, glass in hand, alone. Barbablanca. The old man with the dagger. There. And when I discovered him watching me, I shuddered.

"You vulture!" I shouted with intoxicated boldness, waving my forefinger at him. "Stop following me."

He just looked at me. For a moment I thought he was going to smile, but he didn't.

"Get out of here!" I yelled at him again.

My mother wanted to know what was going on, but just as I was about to tell her, the man got up and left, and I decided that it would worry her too much.

CHAPTER 29

Our enormous bed faced south, toward Montjuïc. María del Mar collapsed onto it in her underwear. The effort of taking off her dress, even with my help, was too much for her. In a few seconds she was snoring softly.

Older people can take just so much alcohol, I thought to myself. Or maybe it was that they drink more. I stretched out by her side and enjoyed the magnificent view through the wide picture window.

The first rays of daylight were trying unsuccessfully to assert themselves through the heavy clouds. The lampposts on the docks were still lit, their reflection playing a game of hide-and-seek over the gleaming black water. Farther up, the lights on Montjuïc followed the mountain's paths, its dark vegetation offering a contrast with the bluish-gray of the misty sky, waiting for the dawn to finally arrive.

The presence of Barbablanca at the restaurant had put me on guard, chasing away the drowsiness caused by the alcohol. My God, I'd had a lot of surprises lately. Enric and María del Mar. What an incredible story. She must have suffered so much. She slept by my side, curled up in the fetal position, as if trying to protect herself from the next blow life had in store for her. I lifted her hair, dyed light brown in a vain attempt to recapture the hue and shine of her youth. I planted a kiss on her forehead.

I couldn't wait. I unwrapped the painting of the Virgin. She seemed more intriguing than before. I compared her ruby ring to the one on my finger. I was struck anew by their similarity. I glanced again at the hesitant dawn over the port and the city, still asleep at my feet, and finally felt that I was about to fall asleep. But my last thought before closing my eyes was not of the Virgin's *Mona Lisa* expression nor of our ruby ring. It was of the old man. I had the feeling I knew him from some other, earlier time. But when? Where? Why was I still afraid of him after he had saved my life as I left Del Grial?

Artur Boix called me the next day. He apologized for having gotten carried away by his emotions during our last meeting. He asked me to imagine, considering how I felt about my godfather's death, how it was for him to lose his father and his uncle. I admitted that I had gotten too worked up as well.

He invited me out for dinner and I told him that I didn't dine alone with men who weren't my fiancé and that, besides, my mother was in town. After a slight hesitation he replied that he'd love to invite Mrs. Wilson, Mr. Wilson, and my entire family; I could sense his smile through the phone. He added that he was a formal young man and that he had good intentions.

"If that's the case, let's meet," I replied, laughing. The truth is, I love guys with a sense of humor. "For lunch, and after my mother leaves."

"You won't regret it. I have a lot to tell you."

María del Mar spent three more days in Barcelona, days that I had to devote exclusively to her. We did a nostalgia tour of the city: the place where we used to live, Grandma and Grandpa's house, our favorite streets. We went for hot chocolate at the *granja* we used to go to, explored our favorite restaurants; she told me anecdotes about when she was a girl, and then a teenager and a newlywed. Some of the stories I knew, others I had never heard before. We laughed like schoolgirls and the camaraderie that had sprung up between us grew. We even had dinner with Luis and Oriol one night. That was when she gave us an unexpected gift.

"Here is the X-ray of the painting of the Virgin," she said, offering us an enormous envelope whose contents she hadn't wanted to reveal to me before then. "Your friend Sharon did it and I give it to you three with my heartfelt wishes that you find Enric's treasure."

María del Mar's eyes were teary, but I doubted the two cousins noticed. Their eyes were focused on the envelope. I opened it carefully and immediately looked at the inscription hidden at the Virgin's feet.

And there it was: "is in an."

"The treasure is in an underwater cave," Oriol declared with disappointment.

"We already knew that, that doesn't give us anything new," said Luis.

We politely thanked her for the gift. It wasn't the clue we'd been hoping for; we'd have to search further.

Just as I was expecting, my mother didn't want to see Alicia. Nor did she change her opinion, which she repeated to me a hundred times, about Oriol. I should forget about him and go back to Mike.

But she had the good sense to leave just before I tired of her or got antsy to resume the treasure hunt. I'll admit that I enjoyed her company. Those were days very well spent, but as soon as I dropped her off at the airport, I returned to the hotel, packed my bags, and moved back into Alicia's house.

CHAPTER 30

Would you be interested in seeing a galley?" asked Oriol
suddenly.

"A galley?" I repeated. The question had caught me by surprise. I remembered that a galley was a kind of ship and that it had been mentioned in the document we'd read.

"Yeah, a galley, the type of ship commanded by the Templar sergeant monk Arnau d'Estopinyá," explained Oriol when he noticed my hesitation.

"I already know what a galley is," I replied, offended.

"Well, do you want to see it or not?" he said with a disarming smile. That boy, well, that man, still had a hold on me.

It was an enormous wooden vessel, spread out in one of the wings of an old building with large arches that supported a tile roof. The building, once Barcelona's shipyard, today houses the Maritime Museum. This galley was a reproduction, but the original had supposedly been built on that site more than four centuries before.

Apart from my curiosity about what Arnau d'Estopinyá's

ship had looked like, that museum visit had added interest for me: it was the first time in my life I'd gone out alone with Oriol. Well, if going to see an ancient ship could be considered "going out." Anyway, for an engaged woman like myself, a "cultural outing" wouldn't be considered a betrayal, not even a temerity. I looked at my engagement ring, and was surprised to see that, once again, the old Templar ruby was shining more brightly than the recently cut sparkling diamond.

A galley is like a gigantic cutter, with a relatively low gunwale so that its long oars can reach the water easily. It's nothing like those ships with high decks loaded with cannons, or the typical caravels on which Columbus sailed to the New World. This ship was bristling with oars. It seemed as if there were hundreds.

"This was a typically Mediterranean ship, designed for war," explained Oriol, pointing out the timbering. "This is a full-scale exact model of the one built here for John of Austria, Emperor Philip II's stepbrother, and which participated in the famous Battle of Lepanto on October seventh, 1571, in which a combined Spanish, Venetian, and papal fleet managed to definitively defeat the Turks. They spread out through the Mediterranean, taking Cyprus and Crete and threatening Italy, particularly the kingdom of Naples and the large Italian islands, which at that time belonged to the Spanish crown. Curiously, galleys from the Hospitaller Order, some of the rivals of the Poor Knights of Christ, and the inheritors of a large part of their assets, also participated in that battle. Three centuries later, the Hospitaller Order still existed under the name of the Order of Malta. They had been banished from the Holy Land by the Turkish advance and then from Cyprus, Rhodes, and Crete, and they established their headquarters on the island of Malta, which up until then had belonged to the crown of Aragon."

He looked at me, smiling, catching his breath for a second.

"In Spain people say that we led the fleet, but if you visit the Naval Museum in Venice, you'll see that the Venetians claim that the commanders were theirs, and I'm sure that the pope thought he was in charge. Some allies."

I laughed discreetly at the irony of it, avoiding those blue eyes that drove me to distraction. I felt the taste of salt on my lips, a reminder of my first kiss. But he didn't seem to share my flight of fancy and continued with his lecture.

"Of course, history depends on who writes it, but it is true that Venice contributed many more ships than the entire Spanish empire."

I thought that Oriol was so turned on by visiting the past that the chances of a flesh-and-blood woman, me, for example, catching his attention in the face of the sensuous curves of a galley were practically nonexistent.

"The ship style changed little in six hundred years," he told me. "In Byzantium, around the year one thousand, there were already ships similar to this one, representing the culmination of the best technology in ancient naval combat. It was the direct heir of the Roman triremes and before that, of Greek and Phoenician vessels. Galleys dominated the Mediterranean for two thousand years. They were built for speed and maneuverability. They could sink an enemy ship by ramming it head-on. This one had cannons on the prow, and some on the stern and sides, but at the time, the artillery was not very powerful. Once cannons were improved, the galley disappeared as a warship. Of course, if you can sink the enemy from a distance with cannonballs, why risk the ship itself in the process?"

"Of course," I said, nodding.

"Arnau d'Estopinyá's galley was what they called a bastard galley because it was propelled by sail and oar. It had two large lateen sails and thirty-four banks of three oarsmen each, on both sides. This one here was a little larger, wider though a bit shorter; it had thirty banks and each oar was moved by four galley slaves. The oars were used only for battle, when they were in a hurry or when there was no wind. Imagine. Seventy-two oars hitting the sea at once. They used a drum to mark the rhythm so that all the rowers went at the same pace."

His eyes shone with enthusiasm. Oriol was envisioning the ship of d'Estopinyá, its keel parting the sea, thrusting itself at full speed against an enemy galley.

"It was the fastest thing on the water at the time," he added.

Oriol continued with his history lesson. And my attention continued to be divided. His explanations weren't uninteresting, but I have to confess that it was the person telling them who really fascinated me.

We walked the boat's length, along the floor, at the height of the keel. From there only the timbering of the hull could be seen and, in some stretches, it was missing planks so that visitors could see the insides of the warship and the equipment stored in each area. Reaching the stern, I admired the aft castle, which rose very high when seen from the ground, and was majestic, decorated lavishly in the baroque style.

"The *Na Santa Coloma* wouldn't have had any of that fancy stuff. What you see here is the flagship commanded by John of Austria, the brother of the emperor of the Hapsburg crown. The second most powerful man in the richest state in the world. The only decoration that Arnau d'Estopinyá's galley would have had was the flared cross or the patriarchal cross of the Templars painted on the stern and on the shields that protected the galley slaves and crossbowmen."

We went up several sets of steps until we reached a platform located above the first rowing banks and at the same height as what's called the companion, the command bridge of the ship. That was where the officers of the galley traveled, along with the pilot and the helmsman. They didn't mix with the gang who rowed, or with the slave drivers and masters-at-arms who made them follow orders.

From there we could see the rowing area and, at the end, the ram on the prow. An audiovisual presentation, which must have been programmed to go on automatically, projected on a screen above our heads, was re-creating galley slaves rowing, making them appear to be on the actual ship.

Then it happened. The ring, I thought. It's the ring again.

Suddenly, the canned images and the sound of the film were surpassed, a thousand times, by the ones that came from inside me.

I heard the beating of the drum marking the rhythm of the rowing, and the splashing of the oars in the water. I smelled the acrid, penetrating stench of the sweat and filth of the galley slaves who, covered in rags and chained to the bank, did their business right there. I felt a breeze, I saw the blues of the sky and the water, and the white foam on the crest of the waves. The day was clear, but the sea was choppy and made the ship lurch.

Ahead there was another galley, decked out in the green of Islam on the ends of its masts, while ours waved the pennant of Templar naval combat: the black flag with a white skull.

The masters-at-arms patrolled the main aisle, threatening with whips those who didn't put enough effort into their rowing. A man on the larger mast shouted something. I heard a voice, perhaps mine, asking them to fire the catapults. The resonant sound of the bulging timbering returning to its natural position began to arrive from the prow.

I felt my heart racing and I clung tensely to the hilt of the sword in my belt; I knew that death would come for many soon, perhaps even for myself.

The enemy ship fled, rowing, while lowering sails, as we had moments before. But I was convinced that we'd catch up to them.

"Row!" I shouted.

And the order was passed along in shouts by the slave drivers throughout the central gangway to the drum that, from the prow, marked the cadence of the rowing. The whips began to fall on the backs of those slaves who couldn't keep up with the rhythm. The rowers, in a chorus, began to groan from the effort each time the oars sank into the sea and the ship accelerated. Cries of pain followed the crack of the whip. The stink of the bodies wafted over to me, more intense now, and I noticed something I had perceived many times before, during similar trances: the smell of fear.

The distance between us and our prey diminished, but it was also a fast ship and the stones that our war machines launched couldn't reach their target. The forward fighting platform on the prow of the *Na Santa Coloma* was filled with crossbowmen waiting to have the Saracens in range. One launched an arrow that managed to stick in the timbering of the enemy's stern, but at that distance the risk of missing was great and I ordered them to stop and save their arrows.

That was when the Moors uncovered the companion of their galley and the sailor up on the highest mast shouted, "Naphtha!" Lines of smoke traced across the sky while jugs of burning fuel began to fall on our ship.

The soldiers covered themselves with their shields, which weren't very helpful against the fire, while the horde of slaves rowed unprotected and, there among banks eighteen and nineteen on the starboard side, a jug fell right on one of those pitiful men, turning him into a ball of liquid fire that splattered those near him. They howled in anguish, and as they let go of the oars, the ship veered port side.

The helmsman tried to correct the direction, the screams of the burning men chilling, but that wasn't the moment for fear or compassion.

"Throw dead leaves on the stove," I ordered.

It wasn't the first time we had used this strategy. While the slave drivers and the soldiers tried to put out the fire with buckets of water, the sailor brought up some sacks of dead leaves and pitch from the hold and threw them on the stove. Soon a column of black smoke rose over the ship.

"Stop the rowing!" I shouted. "Drop the oars in the water."

The order was passed down through the central gangway and the ship stopped, diverted from its chase and rocking. The fire was being gotten under control when the lookout shouted that the Saracens had reduced their rowing and that their ship was turning. For a moment the tracks of smoke from their projectiles stopped and, once they were facing us, they started their firing again, this time from the fighting platform on the prow. Our slave drivers rapidly removed the chains from the wounded and dying in the rowing stations belowdecks and the volunteer rowers, *bonavoglies*, who didn't need shackles, took their places. Our galley, covered in a thick cloud of smoke that the sailors were in charge of feeding, seemed mortally wounded, but we were ready for battle.

The enemy ship came toward our starboard side, attacking us with fire and arrows; they wanted to take advantage of the confusion. They would never have dared board a galley like the *Na Santa Coloma* without reducing its crew first. My people moved among the smoke as if something truly serious was happening, and the Moors' arrows reached the timbering and the galley slaves at the first banks, who began to scream.

We were about six hundred and fifty feet from them when I ordered, "Shoot crossbow. Row."

My orders traveled to the prow, the drum began to beat, along with whiplashes and cries. A cloud of arrows flew toward our enemy and soon screams were heard from the other galley. The screaming reached new heights when we had the good fortune to hit their deck with one of our rocks.

The Saracens didn't realize the trick until, as our ship jumped forward, the fire's smoke, no longer being fed, stayed behind. Then they made their second mistake. Wanting to avoid the clash, they veered toward their port side to dodge us, but thanks to the strength of our rowers and the ship's powerful structure, we managed to sink the ram into their starboard side, making planks and splinters of wood fly. Meanwhile, our crossbowmen, avoiding their galley slaves, who were surely captured Christians, had time to launch a second volley of arrows, now more accurate because we were closer, onto warriors and officers.

At the order to board, our men, expert in these matters, ran over the ram shouting, "For Christ and the Virgin!" and easily jumped onto the other ship. In spite of the losses from Moorish arrows and swords, and forgetting about the violent soldiers who were mostly piled up at the prow, we ferociously attacked the aft companion, where in a matter of moments the officers and midshipmen's throats were cut. When all our men had boarded the ship and advanced toward the prow along the oar banks, the galley slaves were cheering and applauding. I knew then that we had won.

My chest, swollen with happiness and pride, let out a victory cry.

That was when I realized that I was in the museum again. Only seconds had passed and Oriol was still talking.

". . . the type of ship with high gunwales, like Columbus's caravels, was also used in Arnau's time. But they were freight and trading ships. They only used sails, and their deeper hulls allowed them to transport a lot of weight. The most obvious predecessors were the coca, the urca, the caravel, and the entire family of smaller ships called fustas. And in terms of galleys, we can find over twelve different types, from uxers to sagetias, polacres, pinks—"

I grabbed the railing and sat down on the floor, bringing my hand to my chest. My heart was beating quickly and I was having trouble breathing.

"What's the matter?" asked Oriol, startled, interrupting his explanation.

"It happened again," I whispered as I got my breath back. "That ring."

CHAPTER 31

After that upsetting experience I was expecting Oriol to be understanding. I had faith in his sensitivity and the fact that he knew what that strange ring could do to people; I didn't imagine that he'd be the cause of my next panic attack.

We stayed at the Maritime Museum long enough for me to tell him what had happened. When Oriol had made sure that I was more or less okay, he told me that he wanted to show me a very special place. I guess he wanted to cheer me up. We crossed an avenue and entered an area filled with very old houses. We rounded a few corners and went into a tiny bar. It certainly was special; from its filthy walls hung shelves filled with bottles covered by decades of dust and some dirty, depressing paintings of sour-faced women smoking. The framed newspaper clippings, also attached to the walls, confirmed that this was a special place. French music played in the background. It seemed to be coming from an old radio.

"This bar is called Pastís," Oriol informed me after he'd ordered a drink of the same name. It tastes like anisette but is served mixed with water, and I didn't like it.

I guess Oriol was trying to raise my spirits with that brew, but I didn't think he was on the right path. Just thinking of the vision I'd had at the museum gave me goose bumps. My gaze drifted to the ring with its bloody, male stone, perhaps searching for the ghost of the old Templar who seemed to live there.

"I love the legend about this place," added Oriol, distract-ing me from my dismal speculation. His eyes moved around the dive with the same nostalgic air he had displayed in the museum when he was recalling ancient battles and wooden ships and drowned heroes in the Mediterranean. Judging by the look of the place, this new story he was about to tell me must be pretty old too. That's Oriol. He liked to live in the past. I won-dered if he'd ever relived the waves, the storm, and the kiss of our youth.

"This was founded in 1947 by Quimet, a bohemian and an amateur painter, when he returned from Paris, where he had emigrated from Africa as a *pied-noir* at the end of World War Two. There he tried to make it big, like Picasso and Juan Gris had done before him. In those days Paris was still the world's art capital and New York was only dreaming of it. Carme, an energetic woman from Alicante, went with him. Rumor has it that she was his cousin. She was good looking and had a strong personality. She loved him passionately and was convinced of his artistic talent. Carme worked in bars, cleaning, doing any-thing she could to get enough money for them both to live on. But the paintings of existential *nausée* that Quimet made didn't sell. Who'd hang such depressing, terrible images in their liv-ing room?"

I sipped the pastis Oriol had ordered without asking me if it was what I wanted and I looked at the paintings, covered with tobacco soot. Women with empty gazes sat in front of equally empty glasses, the men smoking. Female figures in the street, surely prostitutes waiting for business. I had noticed that the area Oriol had taken me to was part of the old Barrio Chino, the city's bastion of cheap whores.

"Quimet must have aspired to being the existentialist Toulouse-Lautrec of 1950s Barcelona by recording the images that surrounded him on canvas," continued Oriol. "He signed his work as Pastís. It was a time when French culture was admired and Anglo-Saxon culture ignored. The upper-middle class sent their children to the French School."

Like Mamá and Enric, I thought.

"Quimet brought together a group of friends and regulars in a marginal pseudoartistic circle to listen to Piaf, Montand, Greco, and Brel, drinking pastis while discussing the latest trends in the world's capital." Oriol sipped from his glass, looking around before fixing his eyes on me and confiding, "My father used to come to this bar a lot."

I held his gaze—were Oriol's eyes damp? The tiny bar gave me an excuse to get a bit closer to that introverted, shy boy who had grown into a lovely yet ambiguous man. Did I still love him? Did he feel something for me? Had he ever?

We were silent, looking at each other, those old *chansonnier* ballads purring words of love in the half-light, which, in spite of the half dozen patrons who almost filled the place, seemed intimate to me.

I thought I could feel him getting closer too, that our lips wanted to meet, and I longed for the taste of his mouth. I saw myself reflected in his pupils. A thirteen-year-old girl yearning for her first romantic kiss in a September storm. A foolish woman who fantasized about re-creating a romance that distance and time had destroyed. Something that could have been but existed only in the parallel world of my dreams. I got slightly closer, my heart beating like mad.

"He brought me here."

"Who?" I asked stupidly. It was as if I had suddenly woken up, not knowing where I was, as had happened moments before at the museum. Except this time the ring wasn't responsible for the spell, Oriol was.

"My father, Enric," he replied.

Oriol was still very close to me, but the spell had been broken. Did he do it on purpose? Was he afraid of the kiss that our eyes had promised? Was it that he didn't dare? Or was he gay, like they said? I looked over the four narrow walls to hide my embarrassment.

"He was the one who told me the legend. If you read the newspaper articles that hang on these walls, you'll see that there are different stories, but for me the only one, the good one, is Enric's."

"Tell it to me."

"Quimet was a brilliant, charismatic guy who attracted people to him, and a loyal group of customers and friends gathered here regularly. But today no one talks about his dark side."

"His dark side?"

"Yes. He didn't do much besides paint, chat, drink, box, and smoke. Well, except for . . ."

"For what?"

"Giving Carme real thrashings when he got drunk," he said and pointed out a small frame behind the bar. "Look, that's them in the photo."

I looked at the yellowing black-and-white photo. A man with his hair combed back and a good-looking woman, with beautiful long hair in a 1950s-style hairdo and wearing an immaculate white apron, looked out at us, smiling.

"But how could she let him?"

"Because she loved him."

"That's no excuse."

"She supported him in Paris and continued working for him here in Barcelona."

"Why did she put up with the guy not only loafing around but hurting her?"

"Because she loved him."

"That doesn't justify anything . . ."

"He was sick. And one ill-fated day Quimet died, who knows if it was from drinking, cirrhosis, or syphilis," he said, interrupting me. "And that was when this place and Carme's love became a legend."

"Why?"

"Carme decided to leave everything exactly as it was during Quimet's life. Look at the bottles on the shelves."

"They're filthy."

"The walls were never repainted, the music was the same as always, and when you asked Carme, who served behind the bar in her starched, bright white apron, for anything besides pastis she made a face and mumbled under her breath. When you came in she'd receive you with a smile, while she wiped the bar with a rag, and she would suggest, "What'll you have? A *pastisset*?" as if it were the tribute owed to the memory of a saint. When I was a kid, she'd let me have soft drinks.

"At first the painter was missed and one of his friends in the *nova cançó* movement recorded a ballad dedicated to him. It's in Catalan:

"'*Quimet del bar Pastís ja no et veurem mai més . . . ,*'"* and it went on to say, '*però hi ha un fet que no s'entén: cada vegada hi ve més gent.*'†

"The legend of the bar Pastís as a monument to Carme's love for Quimet had gone beyond the drinking painter. And Carme, in spite of all she put up with for love, was a woman to be reckoned with. She always took care to keep up a good atmosphere, kicking out undesirables without a second thought. When she retired in the early eighties, Pastís maintained its popularity, and those who carry on have made sure to uphold the spirit."

Oriol took a sip of his pastís and looked at me again. A slight smiled played on his lips.

---

* "Quimet from the bar Pastís, we'll never see you again . . ."
† "But something inexplicable is happening: more and more people keep coming."

"Would you be able to love that much, Cristina?"

I thought a few moments before nodding.

"I believe in love."

"Do you love your fiancé that way? Like Carme loved Quimet?"

It made me uncomfortable to have him bring up Mike. To myself, I thought that honestly the answer was no.

"I don't know, that's going too far," I mumbled.

"I didn't know Quimet, but when you asked Carme about him she'd say that he was an artist; her gaze floated toward the past, a smile came to her lips, and you could hear the admiration in her words. Could you ever appreciate a man that much? Enough to support him with your work, take care of him in his illness, and on top of it all put up with physical abuse?"

"No," I said, shocked.

Oriol smiled. He seemed satisfied.

"You see?" he said triumphantly. "There are different ways of living. There are different ways of loving. There are those capable of sacrifice for their lover. There are those who would give their own life."

I gave it some thought. What was Oriol trying to tell me? Was he talking about his father? Was he talking about himself? Or both?

We left the bar and walked toward the Ramblas. I let my left hand fall near his, perhaps with the naive hope that they would brush against each other, or that he'd take my hand in his as he sometimes had when we walked on the beach as kids.

I hadn't noticed the presence of a woman who had appeared from behind us. She stopped Oriol by grabbing his arm.

"Hello, baby," she said in a strange voice.

Oriol turned and I couldn't see his expression.

"Hello, Susi," he responded.

Susi wore a short red leather skirt and black panty hose. She was a tall, good-looking woman wearing too much makeup and was perched on impossibly high stilettos.

"It's been a long time, Oriol, darling."

That voice, I thought.

"It has," he replied, and then added, "This is Cristina, a childhood friend who's visiting from New York."

"Pleased to meet you," she said, and without letting go of Oriol's arm she gave me two of those kisses—the kind that don't actually get even close to your cheek, while her lips made a kissy sound. I did the same, though I still sensed something strange. She wore a strong, sickly sweet perfume.

"Charmed," I said. But I wasn't. I was surprised that Oriol seemed to be so well acquainted with such a woman.

"Is she a close friend?" asked Susi, addressing Oriol. The girl had quite a chest on her.

"She is a friend I love very much," he declared, a mischievous smile playing across his face.

"Ah!" she exclaimed. Her thick, sensuous lips opened in a small smile filled with tobacco-stained teeth. She looked at me. "Then we could have a three way."

I was stunned for a few seconds. Then I began to comprehend the incomprehensible. Susi was a prostitute. She launched into selling her wares, explaining what a great time the three of us would have, describing scenes in detail, giving us all sorts of shocking particulars without the least bit of modesty. I looked at Oriol. He was watching me with a smile; he seemed to be waiting for me to make a decision. I felt even worse when I realized I was blushing. I couldn't recall when I had been more embarrassed. Me, who liked to think I was super self-confident and could handle myself in any situation. Although this situation was beyond me.

But the worst was yet to come when, finally getting over my initial shock, I began to understand some of the images Susi was describing. Then I got it.

"You're not a woman!" I couldn't avoid shouting. "You're a man!"

"You're sort of right, darling," responded Susi without losing her smile. Now I noticed her prominent Adam's apple. "Although not entirely. But you're wrong about the other, I'm no man. With these tits?" And she lifted them with her hands. As I had noticed before, they were sizable.

"Come on, Oriol, let's all go," she insisted, looking at him. "Only fifty euros, twenty-five each. And I'll pay for the bed."

I couldn't believe what I was witnessing; it was as if it were happening to someone else, as if it were happening somewhere else. Then, as Oriol spoke, I felt my world crumble.

"How does the plan sound to you, Cristina?" His almond-shaped eyes that I loved so much looked at me, and a wide smile revealed his teeth. "Should we go?"

"Yes, let's go!" exclaimed Susi, taking us both by the waists. "Come on, miss, I know how to please both men and women . . . I'm sure you won't get a chance like this again, to enjoy me and a man at the same time."

For a moment I imagined myself between the two of them. And for a brief instant I felt perversely aroused, and then repulsed.

CHAPTER 32

That night, from my bedroom looking over the city, I called Mike. I hadn't talked to him in two days and he reproached me for it. I accepted his scolding. I needed his love, his devotion, his affection.

"I love you, I miss you," he told me after the reproof. "Forget about that silly treasure hunt and come back to me."

"I love you too." I felt those words deeply. "I would give anything to have you here by my side right now. But I have to see this story through to the end."

That conversation, knowing that Mike still loved me, was like balm on my wounds. Because that's what it was like, I felt wounded. Deeply. Did Oriol really want to get it on with that transvestite? If he really went for that type of thing, and he wanted to have any chance of me actually going for it, he should have at least waited until we were in a relationship. The proposal was absolutely insulting.

No, according to him, that wasn't his intention.

"I wasn't expecting to bump into Susi and I was just improvising on the spur of the moment. It was a joke," he told me. I had set off, almost running, toward the Ramblas without responding to his indecent proposal. He said good-bye to Susi and caught up with me in the middle of the street.

"Well, I didn't like it," I responded.

"Come on, don't get mad, I was just playing along with her to see how you would react . . . I thought it was funny."

His explanations didn't convince me. I was very hurt, and when I locked myself in my room tears came to my eyes. Oriol had really disappointed me.

Where was that shy boy I had fallen in love with?

That night, looking out the window, seeing the lights of the city and still sobbing from the unpleasantness, I couldn't help running the two episodes over and over in my mind. First the one in the bar. Oriol had brought me face-to-face with a way of living and thinking that was the complete opposite of mine. That devotion of woman to man, that voluntary submission. What was he trying to insinuate? And then, the meeting with Susi. Had he set that up? Was he lying when he said it was by chance? I was sure that Oriol was counting on me to refuse the proposition; I'd have trouble imagining a more inappropriate situation in which to propose sex to a woman. Why did he do it? Was my refusal some sort of alibi for his homosexuality? And Susi. That complicity, that trust; they'd definitely known each other for some time. What was their relationship?

When I got into bed I couldn't sleep. The vision I'd had at the museum reappeared every time I shut my eyes. The lines of smoke from the burning naphtha flying toward us, the sickening smell of human excrement, the stench of burnt flesh, the howls of the wounded. I felt sick to my stomach. I got up to get a drink of water and saw that evil ring glimmering on my finger. I took it off and placed it on the bedside table. I would sleep with only the pure, clear diamond from my fiancé that night. I couldn't stand another one of those dreadful visions from the past.

I don't know how many hours it took for me to fall asleep, but when I did, I didn't sleep well. This time I couldn't blame my bad dreams on the ruby ring. At first it was an erotic dream, pleasantly silly, like so many dreams, but because of how I was feeling, it ended up making me even more uneasy.

It began very sweetly, with Oriol coming close to kiss me and me opening my lips and closing my eyes to savor his salty taste, just as I had, so many years earlier, when we'd exchanged our first kiss.

His hand slid under my skirt, making me overflow with desire, but when I half-opened my eyes I saw it was another man who was caressing my inner thighs. I tried to protest. As I pulled away from him, I saw that the second man, with his hands still all over me, was kissing Oriol.

I couldn't escape from the strange three-way embrace where, looking for Oriol's love, I found myself having sex with a person who seemed to be my friend's lover. That man wasn't a transvestite like Susi, but his perfume was the same.

When I woke up I was breathing unevenly, feeling both aroused and upset. How would the dream have continued? I realized that what was really behind that nightmare was the unresolved status of Oriol's homosexuality. Was he or wasn't he?

The uncertainty bothered me. I had to admit that I still had feelings for him. Would my mother's story repeat itself? I started to get depressed. Sitting on the bed, looking fearfully at the ruby ring on my beside table, thinking about Oriol . . .

To hell with the treasure and all these painful old stories, I thought. I'm going to listen to Mamá and Mike. I want to feel loved. I want to be pampered. I began to plan my return trip.

Then the phone rang. It was Artur, inviting me to lunch. I immediately accepted. At least he was gentlemanly, and in many ways more attractive than Oriol.

As soon as we'd ordered a light lunch, I peppered him with

the many questions I had about the events surrounding Enric's death.

"I don't understand," I began. "Why didn't you report the theft of the paintings to the police?"

"How do you know we didn't?" Artur looked at me, smiling. Yes, I said to myself, he's much more attractive than Oriol.

"I have my sources."

He looked at me with interest.

"Was it Alicia?"

"I haven't talked about that with her. It was Captain Castillo. He was in charge of investigating the case. There was no robbery reported. Did it really happen?"

"Of course it did."

"Then how do you expect to recover your stolen goods without reporting it to the police?"

"We have our ways."

"The same ones you used on my godfather's friend?"

"Look, Cristina. We have our way of working and we don't want the police sticking their noses in our business."

"You guys are mafia, right?"

Artur shook his head, displeased, then he spoke in measured words and his smile, now a bit forced, returned to his face.

"Calling us mafia is an insult, dear," he paused. "We are just art dealers with our own business rules."

"Which include murder."

"Only if absolutely necessary."

I stared at his handsome face while I decided if I should just leave right then. I felt my lips purse, a sign that I was angry. This man was obviously dangerous. But the danger didn't scare me much. His arrogance, his thinking he was above the law, made me indignant. I guess that's the lawyer in me. He seemed to guess what I was thinking and hastened to add, "Don't think that they are any better . . ."

"Who?"

"Oriol, Alicia, and the rest of them . . ."

"What about them?"

"They belong to a sect."

"What are you talking about?"

"Yes, they do," he stated with total conviction. "At least I'm honest and tell you my intentions to your face. But they hide theirs."

"Tell me what else you know."

He explained that, led by the romanticism of the late nineteenth century, with its glorification of all things medieval, Oriol's grandfather, a regular in Masonic and Rosicrucian circles, founded his own secret group, resurrecting a very sui generis version of the Order of the Temple. My family, the Colls, and his, the Boix, also belonged to this group. But a few generations later, when Enric was named master of the order, Artur's father and uncle began to feel uncomfortable with the increasingly esoteric and ritualistic nature of the group. It didn't help that Enric managed to change the rules to allow women to be admitted and that the first Templar female was Alicia, a woman with a strong personality who was involved in pseudowitchcraft and the occult, and who enjoyed imposing her opinions on others.

"So that's how things were when Arnau d'Estopinyá appeared."

"Arnau d'Estopinyá?" I asked, surprised.

"Yes," he replied very seriously. "Arnau d'Estopinyá, the Templar monk."

"What do you mean?" I exclaimed. "How could he appear?" I couldn't shake my disbelief. I didn't peg Artur as a guy who believed in ghosts, but his expression was very convincing. "Who did he appear to?"

"To your godfather." I realized that the antiques dealer was enjoying my bewilderment.

"Arnau d'Estopinyá appeared to Enric?" My thoughts were

racing at full speed. Did that have something to do with the visions Alicia attributed to my ring?

"Yes. One fine day a man appeared to your godfather saying that he was a Templar and that he wanted to be admitted into our brotherhood—"

"Wait a second," I interrupted him. "Arnau d'Estopinyá died in the fourteenth century."

"Really?"

"Of course."

"Well, then this must have been another one," he replied mysteriously.

I nodded my head. His jokes were beginning to get on my nerves. I had the feeling he thought I was dumb.

"But no," Artur said suddenly, "it turns out that it was the same Arnau d'Estopinyá from seven hundred years ago."

Obviously, he was pulling my leg.

"Actually, he wasn't Arnau, the old Templar, but he believed that he was," he added with an amused smile. "That can't be possible, right?"

"He must be crazy."

"He is. But, anyway, Enric decided to grant him a hearing and approve his membership. My father too was on the commission that heard his story and, although suspicious, also voted for him."

"But why did they let him in if he was crazy?"

"For the treasure."

"The treasure!"

"Yes. He'd been a real monk but had been kicked out of his order for being too violent. He suffered frequent mood swings, to the point of stabbing another monk during an argument over what TV channel to watch. But he showed up proclaiming himself the continuation of a line of monks who were guardians of the secret of the Templar treasure of the crowns of Aragon, Mallorca, and Valencia. He wore a ring, which I've never seen, but according to what I've been told, it looks very much like the one you're wearing."

I stared down at the ruby, which looked quite dull at the moment.

"Do you think it's this one?" he asked me.

"Yes."

"Well, then it's very important for them."

"For them?"

"Yes. For the sect of neo-Templars Oriol and Alicia belong to. That ring represents the power within the order. According to Arnau d'Estopinyá, the signet comes from the master general of the order himself, William of Beaujeu, who died fighting in Acre and whose ring, symbol of Templar power, similar to another owned by the pope, was collected by one of the Templar Knights who, although badly wounded, managed to get on Arnau's ship. He ended up giving the ring to Arnau d'Estopinyá when the Aragonese and Catalan Templars were captured."

Hearing that story, which fit perfectly with the writings in the sheaf of papers, frightened me. Artur continued his story without noticing my reaction.

"When he died in Poblet, the ring, the painting, and the legend of the treasure were passed down from monk to monk."

"But your father and Enric believed that it was more than a legend."

"Exactly, and they both set off in search of the paintings around the area of the Cistercian monasteries of Poblet and Santes Creus. But your godfather made the best move."

"What was that?"

"Being the master of the order of the neo-Templars, he didn't have much trouble convincing the crazy monk that their sect was the direct heir of the Order of the Temple. So he accepted Arnau as a member and gave him a pension for life, which Enric paid out of his own pocket. The monk was thrilled, he swore eternal obedience to Enric, and he gave him the ring that he thought belonged to your godfather as master of the order. It seems that the man had never considered the ring his property, he was only its keeper."

"What happened when Enric died?"

"My father and my uncle had left the sect months before your godfather murdered them. They took the argument with Enric over the paintings and the disagreement over Alicia's growing power as bad omens. When Enric died, Alicia, going against all Templar tradition with respect to women, took over as master. She kept her husband's promise to Arnau, paying his pension on time each month, and he too, insane but intelligible, swore loyalty to her. Some did it grudgingly, but in the end, all the members accepted Alicia's leadership. I don't know her, but she seems to have charisma. And knew how to link the occult tradition cloaked in the Templar myth with her own schemes to make the rest of the brothers respect and admire her."

"Tell me about the Templars and the occult."

"There have been all sorts of stories. The tragic end of the order, the accusations of heresy, their great riches, all of that has excited the imagination of thousands of people. And if you add the story of the last of the grand masters of the order, Jacques de Molay, placing the king of France and the pope before the judgment of God when they burned him at the stake, and the fact that they both died before the year was out, you have a mysterious and disquieting picture. Others say that the Templars had possession of the holy grail and Moses' law tablets, that they owned *veracruces*, relic crosses containing splinters of Christ's actual cross, which could bring about untold miracles."

"Is there any truth in all that?"

"Do you want my honest opinion?"

"Of course."

"None at all. It's all just stories."

"But you do believe in the treasure."

"That's different. It is written in letters to King James II, which are still around, that when the Templars surrendered Miravet, their last fortress in Catalonia, and the headquarters for the kingdoms of Aragon, Valencia, and Mallorca, the royal agents didn't find the treasure they were expecting. The only things that pleased the monarch were the books they found, which in those days were luxury items. But the fabulous fortune that the castle supposedly housed had gone up in smoke. And it has never, as far as we know, reappeared."

That intrigue remained in the air and, as if there were nothing more to say on the subject, Artur began to ask about my life in New York and to tell me anecdotes of his time spent in the Big Apple. We were soon laughing.

Artur is a subtle man, and I think he just wanted to plant a seed of doubt in my mind about the Bonaplatas. Surely he had his reasons: they were mysterious people. What more were they hiding from me?

I told myself that, whether his stories were true or not, Artur had managed to lift my spirits. He smiled and complimented both my mind and my body. Normally, I wouldn't have paid much attention to that kind of flattery, but my self-esteem needed just what he was offering. He kissed my hand as we said good-bye.

"Don't be tacky," I chastised him, but I was secretly pleased. I stamped a kiss on each of his cheeks.

Later that day I called Mamá.

"Yes, it's true," she confirmed. "Both your grandfather and Enric's father belonged to some sort of religious association. I remember that they called themselves Templars. It's normal that Oriol, being the firstborn son, would continue the tradition."

That night, again I tossed and turned in bed. Artur could be right. His smile kept appearing to me in the darkness. What a mess.

CHAPTER 33

I was awakened by a scream. I tried to determine where it had come from, but then realized that it had come from me. My dream had been so real I wasn't worried I'd ever forget it. I turned on the light to prove that I was awake. The ring was burning my finger, its stone glowing like embers. I needed to take it off and go to the window to breathe some fresh air. The lights of the city, still in darkness, confirmed that I was awake. Well, unless what I was experiencing was a larger dream, the hallucination of someone who'd been dead for years. Someone who was making his dreams of treasure hunts a reality, even momentarily, for the three of us, just like he had when we were kids.

I couldn't see my face. Just the door I was knocking on while holding a suitcase. I knew that behind that door my end awaited me. My last port of call. Death. I had no chance of surviving. But I had to do what I had to do, fulfill my promise that bound me to my lover even beyond life. Like the ancient Templars, like the noble young Thebans of Epaminondas. You never leave your partner, and if he is killed, you must avenge his death. That was what I had sworn and that was what I would do. I belonged to a race of champions and this was my final round. While I waited for the door to open under the one-eyed scrutiny of the security cameras, my heart cringed at the thought of my murdered friend and of the son I would never see again. I felt a knot in my throat, my eyes filled with tears, and I began to say a prayer for them.

When the door opened, two men in suits and ties were waiting for me. One kept his distance while the other pushed me against the door, forcing me to let go of the suitcase. He frisked me. One, two, three times. He went through my wallet, checked my fountain pen and my keys. When they were sure I had no weapons, they inspected the suitcase.

"Okay, you can go in," said the older one. And he took the suitcase and the lead.

"One moment," I said, holding him back. "That's mine and it will be until the transaction is finished."

The man looked into my eyes and saw my determination to not give in.

"Whatever," he said to the other man, who now hovered over me as the older man shrugged his shoulders. "Let him have the damn suitcase. There's no danger."

The room was large and decorated with expensive, eclectic objects. Jaime Boix was sitting on a lovely Chippendale sofa. He was the youngest of the brothers. Arturo sat behind an impressive Imperial-style desk.

They both got up as they saw me come in, and Jaime, smiling under his small gray mustache, offered me his hand. "Welcome, Enric."

I refused the handshake. "Let's get this over with as soon as possible."

Jaime's smile disappeared. His brother was also serious as he pointed me to an armchair.

"Have a seat, please." In spite of his courteousness, it wasn't an invitation.

I obeyed, keeping the suitcase at my feet. Jaime sat on the sofa to my right, and the older brother sat behind the Napoleonic desk. At his back, on the wall, I could see the two other pieces of the triptych hanging: the paintings of Saint John the Baptist and Saint George. My gaze rested on them for a few moments. I was sure, that was them. The other two men remained standing; I watched them with resentful curiosity: they must have been the actual killers of my beloved Manuel. One placed himself to my left and the other in front of me, blocking the exit.

"Are you sure he's not wearing a microphone?" Arturo asked the thug at the door.

"No microphones, no weapons. He's clean." And then with a twisted smile he said, "I even checked his nuts."

"Before finalizing the transaction we want to tell you something," said Arturo, exchanging a look with his brother. "We didn't want this to happen. We're sorry that your boyfriend died. He got hysterical and fought back, and what happened was an accident. We're pleased that you're much more sensible and know how to close a gentleman's deal. A Templar gentleman knight," he added a bit sarcastically.

"You threatened my family." I felt the blood rush to my head. I hated this man, I detested him with all my strength. "That's not gentlemanly; it's despicable and disgraceful."

"I want you to know that we have nothing against you, or your family. And we didn't have anything against that guy." He paused. "It's just that you weren't reasonable—what happened is your fault. We gave you one chance after another. We are businessmen and this is our business. We couldn't let it get past us because of your stubbornness. I'm sorry."

He paused to open a drawer and take out several piles of blue bills.

"My brother and I had decided to add half a million more pesetas to the amount. The price we agreed on was already twice the value of a fourteenth-century Gothic painting. We didn't have to do it, but it's our way of saying that we're sorry about what happened to your friend and to settle the account."

Settle the account, I thought, and my insides twisted in anger. Half a million pesetas and they call that settling the account. My hands shook and I held one over the other to steady them.

"Well, it's time for you to show us the merchandise," said Jaime. "We're anxious to see that famous Virgin."

I opened the suitcase and took out the painting, resting it carefully on my knees. All eyes went to the image. I didn't give them time to discover it was a fake. I tore the cardboard that covered the back and took out the pistol I had hidden in there. My hand shook as I held it and I stood up as the painting fell to the floor.

I had planned on killing Arturo first and then Jaime. I had calculated that I had just enough time before the bodyguards blew me away. But at the last minute, perhaps it was my fear, perhaps it was my survival instinct, or perhaps both at once, I changed my plans.

The first shot went into the guts of the hit man on my right. Strangely, hearing the bang restored my calm and I shot the second bullet into his face. Now I could deal more coolly with the thug I had in front of me. He already had his gun in his hand. My father had taken me as a kid to practice target shooting, and the shot that went through his head was worthy of Olympic gold. I had four bullets left. More than enough to finish the job. I confronted Arturo, who had scattered the bills on the table in a frenetic attempt to use a gun he had just taken out of a drawer. I let off a couple of shots in his chest.

And there was Jaime, his mouth hanging open. He had peed on the Chippendale settee. What a waste.

"Please, Enric," he begged in a stutter.

"Didn't you want to see the Virgin?" I paused.

"Please . . . ," he stammered.

"Did you see her?" His eyes were popping out of his head. He was seeing his death in mine and his mouth moved without saying anything. "Well, now you'll see Satan," I declared.

As I shot him, I felt better than I'd felt before. A few seconds later, worse than I had ever felt. I couldn't believe I was still alive. I collapsed on the sofa and began to cry.

CHAPTER 34

I don't get frightened easily. Actually my mother thinks I'm too daring. The truth is that sometimes, unnecessarily, I get myself into situations that are stressful, and, well, dangerous. And whenever I find myself in one of those, I realize that I shouldn't be there. I have to admit that this time I'd really stuck my head in the lion's mouth. I was truly frightened, and prayed to get out unharmed.

I saw Artur Boix a couple more times. He was entertaining and attractive and always gave me new details about the Bonaplatas and their secret activities.

He confessed that he had set up the mugging when we left the bookstore and that he didn't accept Oriol's refusal to negotiate the dividing up of the treasure. He swore that under no circumstances would his thugs have done me any harm, that he was still furious with those incompetents for fleeing, but that he was partly to blame for not taking into account the reaction of the madman following me.

That led him to proclaim that the neo-Templars were a dangerous sect, fanatics, crazy, ridiculous poseurs. I still didn't know how the order worked, but just based on my sympathies with Enric and Oriol, I replied that he was exaggerating and that it was convenient for him to paint them as bad guys.

This seemed to irritate Artur. He said they had secret ceremonies that only the initiated knew about. This was why they had kept me on the margins, even though I was living with members of the sect and wore the ring that gave me the right to not only membership in the order, but rank. He insisted, and I was somewhat bothered by the possibility, not so much that Alicia, but that Oriol was keeping me in the dark on purpose. I said it was a ridiculous notion.

Artur's handsome smile vanished and he took on the expression of a pouting child. Then he said, "I bet you wouldn't dare show up at one of their secret chapter meetings."

I replied that it would be impolite to go where I hadn't been invited. He answered that I could go and observe without being seen. I said that wouldn't be right, and he countered by saying I was afraid, adding that he knew how to get in and out without being seen and that it was all a question of my having what it took to do it.

I asked him if he'd go with me and he said yes, but just up to the door, because if we were discovered I would be safe, since I am a friend and the bearer of the ring of the highest Templar authority. But that he, in such circumstances, was much more likely to be treated roughly.

"It's obvious that, even though you refuse to admit it, you believe me and you don't trust them," he added.

I don't know if that was the third or fourth time he challenged me, while his ironic smile increased his attractiveness. His sarcasm made it all the more appealing. "Sure, I'll do it," I said. "Even though you'll only accompany me to the door."

He'd bamboozled me, I knew it. What was he up to, sending me to that church at midnight? He wanted me to see their supposed Templar rituals, thus increasing his credibility and decreasing Oriol and Alicia's. I asked him this straight out.

He said that he wanted me on his side in this treasure-hunting business. And that, if I was discovered, he didn't mind that they'd know it was he who had taken me there. He wanted them to know that he was lying in wait, that it was time to negotiate. He had a right to a large part of that fortune, and the best thing for all concerned was to come to an agreement.

Well, I thought, that's what you think.

It was the Noche de San Juan, the shortest night of the year, the summer solstice, the night of the witches, of magical darkness and luminous shadows, the night of Saint John the Baptist, the decapitated patron saint of the Templars. On that night, according to Artur, the sect would gather in an old Gothic church near the Plaza Cataluña. He told me that the Catholic liturgy celebrated the deaths of all its saints and the birth of only one: Saint John, and that this day falls on the exact opposite point on the calendar from Christmas, the celebration of Jesus's birth on the winter solstice. The dates were not chosen at random. They were meant to replace the pagan pre-Christian solstice celebrations. He said that Templar Knights fully participated in these celebrations.

I felt the city vibrating with an exceptionally intense energy. Fireworks exploded in the sky above streets filled with people, as if it were daytime, and groups of children threw firecrackers, running and laughing. It was a night of fire, of sparkling wine and *coca*, a hard, glazed cake covered with crystallized fruit and pine nuts.

Artur gave me a map of the church and explained its interior layout. The faithful enter the church of Saint Anna through what is today its main entrance, located on the extreme right of the crossing. Five Gothic arches mark its portico, each resting on a small column. A statue of the Virgin presides over this entrance, which opens onto the small Plaza Ramón Amadeu.

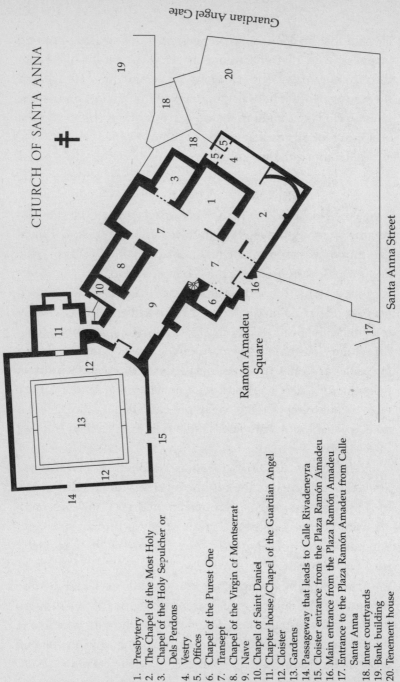

CHURCH OF SANTA ANNA

Guardian Angel Gate

Santa Anna Street

Ramón Amadeu Square

1. Presbytery
2. The Chapel of the Most Holy
3. Chapel of the Holy Sepulcher or Dels Perdons
4. Vestry
5. Offices
6. Chapel of the Purest One
7. Transept
8. Chapel of the Virgin of Montserrat
9. Nave
10. Chapel of Saint Daniel
11. Chapter house/Chapel of the Guardian Angel
12. Cloister
13. Gardens
14. Passageway that leads to Calle Rivadeneyra
15. Cloister entrance from the Plaza Ramón Amadeu
16. Main entrance from the Plaza Ramón Amadeu
17. Entrance to the Plaza Ramón Amadeu from Calle Santa Anna
18. Inner courtyards
19. Bank building
20. Tenement house

The second entrance is located at the foot of the Latin cross that makes up the original ground plan of the church. That entrance leads to the cloister, a lovely two-level construction with Gothic arches covering a hallway that surrounds a square garden. The cloister is entered through the small plaza as well, although that entrance is closed by an iron gate.

Tall modern buildings surround the church and the plaza, enclosing them in a timeless, hidden space that inspires nostalgia for distant, much more prosperous times. The Plaza Ramón Amadeu also closes at night with two metal gates, one located in a doorway that opens in the middle of a tenement house, several hundreds of years old, and then on Calle Santa Anna, and another much more modern one that lets out onto Calle Rivadeneyra, which connects to Plaza Cataluña.

The church is a hidden building, intentionally overprotected. An understandable strategy given the financial ups and downs and violence suffered by this venerable building. First it had been a monastery of the Order of the Holy Sepulcher, then a collegiate church, and finally a parish church. All the land and houses surrounding it were once the property of the monastery and were sold off according to the financial needs of each period. The church was closed by the French during the Napoleonic invasion and suffered various attacks before and after. Few people know that in the early twentieth century, a stylized neo-Gothic extension of the current church was built on what is today the plaza. It survived for twenty-two years before it was burned in a riot during the Second Republic and blown up afterward.

The old building was also affected by the explosion, and in spite of suffering the collapse of part of its roof, it probably escaped the dynamite only because it was a national monument. The rector and several other people involved with the church were not so lucky; they were killed during those chaotic days.

The church has a third entrance, used only by the religious

staff, that begins on Calle Rivadeneyra and passes alongside the parochial house, opening out into the cloister. The entrance is closed off by a railing, and serves as a parking place for the parish priest. It's separated from the end of the cloister by a gate.

The chapter house, which used to be called the Chapel of the Guardian Angel, was where the neo-Templars met to officiate at their ceremonies. It's connected both to the church's nave and the cloister. That's where I was headed.

But there is another entrance that almost no one knows about. Attached to the main altar, and located on the short arms of the cross, there are two chapels. Through the Chapel of the Most Holy, on the right, you can get to the vestry, where there are two small offices at the end. One of them has a glazed door that opens onto a courtyard surrounded by the church walls, a large bank building, and a tenement house several stories high that completely hide the medieval structure on that side. The courtyard is divided in two by a wall separating the area that belongs to the church from the area that belongs to the bank. In the wall there is a large gate that is no longer in use. In the bank's area, a solid metal door leads to an alley between the bank and the tenement house. The door opens out into a wide pedestrian area on the Portal de l'Angel. That was where I was supposed to enter.

The taxi left us on the eastern part of Plaza Cataluña and we walked the short distance to that mysterious entrance.

On the way, Artur went over the church's layout with me and gave me the keys to the gate that separates the courtyard from the back entrance to the vestry. He said that he'd wait for me in the alley. At that moment, I wasn't feeling so gutsy and only my pride kept me from backing out. What if I got locked in? Among the other lovely details he'd given me about the place, he'd mentioned that it also was an old cemetery. I thanked him for his gentlemanly gesture of waiting for me outside, but I insisted he also give me the key to the metal door that opens onto the street. He looked at me with his cynical smile, saying, "Are you afraid?"

"I'm just being careful," I replied, although in a situation like that it was hard to tell the difference.

"Good luck." He continued smiling and, stroking my cheek, leaned over and kissed me on the mouth, tongue included. I wasn't expecting that, but I accepted it. Really, I didn't pay much attention to it; I was worried about other things.

"Enjoy the experience, sweetheart," he added. I wondered if that conceited man was referring to the adventure I was about to begin or his kiss.

CHAPTER 35

When the door closed behind me, I felt as if I were in another place and time. It must have been my imagination, but I sensed a slight vibration in my ruby ring. There was enough light for me to find the door without a flashlight. The small wall was low and didn't cover the church walls, and there, in the stone buttress, I thought I saw a sculpted relief that gave me a start. I shined my flashlight on it for just an instant. It was a cross, a double-crossbar cross, worn by time. It was identical to the one on Luis's painting—seen on the staff held by the resurrected Christ emerging from the holy sepulcher. But then, and I still don't know why, when I turned off the flashlight, I looked up. There, silhouetted against the starry sky, I saw another stone cross crowning a roof. That one was the same as the one in my ring, a flared cross. I shone the flashlight on my ring, and it responded with a red twinkle. Was it warning me of impending danger? I shook my head, thinking that there were too many coincidences, and it was then that I noticed movement in the courtyard. There was someone there. My heart sped up, while my back sought protection against the wall. I aimed my flashlight in that direction and a pair of slanted eyes fixed on me momentarily, then vanished in the darkness.

A cat, just a stupid cat, but it had given me quite a scare.

I'm not fearful or superstitious, but I would have sworn that damn cat was black. I remembered stories of witches transforming themselves into black cats. What the hell was I doing? It was a night of witches, and here I was, about to enter a church cemetery filled with lunatics who practice the occult and think they're Templars. I placed my hand on my chest to slow down my galloping heart. I breathed deeply, and when I felt I had regained control of my breathing, I put the key, a piece of metal so enormous it looked like a hammer, into the lock. I had trouble turning it and opening the gate. The loud squeaking of the hinges made me jump. Obviously, this entrance was rarely used.

I considered the possibility of going back out to the street. But I realized that I was more afraid of confronting Artur's handsome, cynical smile than a bunch of Templars dressed, I imagined, in tunics and pointed hoods à la the KKK. Besides, I was so curious that I would never have forgiven myself if I ran away now. So there was only one way to go.

Where did Artur get the keys? Then I remembered what he had said about how he bought people off.

I decided to leave the door ajar, partly to avoid making more noise and also because I didn't want any obstacles in case I had to run out of there. I found myself in a narrow courtyard where pieces of sculpture were piled up. There was another door; the upper part was glass, protected by bars. It was much more modern than the last one and it opened easily with a small key. This was the office indicated on the map. I continued through a large room with furniture stacked up against the walls. It was the vestry. Another door, and I found myself in a chapel that, according to my diagram, was the Chapel of the Most Holy. Slowly, using the flashlight only briefly to get my bearings, I walked to what should have been one of the arms of the transept. To my left, there was a wooden structure that, again according to my map, was the vestibule that led to the Plaza Ramón Amadeu. Turning to the right I arrived at the crossing. I stayed in the darkness for a few moments to make out the inside of the church. There was no light at all except for a candle that marked the position of the large altar to my right, in the presbytery. I was able to orient myself easily. In the opposite direction, to my left, was the largest space in the church, the nave, and at the back of that, at the base of the cross that creates the building's shape, the exit to the cloister. There, to the right, was the chapel where the Templars supposedly met. I thought I could see some light in the area and hear murmuring. There was definitely someone there.

I shined my flashlight through the nave to see how the benches were arranged and to plan my route. Then I walked through the darkness making sure not to trip. At the end of the aisle, I could see where the light was coming from. To my right, at the end of a short hallway, there was a wooden door, rounded on the top into an arch shaped like a cross in the center, with the four spaces between the sides of the cross and the edge of the door covered in fogged, but translucent glass. The voices came from there, the chapter house. Mass was being celebrated, but I couldn't understand what was being said. I pressed my ear to the door. They weren't speaking Spanish, or Catalan, and I concluded that it must be Latin. I wanted to spy on them, but I realized that if I opened that door I would emerge near the altar, on one side of the oratory, and that I'd be seen immediately. That idea wasn't very appealing, so I decided to watch from the entrance to the cloister, which they should have their backs to. I returned to the small wooden hallway that connected the church to the cloister. None of the doors was locked, so I had no problem crossing to the courtyard. Through the garden in the center, I saw the lights of the city reflected in the sky and the flash of fireworks against the silhouette of a palm tree, reminding me of what night this was. Without having to turn on the flashlight, I could make out the dense shadows of the thin columns supporting the Gothic arches that marked the edges of the cloister. To my right I saw the half-open door of the chapter house, with two pointed windows on each side. As I set off toward that entrance, I sensed a movement in the darkness behind my back. My first instinct was to back up against the wall. My heart was racing again. Another cat? I shot a beam of light in that direction and saw nothing. I got closer to the columns that surrounded the cloister, lighting the passageway on the right side, and I didn't see anything there either. I had turned to check out the other side when, out of the corner of my eye, I thought I saw, through the vegetation, a shadow trying to hide behind the pillars on the opposite side of the courtyard. There was someone there. My heart was beating faster and I realized I was scared to death. What the hell was I doing in that church/cemetery at midnight on Saint John's night? I cursed my stupid pride, which had led me to that moment.

I turned off my flashlight and looked for a hiding spot behind a column. The shadow moved along with me. I moved forward several more columns, and whatever or whoever was following me did the same. I would have started running if only I'd known where to run. So I was still watching, with eyes like saucers, the darkness on the side where I had noticed the last movement. My heart was in my throat. I tried to breathe deeply and calm down. I would have given anything to be somewhere else at that moment, so much so that I decided to enter the oratory. What did it matter if they found me? Really, what I should have done from the beginning was to go and ask Alicia and Oriol face-to-face about their neo-Templar sect.

I moved toward the half-opened door carefully and opened it an inch more to see what was going on inside. A group of people dressed in white and gray capes had their backs to me, looking toward the altar. I didn't have time to see more. Someone grabbed me from behind and I felt the cold prick of a knife on my neck. The flashlight fell from my hand as I struggled to free myself and see my attacker's face.

Sweet Jesus! It was Barbablanca, Mr. White Beard himself. The man who'd been following me since my arrival.

I let out a bloodcurdling scream of terror. I don't remember ever having shrieked like that before.

The congregants turned around, startled. White Beard, with his dagger at my throat, pushed me into the chapel. I have trouble imagining a more spectacular entrance, but, to be honest, at that moment I was more worried about things other than making a fool of myself. We stood there for a few seconds looking at each other.

Finally, from the back of the room, Alicia spoke. She wore a white cape with the same double-crossbar red cross I had seen sculpted into the stone.

"Welcome, Cristina," she said, smiling. "We've been waiting for you." Then she addressed the man. "Thank you for your diligence, Brother Arnau. You can let the young lady go."

Brother Arnau? This is crazy, I thought.

She came toward me and kissed me on both cheeks.

"Brothers," she said, addressing the group of some fifty people who filled the chapel, "let me introduce you to Cristina Wilson, bearer of the master's ring and a full member of our order."

Some of them bowed their heads. They all had the red cross with the double crossbar on their right shoulders. I saw Oriol, who was dressed just like the other men, in a suit and tie below his white cape. He was smiling, amused. I also recognized the cranky old bookseller from Del Grial, who frowned at me, and Marimón, the jovial notary, smiling paternally.

"That is," added Alicia, "she will be admitted into this community if she so desires and completes our rites of initiation."

"Pleased to meet you. I'm sorry for the interruption," I faltered like a student who'd entered the wrong classroom. "Please, continue."

Alicia led me to the first bench, where she was seated, and made a gesture to the priest. He continued the mass in Latin. Arnau, I was thinking. Arnau d'Estopinyá. Since Artur had told me the story, I had suspected it would be him, and now I was sure. The man from the airport, the one I called Barbablanca, and the ex-monk who thought he was Arnau d'Estopinyá, were one and the same.

CHAPTER 36

I had gotten two invitations to two different Saint John's Night celebrations. One was from Luis, who offered to take me to a party at a spectacular mansion on a cliff overlooking the sea, near Cadaqués. It was easy for me to decline his offer sweetly. It was harder with Artur. His party was at a big house in Sarriá, formal dress required. I have to confess I was attracted to that man even though I knew he was a bastard. Well, he was like a criminal wearing kid gloves, and maybe that's what made him so appealing.

But the invitation I was hoping for never arrived, so I told Artur that I'd decide later, that it depended on what mood I was in coming out of the Templar lair. And he was kind enough, or interested enough, to accept my ambivalence. Really, I was still secretly hoping to spend La Noche de San Juan with Oriol.

After the mass, Alicia closed the evening with a few words. I imagine that if they had actually participated in any kind of occult or esoteric thing, it had happened before I came in. What I saw was pretty straightforward. They carefully folded their capes and left through the door that opens onto Calle Santa Anna. Brother Arnau demanded the keys I had used to get in. "From now on, we'll bolt it from the inside," Alicia said with a smile.

As I was leaving I saw Artur watching from a distance and I gave him a sign to say that everything was all right. I stuck to Oriol and started to quiz him on his plans for the evening. He told me that he was going home with his mother to change his clothes and then later he was going out to celebrate with some friends. Seeing that he showed no intention of inviting me, I decided to take the initiative and ask if he'd take me along. He didn't seem thrilled about the idea, but Alicia, who hadn't missed a word, said that it was the least one could expect from the Bonaplatas' hospitality. Finally he agreed, but I knew that I'd better not expect him to open the car door, like a gentleman.

On the way back to the house, Oriol was silent and Alicia was friendly. I felt uncomfortable because of the scene I had made at the church, but Alicia reacted as if it were the most natural thing in the world.

"The man who found you in the cloister is Arnau d'Estopinyá," she confirmed.

"Yeah, White Beard. That man has been following me since I got to Barcelona."

"Yes, darling," replied Alicia. "Following you and protecting you. Remember what happened outside the Del Grial bookstore. He saved you from your friend Artur's henchmen."

"In the church you said that you had been expecting me . . ."

"It was likely that Artur would suggest you do what you did. We knew that you were seeing each other and I suspected he had keys to the alley."

"Then why didn't you change the locks?"

"I thought that perhaps your friend might be interested in some of the antique pieces in the church." Alicia smiled. "Had he fallen into temptation he'd be in jail now."

I was quiet, thinking. That woman seemed to control every-thing. She had set a trap for her enemy. I was glad that Artur had been too smart for her.

* * *

Once we were alone in the car on the way to the party, I apologized to Oriol for my inopportune appearance in the church. He laughed and said that he wasn't surprised at all. He said his mother had predicted it and that, knowing about my relationship with Artur, she had kept the Templar meetings secret, hoping that he'd show his cards. I felt annoyed. It seemed that everyone was manipulating me. To counterattack, I ridiculed his Templar outfit.

"It's tradition," he assured me without losing his smile. "That's how our grandfathers wanted it."

"And how is it that someone so unconventional as you would take part in that game?"

He was silent for a few seconds and then said, "To honor my father."

We were both silent. It was a definitive argument. The traffic was heavy and I didn't know where he was taking me, but I was with him and that was all that mattered.

"I want you to know that I don't have a relationship with Artur." I don't know why I felt the need to say it. "He's been insisting that he can sell the pieces of the treasure better than anyone else, that he has as much right to it as we do, and that he wants to reach an agreement—"

"It's my father's treasure," Oriol said, cutting me off emphatically. "If he didn't make any agreements with the Boixes, I won't either."

I was surprised by his "you're either with me or against me" tone. I was beginning to have a clearer image of the situation. I remembered Artur saying that there would be blood to pay. I sighed, thinking that the whole matter of the treasure could end very badly. I only hoped that tragedy wouldn't befall the Bonaplata and Boix families as it had years before.

CHAPTER 37

A dense pine forest that went all the way to the beach flanked the spot, and the ground was covered with very fine sand and carpeted in stretches by pine needles. When we arrived, a bonfire was already burning on the sand, near the sea, away from the trees by a fair distance. Some folding tables displayed *coca* fruitcake, drinks, and paper cups, but there were no chairs and everyone sat on the sand. There were maybe sixty people and they all greeted Oriol, who was obviously popular with the crowd. They drank and chatted. Oriol started a conversation with a group of dreadlocked people about the program of activities at an abandoned house that, by the sound of it, they had taken by force. What I'd call squatting, they call *okupar*. He argued emphatically and seemed to be the leader in the exchange. It was hard to believe he was the same person who, hours earlier, had been wearing a suit and tie covered by a white cape adorned with the cross of a Templar Knight. Since I didn't know anyone, and I didn't have anything better to do, I listened to the debate. But it wasn't very interesting and I had nothing to contribute unless I let my inner lawyer express itself, and warn the group that squatting is a misdemeanor punished by law.

What a drag, I thought. If this is Oriol's idea of a Noche de San Juan, I'm really in for it.

A young woman who was also listening to the conversation passed me a joint that seemed to have traveled quite a ways. Hand rolled, with one end smoking and the other filterless, it looked slimy and vile. I flashed a friendly smile to accompany my "No thanks."

I took a good look at the woman. There was no way she could pass any halfway decent airport's security inspection. She sported many earrings, ending in spikes on one ear, and piercings on her eyebrows, nose, and chin. And I imagined she was hiding some additional metal in her hard-to-find places. Let's just say that even passing through the metal detectors in her birthday suit, she'd set off all the alarms. She was also sizing me up, from top to bottom, hands on her hips, the joint impressively balanced on the edge of her lips. When she thought she had me pegged, she spat out, "What's your deal, man?"

Oriol hadn't gone to the trouble of telling me who we'd be hanging out with, or how to dress, or anything else. I realized that I was the one who was out of place, not my unexpected opponent. She must have perceived me in the same way I'd have her if she had showed up looking that way at my birthday party in Manhattan.

Oriol seemed to have lost interest in his intellectual conversation and was watching us. He didn't try to hide his smile of enjoyment for what he surely thought was the punishment I deserved for having imposed myself on him that night. But I have to admit that even if I'd been warned, and had searched through my suitcases, there was no way I could have camouflaged myself to fit in with that crowd.

"Well, I . . . ," I replied uncomfortably. "I'm visiting Barcelona."

"A tourist!" she exclaimed while Oriol came over, pulled the joint from her lips, and took a long drag. "What the fuck is a tourist doing here?"

I can be pretty aggressive if I need to be, or if I'm provoked, but at that moment I felt intimidated. I looked at Oriol and, knowing he wasn't going to help me, I just wished I could vanish into thin air. But then, from the other side of the bonfire, somebody started to play the bongos. More drumming soon joined them, and then more, until my opponent lost interest in me and, taking the joint back from Oriol, moved on. The controversy over the social services at the occupied house had come to a close; the squatter leaders couldn't make themselves heard about their utopia du jour. People sat down and, to my surprise, more percussion instruments appeared. Almost everybody had one, and they drummed faster and faster, soon reaching a frenetic pace.

The gentle hum of the waves was lost amid the thunderous noise on the beach. The bonfire threw long flames upward, letting loose a barrage of sparks that for a few seconds pretended to be stars. Shooting stars, an *ignus fatuus* of pine resin. It was lovely; I felt as if I were part of another civilization, in another world. A woman with her hair pulled back into several braids, wearing a T-shirt and a long, tight skirt, got up and, as if in a trance, began to move her arms and hips to the beat of the drums. Her silhouette stood out against the flames in the background, like a priestess of a pagan cult, a dancing siren who drew the sailors of the night into the fire. She reminded me of my friend Jennifer who, just like her, booty shaking, got the party into high gear.

Those who didn't play the bongos were dancing, and the night became a sort of voodoo séance. I felt myself pulled into the mayhem and my body moved along with the others. Then the air vibrated with a high-pitched sound that bored into my bones, and just as the percussion made me move my feet, that sound moved my soul.

"That's a *gralla*, a—," Oriol said as I pulled him to the dance floor.

"I know what a *gralla* is," I interrupted. "It's a wooden clarinetlike instrument. I didn't forget *everything*, you know." Its sound was enthralling. I was in a frenzy. I took off my shoes and threw them away. I felt like a cavewoman dancing by the fire.

I don't know how long we danced. My bare feet sank into the cool, fine sand, slowing them down and massaging them. Faces shone in the light and heat of the bonfire. Above us, the starry sky became even more festive from the multicolored flashes of far-off fireworks.

Oriol was not a faithful dance partner and switched among various people. He danced with men as well as women, with individuals and groups. I watched him attentively. It was obvious that he didn't have a steady lover—man or woman—or at least not in that group.

The flames of the bonfire had dwindled and the drumming died down. I looked around for Oriol and saw him grab a man by the hand and whisper something in his ear. The man smiled and my heart turned over in my chest. Despite the sparkling wine I had drunk from a plastic cup, and the euphoria of the dance, I hadn't missed a beat of what was going on around me. I had noticed that several couples, some of the same sex, had gone into the forest, with beach towels to use as sheets over the sand and pine needles.

What's wrong with you? Don't be an idiot, I thought, criticizing myself softly. You're engaged to Mike. You love him. What is it to you if Oriol is happy with a man?

But I couldn't get rid of the lump in my throat as I watched them head toward the forest holding hands. Good-bye to my most beloved memories.

"My mother was so right," I murmured. "She understood it all from the beginning."

But then they turned around and, still holding hands, ran toward the bonfire and jumped over it. They fell to one side, raising a shower of sparks. Then, when they were out of the way of the flames, they gave each other a high five, laughing and celebrating their leap. Other couples followed their lead. Oriol jumped again, with both men and women. They always did it in the same direction, from the forest toward the beach. I saw the logic in that. The bonfire hadn't died down completely, and if two couples crashed into each other, in the middle of the pyre, they would not only have the collision to contend with, but also some serious burns. Besides, it was obvious that in case someone did get singed, the direction to run toward was the sea.

At that moment, Oriol, after having left me for most of the evening, came toward me.

"The fire symbolizes purification, renewal, burning the old to start anew. You throw all your shit into it," he said, smiling. "And when, on the magical Noche de San Juan, you jump over the bonfire with someone, you make your peace with them, you burn all the bad stuff, you try to perfect your friendship, or your love. You'll also see people throw things into the fire; they represent things you want to be free of, things you don't need in your life."

"Will you jump with me?" I asked him.

"I'm not sure." He winked at me. "Everything forgiven, everything asked for as you jump over the fire on Saint John's Night is recorded by the witches in a big book. It's a commitment you can't back out of."

"Are you afraid to commit to something with me? Or maybe there's something I have to forgive you for?"

"You never say it before you jump. If you do, it doesn't count."

I looked for my shoes, wondering how they'd hold up through my fire leaping. We held hands and went toward the pine forest where the line of couples was forming. Now the sound of just a few drums could still be heard. I took a deep breath and squeezed Oriol's warm hand. I felt I was living an extraordinary moment. I was high on emotion, my adrenaline surging, my heart racing. My senses were filled with the aroma of burned pine resin, the glow of stars up above, and the ancestral music. I'd remember that jump with almost the same emotion I remembered our first kiss.

We flew over the flames. I came to the ground a little bit behind Oriol, at the edge of the embers, but I wasn't there for even half a second, saved by the tug he gave me.

I wanted to know what he had wished for, and to kiss, as some of the other couples did after they leaped. But he turned to talk to someone.

The bonfire jumping was still going on when a woman approached the fire and threw in a bundle of papers, followed by a man who flung in what looked like a wooden box. Then the sexy siren who had gotten the dancing going before took off her shirt and tossed it into the fire, revealing her large, shapely breasts. I don't know if that was a traditional custom or just spur of the moment, but it caught on and more women followed suit, going topless but without such spectacular results.

Some guys also burned their T-shirts. I saw Oriol burn some papers. Naturally I was intrigued.

When people stopped throwing things into the fire, the drums picked up the beat again. The players were intent on creating as much pandemonium as possible while trying to achieve the same rhythm. The dancing got livelier and the woman who had taken center stage earlier returned for an encore, this time swaying her breasts. She had a large tattoo covering one of her shoulders and part of her back. Oriol, sitting on the sand some distance from the revelry, contemplated the flames and the silhouettes of the dancers against the light. I went over and sat beside him.

"What was it you burned?"

He looked at me, surprised, as if he didn't know I was

there, as if he didn't know he was there himself. In the gleam of his eyes, reflecting the light from the bonfire, I could see tears well up.

"I can't say." He smiled at me timidly.

"Yes, you can." I took one of his hands between mine. "Before you jumped you couldn't, but now you can. It always feels better to share your pain. Do you remember how we used to tell each other everything when we were kids?"

"It was a letter," he confessed after a brief silence.

"What letter?" I suspected what his response might be.

"The letter from my father, the one I got at the reading of the will."

"But how could you burn that?" I asked, worried. "The last letter from your father? You're going to regret it."

"I already do."

"Why did you do it?"

"Because I wanted to forget. Or at least not remember him so often, and so painfully. His death was the tragedy of my childhood."

"He must have had his reasons," I said to comfort him. "You know that he loved you more than anyone else. He didn't want to abandon you."

Oriol didn't reply. He lit up a joint and took a thoughtful drag. Still silent, he passed it to me. I took a puff.

"You know?" I asked him after a while. He didn't say anything.

"Remember the letters?" I insisted shortly after.

"What letters?" he finally replied absentmindedly.

"Ours." What did he mean by what letters? What letters could possibly be more important than our letters? "The ones I wrote to you and the ones you wrote me."

"Yeah?"

"I know now why we never received them."

He became silent again. But I didn't. I told him of my

mother's love for his father and how she was afraid to remember those times, afraid that her experience would be repeated in me. She had wanted to keep us from loving each other. That's why she'd intercepted the mail and kept it, that's why we'd never gotten it. I didn't mention that María del Mar also thought he was gay.

"It's a shame," said Oriol finally. "I put a lot of feeling into what I wrote, especially when my father died. I remember it well. I was so lonely and I insisted on writing to you, desperately, in spite of never getting any reply. I had the hope that you at least read them. I needed to communicate with you. I'd have loved to be able to talk to you, but I didn't even have your number."

I moved closer to him and said, "Maybe one day we could tell each other again all the words we lost . . ."

Then the dancer with the fabulous body, now gleaming with sweat, came over to us and sat on the other side of Oriol. She took a hit from the joint that was now just a roach and whispered something in his ear. Actually, it seemed as if she was nibbling on it. She giggled and he joined in every once in a while. Finally she got up, taking Oriol by the hand. I trembled. That girl wanted him to go with her to the forest. They wrestled and joked and finally, she carried him off.

You can't imagine how upset I was. Moments before I'd been giving up hope, thinking he was a homosexual. Now I was giving up hope because he wasn't and, like any man, was bedazzled by a nice pair of boobs. I should be happy, I thought, he's not gay. But what do I care? It shouldn't matter to me in the slightest. I'm engaged and I'm going to marry Mike as soon as I get back to New York. Mike's an incredible guy, a cut above anyone here.

But when I saw him return a few minutes later, too soon for any hanky-panky to have taken place, and carrying a guitar, my heart fluttered with relief. I was so glad that the girl hadn't gotten her way. I was sure the slut would find some horny beast in that dark forest to satisfy her nymphomania.

Oriol sat on the sand about three feet from me and strummed a few chords softly. Suddenly, it hit me again. He must be gay. That was the only explanation for a healthy young man resisting Miss Perfect Tits over there. I gave up.

Some people were still playing drums at the other side of the bonfire, but no one was dancing anymore. Since the burning of the unwanted objects, the enthusiasm and energy level of the crowd had begun to fade. The percussion was soft, thoughtful, and intimate. Oriol played a classical piece that I didn't recognize, followed by a melancholy version of "Cants dels Ocells" that was full of feeling. Then he sang, just for the two of us, "*Quan surts per fer el viatge cap a Itaca . . .*" His eyes were misty. I knew that wasn't just any old song. It was the last one Enric had heard before dying. I listened attentively.

When he finished, everyone clapped and wanted more, but he refused. I had the impression he felt that the audience had interrupted his private moment. He passed the guitar along to someone else. It ended up with the punkish girl who'd confronted me earlier. She passed her slimy joint on to someone else to free up her hands and sang a much more lighthearted song, about someone named Inés who said men could do whatever they wanted with her or something like that. I thought the song fit the singer.

Since Oriol was no longer the center of attention, I took the opportunity to whisper in his ear, "You were thinking about Enric while you were singing."

"My father loved that song. He listened to it before he died."

"How do you know?"

"It was on the record player when they found him. I'm sure he listened to it. Did you understand the words?"

"Of course, it's about Ulysses and his voyage back from

Troy. He sailed for years, trying to return to his island home, Ithaca."

"Yeah, the lyrics are based on a poem by the Greek Constantin Kavafis." And slowly, as if remembering, he began to recite, " 'When you set off for Ithaca, hope for a long journey that lasts many years, don't rush your voyage, and when you dock at the island, older and wiser from the lessons learned along the way, don't expect Ithaca to offer you any riches. Ithaca gave you the journey, and although you may find it lacking, Ithaca hasn't deceived you and thus, in your wisdom, you'll know the meaning of the Ithacas.' "

He wasn't looking at me. His gaze was fixed on the bright red embers. He took some time to reflect before continuing.

"We spend our lives hoping to reach something, chasing dreams, believing that once we have them we'll be happy. But it doesn't work that way. Life is the journey, not the destination. It doesn't matter how beautiful, or how important, or how spiritual our goal is. The final destination is always death. If we don't know how to be happy, how to be better people, how to be who we want to be along the road, then we won't find any of them at the end of the journey, either. That's why we have to enjoy the moment. Life is full of treasures we pursue, things we think will make us happy, but they usually turn out to be illusions. And sometimes, when we reach what we've sought for so long, we find ourselves empty-handed."

"Are you suggesting that your father's trying to trick us with the treasure, as he used to do when we were children?"

"I don't know," he said with a sigh. "But I do know that according to his philosophy, the true treasure is the journey, the excitement of the search, the energy of longing as opposed to the repose of satisfaction. He believed in the ancient Roman idea of carpe diem—seize the day. I remember that when we played hunting treasures, all we found at the end were a few pieces of candy. But we did have fun searching."

My eyelids were heavy, my speech slow, and my thinking dull. I was falling asleep. It had been a night of extraordinary emotion and now suddenly I was crashing. My surreptitious entrance into the church of Santa Anna, my capture by Arnau d'Estopinyá, my introduction to the Templars, the primal dancing, the jump over the bonfire, and my uneasiness about who Oriol would end up with in the forest, then this philosophy about journeys and destinations. Too much for just one evening. It was time to carpe bed.

Oriol was listening to the woman singing and I was sitting on the sand, covered with a beach towel, trying to fend off the cold night air and stay awake. I couldn't see the hands of the clock, but it must have been close to six A.M. Someone pointed to the horizon. A blue-gray line was beginning to appear between the black sea and the navy blue sky. Several drummers got a second wind and played their drums again, trying to create a consistent rhythm. When the sky broke into pale tones and the light seemed to fade instead of increase in intensity, everyone began to beat on whatever was handy, making a deafening, joyful noise unto the dawn. Then a point of gold twinkled on the horizon. The jubilation rose even louder and everyone started shouting, greeting the sun. I did too. They were like Stone Age humanoids worshipping their god, and I was one of them. Gradually, the sun rose until it achieved liftoff above the horizon. It started its ascent, multiplying itself on the reflections the gentle waves carried toward us. A couple ran into the water naked, jumping and shouting. Others followed, and then more joined in. I saw Oriol taking off his clothes. I was now fully awake and couldn't help noticing that my friend was rather well-endowed.

"Are you coming?" he asked.

I'd never been naked in public before, and very rarely even topless, but I didn't wait for a second invitation. I threw the towel aside, took my clothes off, and tossed them carelessly on the towel. Wearing nothing but the two rings, I ran into the sea holding Oriol's hand.

The water was warm and you could walk out for quite a way, except for a few unexpected gaps, with your head above it. Everyone was naked, splashing around and laughing.

Afterward, a lot of people stayed to sleep on the beach, but we decided to go back to Barcelona. As I was getting dressed I couldn't find my shoes. I was searching for them when I heard a voice behind me.

"Hey, blondie, what'd you burn in the fire?"

I turned around and saw that it was that Inés woman with all the piercings. She was drying herself off with a towel and a simple glance confirmed my suspicions from earlier in the evening. She had rings in her nipples, belly button, and doubtless in other, more hidden, places.

She's jerking my chain, I said to myself, deciding whether or not to answer her. I was tired from the long night and not in a very good mood. I wanted to be polite and I responded, "Nothing."

"You're wrong," she replied, smiling. "You burned some expensive shoes."

"What?" I thought she was joking.

"Tonight's lesson is that you can walk the world without two-hundred-euro shoes," the punk bitch gloated. "I threw them into the fire when you went skinny-dipping."

"You're not serious."

"No, blondie. You'll see how it's better to walk barefoot."

I was sure she was joking, but just to be sure I went closer to the bonfire, which was still burning in some areas. And there, among the embers, were my expensive shoes, one scorched, the other a piece of charcoal. I could hardly believe my eyes.

The woman was laughing; I guess she was bragging about her daring deed with her gang of friends. I have to admit that she was right. You can walk without shoes. And run. I don't remember the details, just that I was so pissed off I lost all sense of boundaries, social conventions, tiredness, caution. She wasn't expecting it from "blondie." She had her back to me, talking with her buddies, still undressed. I grabbed her long braid and knocked her to the ground, then dragged her on the sand for a good distance, calling her a fucking bitch every step of the way. I don't know what I might have done next if Oriol hadn't held me back, while several others held Mama Inés or whatever her name was. I wanted to throw her into the embers, or at least rip out one nipple ring. She shouted some insults back at me, but soon everything was under control and we left.

Oriol laughed the whole way back to Barcelona. I felt the rubber of the floor of the car with my toes as I weighed the situation. Cave girl. I had behaved worse than a caveman.

"Will you be able to walk through life without two-hundred-euro shoes?" he chided me with amusement.

I laughed out loud. The night's adventure had been worth much more than two hundred euros.

Carpe diem.

CHAPTER 38

I was awakened by the singsong of my cell phone. I have to
change that music, I said to myself. I was sick of it and, at
that moment, of a whole lot more. Who was calling at this hour?
Couldn't they wait until I was awake? It was Artur Boix asking
me how my night had gone. Night? For me it was still the night.
Yes, it definitely was too early. No, the Templars had treated me
fine. Have lunch? No, of course not. It's already one? Sorry, but
I want to sleep, call me when I'm awake. I wasn't very friendly.
I remembered that I'd gone to the bonfire without my newly
acquired cell phone and that Artur must have called me to see
if I was okay. I thought about the dawn, the splashing around
in the sea, and Oriol buck naked. I felt sleepy. The damn phone
rang again. Why hadn't I thought to turn it off? This time it was
Luis. He was excited.

"I've got it!" he screamed at me.

"What?"

"The clue, the clue to continue."

"Continue what?"

"Last night, all of sudden, inspiration hit me!" he exclaimed
enthusiastically. "I saw it all clearly. Enric's letter explains it."

I was silent, trying to absorb that, but Luis wasn't willing to give me enough time to recover my senses.

"I'm in Cadaqués and I'm coming straight to Oriol's house. Will you be there?"

"Yes."

"Well, let him know and I'll see you soon."

I raised the blinds and saw Barcelona bathed in the afternoon sun. For a weekend, it seemed sleepier than usual. Maybe it was a reflection of my own state. I showered, and by the time I got downstairs it was already three in the afternoon. If it weren't for Luis, I'd still be sleeping, I said to myself. I didn't appreciate his wake-up service.

Dear Luis:

Remember when we played treasure hunt with Oriol
and Cristina and I hid clues in the garden of the house
on Avenida Tibidabo? It's the same game. Only now it's
for real.

    Enjoy your time with Cristina and Oriol.

Your uncle,

Enric

That was it. That was all Luis's letter said. He read it out loud and then passed it to us so we could confirm with our own eyes how well he knew how to read. And of course, first I, and then Oriol, looked it over carefully, in silence. That was what it said, and nothing more. We were seated around the garden table, perhaps to avoid Alicia or perhaps because as kids the garden had been our territory. We were silently looking at Luis, who looked back at us with the beaming expression of someone who knows, or thinks he knows, more.

"Isn't it obvious?" he asked.

It didn't seem obvious at all to me and it seemed as if

it wasn't clear to Oriol either. We looked at each other and shrugged our shoulders.

"The clues, he hid clues for us in the garden," he explained finally. "And what was his favorite spot?"

"The stone in the parapet!" we both shouted at once.

Just about ten feet from where we were, there was a section that had been cleared of trees. In the middle of it was a well that had been in use until the late nineteenth century, when running water had finally reached that part of the city. We always thought it was just decorative, but it had a magical trait: one of the stones at ground level, on the small sculpted parapet, moved, creating a hole that played an important role in many of our treasure-hunting games and which only one adult knew existed—Enric.

"You think he left a clue there?" As soon as I said it I realized I was stating the obvious.

"Of course. That's what it says in the letter, right?"

Well, yes, I accepted that. That was what it said if that was what you wanted to read.

We jumped up and ran to the well, like little kids. We'd always fought to be the one to move the stone. I'm sure Luis was remembering that, as he made it very clear that this time that job belonged to him. There was no argument and he began to carefully pull out the stone. My heart was beating wildly, and after a moment that seemed to last forever, Luis removed the stone. He stuck his hand in and looked at us, first at one, then the other, giving us a smile. I could have killed him. Some people never change, and he was still that insufferable chubby kid who enjoyed being the center of attention.

"There's something here," he said finally.

He pulled out a plastic-wrapped package and undid it carefully. There was a gun inside. There was also a note: "This time it's not a game. Use it if necessary."

That gave me goose bumps. I had an ominous feeling I chose

not to share. I was sure that must be the weapon that Captain Castillo was looking for. The revolver that had killed four people, the one I'd seen in my vision. And Enric was suggesting that it could kill again.

But the gun didn't give us any clue about the treasure.

"Is there anything else?" I asked impatiently.

We had to put up with the same searching ceremony and, finally, Luis said, with his hand still in the hole, "Yes."

"Well, take it out already, goddammit," I said, blowing up at him.

Luis looked at me, hurt, but he did it. It was another package, much smaller. Inside was a piece of paper that said:

TU QUI LEGIS ORA PRO ME.

"That's Latin," Oriol announced. "It says, 'He who reads this, pray for me.'"

"Typical of a learned Templar Knight," I muttered.

We looked at each other. I saw surprise and grief on my friends' faces. Enric was asking that we pray for him. And we did, silently. I imagined him hiding the pistol, perhaps with a guilty conscience, knowing that he was going to die. He also knew his sins were so great that he'd need our prayers. I tried to imagine what he must have felt leaving that posthumous plea for us to find. Perhaps fear and infinite loneliness: for what he did, for what he was about to do, and for what would come after that. But why? Why did he go through with the suicide?

"I suggest we go to mass," said Oriol, cutting short my dismal speculation.

When we went into the church the sun was still shining, but the surrounding buildings kept the church in shadows.

I now saw in the light of day the place I had left the night before in no mood for contemplation. The small plaza seemed peaceful. It had a stone pedestal for a cross that would once

have marked a boundary, and which faced the entrance leading to the cloister's central area. There was only the large stone
trunk left; it had lost the upper part, perhaps in one of those
anticlerical scuffles so common in Barcelona in the late nineteenth and early twentieth centuries, maybe in an act of van-
dalism by common punks. It was a shame. I would have liked
to see what its arms were like. The sheet of paper printed with
the mass schedule had a cross with four crossbars, just like the
crosses carved into various parts of the church. The same cross
that the New Templars wore on their capes.

"The Poor Knights of Christ used two types of crosses,"
said Oriol, launching into one of his exhaustive lectures when I
mentioned it to him. "The four-armed cross is called the patriarchal cross, for the patriarch of Jerusalem, also called the cross
of Lorraine, and of Calatrava, and it may well have a couple
more names. Besides that one, the Templars also used the one
on the seal, with four equal sides and the ends flared. Like on
your ring."

"And why is it that this church has Templar crosses?"

"Because the patriarchal cross was highly disputed. It was
worn by knights from both the order of the Holy Sepulcher and
the Templars, by the Hospitallers for a while, and of course
by the Order of Calatrava. And it turns out that the Church of
Santa Anna was the headquarters in Barcelona of the Order of
the Knights of the Holy Sepulcher. Now, that order's emblem is
a red cross surrounded by four smaller crosses as a reminder of
the five wounds of Christ. Officially, this church continues to be
their headquarters in Catalonia."

"And unofficially?"

"You already know," replied Oriol with a complicit wink.

It had been a while since I had followed a religious service
with such intensity. Enric's plea had pierced my soul. And the

gun had given me a feeling of deep, solemn sadness; it brought back painful memories of the murder of the Boix brothers. How could someone like Enric, someone who loved life with such intensity, kill and then commit suicide? He must have been quite desperate. Quite lonely. And how could he abandon Oriol? I spent most of the mass crying silently while I prayed for his soul. Every once in a while I watched my friends. Oriol seemed to be concentrating as hard as I was. Luis was distracted, looking around, but I'm sure there were moments when he made an effort to do the best he could with his prayers. Well, that is, if he even remembered any.

The religious service was good for me. When it was over, I felt much better. Some deep sighs and the tail end of my crying still rose from within me, but I was relaxed, almost happy. I'd done what Enric had asked, prayed long and hard. I promised myself to return to it periodically. I was hoping I'd helped his soul as much as the ceremony and praying had helped my spirit.

Oriol led us toward the door that opened onto the cloister. To the right was the hallway that led to the entrance to the chapter house where the Templar services had been held the night before and I felt a shiver as I remembered my adventure and the encounter with Arnau d'Estopinyá.

"My father's note was not only a plea for his soul," Oriol said in a soft voice. "I'm sure our prayers did him good, but I think the note was a clue."

"A clue?" asked Luis in a loud, excited tone of voice.

I tried to think at lightning speed.

"How do you know that?"

"Look to your left."

And we did. There on the wall was a recumbent statue. It was of someone named Miguel de Borea, admiral general of the Spanish galleys, who had been dead for many centuries. We moved closer. Oriol pointed to a stone plaque on the ground with the inscription:

TU QUI LEGIS ORA PRO ME.

Luis and I fell silent with shock.

"When did you realize it?" asked Luis after a little while.

"Right away," he said with a mischievous smile on his face. "I've been coming to this church since I was a boy. I know all its details."

I didn't say anything. I had worn myself out praying and crying because of that note and now it turned out that it was just another piece of the game.

"What are we going to do now?" insisted Luis.

"For the moment, get out of the cloister. If the father catches me whispering in his church, he's going to get mad at me like he did when I was a kid."

We went to a *granja* on Calle Santa Anna to discuss our next step.

Luis and I decided that we had to lift up the stone plaque to see what was under it. A dead guy, answered Oriol. "And what else?" we replied. "We have to see if there's anything else." Oriol said that would be desecrating a grave and that opening graves had a religious, legal, and ethical procedure. Luis replied that someone who squatted on other people's property shouldn't be worried about such details, that the owner of the building obviously wasn't going to sue. Oriol responded that the owner wouldn't but that the priest most certainly would.

"Well, let's do it at night, when he's not around," insisted Luis.

Oriol said that he couldn't trick the priest, since he was "one of us," a member of the sect. "Well, if he's one of yours, then he should help us," Luis and I argued. And that's what we agreed on.

When we went to see the priest, he hit the roof.

"You want to open up the admiral's grave? Don't even think about it," he said to Oriol. "Your father wanted to do the same thing and I stopped him. Besides, there's nothing underneath the statue; it was temporarily on display for many years, in the Maritime Museum."

"My father wanted to open that grave?" asked Oriol.

"That's what I said. He wanted to put something inside. I didn't let him."

"And what did he do?"

"He gave it to me so that I could give it to you when you came to me wanting to open the grave."

A few minutes later we had a file in our hands, in the same style and with the same seal as the one from the Del Grial bookstore.

We looked at each other, beaming. The missing piece.

CHAPTER 39

We felt like kids again.

Luis drove us to his apartment while we all prattled on excitedly. Once there, we broke the wax seals that were exactly like the ones on the first file, and found the same handwriting and the same type of paper. Oriol insisted that we begin by reading the last sentences of the first document, so Luis did and the words of old Brother Arnau d'Estopinyá were once again on his lips:

" 'Brothers Jimeno and Ramón had reserved a very special honor for me. Now that all the most valuable possessions of each fiefdom had been collected in Miravet it would be easier to protect them. If the situation got worse, my orders were to head out toward Peñíscola with the treasure, load it onto the *Na Santa Coloma,* a fast ship that no royal galley would be able to catch, and hide it in a safe place until the uncertainty passed. I promised, on my soul's salvation, to never let anyone who wasn't a good Templar get hold of these treasures. Ramón Saguardia gave me his ring, the one with the flared cross etched in the ruby, as a token of my promise and my mission. I was moved by the trust placed in me by these monks. I spent days waiting for the treasure to arrive, fasting and praying to the Lord to make me worthy of such an undertaking.

"'I would give my life, I would give everything, to succeed in my endeavor.'"

Luis paused and, picking up the first page of the second file, continued:

"'On November fifth Brother Jimeno de Lenda met with our King James II to ask for his support and the monarch assured him that he believed in our innocence, although he wouldn't decide if he'd help us before taking it up with his council. But the King reproached our Master for supplying the castles with military equipment. Obviously, he had had us watched.

"'That meeting with the monarch did not assuage Brother Jimeno's fears. He ordered his lieutenant and friend, Brother Saguardia, to postpone his return to his fiefdom in Masdeu, Rosellón, and to stay at the Miravet headquarters. The Master stayed with the monarch in order to intercede on behalf of the Order, meeting with him again on the nineteenth of November in Teruel. While we were anxiously waiting in Miravet, Brother Saguardia received news that the King had asked for the Dominican Juan de Lotger, Grand Inquisitor, who wanted us jailed. Saguardia immediately sent a note to Brother Jimeno. "We believe that you, sir, and any monk at the court are in grave danger." But Brother Jimeno was not concerned about his own safety. He wanted to save our Order and, throwing caution to the wind, stayed close to the monarch.

"'After first mass the next day, with Brother Saguardia's blessing, I set out toward Peñíscola with a good number of guards. We went as fast as the carts could carry us, but I didn't feel safe until I felt the solid planks of my galley underneath my feet and the treasure loaded in the hold. I asked the commander of Peñíscola, Pere de Sant Just, for a special guard that night, and at dawn the next morning we set out to sea. Days later we returned, by sail. I was satisfied that I had completed the Master's assignment well, but sad because I had to eliminate the galley slaves who had helped me hide the treasure. Some of the Moors had been our slaves for many years and slitting their throats was very painful for us.'"

"Hold on a minute," I said to Luis.

I had gone through that before. I locked myself in the bathroom and sat on the toilet. My God, it was happening again! The dream about the slit throats. The beach, the restless sea, the clouds racing across the sky, and the monks slicing the throats of those wretched men in chains. How horrible. And Arnau d'Estopinyá was telling it as if it were the most natural thing in the world, hardly giving it any importance. I breathed deeply, trying to soothe my spirit. I'd never get used to that, it was impossible. I looked at the ring, responsible for my anguish. It glimmered faintly. I wasn't surprised that this ring had driven Arnau d'Estopinyá crazy, not the fourteenth-century monk who'd dictated these writings, but the modern one, mad Barbablanca, who thought he was Arnau. But he couldn't be that demented since he'd gotten rid of the ring by giving it to Enric in exchange for a pension. I wondered if that damned ring had pushed Enric to murder and suicide. I looked at it again. There it was, impassive, looking innocent, beautiful even, with its six-pointed star shining inside. Then I remembered Alicia's warning about it. I concluded that she was right: Mars, violence, and blood ruled this male ruby.

When I returned, Luis was making coffee and telling Oriol that Arnau must have been being merciful to just slit his rowers' throats and not take their heads off. It's commonly believed that in Islam, the decapitated cannot get into paradise. Luis must have felt clever after this observation, for he immediately made a joke about my trips to the bathroom. Oriol smiled at me as if endorsing his cousin's remark.

"Does your finger still hurt?" he asked, pointing to my hand. Then I got it. He knew about the ring and sensed my pain.

Luis started reading again. Once again, Arnau d'Estopinyá's voice came to us through the centuries:

"'Upon my return, I learned that our Master had decided to follow the King to Valencia to continue interceding on behalf of the Order. And it was there, in our monastery in the capital, where the King, in spite of his previous good words, jailed him on the fifth of December. The monarch did not stop there; two days later he jailed all the monks of Burriana, then he took Chirivet Castle, which didn't put up a fight, and headed north toward the fortress of Peñíscola. The King's trickery caused many brothers to be taken by surprise, unprepared to fight. When I learned that the King's forces were coming, I thought about sailing south immediately. But the weather was not right and I was short on galley slaves, although *Na Santa Coloma*, true to her name, knew how to sail perfectly, and my crew was loyal to me.

"'But that flight would have meant not being able to dock in any Catalan, Valencian, or Mallorcan port. Maybe nowhere in Christian territory. I'd have had to survive conducting pirate raids against the Kingdoms of Granada, Tlemcen, or Tunis. And I'd have to wait until the Order of the Temple was given back its freedom and honor. But if Pope Clement V, as was rumored, backed the King's actions, my rebellion would be punished by excommunication, and my fate and that of my men would be attacking Saracen ships until we died in combat, decapitated at Moorish hands or, even worse, hung in Christian nooses. But I didn't fear any of that. What made me discard my plan of escape was the realization that I could never abandon my brothers in such a predicament.

"'And what can I tell you? I spoke with Brother Pere de Sant Just, commander of Peñíscola. He told me that he was too old to fight and had decided to surrender to the King. I asked him for permission to travel, along with those who wanted to follow me, to the fortress of Miravet where surely Brother Ramón Saguardia would fight against that double-crossing King. With his blessing, three sergeants, a knight, and seven laymen, we set off at a gallop. In spite of knowing that ten days earlier King James had given the order to imprison all of us and seize the Order's assets, we defiantly wore our habits emblazoned with the red Temple cross and didn't hide our weapons. No one, not the soldiers, nor the local militias, dared to stop us at any of the road checkpoints.

" 'Two days later, on the twelfth of December 1307, with the capture of Peñíscola, all the properties of our Order in the Kingdom of Valencia had been confiscated and all the monks imprisoned.

" 'As I expected, Brother Saguardia refused the royal order to hand over Miravet Castle and, by the time we arrived, the siege had begun. The militias from Tortosa and its neighboring villages, who, following royal instructions, were formalizing the last details for the siege didn't dare to stop us either.

" 'Brother Saguardia was happy to see us. He embraced me and expressed his relief at my having completed the mission of hiding the treasure. He wanted me to keep the ring. He said that no one should know why I wore it. At that moment, in spite of having lost my beloved ship forever, I was joyous. I knew that I was where I should be. Fighting alongside my brothers. The commanders of Saragossa, Grañena, and Gebut had also taken refuge there and we all prepared ourselves for a long siege.

" 'At year's end, news arrived that Masdeu, Brother Ramón Saguardia's fiefdom, along with the other Templar properties in Rosellón, Cerdanya, Montpellier, and Mallorca, had been confiscated by King James of Mallorca, uncle of our own King James.

" 'At the start of the year 1308 there were only two castles holding out in Catalonia: Miravet and Ascó. In Aragon, the fortress of Monzón and various castles still held up. One of them, Libros, was able to withstand a six-month siege heroically with just one Templar, Brother Pere Rovira, and a group of loyal laymen.

" 'The King sent a letter on January twentieth commanding

us to obey the Pope's orders, and Brother Saguardia asked to negotiate, but the monarch didn't answer. Then the King threatened the gallows, confiscation of goods, and retaliation on the families of the soldiers who defended us. Brother Berenguer de Sant Just, commander of Miravet, proposed letting the soldiers in his service go, paying what was owed to them. Saguardia agreed and negotiated with the King's officials for the removal of these troops without harm or slight to their persons or property. We didn't want those innocents and their loved ones to suffer for their loyalty to our Order. With a heavy heart, I bade farewell to my last sailors.

"Then Brother Saguardia asked the King to send messengers to Rome to defend our cause before the Holy Pontiff. The King responded by stoning our castle with huge catapults. He had reinforcements come from Barcelona and asked his uncle, the King of Mallorca, for additional help.

"'And thus continued the siege of Miravet, with unsuccessful attempts at negotiation, with betrayals, diminishing provisions, and daily growing royal pressure on us. It was useless to remind the monarch of the services we had lent him and his ancestors in reconquering his kingdoms, and that we had been faithful to his father when the Pope excommunicated him and sent a crusade against him. In October, we managed to get our attackers to allow the safe removal of the young knights and novices who had not yet taken their ecclesiastical vows. They were able to return freely to their families.

"'Brother Saguardia didn't trust the King, but he still believed in the Pope. Our community prayed and prayed for the Pontiff to see the light, realize our innocence, and return us to his favor. With the support of Pope Clement V, Saguardia felt he'd be capable of defeating the King himself. On the other hand, Brother Sant Just and the other commanders thought that the evil stemmed from the Pope himself and wanted us to accept the conditions negotiated with the monarch.

" 'Finally, majority opinion won out and, very much in spite of himself, Lieutenant Saguardia, after over a year of resistance, had to surrender Miravet and Ascó on the twelfth of December.

" 'At first our imprisonment was manageable. I shared a cell with four other monks: a knight, a chaplain, and two sergeants, in Peñíscola. I had requested that I be imprisoned there so that I could see the sea. *Na Santa Coloma* was no longer there; they had taken her to Barcelona.

" 'Two months later, my turn to be interrogated by the Inquisition arrived. They had a questionnaire with queries such as whether I had ever spit on the cross, whether I had renounced Our Lord Jesus Christ, whether I had kissed my brothers on the rump or other improper places, if I had ever committed impure acts with other monks, and similar indecencies.

" 'What can I tell you? In spite of having heard of such questions, I couldn't help becoming angered. I, who had seen my companions die boarding Saracen boats, who had witnessed how the Egyptians breached the walls of Acre; I, who knew hundreds of Templar brothers who died in defense of the faith; I, who had the scars to prove I'd shed blood for Our Lord Jesus Christ. I had to answer those filthy questions from those Dominican monks, those clerics who had never seen their own blood except when they accidentally wounded themselves with the instruments they used to torture other Christians.

" 'We tried to negotiate with the King to be treated with respect. That traitorous monarch once again failed to keep his word; not only were we more guarded than those who'd surrendered voluntarily but he had us all chained.

" 'What can I tell you? Unless you've lived through it, you cannot know how it feels to spend months and months loaded down with iron chains, unable to move, your skin torn from the metal cuffs and your limbs swollen. The bishops met in Tarragona and asked the King to free us from the shackles, but the

Dominican inquisitors demanded the opposite, more rigorous punishment for us.

"'They took us to Tarragona for a new council where the Bishops once again asked the King to relax the severity of our treatment, but soon thereafter a letter from the Pope arrived, requesting that we be tortured.

"'We were taken to Lleida and I was subjected to the rack one foggy morning in November.'"

This time I didn't interrupt Luis's reading. Since the last time, I'd been sure that the torture vision would appear in Arnau's story. I just shut my eyes, breathed deeply, and, controlling my fear, listened attentively.

"'We knew that we had to endure, to not give in to the pain as some of our French brothers did.'" Luis continued reading without realizing my anguish.

"'The hours seemed endless, the torturers worked in shifts so that each monk received three sessions of torture a day. The inquisitors asked me the same obscenities as they had the first time, only this time the King's officers were present, wanting to know where we had hidden the treasure. Lying, thieving, murderous monarch. None of us confessed to breaking the rules, renouncing Our Lord Jesus Christ, worshipping "Bracoforte," or fornicating with our brothers. Nor did we admit to having hidden any treasure. I would rather have died than have allowed that disgraceful King, that cowardly and cruel Pope, and those contemptible inquisitors take what was rightfully ours.

"'None of the Catalan, Aragonese, or Valencian monks gave in to torture. We all maintained our innocence. Some died from the abuse, others were crippled for life. Then our hypocritical monarch, to ingratiate himself with our supporters, sent doctors and medicines. What a fraud.

"'Finally, almost a year later, they gathered us all together in Barcelona where the Council of Tarragona declared us innocent.

" 'But the Templars no longer existed. Months earlier, Pope Clement V had proclaimed the bull *Vox in excelso* suppressing our Order forever, our Order, which had brought such glory to Christianity. He also forbade, under penalty of excommunication that, "anyone should pass himself off as a Templar." In other words, we couldn't even call ourselves Templars any longer!

" 'The King assigned us each a pension according to our position; as a sergeant I was owed fourteen dinars. We had to live in houses run by clerics who had not been Templars, and maintain our vows of chastity, poverty, and obedience. We had to renounce the fourth vow, the one about fighting against infidels. Anyway, we no longer had the means to do it.

" 'It had been five years since I had set foot on the planks of the *Na Santa Coloma* and throughout all that time of terrible penitence I would close my eyes and see the swollen sails of my ship, lit up by the morning sun, en route to Almería, Granada, Tunisia, or Tlemcen to board or sink Saracen ships. That vision would seize me while praying at matins, eating, strolling, at any moment of the day. When I regained my freedom I considered fleeing with some of the monks, getting a galley and returning to the fight against the infidels. I dreamed of doing that and even spent time making plans with other brothers. Some had never even set sail before. But we all wanted to be useful again, regain our dignity. But in the end, we did nothing. They were just old men's fantasies.

" 'I was already more than forty-five years old and my body was wracked by years of torture and prison. I felt like a coward, but the idea of praying till the end of my days became sweeter and sweeter. A monk taught me the basics of the art of painting and my pension gave me enough for wood, stucco, glue, and paint. I thought that in this way, my humble and awkward work could better serve our Lord, drawing his saints so that people could pray to them.

" 'Meanwhile, news arrived that the pope and King James II were fighting, like vultures, over the remains of our patrimony. The king had managed to get the papal bull *Ad providam Christi* of that year, in which the pontiff bestowed the Order's assets to the Hospitaller monks, to expressly exclude the Spanish kingdoms. And then he got the pope to create the order of Montesa, which would be loyal to him and inherit the Templar properties in the kingdom of Valencia. Finally, he accepted the handing over of what was left of the assets from Catalonia and Aragon to the Hospitallers, but he kept everything he could, with the excuse of covering the expenses we caused him. He appropriated money and jewels from us, to the extent that in some churches, priests couldn't celebrate mass because they lacked the necessary liturgical objects. The rents from our properties were also added to his private wealth, as he managed them for the ten years of his dispute with the Pope. And finally, he made the monks of Saint John of the Hospital pay our pensions until we died.

" 'We couldn't publicly use the name Templar, but none of us agreed to join another order.

" 'Almost two years after our liberation, the news arrived from France. That wretched king, Philip the so-called Fair, had sent Temple Master Jacques de Molay and two of his dignitaries to be burned at the stake. There, the old man regained his dignity, proclaimed the purity and integrity of the Order and cursed the King and the Pope. He died consumed by the flames, shouting out his innocence and ours. Witnesses say that in his last throes Jacques de Molay summoned the French King and the Pontiff before the court of God. That same year, both perished under strange circumstances.

" 'King James lived much longer. A year ago he went to the monastery of Santes Creus to die. They say that he gave up his soul at nightfall the moment the oil lamps were lit. In his funereal record it says, *"Circa horam pulsacionis cimbali latronis."* I don't understand Latin well, but that's what they call dusk: the hour of the thief.

"'And thus, with final justice, God's justice, I end my tale. I also hope to appear before Him soon and I pray for his mercy. I also pray that He allow the Order of the Temple to return, in some way, to fight for enlightenment, for what's good.

"'And what can I tell you? At the end of my road, after pride, grandeur, victory and defeat, suffering and passion, I have discovered that the secret of what I hid is found in God. It is hidden in the land the saints once trod upon and in the divinity of the Virgin. May Our Lord God forgive my sins and have mercy on my soul.'"

CHAPTER 40

We looked at each other in silence. I was moved by the story. When Oriol finally spoke, he did so as an expert historian. Again.

"The story sounds authentic. It is as if a true Templar monk had offered us his testimony, but in modern language. He even uses colloquial questions to engage the reader, such as, 'What can I tell you?'

"Maybe the text is a copy of an older translation, or maybe someone wrote it down from an oral rendition. I'd go with the first one, because the details are so precise. I know that historical period very well and everything happened exactly as Arnau tells it. And although he paints James II as a despicable bastard, the truth is, he was a very clever king. Instead of confronting the pope as his father and great-grandfather had done, he handled it very well, convincing the pope to allocate Corsica and Sardinia to him. With him, the power of the house of Barcelona and Aragon in the Mediterranean was definitively consolidated. The pope couldn't keep any of the Templar possessions from Aragon and Valencia, but James II sure made out like a bandit! A logical defense tactic against his French rival, who received a fortune thanks to the Templars. Money was, and still is, a fundamental element of war strategy, essential for equipping armies.

"And finally, in spite of Arnau describing his comrades as heroes withstanding torture, in Aragon, torture was applied lightly. It was torture, let's not kid ourselves, but there's torture you can withstand and there's torture you can't. In France, for example, torture methods were so harsh that one French Templar Knight said, 'If they want me to confess to killing Christ, I'll do it, but I cannot take this anymore.'"

"This story is all very well and good," interjected Luis. "But it doesn't give us any clues."

"Maybe it does," replied Oriol thoughtfully.

"The second to last sentence, right?" I asked.

Luis picked up the document again and looked for the last page.

"'The secret of what I hid is found in God. It is hidden in the land the saints once trod upon and in the divinity of the Virgin,'" he read.

"'The land the saints once trod upon'!" he exclaimed. "Under the feet of the saints and the Virgin was where we found the hidden inscriptions in the paintings."

"Yup," confirmed his cousin.

"Oriol," I cut in; I had an idea. "We haven't completely X-rayed the paintings."

"Of course we did," he replied. "You saw the X-rays."

"Let's look at them again."

Oriol showed us the X-rays of the three paintings. It was hard to recognize them, and I asked, "Is it true that the more opaque parts of the X-rays are the areas of the painting where there's a lot of white?"

"Yes."

"And if it's completely white, then there must be metal blocking the view?"

Oriol smiled. "I get where you're going with this."

"What is it?" asked Luis impatiently.

"Simple," I replied, beaming. "There is a part of the middle painting that hasn't been X-rayed. Do you see a totally white area in the X-ray?"

"The Virgin's crown!" exclaimed Luis.

"Yes," said Oriol. "In the text it says: 'The divinity of the Virgin.' That must be a clue. It should say 'the holiness of the Virgin,' since the Virgin is human, not divine. And in Christian iconography, a halo or a crown represents holiness. When it appeared in the X-ray, I didn't focus on it because it seemed normal. In some paintings of the period, especially Italian ones, and in some Greek icons, the halo is not stucco with gold plating, but metal, gilded pewter with etched floral designs or an inscription."

Oriol went for a toolbox while we looked at the Virgin's crown in the painting. It definitely could be a piece of pewter.

"It was stupid of me," said Oriol. "If I'd used infrared, instead of X-rays as my father suggested in his will, we'd have also seen if there was a drawing or inscription below the metal. But we're not going to wait till tomorrow to use reflectography . . ."

None of us wanted to wait. We laid the painting on a table and with a fine blade Oriol began to tease out the sides of the crown. Soon an edge lifted up. It was true. It was made of a thin and somewhat flexible metal. With the utmost care he loosened the crown, which came out whole. And beneath, *"Illa Sanct Pau"* could easily be read with the naked eye.

"Saint Paul's Island!" I shouted. "The treasure is in an underwater cave on the island of Saint Paul."

"The island of Saint Paul?" questioned Luis. "Never heard of it."

"It's true," agreed Oriol. "I haven't either."

My smile froze on my lips.

* * *

Saint Paul. An unknown island. It must be very small or very far away. The next day, we looked for it everywhere. I checked all kinds of maps and atlases, and my two partners asked anyone who might know, from boat skippers to geographers. When we met that afternoon, we still had no clue as to where such an island might be located.

"I haven't been able to stop thinking about it all day," said Luis. "Maybe the name has changed? Didn't the Templars, because they were so religious, name islands after saints?"

"It's quite possible," agreed Oriol.

"On the map there's a San Pietro and a San Antioco in Sardinia," I read from my notes. "Farther away, in Italy, there's another San Pietro Island on a small archipelago in the Tyrrhenian Sea called the Lipari Islands, and in the Gulf of Tarento there is a San Antico. Then we'd have to go to the Adriatic or the Ionian Sea to find more islands named after saints."

"No, that's too far," said Oriol.

"I've also looked for names in the index of an atlas, and I didn't find any island called San Pablo, Sant Pau, Sant Pol, Saint Paul, Santo Paolo, not even taking off the word 'saint' and just looking by name," I concluded.

"It has to be relatively close to Peñíscola," said Oriol.

"Why?" we asked.

"The dates written in the story give the clue," explained our historian. "Arnau d'Estopinyá mentions the meeting between Brother Jimeno de Lenda and King James II in Teruel on November nineteenth as the moment in which he made the decision to hide the treasures. That's too late in the year for a galley, they usually only sailed between May and October. Although they were very fast ships, they had a shallow draft and weren't prepared for rough seas.

"An expert galley captain like Arnau wouldn't risk his ship

and cargo sailing very far at that time of the year. Besides, on December fifth, when the king imprisoned the master, Arnau had already been back for a while, so he could have been at sea for only about ten days total. I would focus the search on the radius of a two days' voyage by galley from Peñíscola; that area includes the coasts that were most familiar to Arnau. Take a look . . ."

He went over to a map of the Mediterranean that we had spread out on the table. Taking a compass, he placed the needle on Peñíscola and extended it so that the other end reached Cap d'Agde, then traced a circular arc that included the Balearic Islands and reached Mojácar to the south.

"I don't think he'd have gone close to Cap d'Agde. A Templar ship in French territory would be in danger, and the north was toward the cold and storms. An expert sailor such as Arnau would never have risked crossing an area hit by the north wind at that time of year. I think he went to the east or the south. That includes the Columbretes Islands, the Balearic Islands, and the whole southern coast, but no farther than Guardamar, maybe up to the Cape of Palos. From that point on, it was Moorish territory."

"There are no islands with saints' names in the Columbretes, or the Balearics, or on the Murcian or Valencian coasts," I declared. "But there are some little ones before Cabo de Gata: San Pedro, San Andrés, and San Juan."

"That's too far, and those don't have the saint's name we're looking for," said Oriol.

"There's a town on the Catalan coast called Sant Pol and in Alicante, Santa Pola," Luis commented.

"Near Santa Pola there is an island that's a good candidate," I told them. "But it doesn't have a saint's name; it appears on the map as Nueva Tabarca, or Isla Plana."

"I know something about that," said Oriol. "Charles III, tired of that island being a permanent pirate base, had a walled

city built there in the eighteenth century. He repopulated it
with freed Christians of Genovese descent, held captive by the
Algerians who had come from the island of Tabarca, a former
Spanish possession in North Africa. That's where the name
comes from."

"So the island was a nest of pirates. Saracen pirates, right?" I
asked. "What happened to the island before it was Christian?"

"The Muslim chronicles of the kingdom of Murcia, which
that area belonged to before the reconquest, say that it was un-
inhabited, but that it had a good port that the enemies of Islam
took advantage of for pirating."

"Does that include Arnau d'Estopinyá?"

"I'm sure," affirmed Oriol. "In the mid–thirteenth century
the king of Murcia began to pay homage and fealty to the king
of Castile, until a Mudejar uprising made James I, the grandfather of James II, intervene to help the Castilians. The area was
annexed definitively by the Aragonese crown a couple of years
before the fall of the Templars. I'm sure that Arnau knew that
island well."

We agreed that Oriol would review the history of the is-
lands in search of one that could have been called Sant Pau, San
Pol, or San Pablo. The first candidate was the island of Nueva
Tabarca.

The next morning he called me on my cell.

"Write this down," he said, but without waiting for me
to grab a pencil. "The historians Mas i Miralles and Llobre-
gat Conesa believe that the name Santa Pola is pre-Arab and
that before it must have been named Sant Pol since the Arabs
changed place names to the feminine. They wrote Shant Bul,
whose pronunciation is very close to Sant Pol. The name of the
saint comes from the fact that he supposedly disembarked in

Portus Ilicitanus, the Roman name for Santa Pola, in the year AD 63 to evangelize Spain. Because of its proximity, the island came to be called the island of San Pablo and, according to other historians, the inhabited area of Tabarca appeared for many years in the parish books as the town of San Pablo."

My heart leaped.

"We've got it," I whispered.

CHAPTER 41

We saw it as evening approached. The sun lit up the island, which stretched out almost parallel to the horizon, floating on deep blue waters. The wall rose on its right side, above the sea, enclosing the town within. Its main building was a church that looked like a fortress. Walls and roofs shone with the reddish light of the waning of the day. The town looked like something out of a pirate tale. The island is several times longer than it is wide and it narrows in the middle, where there is a port that looks north, toward the continent. The left side seemed sparse and brown, with a couple of towers, one of which, on close inspection, turned out to be a lighthouse.

We were on top of the Santa Pola mountain. Luis had driven us to the lighthouse, where the view was spectacular. The island, filled with light, contrasted with the beach, now in shadows at the foot of the precipice. Leaning over the edge gave you vertigo.

"Treasure island," I thought out loud. "It looks so pretty."

It smelled of pine. Suddenly, out of the lower part of the cliff, a butterfly with stiff wings, multicolored and gigantic, rose silently and floated in the air above our heads. It was a girl, paragliding, followed by a boy, and then another. They emerged from the shadows below, allowing the late-afternoon sun to fully illuminate them. It was a lovely image.

Luis said that the sea breeze hitting the mountain created an air current that was almost vertical and that was why they were able to rise so high. I wasn't sure why, but I identified those apprentice angels with the three of us. They hung over the abyss by fragile cloth wings, and we floated on an adventure made out of stories from the distant past. It was scary to watch them. Maybe I was sensing the danger in our own quest? I had a desire to hug Oriol who, like Luis, was enjoying the view in silence. I had them on either side of me and I embraced them both around the waist. I didn't want to play favorites. They held me around the shoulders and I felt their warm bodies and the camaraderie we had shared as children. Carpe diem. I remembered the words, and knew I had to live this moment of excitement and hope. I had to enjoy every second of the days to come. I focused on the beauty of the landscape and the warmth of my feelings toward my friends. I filled my lungs with air in a vain attempt to hold it all in, to keep it forever: the light, the friendship, the emotion, and the color of the sea . . . I sighed.

"I wonder what this adventure has in store for us," I said.

The guys didn't respond. Maybe they were asking themselves the same thing.

From the prow of the vessel making its way from Santa Pola, we saw Nueva Tabarca approaching. The day was clear, the sea was calm, and the sun, although still low in the sky, reverberated over the water in such a way that the island appeared to be in the middle of a lake of light. From that side some reefs led to the island, then the town appeared above the walls, and, immediately, the massive church, standing out above all the rest. Its four large baroque windows, higher than the roofs of any of the other buildings, reminded me of the portholes of a brigantine ready to stick out its cannons. Seagulls flew above our heads and in the crystal-clear water we saw a purple jellyfish, almost as big as a soccer ball, floating.

The boat wasn't very full at that time of day. With us were tourists making day trips and, in their honor, as we arrived at the port, the sailors threw bread into the water so that hundreds of beautiful, voracious silver fish swirled around.

"Don't stop to watch the fish," Oriol said to me. "We're going to see more of them than we'll want to."

We went ashore and headed toward the town. We passed through an open door in the thick wall of yellowed and worn limestone. Inside the door, there were two niches, one dedicated to the Virgin and the other holding various images of saints and plastic flowers. We left our things in the hotel and hurried to have a look around. Oriol and Luis had visited the island a couple of times with their families, so it wasn't entirely unfamiliar to them.

Nueva Tabarca lived up to its second name, Isla Plana, which means Flat Island. It's actually two islands, which together stretch almost a mile, with a central plain on each one rising about twenty-six feet above sea level. The smaller one, to the west, where the walled town is located, is the higher one. In most sections, the walls are built just above the crags that hang out straight over the sea. In the center, the isthmus below has a beach to the south and the port to the north, facing the continent. There, my friends could see changes: an urbanized area with ramps and several restaurants facing the beach. On the other, larger part of the island, there was a defense tower, built around the same time as the town but of Roman foundations; a lighthouse; and on the farthest end, a cemetery. There were also the remains of an old farm, but the only thing that grew in that area these days, apart from shrubs, was prickly pear cactus. Given the abrupt rise of the island from the sea and the erratic shapes of the rocks, there definitely had to be caves.

Our exploration from the water began that afternoon. We equipped ourselves with some simple snorkel masks and water shoes, which would allow us to swim and also walk on the shore, and would protect our feet from sea-urchin spines and underwater rocks. We looked just like the many tourists who came to enjoy the fascinating underwater surroundings.

We left the town through the door on the west wall and soon found a jetty, almost joined to an islet called La Cantera. It was too low to hide caves, so we decided not to explore it. In the afternoon, as usually happens at that time of year, the *llebeig*, the southwestern wind that makes the sea on the south side choppy, picked up. Even so, on the north side of the island, the water was still calm and there, below a stretch of wall that rose vertically above our heads, we went into the water.

We were all excited and in a very good mood. Once in a while the boys would race each other, leaving me behind. Taller, slimmer Oriol always won, even though Luis seemed to be much more muscular than his cousin. On one occasion, when they were distracted by observing a school of fish whose silver and gold stripes sparkled in the sun, I shot out ahead. Once I had some distance I teased them for being slow. I felt like I had when I was a girl, and the only thing that showed time had passed was seeing their fully developed bodies.

We covered about a hundred feet toward the east, until we got to the port, and we noted a couple of places where the walls had openings at sea level that could be old buried caves. We decided to come back later to explore further. Now far from the fortress, we found a small cave that didn't look very promising. After we checked it out, we realized we were near the port, and we continued the route, walking up behind the jetty.

The next stretch began on an islet, where a ragged edge of rocky plates jutted out into the sea, and a slope of ten to twelve feet separated the coastline from the higher plane. On a stretch farther along, we found an underwater arch that separated the reefs from a large rocky pool, filled with warm water. There, we saw a beautiful underwater landscape filled with rocks, green and yellow anemones, red starfish, sea urchins, fan worms, and corals. At one point it got deeper, revealing vast fields of green *Posidonia oceanica*. It grows on white sand, not far from the surface, and countless fish peacefully grazed among its leaves. There were schools of saddled sea bream, salemas, giltheads, silver porgy, and green and multicolored Mediterranean rainbow wrasse that sometimes came close to peek through my goggles. The sea was calm and the sun filtered through the surface, diffusing reds and yellows deeper down, but maintaining colors near the surface where we swam. It was a delicious afternoon. Even though we didn't find any caves, we decided to call it a day when we arrived at the rock called La Tanda on the western end of the island, our spirits still filled with hope and anticipation.

Before dinner we struck up a conversation with an old fisherman, native to the island, whose last name, Pianelo, bore witness to the history of the place. He told us about the *cova del llop marí*, a cave located not far from where we were standing. There were stories of pirates, smugglers, fishermen, and kidnapped damsels who wailed in distress on the long, windy winter nights. The cave was at sea level and went several feet under the island. Luis suggested that we head there first thing in the morning. Oriol preferred to continue our exploration systematically, starting at the La Tanda rock, and advancing along the southern coast toward the west until we reach the *cova*. It was up to me to decide. Oriol's suggestion won out.

I remember that dinner with special fondness. My body was worn out and aching from the exertion, but we ate and drank. We laughed a lot, in spite of, or thanks to, the sexual innuendoes that Luis directed at me. Once again he became the cock of the walk, amusingly aggressive, and seemed to exclude Oriol as a possible rival in pursuing me. He appeared to be quite sure about his cousin's sexual orientation. Too sure.

I looked at Oriol. I was hanging on his every word, wanting to see how he'd react to his cousin's silly remarks, wanting to see that smile he'd often direct at me, and sometimes at Luis. I wanted to hear his sometimes noisy laugh that revealed his perfect teeth. It was true that some of his mannerisms could be misinterpreted, but I couldn't help feeling something very special in my stomach when our gazes met, lingering in the pleasure of exploring each other's eyes.

We decided to take a walk before going to bed. Luis said he had to go up to his room for a minute.

But we didn't wait for Luis. We kept walking, out the door and into the night. The island's small; he'll find us, I thought.

CHAPTER 42

Oriol and I walked toward the north wall, passing narrow streets with fences hiding secluded gardens from which bougainvillea tried to escape. The streetlight revealed the mauve and cinnamon tones. The four-o'clocks bloomed in the small church plaza and a palm tree's exotic silhouette stood out against a starry sky. It was a warm night in early July and the island, once the tourists had left in the last boat, was intimate and peaceful.

I took Oriol by the hand while my heart beat with excitement at my own boldness and for the pleasure of feeling his warm hand in mine. We walked in silence toward the path at the top of the wall.

The bay extended before us, its black water cleaved by the occasional fishing boat and outlined by the lights of the coast. Santa Pola was ahead of us, the lighthouse crowned the mountain to the right, and farther off, Alicante could be seen.

We sat on the balustrade of the path on the top of the wall, a good fifteen feet above where the waves beat gently against it.

After a few minutes of silence, he began to speak suddenly and softly. It might have been a continuation of our conversation from Saint John's Night.

"My father's death, his abandoning me, still hurts."

"I'm sure he didn't want to abandon you. Maybe he was honor bound to a commitment." Oriol looked at me questioningly. "Maybe he had made a promise to a friend." I had ruled out telling him, at least for the moment, about the vision in which I had learned that his father had decided to die to avenge his lover's death.

"You know," I continued in the face of his silence, "the Templar vow, the one from the sacred Theban legion that you told me about . . ."

I remembered what Oriol himself had told me: "Isn't it beautiful to love someone so much that you would give your life for him?"

"That story's not over," he said after a little while, pensive, perhaps guessing my thoughts. "Between us and the Boix family more blood may be shed."

I shuddered. Artur had used almost the same words.

"You feel this peace, the beauty of this moment?" he continued. "To me it feels like the calm before a storm. Artur Boix won't give up the treasure. I don't know how, but I'm sure he's spying on us."

His hand still held mine, and as he said those words he grabbed it tighter. I was silent. Suddenly he said, "The promise, the one the Templar Knights made. Would you swear that with me?"

His proposal left me speechless and thoughtful. Historically it was a pact between warriors of the same sex. Was Oriol insinuating that that was our case? I didn't know if I wanted to answer him, or at least not in words, and I decided to risk kissing him. I really wanted to. And with my heart racing I began to bring my mouth closer to his. I wanted to feel the taste of the sea, the taste of innocence again.

"So there you are."

Luis. There he was, at the edge of the path, coming closer but still too far to make out what we were doing in the half-light.

The distance between Oriol and me suddenly increased and I let go of his hand. I don't think Luis had realized anything and I didn't want to give rise to any of his stupid jokes.

When we went to our rooms shortly after, I still felt the warmth of Oriol's hand on mine and the desire of that frustrated kiss. I sighed, and was leaning on the sill of the window that opened onto the south and the open sea, watching the distant lights of some ship, when I heard discreet knocking on my door. My heart leaped.

I told myself that it must be Oriol, that he felt the same way, and that his cousin's showing up had spoiled the moment for him as much as it had for me. I ran to the door, and when I opened it, I found Luis there. His smile was half joking, half seductive.

"Would you like a bit of company?" he offered.

"Go to hell, moron!" I spat out at him, slamming the door, hopefully in his face. Did that idiot really believe his own jokes?

Indignation, frustration, anxiety, I don't know how to express what I was feeling at that moment, but my rage passed quickly. I was upset; I had wanted that kiss and was sure Oriol would have accepted it gladly had it been a few minutes earlier. Something in my gut was telling me that. No, I couldn't accept that failure. I looked at my rings. The diamond one shone innocently, purely, reminding me of my commitment to Mike, and the red ruby, now the red of passion, sparkled with irony. I took them both off, put them on the bedside table, and angrily covered them with a pillow. I didn't want to see them.

I thought of my mother and what had happened between her and Enric. At least she had had the courage to try. It had turned out badly, but it wasn't her fault. Was I just a coward?

I opened the door and went out into the hallway cautiously. There was no trace of Luis and I stopped in front of Oriol's door with my knuckles poised to knock. I stayed frozen in that position, like an idiot. What was I going to say to him? "You want a little company?" "You owe me a kiss?" I realized that this was what María del Mar had been trying to avoid for the last fourteen years. Suddenly I got scared. What would Oriol think? Maybe he really was gay and would reject me. Or even worse, would he accept me as Enric had my mother? And what about Mike?

I'm embarrassed to admit that I beat a hasty retreat back to my room. I thought about Mamá. That night I cried out my cowardice all over the pillow, the two rings locked in the drawer of the bedside table.

The next day dawned bright and clear, with calm seas. I opened the window and let my bad mood of the previous night stream out. I decided to enjoy the day. After a good breakfast, filled with laughter and a few loaded looks, all three of us were brimming with happiness.

The morning was a continuation of the previous, unforgettable evening. The sun caressed our skin even underwater, illuminating fields of green Posidonia on white sand that contrasted with the rocky walls running vertically to the invisible bottom, hundreds of fish swimming at different levels.

Although we enjoyed the sea, the exploration of the stretch from the east end of Tabarca to the beach didn't offer any clues. But the southwest area, below some of the enormous rocks that the town walls rested upon, held a surprise. Where we'd hoped to locate the *cova del llop marí* we found not one, but two caves, separated by a cove. They were similar, although one was deeper than the other. We entered swimming across the floor, which was underwater for quite a distance, then rose above sea level to expose a bottom covered with stones. Large rocky outcrops closed off the back of the cave. We had come prepared with flashlights, but our exploration didn't lead to any promising results.

In the following days, we conscientiously checked all the caves we could find, even using tools to dig out the small stones and sandy bottoms that were above water. Our spirits progressively flagged as we lost all hope of finding anything. Our laughter stopped and, little by little, with discouragement came fatigue and disappointment. We tried to fight it, but we finally arrived at the painful conclusion that we'd come to the end of our adventure.

CHAPTER 43

On the way back to Barcelona, Oriol wanted to stop in Peñíscola to visit the Templar naval base from which Arnau d'Estopinyá had fought the infidels.

"Maybe we'll find some clue," he argued to convince us.

The truth is, we weren't really up for tourism. Our spirits were at an all-time low. The excitement of treasures and pirates had slowly dwindled as we made our last trip around the island. We were meticulous, we checked every crack, we moved rocks, we dug in the sand. Nothing. We were like kids playing with rainbow-streaked soap bubbles that suddenly burst, leaving us with wet, disappointed faces.

"We're not going to find anything here," said Luis, discouraged. "Let's go back to Barcelona."

Although I agreed with Luis, I took Oriol's side again and we continued looking. Was he always right or was it just that I wanted to make him happy? The answer was obvious.

We went through the old part of the town and its fortress. Oriol was surprisingly energetic and good humored, while Luis and I were practically dragging our feet with discouragement. We saw the castle of the Papa Luna, the schismatic, built a couple of hundred years after our Arnau. It had been on December 12, 1307, when the old commander Pere de Sant Just had surrendered his fortress, port, and town to James II without any resistance. A lot had been built since the time of the Templars, but you could still make out architectural elements from the thirteenth century, the same stones that Arnau d'Estopinyá had seen. If he ever existed, that is.

Then Oriol suggested taking a look from the beach at the old part of town, and although Luis was in a foul mood and I was tired, we followed him. We stood by the seashore and looked at the fortress in the distance, not sure of what we were looking for.

Suddenly, Oriol said, "I think we found the cave."

"Whaaat?" we both responded at once.

"We've got it," he said, smiling with satisfaction when he saw our faces.

"But we haven't found anything!" I exclaimed.

"Yes. Yes we have." His smile widened. He was enjoying this.

"What exactly have we found?" demanded Luis with a touch of impatience.

"A clue. An important clue."

"What is it?"

"Stones."

"Come on, Oriol." Luis was getting mad. "We've seen millions of stones. My hands are wrecked from turning them over."

"Yeah, but very few granite or marble ones."

"Granite or marble?" I asked, trying to get more information.

"Round stones. Like six- to nine-pound rocks."

"We saw mountains of round stones," I replied.

"But they have to be granite or marble," repeated Oriol.

"We didn't notice what kind of stones they were, okay?" Luis let fly. "Where are you going with this?"

"Granite and marble are not natural to this island. What does that tell you?"

"That it doesn't fit," I replied. "That they're out of place."

"Maybe they were brought by the tide," guessed Luis.

"You think the tide can lower stones to the bottom of the sea and then lift them back up again?"

"Maybe."

"No. Those stones were brought by someone, and they are covering the entrance to an underwater cave."

Luis and I looked at each other in shock.

"Yup, and they're round because they were projectiles," continued Oriol. "Catapult projectiles that were also used as ballast for galleys."

He was quiet, watching us.

"Get to the point!" Luis was exasperated.

"Okay. Listen to my theory. On the southern part of the island, on the east side, facing a cliff and a foot and a half underwater at low tide, there are a ton of very similar round rocks. They're all about the same size and they're made of minerals that aren't found on Tabarca. In that area there are only metamorphic rocks, mostly dark greenish and occasionally ocher. They used to mine the island for that mineral. They caught my eye the first time we went around and I confirmed it on our later trips. Someone took the stones I'm talking about there. Who would bring those rocks, of a different composition and so uniform? I arrived at the conclusion that it must have been a galley because they used them as ballast and for ammo."

"Ammo?" asked Luis.

"Yes. Projectiles. Galleys had regulated equipment, depending on their size. The written inventories that have survived are very strict, listing how many oars they had, how many spare rudders, helmets, shields, lances, crossbows, bows, arrows, war machines, and . . . projectiles were to be carried. In the late thirteenth century Venetian galleys were already equipped with artillery, but most likely Arnau d'Estopinyá's *Na Santa Coloma* still used the old catapults. And they launched round rocks to bust holes in the enemy ships and jars of lit naphtha to burn them. But it doesn't matter, even if Arnau used artillery, at that time the cannons still shot stones. Look, it's simple.

"If you want to hide the mouth of a cave that opens near the surface, you move some big rocks first. Then you cover them with the smaller rocks you are using for ballast. So the cave's entrance is hidden, but you can always get in it by moving those manageable-size rocks. What do you guys think?"

"Amazing," I exclaimed, really impressed. "So you think there may still be a treasure?"

"Well, yeah."

"And why'd you wait so long to tell us this?" Luis's voice showed his excitement, but he still seemed resentful.

"Because I'm afraid of Boix and his men. I've been extremely alert during this whole trip. I haven't seen anyone or anything strange, but I'm sure they're watching us. Artur Boix isn't going to give up. I've decided it would be better if they thought we'd left, discouraged. I'm surprised I haven't seen anything, but I'm convinced that he knows what we're doing. I'm even worried that the car might be bugged, which is why I wanted to talk here on the beach. I want to ask you guys to not talk about it again, not in the car or at home."

"But sooner or later we have to come back to Tabarca," I said.

"Sooner," replied Oriol. "I've been thinking about our next step for a few days now. And this is the plan: tomorrow we'll act completely normal, making it look as if we're going about our regular routines. The day after tomorrow, Cristina, you'll rent a car and go do some sightseeing along the Costa Brava. And, Luis, you'll go to Madrid on a business trip. We'll make sure to shake off anyone who might be following us. Your luggage should be minimal, a carry-on bag or something like that. I'll go on a roundabout route to Salou, where a friend will lend me a forty-foot boat equipped with a Zodiac motor launch and I'll take it to Valencia. There I'll pick up Cristina at the marina. I suggest you leave the rental car parked with the keys hidden inside, near the train station of one of the towns you visit. Take the train and switch in Barcelona to connect to the airport, and once you're there buy a ticket to Valencia, using the boarding pass at the last minute, so no one will know your destination until it's too late to follow you. I'll pick up Luis at the port of Altea. Luis, I suggest you use the same strategy as Cristina, but twice, once for the flight from Barcelona to Madrid and again from Madrid to Alicante. If someone follows you guys, and only in the case of an emergency, call me on my cell to change plans. If you don't call, then I'll assume everything is going smoothly. On the boat there'll be diving equipment to make the underwater work easier."

"Don't you think you're going a bit far with so much precaution?" I asked him.

Oriol looked at me with an intense look, and I felt a shiver run through me.

"You know Artur." He knew I did and I only responded with a slight nod.

"No. You don't know him," he continued. "You don't really know him. He's clever and cruel. He's a criminal, and he thinks that the Bonaplatas owe a debt to his family and he wants to get back at us. He's not going to quit, he's never going to give up."

Artur's words about the blood feud came to mind, but I kept my peace.

"He's a dangerous guy, very dangerous, and any attempts to keep him away are too few," continued Oriol.

* * *

Artur Boix, who according to Oriol was a dangerous man, was definitely pursuing me. And he was very appealing. And he knew it.

I had noticed it in our previous meetings. He employed all his good looks, class, and sophistication to make you feel like a queen.

And that's how he acted during the first part of the lunch he invited me to the day after we came back from Tabarca. As if he were expecting me. Although we didn't mention it, we both remembered that good-bye kiss he had given me before I sneaked into the back door of the Santa Anna church.

I must confess that by the time dessert arrived I was feeling attracted to him. Artur is a very seductive person, and even though I knew I shouldn't be affected by his charms, I couldn't help but be drawn to him.

I was thinking about this when Artur stretched out his hand in search of mine. Once he held it, he kissed it. That ended my ruminations. I closed my eyes and sighed. I told myself that even if my ability to control my feelings had been a bit off lately, I could wait to fix that for a few more days.

"How did the treasure hunting in Tabarca go?" I was shocked by the unexpected question.

"How do you know I was in Tabarca?"

"I know," he said, smiling. "I watch out for my business. Part of that treasure belongs to me."

"You've been spying on us?"

Artur shrugged and gave me one of his beguiling smiles—like a little boy caught being naughty.

"Then you'll know that we didn't find even one crummy clue," I lied.

"So it would seem. But I'm disappointed—I had high hopes for you."

"For me?"

"Yes, of course. We're partners." He took my hand again.

"And we could be more, if you'd like. I'm entitled to two-thirds of the treasure as the rightful heir to the two paintings Enric stole from my family. The other third belongs to the three of you, but Oriol has always stubbornly refused to negotiate with me. He's just like his father.

"Let's you and I come to an agreement," he said. "I'm willing to give you part of my share if we become a team. I'll even give the others something just to make peace."

"That's all very well," I replied. "But there's nothing to negotiate. There is no treasure." I liked Artur, but I didn't want to betray Oriol. Although maybe he was right; maybe we should come to some agreement. We'd have to talk about that.

"And now what are you going to do?" he asked me.

"Make the most of my trip and visit the Costa Brava for a few days. I leave tomorrow."

"Alone?"

"Yes."

"I'll go with you."

I looked at him again. Was he trying to seduce me or did he suspect that that wasn't my real destination?

"No, Artur. I'll see you when I return."

As we left the restaurant he invited me to his house. I'll confess that I hesitated for a few seconds before declining.

CHAPTER 44

This time, it was the eastern end of the island that first appeared. We were sailing from the port of Altea, where we had picked up Luis. We had spent the first nights in its sheltered waters. The boat was large and had an enormous bed below the prow, which the cousins had chivalrously let me have. They slept in the anteroom, a large room that held the kitchen and two fold-out beds. Oriol made us get up early and, with a skill that surprised me even after I found out that he had a yacht-skipper's license, he made all the necessary maneuvers to set sail and in a few minutes we were heading south.

When I made out Tabarca's earthy color in the distance, lit by the sun on our backs, my heart leaped. There was our treasure island, and this time we would find it.

We laid anchor on the southeast side, the boat's sonar marking a depth of twenty-three feet about eighty feet from the shore. There, opposite us, was the place where the catapult projectiles from Arnau's galley hid the Templar treasure.

"We should use wet suits, water shoes, and gloves. They'll protect us from bumps, scrapes, and the cold," Oriol informed us. "But fins would be a hassle. We'll use plastic sandals on top of the water shoes for better protection against the rocks."

We began our work enthusiastically. The sea was flat and the bed of round, similar rocks, just as Oriol had said, extended from the foot of a stack that rose almost vertically some sixteen feet above the sea. The first thing that Luis and I did, after jumping from the boat and swimming to shore, was to check the composition of those rocks. Some were granite or basalt, others seemed to be marble or quartz, although there were also some greenish volcanic rocks and ocher limestone, stones native to that part of the island. Although we trusted Oriol, it was satisfying to check for ourselves.

We had some friendly, although noisy neighbors—a group of white-bellied sea birds that nested on the cliff above our heads and came and went as they fished.

At low tide, the rocks were at about twenty inches deep and at high tide almost three feet. We started to take the rocks to an incline a little bit farther out to sea. This assured that the waves wouldn't bring them back. A small reef of larger rocks that, just as we had suspected, could well have been put there by someone, created the border between the pebble-covered bottom and the deeper area.

In the beginning, we placed ourselves on the edge of the reef to throw the stones to the other side, especially when the water was low and we didn't have to breathe through the snorkel tube. But when we had to move stones for longer distances, it was very uncomfortable walking over the rocks, so we decided to make a chain. One person picked up the stone, passed it to the second, and the third threw it above the barrier. Soon our lower backs and arms began to feel the effects of this effort and we realized that the job would take us a few days. We took frequent breaks and stopped for several hours at high tide.

* * *

Oriol stayed on constant alert and his uneasiness was contagious.

"I don't think Artur can be tricked so easily," he repeated. "He could show up at any minute. And if he does, things are going to get ugly."

So we looked suspiciously at any boat that came close, but luckily that area was not zoned for anchorage. Everyone went to the south beach, located about a quarter of a mile west of where we were. From there, with the help of an inflatable dinghy, or sometimes by swimming, the tourists went to the restaurants on the beach and in town.

I felt guilty about not telling Oriol of my meeting with Artur in Barcelona. But I wasn't sure whether it was because of personal or business reasons.

At midday, we moved the boat to the beach area and, just like three more tourists, we put out the dinghy and went to eat a delicious Tabarcan fish stew in one of the restaurants.

"We don't want to forget to enjoy ourselves; we can't let all this work ruin our adventure," Luis warned Oriol at lunch when a controversy arose over his asking for a second pitcher of sangria. "Remember your father's philosophy. Take pleasure in the journey. When you arrive, there's little left to enjoy. The goal is the adventure, the treasure is just a question of luck."

"You're right," conceded Oriol. "But I'm nervous about Artur. I'm afraid he's going to show up, and I'm not going to relax until I can get into that cave."

As a spectator, the role switching between the cousins was very peculiar. The squatter, the rebel against the system, was worried about material goals, and the prosaic capitalist, slave to the almighty euro, was busy enjoying the moment when he had a fortune within arm's reach. Who'd have believed it?

At dawn on the third day, the *mestral*, the northwestern wind, began to blow, but since we were anchored on the southeast, the island protected us and we could continue our work without major inconvenience. We had cleared a small entrance in the rock, at nearly thirty inches below the surface during low tide. But there were still many rocks to remove. We took turns in each of the positions to avoid getting tired out by repetitive motions, but because we had lowered the level of the bottom, the work became more difficult and we now had to struggle with goggles and snorkels.

That afternoon we worked harder than ever. The tunnel was opening up before our eyes and in spite of our exhaustion, the excitement made us keep removing stones from the entrance. Meanwhile, the wind had veered to a *llevant* that came from the east, raising waves that broke against the cliff. Finally we had no choice but to use our scuba equipment and flashlights to look into the cavity.

By sundown, the tunnel seemed almost accessible but we decided to wait till the next morning to go in. We were too tired to reach the climax of our adventure that night and the waves beat too furiously against the rocks.

"The *llevant* usually blows for three days," Oriol said. Isn't there anything he doesn't know? I thought. "And it will get worse. We're going to have a rough night. It would be wise to take shelter in the port."

We didn't want to. Having the treasure within our grasp and abandoning it was too much for us.

The weather report announced waves at a strength of two or three knots, uncomfortable but not dangerous. Oriol decided to move the boat away from the shore about thirty feet more and drop anchor at a depth of about thirty-five feet. I doubled my seasickness medication. Showering was quite a challenge. The water went from one side to the other depending on the boat's rocking. I had to chase after it, and getting it to land on my body was a victory. We took care of dinner with a few sandwiches, not speaking very much. The sea wears you out, especially when it's rough. The previous nights we'd fallen into our beds exhausted. Tonight we simply collapsed.

But I couldn't help thinking that the next day would be the day we'd been dreaming of. The day we'd find the treasure. I fell asleep praying that the wind would die down, that the waves would abate and that we'd be able to get into the cave. But I was uneasy. Was it the excitement or a premonition? Something was going to happen.

In the middle of the night, I heard a loud bang. I must have been sleeping lightly, because I woke up with a start. I looked for the light to get my bearings and I saw that everything was moving, even more than when I'd gone to bed. What was going on? Had we hit something? Before we'd gone to sleep, we'd checked the anchor, and from the tugs I felt I didn't think it had come loose, so we couldn't be adrift. I thought I should investigate. I drew back the folding door that separated me from the other room. When I turned on the light I found Luis sitting on the floor, trying to figure out where he was. He'd been thrown out of bed with a lurch, and in his stunned, sleepy expression I saw the chubby little boy from my childhood. Not even my roars of laughter woke up Oriol.

CHAPTER 45

The *llevant* continued to blow, although it had veered slightly
to the south, bringing a dawn without mist and a sun that
appeared without warning over the horizon.

I looked toward the island. The waves beat mercilessly on
the cliff; they weren't extreme but they were dangerous. I told
myself with disappointment that we wouldn't be able to reach
the cave under those conditions. The seabirds nesting in the
crags were already awake and flying against the wind, competing with seagulls for the fish du jour.

I was surprised to see tourists on that part of the island so
early in the day. All the time we'd been working there, even
though the high season had already started, we hadn't seen
so many people. We were in a spot far from the town and the
beach, which wasn't very popular because of that. But I didn't
think much of it.

I went to the bathroom and while I rode the toilet I decided
to take another seasickness pill and then go back to bed. But I
thought I'd look outside again. I saw two boats about the same
size as ours, coming straight toward us at such a speed that it
made them leap over the waves. I didn't realize what was going

on until I recognized one of the crew members: it was Artur.

"They're going to hit us!" I shouted to the sleeping guys. "It's Artur!"

The two cousins were slow to react, while the others were coming at full speed. They maneuvered skillfully and Artur's boat hit our stern, but not too hard.

Suddenly Oriol seemed to understand what was going on. He leaped up and, without the slightest hesitation, grabbed the boat hook and headed out on deck, swinging it above his head to keep Artur's men from boarding our ship. Oriol landed a lucky shot on the head of one of the goons, making him fall overboard. But that didn't prevent a couple of the others from jumping on deck.

"Call the police!" yelled Oriol.

I rushed to the radio, but Luis, who'd left his cousin alone in the commotion, pulled at my arm, making me come down off the bridge.

"Forget about that," he said. "If the police come, we can say good-bye to our treasure. It's better to negotiate with them."

"Negotiate?" I repeated, surprised. "How can you—" I didn't finish my sentence, as one of Artur's thugs had gone around the cabin on the starboard side and was coming up on Oriol from the back.

"Behind you!"

I shouted at him and he turned, quickly spinning the boat hook, but the guy was already on him and was able to stop the blow with his arms. Artur and the other man were right behind Oriol, who turned and without a moment's hesitation, slapped Artur in the mouth. I was impressed. It looked like the squatter knew martial arts. The other two guys, who were almost as tall as he was but much stockier, held him down. They suggested he calm down, giving him a couple of punches in the pit of the stomach. The hit Artur had taken hadn't been very hard, but he brought his hand to his lips to see if they were bleeding. They weren't, and Artur quickly regained his sophisticated manner, flashing me a smile.

"The Costa Brava is farther north," he said to me. "Didn't you know, sweetheart?"

"Yes, dear," I replied in the same cynical tone. "Change of plans."

He nodded his head slightly, politely accepting my explanation.

"Mr. Casajoana," he said to Luis. "I see that you are a man of your word."

Luis! I thought. Luis in cahoots with Artur? How could that be?

"Agreements are meant to be honored," Luis replied. "Now it's your turn to keep your word and negotiate with my friends."

"I've already tried, unsuccessfully. Do you think they'll be more receptive now?" Artur smiled maliciously. He was enjoying his victory.

"Yes. I'm sure they'll listen to you," said Luis, giving me a pleading look.

"But how could you?" I reproached him. "Why did you betray us?"

"I think that Mr. Boix also has a right to part of the treasure," he said, lifting his chin and trying to look dignified.

"You acknowledged that?" I asked. "On behalf of all of us?"

"And he also sold me his share," clarified Artur. "A few months ago your friend, who had invested in Internet companies, lost a lot of money, money that wasn't only his. He was in a bind, so we made a deal and I bought his part of the treasure."

"But how could you . . . ?"

"I had to do it." Luis was upset. "He was threatening to kill me."

God, I thought, he better stop whining or I'll bust his face.

"And now he's going to kill us all," interjected Oriol. "Don't you realize that, you idiot? Don't you get it? Even if we cut a deal, he could never resell the pieces with three witnesses who could turn him in before he even had a chance."

"You think you're so smart," Artur said, approaching Oriol, whose arms were still being held by the two thugs. "You thought you had me fooled, that your pervert father's crime would go unpunished, that you'd get everything . . . And on top of it all, you dare to hit me . . ." He raised his right fist and smashed it into Oriol's mouth. Oriol couldn't defend himself. I heard a thud and something breaking. I ran to put myself between them, but Artur pushed me to one side.

"Get out of the way," he roared. "This is between the two of us."

As a lawyer, I'd never advise anyone to seek out this situation, and even less to provoke it, but if a woman's hesitating between two men, there's no better way to know her true feelings than by watching her suitors go head-to-head. Her heart chooses sides immediately. Seeing Oriol held by those thugs, his lips covered in blood and Artur triumphantly hitting him, even knowing that Oriol had started it, made me feel great tenderness for the blue-eyed Oriol and hate his opponent. So my heart, predictably, chose Oriol and, at the same time, I got my money's worth for a self-defense course I'd taken but had never had the chance to use before. It was instinctive. I let loose with a well-aimed kick to the groin. It was a sharp impact, followed by a quick intake of air and a scream that never made it out of Artur's throat. He fell onto his knees, protecting himself with his hands, even though it was too late, and then curled up in a ball on the ground—still able to do it with style and elegance.

Oriol took advantage of the confusion to break loose from the guy who held his right arm and jam an elbow into his face. The guy fell backward while Oriol launched a punch at the other one, who in trying to dodge it, also let go of him. Oriol didn't stop to think for a second but jumped overboard. I immediately knew what he was going to do and panicked. Oriol was swimming, without any type of equipment or protection, toward the cave's entrance. It was suicidal. We didn't know what was on the other side. It could be a cave blocked by a landslide, or flooded. Tired out by the fight and swimming in that swell, he might not have the strength to overcome the current, or the waves might smash him against the wall, or he could die in a thousand other ways. Coming out of that alive would be a miracle.

Since our conversation that night, on our first trip to the island, I hadn't stopped thinking about the Templar promise, to never abandon one's partner, Oriol had proposed we make to each other. Maybe I'd been waiting for the right moment to seal it with a kiss, the one Luis had ruined.

At that moment, as I watched the shy, skinny boy I had loved so much struggling against the waves, the pledge bubbled up from deep within me.

"I swear to you."

The night before, exhausted, I had collapsed on the bed without following the basic rule for all diving equipment: take it apart and clean it. My water shoes and wet suit were there piled on top of the weights and the vest, with the air tank and regulator still attached. I had only closed the air valve. Taking advantage of the confusion and the fact that everyone was focused on Oriol, I rushed into my room and toward my equipment; when I opened the valve I saw that there was still a little over a hundred atmospheres. Enough to save us both. I put on the water shoes, goggles, and snorkel and, resting the vest and tank on one of the beds, I managed to get them on too. There was no time for the suit or the weights. That was when I heard the first shot, and then another. My heart began to race. They were going to kill him.

"Stop, you idiots," I heard Artur shout, making me glad I hadn't kicked him any harder. "Don't make any noise. Damnit!

Don't you see, he can't escape? We've got plenty of our people on the island."

I didn't like his confidence about our being trapped. I liked even less the fact that the only thing that bothered him about the shots was the noise. But that didn't change anything. That didn't change my promise. And, just as I was about to jump in, I looked at the coastline and, sure enough, I saw several men standing guard.

Then I felt myself being held tightly from behind, and someone asked me sarcastically, in a voice loud enough for everyone to hear, "Hey, pretty lady, where do you think you're going?" It was one of the thugs.

I struggled to get loose but he held me tight. Desperate, I tried to kick him. It was useless, he only held me tighter.

As a girl, I had always thought that Luis liked me. More than just liked me, that he'd been in love with me. And that that was what made him act so difficult with me, so that he could prove to himself that it wasn't love, but hate. Maybe at that moment, he felt for me what I had felt for his cousin seconds before. I saw him appear on my right, hoisting a buoy. He hit my assailant with it, giving him a tremendous whack that sounded hard and hollow.

"Jump, bossy-boots," he ordered as he helped me with my gear. I put on the goggles and a second later I was filling up the vest with as much air as possible while I fell into the water.

Swimming, I felt a strange happiness. For him, for Luis, for what he'd done. For his newfound dignity. I didn't know if his action would help us—maybe we were already doomed—but ol' Chubby had had his moment of glory and redemption. Oriol and I were going to have a rough time. But now Luis was definitely going to have a worse one. He was the one in the pirates' hands. Surely they'd take out their frustrations on him.

CHAPTER 46

I swam and swam. Without fins, swimming with gear is exhausting and I had to let some air out of the vest so I could use my arms better. For a moment I thought I saw Oriol suspended above the waves, about forty feet ahead. He must have been right in front of the rocks that broke the waves. As I approached, I studied the rhythm of the swell. It was more violent than the previous night. I let the force of a wave carry me along, but I went under before the undertow dragged me back. It wasn't very deep, and down below, the strength of the swell was reduced considerably, so I was able to safely approach the tunnel. I let all the air out of the vest, let go of the snorkel, put the regulator in my mouth, and breathed in a calming mouthful of canned air. It worked. I went under just as the crest of a wave passed, putting my hands down and my legs straight up, without kicking, to descend. Below, everything was confusion. In spite of the rocky bottom, shreds of dead Posidonia leaves and thousands of other suspended particles mixed with the foam and the bubbles that came from it. I found myself trapped in the current going out to sea. I moved backward and forward without being able to see practically anything. I thought about

Oriol. He didn't have an air tank or even goggles. There was no way he could have gotten through, I thought.

I swam desperately, forward and down, with one hand in front to protect myself from bumping into anything. I continued swimming until I finally saw the outline of the cave's entrance. After all I'd gone through that night, that was the first time I felt really scared. What if Oriol hadn't been able to enter the cave? Or worse, what if I found his dead body inside? For a moment I imagined his body blocking the way, floating against the tunnel's roof. I shuddered. But there was no turning back. I faced the darkness. "Damnit," I said to myself, "I forgot to grab a flashlight." But that didn't stop me. I noticed the current inside the tunnel right away. It pushed me backward and then forward, but I still managed to advance and I saw indications of the possibility of a pocket of air in some part of the cave.

I hadn't gone much more than three feet when I got stuck. My heart sped up. I couldn't move forward. I pushed backward with my hands, off the floor, and I still couldn't budge. I started to panic. I struggled desperately and wasn't getting anywhere. Claustrophobia was setting in. I'd have given anything to get out of that wet, dark, cold tomb. I was trapped, I couldn't move, but I could touch the side wall, only twelve inches from my hand. It was torture. I frantically tried to move forward. Nothing. The same thing backward. I felt as if I was suffocating even though I had air, and after some more unsuccessful jerking around I started to pray. I remembered seeing a diving rule: never enter a closed space, underwater, unless you've had special training. I didn't have any.

I only had my vow, to die before abandoning Oriol. That thought made me try again, hopelessly. I ended up out of breath, without having moved an inch, in the same spot in that murky grave.

How long did I have? Maybe a half hour's worth of air. It was already getting harder to inhale. Soon there'd be no more.

I promised myself that when that happened I wouldn't struggle, I'd just spit the mouthpiece to one side and take a deep breath of water.

It's strange. That idea of facing death with dignity, of accepting my fate, helped calm me and I breathed more easily. If I was relaxed I used less air. Little by little I was able to maintain control. I was trapped. Or, better put, I was stuck because of my gear. Without it I could definitely get through. I could let go of the straps, take a big breath of air, and swim forward, trusting that the exit on the other side was close by. Otherwise, no one would have been able to get in there, especially without gear. And in the thirteenth century they would have entered on lungs alone. Then I remembered that we'd been working the night before until after it had gotten dark. We were using flashlights. Where did I put mine after we got back to the boat? Maybe, after all that, I did still have it . . . in my vest pocket . . . I felt it and there was something hard on the right side. I had light! The first thing I looked at was the pressure indicator. Seventy atmospheres! I still had a little bit of time to live. The next step was to check my situation. There, surrounded by rocks, visibility was better than outside and I discovered that just a few inches above my head the tunnel rose up. I even thought I could make out some light on the other side. The problem could be that we hadn't taken all the rocks out of the passageway and my air tank had gotten stuck in a cavity in the roof. My own ability to float had kept me from lowering myself the inches I needed to escape. I devised a plan, repeated it to myself once, twice, three times, reviewing possible setbacks. Then I decided to act. I released all the buckles on the vest, then put the lit flashlight into my underwear, took a deep breath, and, letting the mouthpiece go, I swam forward and down. The vest came off relatively easily. Barely six feet and I saw the surface on the other side, just above me. I didn't want to leave my gear behind, it still could save my life. So when I had space to maneuver, I turned around, went into the passageway, and pulled out the vest. It took me what seemed like an incredibly long time, but I finally found the inflator and, with a hand above to keep me from banging my head, I went up to the surface, which was surprisingly close. I was saved. For the moment.

It was a remarkable place. I was in a cave with a relatively high roof that seemed to drop and rise with the water level, responding to the ebb and flow of the sea outside. From somewhere in the roof, a tiny ray of sunlight came in. It made me unexplainably happy. To one side of that secret little lake, I saw a large rock. I climbed up, pulling the vest along with me.

I saw him right away. He was stretched out, faceup, in a spot out of the reach of the rising water. My heart jumped with joy. He was alive! He wasn't moving, but if he had managed to reach that spot, he must be alive. I focused my flashlight on him. He didn't react. He was a sight. Besides his bleeding lower lip, he had bruises all over his body. He was wearing only the underwear he had slept in, which had one torn leg. I knelt beside him and stroked his forehead.

"Oriol," I said softly. There was no response. I was afraid he wasn't breathing.

"Oriol!" I raised my voice.

I don't know if it was the cold that had gradually seeped into me, or fear, but I started to tremble like a leaf. He didn't react. I checked for a pulse on his carotid artery and couldn't find one.

"Oriol!" I shouted.

I was panicking again. I gave him mouth-to-mouth resuscitation, tasting the sea on his lips. Like that day of the storm. Only this time it also tasted of blood.

But he was breathing. What a relief! I thanked God as I

hugged him and got on top of him, being careful not to obstruct his breathing, so we could share body heat.

I searched again for the taste of his lips.

Maybe my touch gave him strength, because soon his eyes opened. I didn't say anything. I just held him tight, being careful not to rub against any of his wounds, and I waited.

"Cristina," he said finally.

"Yes, it's me."

He looked around again and, as if he suddenly understood the situation, said, "But what are you doing here?"

"I'm here with you."

"But how did you get in here?"

"Through the tunnel, just like you," I said, stroking the hair off of his forehead.

"Are you crazy?"

"Are *you* crazy?"

"I had made a promise to myself that it would be me and not Artur who found my father's treasure."

"Well, I swore, like the Theban warriors and the Templar Knights, not to abandon my partner."

"You swore that?" He loosened himself slightly from my embrace and tried to look into my eyes.

"I made the promise when I saw you jump off the boat."

He didn't respond. We stayed there for a little while in silence.

"Thanks, Cristina," he said finally. His voice was filled with emotion. "He's going to kill us anyway. But dying this way will be lovely."

I couldn't help kissing him again. This time he responded. Once again there was the salt of the sea on his lips. But the taste of blood was a sinister omen. I ignored it and let myself get carried away by memories of my adolescent dreams in which, hand in hand, we set out to discover the world together. I thought of the letters I'd sent, filled with love poems, that he'd never read and never would. None of that could happen now. Oriol was right, Artur was going to kill us.

Suddenly, I remembered the treasure. I had completely forgotten about it, but it made sense. I hadn't gone into that cave for the treasure. I'd done it for him.

Oriol didn't seem to be in any rush to find the treasure either. When you think you're about to die, your whole value system changes. What would we do with a treasure? Our friendship, our affection, and the few minutes we had left were the only things that had any value inside that cave. Well, maybe Oriol still needed to find that treasure. For his father. That did still have value.

And there we were—I don't know for how long, but for me it went too quickly—caressing and kissing each other, gently but with the intensity of knowing it was for the last time. We were in a dry spot, so holding each other warmed me up a bit. Then something unexpected happened. I felt a familiar pressure against my lower abdomen.

"Oriol!" I exclaimed in surprise.

He didn't say anything, but the pressure kept increasing.

"Oriol," I repeated deliberately, pulling away from him enough to be able to see his eyes.

"As you can see," he said, "I'm getting my strength back."

I didn't know you had that kind of strength, I thought.

"Are you sure?" I asked.

"Of what?"

"That this is about me."

"Absolutely."

And that's where the discussion ended. We sealed it with a kiss, forgetting his bleeding lips, our bruised bodies, the treasure, and even death. We didn't even feel the rocks on the floor. And as for the cold, it disappeared once I took off my wet clothes.

Our lovemaking was passionate. I don't remember anything

like it before. If I still had any doubts about Oriol's sexual preference, they vanished that morning. It was obvious that he wasn't making an exception based on the circumstances, and that this wasn't the first time he had slept with a woman. He knew what to do every step of the way.

We made love with the urgency that had been stored up for over fourteen years. As if it were the first time. As if it were the last. With no worries, and no precautions. There was no tomorrow.

I'm not usually like that. I'm not often overcome by fits of passion. But did critical situations arouse me? Like the night of September 11 with Mike. Or is that a normal reaction? That the smell of death drives us to seek life? Maybe it was just an attempt to fight off fear, banish it for a few seconds by taking refuge in love and passion.

And there we stayed, body against body, holding each other, throbbing as the fire went out and our bodies became aware of the bruises. I searched his lips again. I felt moments of intense happiness followed by even more intense grief. My breathing was shallow, more like hiccupping, as I struggled not to cry. With death almost a certainty, now I knew we'd never be able to enjoy our love. But I promised myself that I would make the most of each and every second we had left.

Carpe diem.

CHAPTER 47

We held our embrace for a few more minutes, then released each other gradually.

"We have to see if the cave has another exit," Oriol whispered into my ear.

We got up and checked the cave. The inner lagoon continued its rocking motion. The swell outside hadn't stopped. Its tireless murmur made its way to us.

We were on a relatively flat platform, although it was dotted with little stones. The ray of sun that came in through a crack some ten feet above our heads had moved down and toward the right, against a rocky wall on the island side.

And there it was, three feet beyond the illuminated spot, painted on the wall: a flared red cross. Like the one in my ring.

"Look," I said, pointing.

"It's placed so it receives the midday sun," he commented after looking at it. "This cave is a perfect hiding spot."

Then that ray of hope went out as the opening on the rock darkened. We looked up, startled.

"It's the seabirds that nest in the crevice," Oriol declared.

"They have a good, safe spot here." The flapping of wings underscored his words.

He held me around the shoulders, and added, "Don't worry. Artur's thugs won't come in, not with this rough sea. They'll wait for us to come out."

He looked into my eyes.

"I'm sorry. I'm really sorry that I got you into this."

"It's not your fault," I replied. "I'm the only one responsible for what might happen to me."

I hugged him and our naked bodies took on new heat and energy. It was another long, unhurried embrace. After we let each other go, we began to think again about a way out of the cave. The crack through which the light entered was above the water, on an almost smooth wall; it was inaccessible and small. It would be impossible to get out that way. To the left of the shelf where we had come in, large stones, too heavy to move, blocked the cave. Toward the right, along the path the ray of light would follow, the cave continued, its rocky bottom entering the water and then coming out about ten feet ahead. Along that path, about five feet above the surface of the water, there was a parallel, deeper shelf. It was dark and I focused my flashlight down on it. I saw a chest.

"The treasure," I said without much enthusiasm.

Oriol said nothing, and without stopping to check what we'd found we continued in that direction, looking for an exit. The rock wall narrowed and the floor rose until there was only a short passage blocked by large rocks. There was no way to continue.

"You and me, the treasure, and death," I mused.

"At least we'll die rich," he tried to joke.

"Don't you want to see it?"

"Sure, of course."

I focused the beam on the trunk. It was a medium-size chest, made of reinforced wood with metal riveting. It was in surprisingly good shape.

"It has no latches or locks," commented Oriol.

"It doesn't need them." He put his hand on the lid and opened it easily.

The flashlight revealed . . . a pile of rocks. Regular old rocks. A ton of rocks, common rocks, small pebbles . . . just like millions of others on that part of the island.

Oriol started taking them out and throwing them on the ground. It looked as if he'd lost his mind.

"There's no treasure! There's no treasure!" he kept repeating as he reached the bottom without finding anything more than rocks.

He turned and looked at me with a happy smile. He had something in his hand.

"We're saved!" he shouted. "There's no treasure!"

"Artur," I said in a daze. "He's not going to kill us?"

"Not anymore! Why would he? Artur's a rational guy, a businessman. No, he won't do it, he's not going to put himself at risk for nothing. Maybe he'd like to, but for him this is a game of probabilities and rewards. If there's nothing to gain, he won't take the risk."

I wasn't so sure. This was more than business for Artur. I remembered his words about the debt of blood, but I didn't want to discourage my friend.

"What have you got in your hand?" I asked him.

"Looks like a note. A note protected in plastic."

It was from Enric, and it said:

My dears, I hope and trust that one day you will read
this. You've found the treasure! You are too grown up
for chocolate and candy, but I hope that you're neither
too young nor too old to enjoy this experience. If you've
made it here, you've lived days you will never forget.

That is life's treasure. May you know how to live the
rest of it fully.

> I love you,
> Enric

We were silent. It was all a game, a joke. Just like when we were
kids but on a larger scale.

"Carpe diem," I muttered under my breath.

Thank God for the game that saved our lives. Now I could
think beyond those rock walls, beyond the sea and the ocean.
I still wasn't sure about Artur's reaction, but our survival was
looking more likely. Everything began to change. I realized
that except for the water shoes, I was completely naked, and
I regained the modesty I had forgotten. With the flashlight I
looked for my pajamas and headed toward them. I felt guilty.
It was I who had initiated our lovemaking. Maybe I had forced
him. Me, with an engagement ring sparkling on my finger.
That was bad, very bad. One thing was to want it and another
to do it. Maybe Oriol could read my guilty face, because he
took me by the arm, pulled me toward him, and kissed me. I
let myself get caught up in it and we made love again. It was
good, but not like before. The second time, I did feel the rocks
on my back.

We were sitting side by side, touching each other after the passion had waned. I started to feel cold.

"There were some very strange details." Oriol began to talk
while he strung his ideas together. "But I was so obsessed with
the adventure that I didn't want to see them. Ancient messages
hidden under paint. How ridiculous! That's like something out
of a novel, not very original and not at all realistic. Nowadays,
in the twenty-first century, we have the means to uncover
scrapped drawings that were later covered with paint. But in

the thirteenth century no one would have thought to hide a message that way, unless they wanted it to be hidden forever." I could hear the disappointment in his voice.

People are strange, I thought. Minutes earlier we were bursting with joy when we found out that it was all made up, that our lives were saved. And now that Oriol has forgotten his fear, he's complaining.

"But the paintings are authentic. Right?"

"Yes they are, but my father, who was a great restorer, altered them. He wrote those inscriptions so well that he fooled everyone. He also did a great job writing Arnau's saga."

"It's a fake too?"

"The trick with the paintings seems to point to that. Even though there are surprisingly realistic details and the descriptions coincide perfectly with history, it could all have been made up."

"Do you think that Arnau d'Estopinyá is a fictional character?" Now I felt disappointed too. "And the ring? Where did the ring come from?"

"I don't know where the ring came from. But Arnau did exist. His name appears in the documents of the Templar fiefdom of Peñíscola and in Inquisition reports. What I can't be sure about is what parts of that story are true and what parts my father invented."

"But Enric was convinced that there was a treasure. He killed for it."

"I don't think he killed for money. Maybe he did it for his own particular principles, for his own code of honor. He was searching for a treasure, but everything seems to indicate that he wasn't able to find it and instead set up this posthumous game." He was quiet for a moment before crying out, "I should have realized!"

"What?"

"My father brought us to this island several times. He knew

it well, snorkeling and diving here. It's too big a coincidence."

"What does it matter now?" The sun was illuminating the cross. I smiled at him. He smiled back. "We're going to live. Don't you realize that?"

I felt terribly thirsty. We had to get out of that surreal, cavernous wonderland before we got any weaker. Now we could leave the way we'd come in since it didn't matter that Artur would be waiting.

The sea outside, judging by the ups and downs of the inner pool, was still rough. Oriol wanted to leave first, without gear, but I convinced him to wait half an hour so I could get out before him. Artur would be more likely to believe me. I hoped his sore groin was better and that he didn't hold much of a grudge toward me.

I had no major difficulty getting out. We both went down to the tunnel, taking turns breathing what little air was left in the life vest through one of the mouthpieces. Then he handed me the life vest and I gave him the flashlight. From that point on, the light outside showed my way.

I was breathing well. I swam downward and toward the open sea to get around the waves that crashed against the cliff. When I felt like I had gone a reasonable distance and the undertow had lessened, I filled the life vest, rising to the surface with it. I began to breathe fresh air through the snorkel while I got my bearings. I saw the boats a short distance away. I swam at a relaxed pace and wondered how Artur would receive me.

He took it badly, very badly. But he had recovered his suave manners and acted with strained politeness. It was poor Luis he hadn't treated well at all. My last-minute hero had paid dearly for his derring-do. His face was black and blue, but at least he was alive. He smiled when he saw me and practically laughed once he understood that the news I brought would save our lives.

Oriol had guessed right. Artur, hiding his displeasure admirably, ended up believing my story. He agreed to send an inflatable dinghy, which was secured by a cable to one of the boats to keep it from crashing into the rock wall, with a couple of men in diving gear to get Oriol.

We became Artur's involuntary guests until his men returned from the cave after taking it apart stone by stone. They came back by midmorning with Enric's note that Oriol had left where he'd found it.

Oriol was now willing to negotiate, and he proved himself very persuasive. He recognized that there was an unpayable debt between the Boix and Bonaplata families, but that the debt was better left to the dead. They had to answer to God. Meanwhile, the living could settle material accounts. Oriol acknowledged that his father had stolen the two side paintings of the triptych. He was willing to buy them, as a souvenir, for an amount that included the debt his cousin had with Artur. The central painting had always been Enric's property; now it belonged to me and on that point he was unwilling to compromise. In the amount they were discussing there was a hefty surcharge so Artur would renounce any revenge. It was a tough negotiation that didn't end until the next morning. I was impressed by how little importance Oriol seemed to give to money and how generous he'd been with his cousin.

During the return trip, I didn't know what to do or how to act with Oriol. We both pretended nothing had happened inside that cave. I even wondered for a moment if it had all been just a dream. Only the pain in my back and the bruises from the stones bore witness to the truth.

I casually commented that once we got back to Barcelona, I'd have to start packing for my trip to New York. I watched for Oriol's reaction. He didn't say anything; he seemed distracted, as if he had more important things to think about. I was expecting him to at least invite me to stay for a few more days. He didn't, and that hurt my pride. Or something more. I came to the conclusion that he could care less about what had happened between us. It seemed as if he just wanted to forget the whole thing.

As far as Luis was concerned, Oriol wouldn't listen to any of his excuses for telling Artur where they were. He said it was over. The Saint George painting now belonged to him and he didn't care if the price had been obscene; that's what the other inheritance his father had left him was for. And he gave Luis a hug.

CHAPTER 48

The next day, I realized it was all over. Oriol had disappeared the night before without saying good night. Maybe he was afraid I would follow him to his bedroom. I went down early to have breakfast, hoping to see him, but Alicia told me he'd gotten up even earlier and was already gone. I was disappointed. I had to make conversation with her, so I answered the numerous questions she still had about what we'd told her at dinner the night before. She was thirsty for information. I didn't mention what had happened between Oriol and me in the cave, of course. But she was known to have powers and she seemed to guess it. Maybe it was the crestfallen way I explained things. There came a moment when I almost started crying and I excused myself, saying I had a headache. I didn't fool her. Did I mean so little to Oriol that he wasn't even there to say good-bye?

I knew it was time to start packing my suitcases. I opened the closet almost wishing that they had disappeared, but there they were. Seeing my luggage made me collapse onto the bed, sobbing. It was the end. The adventure was over. The possibility of our love had died, trapped in an underwater cave, and only my bruises kept me from thinking I had dreamed the whole thing. I noticed two records on my bedside table. One was "Viatge a Itaca" and the other was by Jacques Brel. I shuddered. God! Those were the records Enric had listened to when he died. Who'd left them there? Oriol or Alicia?

It must have been Oriol. It was a message for me. The lesson of the trip, the experience of the search. That's what it was about. I hadn't learned the lesson. The journey was the goal. Life was the final destination. It was hard for me to fully accept it.

When I moved into that room, I'd been surprised to see that, along with the modern stereo equipment, there was also an old record player. It was an automatic one; I put both records on. It still worked perfectly and I stretched out on the bed to listen. I wanted to find the sense of that adventure, some meaning that I hadn't been able to discover.

I held the record covers and, stretching out on the bed, I shut my eyes. I heard the wind and the sea in the background while the music took over. The image of green fields of Posidonia grass on white sand in Tabarca came to me, and among them, schools of fish swimming near the surface with the sunlight making their gold and silver stripes sparkle. The calm, sweet sea at the beginning, and then the rough sea of the last few days I relived my journey to the cave and everything started anew. That's what it was about, right? Living in the moment. And remembering it later. Sometimes forever, constantly, throughout your entire life. Like my first love, the storm, the salt, and my first kiss.

But did the wise poet Constantin Kavafis have advice for when carpe diem left you brokenhearted? I think I stopped sobbing when I fell asleep. And I had another dream.

"Police. How may I help you?" The voice sounded full of life through the phone.

"Good afternoon," I replied. I felt stiff, a knot of emotion gripping my throat. But I had decided to live those moments fully.

"Good afternoon. How may I help you?" insisted the officer.

"I'm going to shoot myself."

There was a surprised silence and I tried to imagine the shocked face that accompanied that young voice.

"What?" stammered the policeman.

"I said, I'm going to commit suicide."

"You're not serious."

"Of course I am." I smiled. His confusion amused me. The young man must not have reached the part of the manual that tells you how to deal with suicides.

"But, why? Why would you want to kill yourself?" There was anguish in his voice.

I let out a mouthful of smoke from the Davidoff I was smoking. From the armchair, through the wide-open balcony, I could see the dark green leaves of the plane trees on the avenue. It was a crystal-clear spring day and life was sprouting all around with the same vigor that astonished me year after year.

Jacques Brel was singing his farewell song: *"Adieu, l'Émile je vais mourir. C'est dur de mourir au printemps, tu sais . . ."**

Yes, it was hard to die on a day like this, when everything in the ancient city of Barcelona was bursting with renewal: the pigeons, the breeze, the trees on the avenue, even the same people I usually saw on the streets were oozing with exuberant energy.

But that was the day I would die.

"I blew four guys away."

"What?"

"I killed them, I shot them."

"Holy shit," the policeman exclaimed and then there was

---

* Good-bye, Emile. I'm going to die. It's hard to die in springtime, you know?

silence until he said, "All right, that's enough, you're pulling my leg. I don't believe it."

"I swear."

"Well, tell me when and where so we can check it out."

"It's been days and now there's no time to check, I'm going to blow my brains out in a few minutes. And, besides, if I tell you everything, then your job will be way too boring."

"No, you don't want to die." The young man seemed to have recovered his cool. "You're calling for help. If you wanted to kill yourself you'd have already done it."

"I'm calling so that nobody gets blamed for my death." Or maybe I was calling because I wanted company, I thought. I didn't want to die alone. I took a sip of cognac and I looked at my favorite painting by Ramón Casas. In it, a middle-class Catalan couple at the end of the nineteenth century, in white summer attire, were having cold drinks beneath a grapevine. They were my grandparents, and they were lovely. The play of light and shadows, the diffuse pastel shades, the drowsiness, and the pleasant decadence. "It's more practical than writing little notes," I added.

"Give me your name and address. Let's talk. No matter how complicated your situation is, I'm sure there must be a way out."

I waited to respond. I listened for the last time to a song I could repeat, word for word, by heart.

> *Je veux qu'on rie*
> *Je veux qu'on danse*
> *Quand c'est qu'on me mettra dans le trou . . .* *

"Enric Bonaplata, on the Paseo de Gracia," I said finally. "And if they hurry and send a unit right away, across the street from the

---

* I want them to laugh. I want them to dance. When they stick me in the grave.

Manzana de la Discordia, they'll hear the shot." Then I spoke to him sweetly. "How old are you, young man?"

"Twenty."

"What color are your eyes?"

"What does it matter? Why do you ask?" he replied, irritated.

"I'm just trying to make conversation. You're trying to trace the call, aren't you? Tell me, what color are they?"

"Green."

"Hmmm . . ." And I took another puff on the cigar before continuing. I imagined a handsome boy with feline eyes. The perfect complement to the drink and the smoke.

"Green-eyed boy, have you ever seen anyone die?"

"No."

"Well, now you're going to hear it."

"Wait."

"I wish you a long and happy life, my friend. Forgive me for cutting our conversation short, but it's rude to talk with your mouth full."

"Wait. Wait a minute!"

I put the telephone receiver on top of the small table, next to the still smoking cigar. And I listened:

C'est dur de mourir en printemps, tu sais?
Mais je pars aux fleurs la paix dans l'âme . . . *

I didn't feel the peace that Brel sang about in his song. My chest was frantic with emotion, my mind was filled with images of my life, each fighting to be the last one. But I had to do it, for my family, for my dignity. I looked at the Picasso painting that hung on one of the walls. A window opened onto a Mediterranean town, maybe Barcelona, someplace up high: houses, palm

---

* It's hard to die in the springtime, you know? But I'm going toward the flowers with a peaceful soul . . .

trees, foliage . . . and the sea . . . Vibrant tones, an explosion of color in long strokes.

I took a last sip of my cognac, holding it in my mouth for a few moments, feeling its flavor, breathing in its essence. Then I put the cold barrel of the revolver in my mouth, pointing upward. I saw two boys, one dead, and one with much of his life still to live: my son, Oriol. Oh, God, please help him get through this! I breathed deeply and looked out onto the avenue, wanting to fill my eyes to the brim with the light and greenness of that unstoppable force of life, springtime. That would be my last image.

The sound of the shot reached young Officer Castillo through the phone wires and made him jump out of his chair. The pigeons on the avenue took off in a swarm, as if on cue. Down on the avenue, passersby looked up in alarm at that beautiful art nouveau building with the balcony window wide open.

I opened my eyes and looked at the ceiling. Jacques Brel was singing the next song and I sat up with a start. Again. It had happened again! I was upset enough about Oriol without the damn rings making me relive dead people's stories. In a rage I took off the damn ring and left it on the table, along with my engagement ring. I didn't know which one was weighing on me more.

I went downstairs to find Alicia. I mentioned what had just happened to me, and she took me to her office. There, with the radiant, sunny city at our feet, I told her everything.

"This will help you get over the vision," she said, offering me a cognac. And she watched me.

"It's, it's . . . ," I stammered after the first sip. It was the same taste as in my dream.

"Yes. I drink the same cognac Enric used to drink."

I felt as if she was using me and I got up to leave.

"Forgive me," she apologized. "It wasn't on purpose—I didn't realize until I saw your face."

I didn't believe her. I remained standing in front of the door, hesitating about whether I should leave or not. She got up and took my hand into her large warm one. Her hands reminded me of Oriol's. She sat me in an armchair.

"I'm sorry, dear." Her voice was deep and persuasive. "Stay here, and as an apology, I'll tell you a story that I'm sure you'll find interesting. You deserve it."

I waited expectantly, a bit tense, for her to try some other move. She began to speak, slowly and deliberately . . .

"At this point you must have realized that Enric wasn't into women and I'm not into men. We got together for our families, and because we wanted to have a son, and that was the only way in those days. We each had our own lives, though we were able to be friends. Having Oriol was worth the effort." She looked at me, smiling. "Don't you agree?

"He's a great kid," she continued without waiting for me to respond. "And, in case you still have any doubts, he's straight. Well," she sighed in resignation, "nobody's perfect." She smiled again.

"Enric and I shared a lot with each other. He made the Templar Order, founded by his grandfather and great-grandfather, who were also Masons, change its statutes so that I could be admitted. But when Arnau appeared with the story of the paintings and the treasure, everything got complicated. Enric was a romantic, and reviving the Templar tradition was one of his passions. It became his obsession. And that was when the dispute with the Boix family began. He also had our Templar Order admit his friend Manuel as a knight. Manuel was his lover at the time, and he was crazy about him. They were joined by the Templar vow, the one from Epaminondas's Thebans." She looked at me to make sure I knew what she was talking about and when I nodded she continued her story.

"When they killed Manuel, Enric lost all hope. I remember him crying inconsolably, right here, on that very chair you're sitting on now. I knew that something tragic was going to happen and I asked him to calm down. He surprised me days later when he told me he'd killed four men and that Manuel's death had been avenged. Your godfather was not a gunman. He must have been lucky." I didn't say anything, but to myself I thought that no one knew that part better than I did.

"But the police began to tighten the net around him. Many people knew that he had made enemies of the Boix brothers, his competitors and former members of his Templar Order. His relationship with Manuel, and Manuel's violent death, were also known.

"For I while I didn't hear anything from Enric, but the police were calling, and they even came here looking for him. They didn't have an arrest warrant, but it was obvious that they suspected him. He never told me what he was doing at that time, but I think he was looking for the treasure, to no avail. One night, he came to the house. He had dinner with us, talked to Oriol for a while, and, when our son went to bed, we came up here to have a cognac. He wanted me to read the cards for him. I agreed; it was something I did for fun in those days. But that night, the first cards I turned over spelled out death. There was the skeleton with his scythe looking right at him. The message was very clear, but I told him that the signs were mixed. He looked at me without saying anything. I shuffled, then had him shuffle and cut the deck. A shiver ran down my spine when immediately, similar cards turned up. The skull was smiling at him. I was upset, I picked up the cards and prayed that the third time something, anything, else would show up. The same combination. The cards are so stubborn when they insist on telling you something. I'm not the crying kind, but when I picked up that damn deck I had tears in my eyes. I didn't know what to say. Enric took a sip of cognac, smiled at me and told me not to worry, that the cards were right. He was going to die soon.

"He told me he'd been diagnosed with AIDS a while back and he was beginning to feel the symptoms. In those early days, there was no treatment for that dreadful disease. He said the police were after him and so was the Boix brothers' art-trafficking mafia. They'd even threatened to kidnap and hurt Oriol. He assured me that he wouldn't die in jail or live the rest of his life sleeping with a gun under his pillow. And that if they didn't have anyone to blackmail, then Oriol wouldn't be in danger. I imagine that was when he planned and put into motion that last treasure hunt for you guys." She looked into my eyes and said, "Enric was a man of very strong opinions and attitudes. He lived and died according to his own rules and his own style. I think he is at peace with himself."

Alicia was silent as she looked out over the city nostalgically, sipping her cognac. I did the same. As I relished its flavor, I thought about what had happened moments before.

"Alicia."

"What?"

"Is my bedroom the one Enric used when he slept here?"

"Yes."

"Was it you who left those records on my night table?"

"Yes, it was me."

"You wanted me to have a vision, didn't you?" I don't think there was anger in my voice, or anything but curiosity.

She didn't say anything, just sipped her cognac and went back to contemplating the city. After a little while she looked into my eyes with her almond-shaped ones, and she asked me:

"He died in peace. Right?" There was pleading in her voice.

"Yes," I lied, after a thoughtful pause.

CHAPTER 49

There was nothing left for me to do in the city. I was overcome with sadness. I went into my room and opened the
window. Leaning on the sill, I ran through my situation again.
Then I understood that I did have some unfinished business to
attend to before leaving Barcelona. Leaving forever and never
coming back, just like my mother tried to do.

Arnau d'Estopinyá. Barbablanca. There was a time when
scanning crowds in fear, searching for him, had become a habit
for me. But recently, the monk had completely disappeared.

Alicia would know where to find him.

This time the shoe was on the other foot. I sat waiting for him
in a tiny bar across the street from his house. It was in a narrow street in the old part of Barcelona, in a neighborhood that
used to be called Barrio Chino, then Fifth District, and now
Raval. Lodging is cheap and it's packed with immigrants. New
storefronts offering long-distance telephone and Internet access
spring up all the time and a colorful, multiracial, multilingual
crowd, many attired in their native costumes, fills the streets.

Alicia had told me that he lived there, in a boarding house or a sublet. When I saw the place I thought she must not be paying him *too* big a pension.

I saw him about fifty feet before he got to his door. He was dressed as usual, a black T-shirt and a dark gray suit. He walked ramrod straight, with a firm military stride. Some pedestrians seemed to step off the curb, as if to avoid him as he passed. He had trimmed his beard, and now the whitish hair on his head was no more than a quarter of an inch long.

I ran across the street, but when I got there he already had his back to me and was sticking his key in the door.

"Arnau," I said, resting a hand on his shoulder.

He turned with a savage expression while his hand reached for his dagger. He fixed his dull blue eyes on mine and again I felt afraid of his crazy gaze.

"Brother Arnau. It's me, the girl with the ring," I told him quickly. "I'm a friend." His face softened somewhat when he recognized me.

"What do you want?" He pronounced the words slowly in his hoarse voice.

"To talk to you."

I saw that he was looking at my hands and I remembered that the ring was a symbol of authority for him. So when he didn't answer I said, carefully using the right words and a tone that I thought sounded military, "Sergeant Brother Arnau d'Estopinyá. I request your presence at lunch."

I saw him hesitate. His eyes traced a path from mine to the ring again and he finally accepted with a grunt.

It was a family restaurant with a daily fixed menu, filled with the smell of fried food. There wasn't much to choose from in the area. I managed to get a table away from the television, the slot machine, and the noise of dishes and spoons that rose above the bar, but in spite of that relative privacy I still couldn't strike up a conversation with the monk. When they brought us the bread, he blessed the table and, leaning on his elbows, began to pray in an audible murmur. He stopped and looked at me, waiting for me to do the same, so I did. When the prayers were over, he didn't waste a second. He dove into the bread without waiting for the first course to arrive. I tried to make conversation, but he replied in monosyllables. I guessed that he wasn't used to talking to people. But his appetite was impressive. It was obvious that he either hadn't enjoyed many fine meals in his life or that he fasted for religious or financial reasons. He also seemed to enjoy a good tipple so, in the hope that it would loosen his tongue, I ordered a second bottle of wine.

And suddenly, as he finished the second course, he started to talk, taking me by surprise.

"I come from a line of mad monks. I know full well why Master Bonaplata committed suicide."

I stared at him. Those were the first two sentences in a row that the man had spoken throughout the whole meal, and I realized that I had never heard him talk so much before.

"Don't believe what they say. The monk who gave me the ring killed himself too, and many more did before him. Everyone in my congregation thought he was insane. Except me. He entrusted me with the ring and then they decided that I was demented too. It began with the visions. Have you been through torture? Did the inquisitors interrogate you? Did you see the wall of Saint John of Acre collapse? Did you feel it when the Saracens stabbed you? How many murders has the ring forced you to see? How many mutilations? Many lives, much pain, that is what it bears. And then they come to live with you and they don't leave you, all day and all night."

"Who are they?" I asked.

"Who?" he questioned me, opening his eyes wide, as if surprised, as if I were asking him something that I should already know. "The spirits of the monks are in the ring. And with each apparition, a bit of them enters you. I am no longer who I once was. One day I had a different dream. I'd had many visions of Brother Arnau d'Estopinyá before, but it was that day when his bereaved spirit stayed inside me. Forever. Ever since, I am Arnau.

"He is a soul in purgatory, suffering for the crimes he committed. But that is not his greatest grief. He knows that his mission has not been completed, that the treasure has not yet been returned to the Templar Knights."

He looked at me with wild, wide eyes and I didn't dare contradict him.

"I am Arnau d'Estopinyá," he repeated, raising his voice. "I am the last Templar. The last real one." And growing silent he looked into my eyes, perhaps hoping that I would question his statement. I made sure not to.

Then his tone softened and he continued in a lower voice, "Be careful, young lady. That ring is dangerous. The day that I finally came across the new Order of Templars and met Master Bonaplata I knew that I had found my home. And when I handed the ring over to him, I felt great relief. They say that Pope Boniface VIII wore a ring very similar to that one and that Philip IV, the Fair, of France declared that a devil lived inside it.

"The king wanted to slander the pope and would resort to anything to accuse him, and, having a good network of spies, the king built his shameful lies on facts. That stone has something living in it, in its six-pointed star . . . No one can hold on to that ring without suffering—"

"Did you give Mr. Bonaplata some files as well?" I interrupted him. I didn't want to hear more about the ring.

"No. I told the master the life of Sergeant Brother Arnau d'Estopinyá, part of which was told to me by my predecessor, the bearer of the ring. The rest, I experienced through my visions."

I stared at him as he emptied his glass of wine. I already

had reservations about the ring, and I was starting to fear him. Whether this deranged man was possessed by the spirit of old Arnau d'Estopinyá or not didn't mean much to me. I already identified them as the same person. For me he was Brother Arnau d'Estopinyá, the last of the true Templars.

"And the paintings?" I inquired.

"The paintings were, along with the ring and the oral narrative, the legacy that was transmitted from monk to monk for hundreds of years. These were stolen in 1845 when Poblet was sacked and burned in the anticlerical riots. We knew that the fire didn't destroy them, since the monks chased the thieves, although the crowd kept them from catching them. Many artworks were burned in that period, but not the paintings. Maybe the person who took them knew their history."

"Why were you following me?"

"Mistress Alicia ordered me to report to her what you were up to. Then, when I knew that you had the ring, I followed you to protect you. Like when they attacked you."

"If you wanted to protect me, why haven't I seen you recently?"

"Because you went out of the city. And here is where the danger is. That's why I didn't follow you."

"What are you talking about?"

"It's here, in Barcelona."

"What?" I insisted. "What danger?"

He didn't reply. His gaze drifted and he murmured something when he saw some men who looked North African at the bar.

"Don't you see? The Saracens are coming back." There was rage in his voice. "One of these days, I'll slit their throats." And then he wrapped himself in silence.

I shuddered. The monk was serious.

CHAPTER 50

When I returned that afternoon, I faced my suitcases again. They depressed me and I figured the best thing to do was just to pack. But then I remembered something. I knew Oriol wasn't home and I went to his room, right next door to mine. I tried the knob. It wasn't locked. I slipped in quickly.

It smelled of him. Not because Oriol wore cologne. That place was filled with his presence. I looked at his bed, his closet, and his desk, facing a window overlooking the city. I had to hurry; I didn't want to be caught. I started to go through his desk drawers. I couldn't help looking at a pile of photos of him with friends, the girl from the beach among them. I had to remind myself of the task at hand. I continued with the night table, then the chiffonier . . . I couldn't find it. It was in the chest. In the underwear drawer. That was where I found it. His father's revolver. The one that killed the Boix brothers, the one we discovered in the hole in the well's secret compartment.

I put it in my belt and headed toward the attic. Once I got there I had no problem finding the painting. The replica of mine. I tore off the cardboard that covered the back and saw that its inside wasn't solid like my painting, although it was thicker and had strips around the edge. There were also strips in the middle, some reinforcing the structure and others making up an elaborate support. I placed the revolver in that wooden case and saw that it fit perfectly. It stayed put, even when I shook the painting, but it came out easily when I pulled. I repeated the motion. I rehearsed it several times, recalling my dream of the Boix murders. Yes, it was true. That was how it had happened. I had solved Captain Castillo's mystery, although he'd never know. But the memory of my godfather in that damn dream, the proof that it had all really happened, just as I had seen it, didn't make me feel better. Just the opposite. I was sick of those bloodcurdling visions. I decided to go back to the task of packing.

But first I called my office in New York and asked if I could go back to work the following week. My boss said that it would have to be taken up with the board. The firm's partners hadn't liked my long vacation, but from his tone I sensed that I still had a job.

Then I called María del Mar to tell her I was coming home. She was thrilled. But when I told her that I was planning to break up with Mike, she hit the roof. I told her what had happened with Oriol and she wasn't at all surprised. She told me that it wasn't a good enough reason to break up with Mike, and that, anyway, I couldn't give back an engagement ring over the phone, so I should wait a bit and put off making a decision until I returned.

The adventure had come to an end. It had been lovely, but my life would go on in New York. With or without Mike. I had traveled through time, space, and inside myself.

Having satisfied the longing for Oriol I had suppressed for so many years, I had healed the wounds of the past and now it was just a consummated summer fling. I'd returned to Barcelona, to my Mediterranean youth, cut short at thirteen, and for a few moments I'd recaptured it and made some adjustments.

Those voyages had changed my way of seeing the world. I wasn't the same person who had arrived. Now I knew I could walk barefoot through life.

It wasn't fair that now, docking at the port, I was sad to find Ithaca lacking, as disappointing and empty as this ending seemed. I'd learned on the journey, I had enjoyed the moments. That's what life was about.

And there was nothing to keep me here. My future was in New York.

When Oriol knocked on my door, the bed was covered with clothes, a couple of open suitcases rested on the floor, and a jumble of things was scattered around the room.

"Mother told me you're leaving," he said.

"Yup. The adventure's over and it's time to go back. You know, family, responsibilities . . ."

He looked at my hands. After the conversation with my mother, I had put Mike's ring back on.

"Where's my father's ring?"

"I left it on the night table. It scares me."

"Alicia told me—" He cut himself short. "When are you leaving?"

"Tomorrow."

"I'll buy your painting from you."

I looked at him sadly.

"The painting isn't for sale, it's a gift from someone I loved very much."

"Name your price."

His insistence offended me.

"I know you're generous, Oriol, you proved that by getting

Luis out of that fix." I felt like crying. "But I don't need money, and I can be generous too. If you want it so badly, it's yours. I'll give it to you."

"Thank you very much."

"If that's all, I'm going to keep packing." I wanted him to leave, I wanted to sob alone.

"Why don't you postpone your trip?"

"Why? There's nothing keeping me here."

"I can't accept such a valuable gift. So if you don't want to sell it, then you have to become my partner. That's going to force you to stay a few days more."

His self-assured look and tone of voice, which I interpreted as arrogant, hurt my pride, which was already in pretty bad shape. But my curiosity kept me from showing that I was offended.

"Your partner in what?"

"In the search for the Templar treasure."

I studied him carefully, trying to figure out whether he was pulling my leg. But Oriol started to tell me excitedly, "When I was alone in the cave in Tabarca, I started thinking, and since then I haven't stopped. The fact that my father put false clues in the paintings doesn't mean they aren't authentic, or that the story of the treasure isn't true. And if it were true, the signs should be obvious, although they couldn't be seen by the uninitiated. If we didn't realize it, it's because we were blindsided by looking for hidden inscriptions without recognizing the real clues. Last night I could hardly sleep, and in the morning, I took your painting and mine to the best restorer's studio in the city. I've been analyzing it and consulting experts almost all day long. Come here."

He took me by the hand and pulled me into his room.

CHAPTER 51

There, on top of his chest of drawers, leaning against the wall, were the paintings.

"Take a good look at them," he said.

I saw what I had always seen. The left side, divided into two rectangles each about six inches wide and twenty tall; above, under a decorative arch of painted stucco, Jesus Christ coming out of his tomb triumphantly, and below him Saint John the Baptist, the Messiah's predecessor in preaching the divine message, wearing lamb fur. In the central painting, also covered by a pointed arch, was Mary, mother of Jesus, and, at her feet, the Latin inscription *Mater* in Gothic letters. She looked forward, her expression sad, and she held the child on her lap. The metal part of her halo was still detached and I could still read *"Illa Sanct Pol."* The child, with a more cheerful expression, blessed the onlooker with his right hand. The third painting's upper square showed, beneath a curious foiled arch, Christ on the cross, flanked by Saint John and the Virgin. Below, Saint George was stepping on that ridiculously tiny dragon.

"To begin with," continued Oriol, "today I checked out the

words at the feet of the saints and below the crown; their paint and the paint that covered them have synthetic components, which didn't exist in the Middle Ages, so those added parts are modern. That proves that the hidden texts are very recent, most likely painted by my father. However, the strange element of the ring on the Virgin's hand is medieval. Everything else on the paintings is also, definitely, from the late thirteenth or early fourteenth century."

"And that confirms that the story has a basis in fact."

"Exactly. It's the first real clue. It's something visible to the naked eye that today looks normal but in its time would have stuck out immediately. The Virgin is a classic Madonna, she doesn't wear a royal crown, just a wimple, but she does have a halo. What makes it unusual is that she's wearing a ring. Like I told you, it was not well looked upon for Christians to wear jewelry. Only high ecclesiastical dignitaries wore rings."

"So it's strange, but not fake," I concluded.

"Right. So, we have two elements that are from the period and which we can assume are authentic: the paintings and the ring. Only through them could Arnau d'Estopinyá, or whomever, send a message through time."

"And what about Arnau's story? You don't think there could be some truth to it?"

"Absolutely. The oral tradition is fundamental in many cultures, and it's surprising how sometimes ancient stories are passed along over many generations. Since this story contains a vital secret for those involved, the real story could have gotten to us with few things added or taken out."

"But we'll never be able to tell what's real and what's made up."

"You're right. But I trust intuition. I believe in the not entirely rational as a source of knowledge. Not all human intelligence is based on science."

I thought about that for a while. I remembered the shiver

I'd felt when I discovered the support structure for the pistol in the back of the fake painting in the attic.

"To someone familiar with the subject, the sign of the Templar Order is obvious in the paintings. In spite of the fact that the Virgin was a common subject in paintings of the period, there is a deep-rooted relationship between the Templars and the Marian cult. That and the presence of their decapitated patron saints, before losing their heads, on the side paintings, proves that this small portable altar belonged to the warrior monks. We also have the two crosses used by the Order of the Temple: the patriarchal cross on the resurrected Christ's staff and the flared cross on Saint George's clothing. That last one is strange. Saint George's cross is the one from the Crusades: thin and red, like the one on Barcelona's coat of arms. That saint is never shown with a flared cross."

"So we've proved the paintings are authentic and that they belonged to the Templars," I said. "Where does that get us?"

"Well, just that if they hold a message, it should be out in the open where anyone could see it. Don't you think?"

"I guess," I replied, not quite convinced. "I don't think there is any clue in the ring. Its surface is smooth; it doesn't have any grooves or engravings."

"So all we've got left is Arnau's story, if we can believe any of it." I didn't want to interrupt him, but I had reasons for accepting the veracity of a large part of the story. "And the paintings," concluded Oriol, looking at them carefully. "We have to look at them with the eyes of a detective from the late thirteenth or early fourteenth century. What elements would catch the eye of a sleuth of the period?"

"You're the medievalist," I said, shrugging my shoulders. "I'm afraid it's up to you to see it."

"Okay, well besides what we've already mentioned, the inscription *Mater* at the feet of the Virgin strikes me as a little weird . . ."

"Why's that?"

"It means 'mother' in Latin and it's redundant. Everybody knows that the Virgin Mary was Jesus's mother. Why did the painter put 'mother' when it was obvious who she was? The inscriptions to identify saints are pretty common, especially when the artist wasn't able to differentiate them with his brush; that happened a lot in the Romanesque period. But in our paintings everyone would have been able to recognize the Virgin Mary, and Saint George stepping on a dragon, and Saint John the Baptist holding a scroll, which alludes to the Old Testament. They are all unmistakable; there's no room for doubt and no need to identify anyone."

"Maybe the artist wanted to reinforce the importance of the Virgin."

"I don't think so. The presence of the Virgin dominates the painting. Besides, in ancient painting, patterns are often repeated, and I've never seen an inscription that referred to the Virgin as 'mother.' They always used Mary or Saint Mary. If the artist was using 'mother' to refer to the Virgin, he'd have written *Mater Dei,* mother of God."

"What do you make of that?"

"That *Mater* doesn't refer to *Mater Dei.*"

"To who, then?"

"If the word is on the center painting, it refers to someone found there. And if it's not the mother of the child, then . . ."

"The mother of the mother!"

"Yes, and the mother of the Virgin was . . ."

Religion wasn't my best subject, but the answer came to me like a flash of lightning . . . maybe it was my memory, or maybe it was intuition.

"Saint Ann."

We looked at each other, our eyes wide with surprise.

"Santa Anna!" I exclaimed. "The church of Santa Anna."

Santa Anna. The church where Enric and Alicia's neo-

Templars met. Did the inscription on the painting really have something to do with that church or did we just want to see the connection? It was too much of a coincidence. Or was it another fake clue that Enric put into the painting? We ruled that out. Oriol had verified that the pigments used in each part of the paintings and the inscription were from the Middle Ages.

My intuition told me that the church of Santa Anna was crucial. Although I thought it was possible I was just seizing on that idea as my only hope for continuing the adventure.

"Let's accept that possibility as a working hypothesis," concluded Oriol, after a long debate during which he tried to rein in my enthusiasm. And his own.

I reproached him because just minutes before he had been defending intuition and instinct as a source of knowledge and now he was getting scientific. I knew that he was right, that we needed a working method, but debate is one of my strong points. And I felt like recovering my advantage with some pointless arguing for a little while.

While I had Oriol engaged in a debate that I already knew was futile, I kept looking over at the paintings trying to find any other strange details.

"The arches!" I suddenly shouted out.

Oriol looked at me, disconcerted. What did the arches have to do with the dispute between intuition and method?

"The arches," I repeated. "Usually the chapel arches on the upper part of the lateral paintings would be the same. Don't you think? That's something out of place."

"Yeah, it sure is," he said. "That foiled arch, the one on the right—it caught my eye from the very beginning."

"Is it that strange?"

"Yeah, it is, very much so . . . I think it's time to go back to the church of Santa Anna. You'll come with me, right?"

I closed my eyes for a few seconds, trying to figure out

where I was in my life. Oriòl and I were in his room, looking at the paintings that supposedly held the clues to the treasure, and next door, in my room, a jumble of scattered clothes were waiting for me to put them in suitcases and accompany me back to the Big Apple. And now, Oriol had just asked me if I would go with him to continue deciphering this mystery. And what could I say?

"Yes," I said.

I realized that, as my mother would say, I had just thrown away my future again. Neither the new commitment I had just made with the firm nor the old one I had made to Mike held me back from saying "yes, I do," again tying the knot with adventure.

CHAPTER 52

The dawn was radiant. It promised to be one of those summer days where the Mediterranean breeze blesses Barcelona with clear air and mild temperatures. The sun came through my window and, stretching beneath its warm caress, I remembered the primal dawn the morning of Saint John's Night, the pandemonium, the skinny-dipping, and all the rest . . . I wouldn't mind doing it again. The city buzzed with activity below, with the blues of the sea and the sky as a backdrop. I saw a shiny airplane making its descent and suddenly it seemed like a bad omen, reminding me of New York, where "my responsibilities" awaited my return. I felt like I was cutting school. I should enjoy it, I said to myself as I ran toward the shower, imagining myself having breakfast with Oriol downstairs in the rose garden. Steaming coffee, fresh croissants, toast, butter, jam . . . and him. My mouth was watering. Carpe diem, I shouted, as an alibi and an antidote against regrets.

We entered through the portico on the south side of the transept, the short arm of the Latin cross that created the shape of the building. On my previous visits I hadn't even noticed the arches, but now they were the focus of my undivided attention.

We situated ourselves in the crossing, below the dome, and suddenly it became obvious that there was only one point in the church from which you could see the three chapels lined up as in the paintings: the apse. The presbytery in the center is much larger than the side chapels. To the left is the Chapel of the Holy Sepulcher and to the right the Chapel of the Most Holy.

"Remember the paintings," Oriol whispered to me. "There are three, and each one, in the manner of the period, has an arch on the upper part, as if it were an oratory. The first chapel, the one on the right with Jesus Christ resurrecting, has a barrel arch, slightly pointed, showing the transition between the Romanesque and the Gothic. The arch doesn't sit on a corbel, instead it rests uninterrupted on a pillar."

"Just like the chapel here on the left," I said excitedly. "Look, it matches the dedication. The Chapel of the Holy Sepulcher in the painting and the Chapel of the Holy Sepulcher in the corresponding place inside the church."

Oriol, smiling and nodding, continued, "The center painting has a similar arch, but it rests on a small border and has another, more pointed, arch above it."

"That matches too."

"And finally, remember that the painting on the right has a strange arch with a center foil. Foiled arches were typical in this style of the period, but they have several foils, not just one as in the painting. And what do we see here, on the right?"

"The Chapel of the Most Holy, but there are a couple of small vaults made up of surbased arches, which rest on corbels that in turn rest on the thick side walls and on the thinner middle wall."

"But if you wanted to draw those vaults from the front, they would appear as surbased arches, and the central wall would look like a column. Don't you think?"

"True."

"So if you take out the dividing column, you have something very similar between the painting and the church. So, it wasn't an arch with a single foil, but rather the common support for two surbased arches that rested on the same corbel. Besides, remember that in the painting the longer post of the cross coincides exactly with where the column is here. It actually represents this small wall."

"Could it be a coincidence?" I asked, just to provoke him.

"No. Hell no!" he exclaimed enthusiastically. "It's no coincidence. The painter did it on purpose. The paintings are a map of this church. The chapels on the painting are representations of the real ones here, looking from the nave to the apse. It's here, Cristina."

We decided to arm ourselves with as much information as possible about Santa Anna, which meant analyzing the most minor details. We divided up the work. I would look in modern sources and he, given his profession, would go to the ancient documents.

I gathered any writing that mentioned the building and its history, from tourist guides of the city to dense academic volumes on Catalan Gothic architecture. Oriol, because of his family ties to the church, already knew a lot about it and supplied me with a real jewel: a thick book on Santa Anna, recently published and of very limited distribution. Everything we could possibly want to know would be in there. I was going to become an expert on that church.

Oriol responded to my enthusiastic statement with a sarcastic smile that surprised me, and left me feeling both somewhat insulted and blissful. He's so handsome, and so pedantic, I said to myself.

The following days were entirely devoted to reading and visiting the church, where we frequently saw Arnau d'Estopinyá. Sometimes he'd respond to my greeting, other times he just grunted. But he never gave in to my attempts to strike up a conversation for more than a couple of sentences.

I'm tempted to, but I won't bore you with all the details of everything I read about Santa Anna. Its documented history seems to begin in the year 1141, as a result of the Aragonese King Alfonso I who gave his entire kingdom to the Temple, Hospital, and Holy Sepulcher orders. In that year, Canon Carfillius came, on behalf of the Knights of the Holy Sepulcher, to negotiate with the heir to the crown by marriage, the count of Barcelona Ramón Berenguer IV, who agreed to exchange goods and privileges with the three military orders so he could get the kingdom back.

So the Holy Sepulcher order found itself, from one day to the next, with vast possessions in Catalonia and Aragon, among which was Santa Anna, a church on the outskirts of Barcelona where the order decided to establish a monastery dedicated to the saint. The monastery went on to have additional possessions in Mallorca and Valencia. It had a hectic, turbulent history, beginning with its early days of splendor and wealth then its centuries of decline, where it stopped being a monastery and became a collegiate church, and then finally a parish church. The church's substantial possessions were sold off over time, including the surrounding plots of land. The church was sacked and closed down during the Napoleonic invasion, desecrated by armed groups, and closed to the public in 1873 during the First Republic, then burned and plundered in 1936 during the Second Republic. It was then, just as Artur had told me, that the new church was blown up. The only remains of that stylized neo-Gothic building are some walls that mark the limits of one of the sides of the Plaza Ramón Amadeu.

* * *

Oriol alternated between his work and his research and we'd get together at night, or when we found the time, to compare notes.

In our first meeting I conveyed my enthusiasm for a photo that showed the inside of the church after the fire: a gigantic flared cross appeared in the remains of an altar that must have been hiding it.

"Our grandfathers gathered here," declared Oriol emphatically. "And unlike the Order of the Holy Sepulcher, our sect has always been secret."

The current group of buildings was built over the centuries. There are documents showing that the presbytery and the transept were built between 1169 and 1177, the nave and some of the chapels in the thirteenth century, others like the Chapel of the Holy Sepulcher and the main portico in the fourteenth, the cloister and the chapter house in the fifteenth century, and the Chapel of the Most Holy in the sixteenth and modified in the twentieth.

But soon I realized that there was an anachronism between the painting and the construction. If the Chapel of the Most Holy wasn't built until the sixteenth century, how could an oratory appear on the right-hand painting? Did we have the wrong church? Besides, in spite of the coincidence of the Chapel of the Holy Sepulcher in both the painting and the church, that chapel was from the fourteenth century, too late for the painter, and none of the other chapels matched in terms of saints. In the presbytery, on the main altar, the patron saint, Ann, is worshipped. She is shown in an image with her arms wide open, protecting her daughter and grandson. That's where she should be. And although the images are modern, which makes sense after the fire in the last century, it must have always been that way: the main altar dedicated to the patron saint. What's more, the right

chapel, the modern one, the Most Holy, doesn't show any cru-
cifixion. Although it does show a pietà framed in a contempo-
rary mural. So there were elements that fit, but many more that
didn't. I was discouraged. It seemed we were following a false
lead again.

"We bought our own fantasies, Oriol," I said to him when
we met and I explained all of the above to him.

"Buildings as old as this weren't always the way you see
them now, and certain things aren't always in the same place,"
he replied. "Besides, Santa Anna hasn't been studied enough."

"You think the books about the church are wrong?"

"In some respects. To begin with, the oldest parts of the
church aren't the presbytery and the transept. They're just the
first documented. When the Order of the Holy Sepulcher took
possession of Santa Anna, it already existed. If not, they'd have
called it the monastery of the Holy Sepulcher and not Santa
Anna."

I nodded in agreement.

"Now, where would the old building of Santa Anna be?"

I shrugged my shoulders.

"Come with me."

We went to the church and he led me by the hand to the
presbytery.

"Do you see something strange about the windows?"

On the wall of the apse, high up behind the large altar,
there is a large Gothic stained-glass window. Farther down,
there are two thin windows with pointed arches, which are
at the same height and similar to the three windows on the
right-hand, south-facing wall.

"I see windows on the right wall, but none on the left."

"And what else?"

I had another good look around before answering.

"Apart from the large window up high," I concluded, "none
of the other windows of the presbytery opens onto the outside.

The ones in the back connect to the vestry and the three on the right with the Chapel of the Most Holy."

"And what does that tell you?"

"That when they built the apse, all the windows opened onto the outside. And that there are no windows on the north side, to the left, because there was another building there. Maybe the original church of Santa Anna."

"Exactly. What's today the Chapel of the Holy Sepulcher was the original church, which must have been built during the eleventh century, in the Romanesque style."

"So why do the modern researchers date it to the fourteenth century?"

"Because they don't know what happened and they are evaluating the construction based on what can be seen today. The old Romanesque chapel collapsed in the fire of 1936, like many other parts of the church and the dome, which blew up and turned into a gigantic chimney. The reconstruction has a pointed barrel arch, like the presbytery and the transept, but the original was probably not as pointed. What's more, I found some blueprints of the church, dated 1859 by an architect named Miguel Garriga, and they show a structure of walls in the Chapel Del Perdons, as it was called then, completely different from the rest of the church walls. They were thicker and had niches, most likely to hold images of saints.

"And the part to the left of the presbytery, the chapel known today as the Chapel of the Most Holy, didn't exist in the thirteenth century because the windows faced the outside. What was built there in the sixteenth century was the vestry. But there were two oratories in that period, whose structure, covered with two small Gothic crossing vaults, we can see today in the entrance to that chapel. They appear in the painting represented by that surbased arch, what we thought was a foil, just above the cross, but which actually represents the two oratories. The main, porticoed entrance is just beside it. It is dated thirteen hundred and its Gothic style seems to coincide with the style of the oratories, so we can assume they were built at the same time."

"So that Arnau, if we're to still believe in him, must have seen four arches, not three like in the paintings."

"That's true. Triptychs were common in Gothic painting, and groups of four just didn't exist. So they put it all into three. The chapel located to our left represents the Chapel of the Holy Sepulcher, with a triumphant Christ resurrecting, holding a staff with the patriarchal cross, the Templar cross, on one end. In the center, which corresponds in size to the presbytery, we have the Virgin; however, the word *Mater* seems to refer to Santa Anna. Following in the same direction, the two oratories from before the fire of 1936 are shown. At that time the first one held the Virgin of the Star, a Gothic sculpture similar to the Madonna on the center painting, and the second one opened into the vestry. And guess who that last oratory was dedicated to."

I waited for his answer.

"To Jesus on the cross," he said, smiling. "There used to be a large cross with a life-size image."

"Like in the paintings," I whispered.

CHAPTER 53

We left the church so we could speak freely, and walking on Calle Santa Anna toward the Ramblas, Oriol continued.

"Assuming that Arnau really had something to do with the ring and the paintings, like my father says in his story—which seems to be based on oral history—and taking into account that part of the portico and the oratories were built around 1300, Arnau must have seen the Church of Santa Anna just as it's reflected in the paintings. The Templars weren't persecuted until 1307, and according to the files, Arnau d'Estopinyá lived till at least 1328, a year after the death of James II."

"It all fits together," I said, convinced. "Someone from the period who knew the church could identify it in the paintings."

"The story would have gone like this," he continued. "Arnau sailed his galley northward instead of south. Unlike the Hospital order, the Templars always had good relations with the monks of the Order of the Holy Sepulcher. It was a much smaller order and there was no reason for them to have rivalries like they had with the Hospitallers. Besides, the Knights of the Holy Sepulcher didn't have a military arm in Catalonia. They were regular clerics. Brothers Lenda and Saguardia had already made an agreement with the commander of the Order of the Holy Sepulcher in Barcelona over the custody of the treasure, and Arnau d'Estopinyá went to shore on a beach near the city, avoiding both the Temple headquarters, located very close to the shipyards, and no doubt under surveillance, and the port of Can Tunis, located on the southern side of Montjuïc and a castle well protected by the king's troops. He allowed only his Saracen galley slaves to see to whom he handed over his cargo and then, on the way back, he had their throats slit so they wouldn't talk after arriving in Peñíscola. He had good reason to fear that the agents of the Inquisition or the king would interrogate his crew. The monks of the Holy Sepulcher order, on the other hand, were free of suspicion and they moved the treasure to their monastery, keeping it in their church, which was then known as Santa Anna. The monastery was located outside Barcelona's walls, so it had its own defenses, but right around that time they were building the second wall to encircle the city, which would end up enclosing Santa Anna within it. I don't know if the wall already protected the fiefdom of the Holy Sepulcher order then, but the monks definitely either had their own door, since their monastery ended up sharing a border with the city's defenses, or they had the privilege of entering without being subject to taxation or searches. That meant they wouldn't have had to give any explanations."

"Or maybe it didn't happen that way," I said.

"Maybe not. Maybe they brought the treasure by land from Miravet Castle. But the final result would be the same."

"Okay, fine. The Templar treasure is in the Church of Santa Anna. And now what do we do?"

Oriol scratched his head. We were in the middle of the Ramblas, surrounded by the brilliance of that summer afternoon and the colorful crowds. He stopped in front of one of the flower stands and, taking a bouquet of multicolored flowers, handed it to me, adding a little spice with a kiss on the lips. I was surprised, given Oriol's coolness in the last few days. But I got my reflexes back immediately and threw my arms around his neck in a passionate embrace.

"We'll have to look for it," he said once we pulled apart. "Don't you think?" He smiled and I saw the happiness in his almond-shaped blue eyes.

"We'll have to," I agreed.

Hand in hand we wandered down the Ramblas, talking about this and that, laughing over nothing, maybe just because we were living that moment of happiness. What did the treasure matter? I asked myself. But what treasure? What treasure were we talking about?

We enjoyed the afternoon, the city, and the night. The next dawn found us seated, naked on Oriol's rumpled bed, with the window open over a hushed Barcelona, looking at the paintings, lit by a pair of small lamps.

After a period of silence, I broke Oriol's state of deep meditation. He seemed to be trying to use his mental powers to extract the paintings' secrets, but I wanted to review my own ideas out loud.

"So, we know that the triptych is a map of the church," I said. "Now we have to find where it leads."

"Yes," he admitted contemplatively.

"We have to find anything unusual—"

"The placing of the baby Jesus to the Virgin's right," he interrupted. "I told you before that that was unusual. The vast majority of Gothic Virgins from that period of the kingdom of Aragon, both in painting and sculpture, were depicted with the child sitting on her left. But not this one."

"Another clue."

"Exactly. Also, the child usually appears engaged in various activities—holding a book, playing with birds, offering fruit to his mother. The most common is blessing."

"That's what he's doing in my painting."

"No. Take a closer look. He's not blessing. The blessing is done with the index and middle fingers of the right hand raised. Like in the left-hand painting where Jesus is coming out of the holy sepulcher."

"The child is only raising his index finger."

"Exactly, he's not blessing, he's pointing."

"But, to what? He's pointing toward the sky and slightly to his left, but not anywhere in particular," I said. And I added thoughtfully, "He must be representing the promise of the kingdom of Heaven to believers . . ."

"No. Look closely. I just saw it."

Oriol turned the painting of the Chapel of the Holy Sepulcher on its nonexistent hinges, closing it like a window over the central painting.

"Where's the child's finger now?"

I looked at the angle created by the two paintings in that position.

"He's pointing to the inside of the tomb, the holy sepulcher."

"Inside a tomb, in the chapel to the left of the main altar of the church of Santa Anna in Barcelona," recited Oriol. "The Chapel of the Knights of the Holy Sepulcher, the Chapel Del Perdons."

It seemed very far-fetched, but it made sense. I tried to remember the church.

"Are you sure the treasure's there?" I asked finally.

Oriol shrugged his shoulders.

"It's the only possibility we've got left."

"And how can we get them to let us dig in the church floor?"

"I'll talk to my mother," replied Oriol. "I'm sure she'd be able to convince the parish priest to let us explore that chapel.

She and the presiding 'brotherhood' are the church's main benefactors. And you should definitely cancel your return trip. You're not going to leave me alone in this, are you . . . ? Remember, we made a vow to not abandon each other."

What a rhetorical question. Leave him alone? Even if all the arches, vaults, columns, and voussoirs in that damn church were about to collapse, giving up this adventure would be the last thing I'd do.

CHAPTER 54

We spent many wonderful nights in his room, deciphering the mysteries of each other's bodies and souls, since the paintings were no longer a valid excuse. My room was still a mess of suitcases to pack . . . or unpack.

And we talked, about our first kiss, the sea, our lost letters, and about what had happened recently. The sexy siren that Oriol had turned down the night of Saint John's happened to be one of his students at the university. He said that because of that and because I was there as his guest, he thought it wouldn't be very classy to go frolic with her in the forest. He knew Susi, the transvestite from the Pastís bar, through one of the charitable organizations he was involved with. He went along with her joke about having a ménage à trois because he was amused by my shocked expression. Laughing, he assured me that he wasn't into transvestites. Then he got serious, telling me that even if he was into that, he wouldn't sleep with Susi; she had AIDS and the goal of the charitable organization was to help those affected by the disease who had no means of support. He did it in honor of his father. I was appalled. How could someone in that condition sell her body? It was dangerous. Why didn't someone do something to prevent it? Oriol shrugged his shoulders, saying that maybe I was right but that in spite of having "that," Susi was still a person, with all her rights, who was free and who suffered, who needed to work to eat and love to live. I acknowledged that all that was true. But I wasn't convinced; we all have our fears. I also wasn't satisfied with his explanation about the joke; I really let him have it about his terrible sense of humor.

The days we spent searching the church were unforgettable. We enjoyed a magnificent Barcelona, the beginning of summer and of our love. It was love that made all the rest marvelous. I stopped using the phone, completely disconnecting myself from the United States. But first I made a call asking for the nearly impossible, more time away from the firm. And another to warn Mike that our relationship was in trouble and that I was sending him the ring by courier service. It was a long, painful conversation and at the end of it, he still refused to give up.

And finally I talked to María del Mar, who was saddened, but resigned to the relentless twists of fate we simple mortals are unable to escape no matter how hard we try. I told her not to worry, that I was having a fabulous time with Oriol and that she shouldn't be concerned about not hearing from me for a few days; I'd be okay. Much better than okay.

We visited Santa Anna frequently, closely inspecting even the slightest details.

"The church has a crypt," Oriol told me one morning.

"A crypt?" I inquired. "An underground chapel?"

"Yeah, I'm sure of it. The original church of Santa Anna must have been built in the mid-eleventh century, only about fifty years after Almanzor devastated Barcelona, taking everything of value in the city and thousands of slaves. The Moorish incursions were still common and the fear of more looting was only logical. Normally a church like this, located outside the protection of the city's walls, would have not only its own walls of defense but also a hiding spot for objects of worship and value, in case of siege."

"But that's pure conjecture."

"No, it's not. I found very old documentation that mentions the crypt of Saint Joseph."

"And where would it be?"

"Under the Chapel of the Holy Sepulcher," he declared.

"Why?"

"Because it's the oldest and most venerated part. In the past, the oratory of the Chapel of the Holy Sepulcher had pilgrim shells on the outside, sculpted into the stones of its walls, referring to the pardon given in that chapel, similar to the forgiveness obtained by making the pilgrimage to the holy sepulcher in Jerusalem. Imagine the spiritual and economic importance of that indulgence for the monastery. In the reconstruction following the church's fire in 1936, during which the old roof collapsed, the shells and other structural elements of the chapel disappeared. But it's very likely that anything hidden under the floor is still there. No one today knows that the crypt exists, or where it's located, but no collapse or fire would have been able to affect it, except maybe to hide its entrance. I'm sure that somewhere beneath these stones there's a secret crypt and I bet it's right below the chapel once known as Del Perdons."

With the help of steel levers, the sacristan, and a small crane like those used in minor construction, we were able to move the chapel's tombstone, which had a clergyman sculpted into it. The result was disappointing. Bones. Oriol's brilliant theory crumbled. He said we should lift up the floor, but the priest refused. The fact that Alicia's neo-Templars were an important economic contributor to the church didn't make the priest

change his mind. Years earlier, they had installed a heating system for the nave under the floor and countless human remains
were uncovered. It was very embarrassing. No, he would not
allow any excavations.

"If there was an entrance through this chapel it must have
been blocked during its many restorations," said Oriol to himself.

So we tried the same thing in the presbytery.

In order to do it, we had to move the pews from the apse
and we discovered four stelae with double-armed crosses and
cardinal's symbols on the sides of the main altar. We assumed
that it was the tomb of cardinals who had been parish priests in
the church, but when we lifted up the first two, the ones closest to the Chapel of the Holy Sepulcher, we found them empty.
When we got to the third, our hopes were rewarded when a
narrow staircase, with deep steps that sank into the darkness,
appeared before us.

"The entrance to the crypt!" I exclaimed. I looked at Oriol
and could see the excitement in his eyes.

He lit a candle and prepared to go down. That seemed silly
and old-fashioned to me, so I told him that he'd be better off
with one of the flashlights we'd brought along.

"It's for the oxygen," he informed me. "Many people have
died going down into wells or underground spaces without
taking this precaution. Carbon dioxide and other gases heavier
than air tend to concentrate in places like this. You have to carry
the candle at waist height. If it goes out, that's a sign that you
can't breathe down there."

My lover was a true Boy Scout. Always prepared. I was
ready to follow him, armed with a flashlight. He went down
facing outward, supporting himself on the walls and roof,
but the stairs were so narrow and steep that I decided to

descend facing the stairs, grabbing the steps with my hands. The idea of tumbling down into that eerie darkness was not appealing.

It was a somewhat smaller place than the apse, with a barrel vault resting on a low wall that gave the space a maximum height of about eight feet. At the back, there was only a stone altar and farther in, on the wall, a large patriarchal cross painted in red. The same one that the Templars and the Knights of the Holy Sepulcher shared. Oriol's candle was still burning and he left it on top of the altar where some small chests rested.

"They might be relics of Saint Ann, Saint Philomena, or the *lignum crucis,* an actual piece of the cross, which was stored in the church after the war," stated Oriol.

"It doesn't look like there's any treasure here," I said.

Oriol didn't respond and began to explore the ground with his flashlight, in search of gravestones. Every once in a while he stopped to read signs carved on some of the stones.

"The cardinals must be buried here," he said finally, pointing to some stelae at his feet. He seemed disappointed.

The sacristan and the father came down, also armed with flashlights, and helped us search. The tombstones in the crypt held only bones. That seemed to be the end of the hunt.

Oriol suggested that we resign ourselves, but asked the priest's permission to continue looking through the crypt, just us alone, at night, promising that everything would be in its place for the first mass the next day. The old priest, with a string of warnings, acquiesced reluctantly. Oriol invited me to go have a bite to eat outside first. I wasn't in the mood. Poking around under tombstones didn't exactly whet my appetite and I didn't feel very well. He insisted; we had to get our strength back.

* * *

"A shell. Did you notice it?" said Oriol suddenly, in the restaurant. "There was a pilgrim's shell engraved in one of the stones on the left wall of the crypt. The slab is almost as large as a tombstone. A man could easily fit through the hole."

"And what does that mean?"

"Remember? That's the sign of the Chapel Del Perdons, what's now the Chapel of the Holy Sepulcher." His eyes shone with enthusiasm. "Like the ones that were on the outside of the oratory but disappeared after the civil war."

"And . . . ?"

"Why would they carve a pilgrim's shell in a crypt underneath the apse, which theoretically has nothing to do with the neighboring chapel Del Perdons?"

"To show that they're related?" I asked, unsure.

"Of course." A victorious smile played across his lips. "It has to be the entrance to another crypt, the older one. The one we couldn't find from the surface. It has to be there."

We ate our dinner hurriedly in order to return to our search. We approached the church from Calle Rivadeneyra, entering through the passageway beside the parochial house that opens onto the cloister. Seeing the cloister so dark as we crossed in front of the chapter house, I felt a shudder remembering my previous encounter there with Arnau d'Estopinyá.

Once we were alone, thanks to the crowbars and after a couple of attempts, the slab with the engraving of the pilgrim's shell began to move and it wasn't too hard to remove it. A stale vapor came from the black opening and Oriol brought one of the candles near it, placing it on the ground, at the entrance to the hole. He stopped a moment to look at me. He smiled, we held hands and kissed. I felt my heart beating wildly. Was the legendary Templar treasure hidden in the darkness?

Oriol made the gallant gesture of letting a lady go through the door first. I realized that in spite of my curiosity I didn't relish the idea of going in there. I looked at the candle burning steadily at my feet. I asked Oriol to go in with me. We held hands, and saying carpe diem to myself, we ducked into the hole. I carried the candle in front of me and below my waist. I relaxed when I saw that it didn't go out. Then I had to lift it above my head to be able to see. Oriol immediately helped me with the flashlight. It was a room quite a bit smaller than the previous one. It had round arches on the ceiling, which rested on the walls and on a central set of three columns that Oriol later told me could be Visigothic. But at the moment, that detail meant nothing. Seeing the contents of the catacomb Oriol cried out, "The treasure!"

CHAPTER 55

I shivered with excitement. Sure enough, we found ourselves in the central part of a small crypt, in a space that was clear but was surrounded by trunks and, farther ahead, a ton of small chests piled up against the wall.

I put my candle on top of one of the large chests and asked Oriol if we should open one. He shined a light on the one closest to me and I pulled at the creaky lid with all my strength. It was empty. Oriol opened another one . . . empty too. Empty, empty, empty . . . all six large chests were empty.

"There's nothing!" I said to Oriol, heartbroken, and he looked at me, crushed.

"I suspect that there is something," he replied after thinking for a few seconds. "There's no gold and silver, but I think the treasure that was most valuable to the Templars is still here. Let's look in the small chests."

There were many of them, and they were lovely. Some were metal with Limoges-type enamel, others were carved with small ivory figures, or covered with damascene work, or made of wood with plaster relief and paintings similar to mine, the one that had brought us here.

"I'm sure that these are still full," Oriol assured me.

I opened one expecting to see the gleam of gold and precious stones, but instead I found a skull that still had dried skin and hair stuck to the bones.

"Oh my God," I exclaimed apprehensively. "These are human remains."

Oriol, who'd already opened two other chests, turned his flashlight toward me and said, "They're relics." He picked up a wooden box with saints painted on it in the Romanesque style. On the lid there was a cross identical to the one in my ring. I shined the light on my ruby. I felt a strange vibration in its blood red stone.

"No doubt about it, we found the lost treasure of the Temple order," said Oriol before opening the small chest.

Inside it were more bones, some still with leathery skin attached.

"In the chronicles of the church that I looked over, they say that in the fifteenth century the Order of the Holy Sepulcher was dissolved and the monastery became an Augustinian collegiate church. Monks no longer lived here, just regular canons without vows of chastity. They were disciplined on numerous occasions for their dissolute lives. They spent amounts that were inconceivable for a mendicant order. The gardens, rents, and charity that the community received didn't allow for even a hundredth part of that extravagance. When I read that, I became convinced that the treasure had been here and the monetary part of it was squandered about a hundred years after Arnau died. But for the Templars, the relics of the saints were much more valuable than gold and silver, and surely the Augustinian canons respected them, or even feared them. So it was unlikely they'd shop with them around."

"I'm not surprised they had reservations. Let's get out of here," I begged. "This is a cemetery."

I felt nauseated. Suddenly I was overcome by a superstitious fear, as if we had desecrated a tomb, as if we should be punished for it. I needed to get out, but I wanted Oriol to come with me. I didn't feel up to facing the gloomy church alone.

But I was wrong. It wasn't darkness that awaited us, but a light aimed right into our eyes, and a familiar voice.

"Well, well, Cristina, I thought you were already back in America." I recognized Artur's sarcastic tone as he kindly took my hand to help me out of that catacomb.

I counted one, two, three of his thugs with flashlights and revolvers in their hands. Oriol, who was following me, also had guns pointed at him.

"You thought you had me fooled, right?" Artur spat out in a tone very different from the one he had used with me before. "I always get suspicious when someone pays too much for something. And especially when they know the market value. How could you think I'd swallow that bait?"

"There's no gold, just relics," I hastened to say. I thought that maybe we could save ourselves again if he were convinced that the value of what was down below wasn't worth the risk of killing us.

"No, dear," he told me. "I've heard enough of your conversation. Dozens of chests, reliquaries from the twelfth and thirteenth centuries. Metal covered with Limoges enamel, plastered and painted boxes in the Romanesque and Gothic styles. Small trunks with figures carved in ivory. That's a fortune for an antiques dealer."

"What are you going to do with the relics?" asked Oriol.

"We'll leave the carrion where it is," he replied quickly. "And that includes you."

It seemed that this time we'd be out of luck. Who had he bribed to get in there? Or did he have more keys? It didn't matter; whoever had helped him wasn't going to help us now. But my brain went into high gear trying to think of a way to get out of this situation. I saw my own corpse, next to Oriol's, lying in the darkness on top of the remains of all those saints dumped from their chests, piled in a corner and locked up forever in the secret crypt.

"I have money, if that's what you want," offered Oriol.

"I don't want your money." Artur looked at him with an expression of disgust, his dignity offended. "Don't you understand? This could be the biggest discovery of medieval art in this century. Besides, I'm not in the kidnapping business."

"But you're in the murdering business?" I asked angrily. I didn't know how I could ever have been attracted to this fatuous, snobby, rich jerk.

"I'm sorry, sweetheart," he replied, pretending to feel bad. "But sometimes that comes with the territory."

"Artur, there has to be some other solution," Oriol negotiated. "Take what you want, hold us somewhere until there's nothing left. No one knows this crypt exists, nothing in it is cataloged, no one can accuse you of anything. We promise, we swear, that we'll never say anything. Take it all."

Artur let his gaze drift into the darkness, toward the ceiling, pretending to think it over.

"No, sorry," he said after a few seconds that seemed an eternity. "I'm truly sorry, not for you but for her, but I know that as soon as you stopped being afraid you would turn me in. I'd never be able to enjoy the loot in peace. It's not just about money. I'll keep the best pieces for myself, just for the pleasure of owning them."

He spoke softly. In spite of the situation we all felt a strange respect for the church.

He was going to kill us. I'd have begged if I thought it would do us any good, but Oriol had tried that, probably for my sake, and it hadn't worked. Perhaps I'd have said something if anything reasonable had crossed my mind, but fear was beginning to take hold. I looked with panic into the black hole we had just come out of.

"I'm sorry, but I don't have more time to chat. Please, go on down. If you don't make a scene, no one will suffer unnecessarily."

They won't get me down there alive, I thought. My hand sought out Oriol's and grabbed it hard. It was cold, almost as ice cold as my own. We had to do something, we couldn't die without trying something. I didn't feel as if I could do anything at that moment, but I squeezed his hand tightly and moved closer to him. I was sure Oriol would react in some way, and I'd follow him till my last breath.

"We're not going down." His voice sounded firm, but tense.

"You've got to understand, Bonaplata," replied Artur, as if complaining about Oriol's lack of civility. "It's just so we won't make a mess in the church."

I'd thought that Artur wanted us to go down with his henchmen so he wouldn't have to watch us die. Maybe he still had some remnants of a conscience.

Just when I thought he was going to give the order for our execution, we heard a scream from the church. It was one of the thugs. Flashlights moved in that direction, illuminating a terrible scene. One of the thugs was struggling with someone who was holding him by the jaw, from behind. Then, a flash of steel and a gush of blood was spurting out of his neck. A shot resounded like a bomb in the closed space. The thug was shooting into the void. I immediately recognized his attacker: Barbablanca. Arnau d'Estopinyá had just cut the thug's jugular and let his body fall to the ground, bleeding to death. God, I thought. He knows how to slit people's throats, just like in the dream. But there was little time to think because the other two thugs began shooting at Arnau. Oriol let go of my hand and threw himself onto one of the shooting men, trying to grab his gun. I saw Artur searching for something in his jacket. I was in a good position and almost without thinking kicked him right where the fly of his pants met with the seat. Bam! Just like in Tabarca. He let out a shriek, his hands covering his wounded parts, late again. Arnau tried to grab the pistol from his victim's hand, but Arnau fell to the ground, shot down about six feet from the flashlight that lit up the carnage. Oriol struggled, holding his opponent's gun with both hands, but the thug wouldn't let go.

"Get out, Cristina!" he shouted to me. "Get away, now." I could see his opponent give him a head butt in the face.

I hesitated for a second. I couldn't leave him alone. I remembered our Templar vow. But I realized that if I managed to get out, they wouldn't dare kill him. So, in almost complete darkness, since only one of the thugs still had his flashlight, I started running toward the door that opens onto the cloister, with the hope that the two wrought-iron gates to Calle Rivadeneyra were also open. That was how we had come in, but when I was already halfway through the nave I remembered that we had closed the gates, that we had left open only the door that connected the church with the cloister and that it was Oriol who had the keys. How had they gotten in? Through the vestry, like I had the first time? It was too late to go back.

"Don't let her get away," said Artur in a weak, but audible, voice.

The thug's flashlight searched for me and the bang of another shot echoed in the sacred site.

"Stop or I'll shoot," yelled the man who had just done so.

I felt the hairs on my neck rising and my knees weakening for an instant, but I continued fleeing toward the trap the cloister had become. I told myself that the darkness of the sanctuary was working in my favor. But that hopeful thought lasted only a few seconds. In spite of the darkness at that end of the church, I had managed to reach the door, with a good lead on my pursuer. Just as I crossed the small wooden vestibule and left the cloister, I smashed right into a man who immediately grabbed me. Artur had another of his henchmen stationed in the shadows.

Then I felt sick. What a sad way for this to end. I made a desperate attempt to break free of my captor, who'd covered my mouth with his hand. Then, I saw more people in the half-light of the cloister. That was when the man holding me said to calm down, that I was safe, that he was a policeman.

I looked for a wall to lean on and realized that I was next to one of the windows that connect the cloister with the chapter house, the one where the neo-Templars performed their rituals. Finally I had to sit on the floor.

What happened next happened very fast. The gunman following me fell into the arms of the same policeman, now joined by a lot more cops who aimed their guns at the thug's head.

Alicia also appeared from the darkness, along with the priest. She'd been the one who'd called the police. It looked like she was in charge. That woman's authority never ceased to surprise me. The captain at the head of the operation asked her to be quiet a couple of times, but everybody, including him, ended up following her directions. She knew what had to be done in each and every moment.

Oriol was bruised and his nose was bleeding, but otherwise he was okay. We hugged each other. The thug still in the church, when he realized what the situation was, threw his gun away. The police never found one on Artur. It's discouraging to think that he got away with just bail and one night in jail. The trial is still pending.

The corpses stayed where they were, in the main hall of the church, a bit before the crossing. They couldn't be moved until the coroner got there.

There was the body of Arnau d'Estopinyá, facedown, in a pool of blood. Scattered around were his dagger, the gun he had snatched from his victim, and a cell phone. It didn't really fit with the old Templar. Later I found out that Alicia had given it to him so he could warn her in case we ran into problems. She said that for Arnau that church was like his home and that he'd spent many a night there in penitence, praying on his knees until he fell asleep on the ground or one of the pews.

He didn't die right away. He had enough time to paint on the floor, with his own blood, a patriarchal cross, the one with four arms, the same one that was everywhere around the church. He died kissing it. I can't help it, but I've always associated him with the historic Arnau. To me they were the same person. What Luis had read in those files, apparently written by Enric based on what he'd heard, intuited, or simply made up, was still the true story of Arnau—the possessed one, the old one, the new, both, one and the same. His crazed gaze had frightened me many times. But when I saw him there, stretched out in a pool of his own blood, my eyes filled with tears. He was a misfit, stuck in the wrong century, a marginalized, lonely, and violent guy, but he was consistent in his insanity, his faith, and his ideals. He didn't hesitate to die for his beliefs. Maybe saving us wasn't his priority, but he did it. He didn't hesitate in offering his only possession as a Poor Knight of Christ: his life, to keep the last treasures of the Temple from falling into heathen hands.

His existence, like that of the other Arnau seven hundred years earlier, hadn't been sweet, or beautiful, or even enlightening, in my opinion. Theirs were tough lives, marked by violence and misfortune. But his last moments had been lovely for a Templar. He died for his faith, in battle against the infidels, saving the life of his companions in arms and in defense of the relics of the martyrs. What more could a Poor Knight of Christ ask for?

Alicia organized a funeral worthy of a hero. The funeral chapel was set up in the chapter house and the coffin was watched over at all times by four knights wearing white capes, the red patriarchal cross on the right shoulder. The same cross that Arnau kissed as he died. He received the posthumous title of Knight Templar and Alicia gave the recognition to the recumbent body. I was also named a Lady of the Temple. The ring gave me that right, but I had already considered myself part of the order from the moment that, jumping into the sea, I had sworn to never abandon Oriol. But what is true is that all those ceremonies, which the attendees take so seriously, still just seem like nonsense to me. The only authentic thing there was Arnau himself. He was the last of the true Templars. And it was ironic that he, who had dedicated his life to that utopian dream, had only been able to wear the dark cape of a sergeant during his lifetime, while those who were rich or of noble birth, without more merit than he, wore the white cape of a knight. What a farce.

Even so, I was moved by the funeral ceremony, which I attended with Oriol at my side. A thought came to me. It was then and there that our ship had finally arrived in Ithaca. The adventure was over.

CHAPTER 56

I'm going to tell this part quickly because it's sad. As sad as the distance that separates reality from dreams.

The days of our second childhood, the days of Enric's posthumous gift of adventure, were behind us. As is often the case, special friends or lovers in exceptional circumstances often don't work once they're back in their daily unexceptional lives. I still love him and he still loves me. We tried, but our love must not have been enough to span the abyss of our differences.

I think our adventure brought us closer. I was no longer the yuppie unable to walk barefoot, if necessary, through life. I accepted that the Susis of this world had a right to live and love too. And I accepted that there were people able to give everything for love, although I wasn't one of them.

He had changed too. He was no longer the contrarian, anarchic, radical man of years earlier. He'd found his father's treasure and with it he'd paid an old debt. I still don't know which of the two, the father or the son, was the creditor and which the debtor. But I am sure that when Oriol closed that chapter, he signed a peace agreement with himself, with the past, and with his memories.

Unfortunately, those changes weren't enough. We were still, he and I, very different. Life had sent us on divergent paths and, as hard as one tries, there is never any going back; time moves in only one direction. The Costa Brava, the storm, and the kiss were now buried forever in the sands of the past.

What a shame.

You're probably wondering what happened to the treasure. Well, I still don't know where it finally will end up and, truthfully, I don't much care, at least personally. I don't want any of those chests. No matter how artistic, historic, and valuable they may be. And much less their contents. The idea of having one of them decorating my apartment in New York gives me the creeps. I'd had enough of that macabre, beautiful ring with its human remains set into it.

It doesn't seem that Oriol, in spite of his passion for the Middle Ages, has any desire to own those historical chests either. He only wants to be able to study them.

He's convinced that the treasure was the adventure we lived through. That, and only that, was the inheritance from Enric. Nothing and nobody in the world can take that away from us. And I think he's right.

As Kavafis says:

Ithaca has given you a beautiful voyage . . .
It has no more to give you.
And if you find it lacking . . .
With the wisdom you have acquired from so many experiences,
You'll understand what the Ithacas mean.

But not everyone thinks the same way.

The police's intervention made the discovery public and that opened up a can of worms. The diocese of Barcelona considered that such a finding, made inside a church, belonged to them. But in its day it had been part of the monastery of Santa Anna, of the Order of the Holy Sepulcher, which still has its headquarters in Catalonia, and its rights . . . But the relics and the chests that hold them belong to the Templar order. Although dissolved by the pope centuries ago, the king of Aragon had ceded the few Templar possessions that were left after the royal plundering to the Order of Saint John of the Hospital, which still exists today under the name the Order of Malta, and they are the legal Templar heirs.

But those chests also represent a historic legacy and the Spanish state has legal authority over them. And since it belongs to the Catalan cultural patrimony, the autonomous regional government has plenty to say about it too.

And let's not forget the authentic, genuine successors of the Poor Knights of Christ. There are hundreds of groups that proclaim themselves the true heirs of the Temple Order. Including Alicia's.

Alicia's very clever and didn't want to get involved with claims of who was the rightful heir to the Templar inheritance . . . what a nest of vipers. But she filed a legal claim for its discovery in Oriol's name and mine. In my opinion, that woman has an unsettling interest in the relics, even more than in their lovely containers. But I don't want to know why.

As a lawyer, I am curious to see how this whole legal mess turns out. Although, if I'm sure of anything at all, it's that Alicia will get most of what she wants. As she always has.

Now, here I am, looking at my bare hand, free of rings, while the plane takes me back to New York. Alone. Who ever said life was simple?

I had sent my engagement ring, with its impressive solitaire, back to Mike when things with Oriol got red hot. The other ring, the beautiful male ruby with its gleaming six-pointed star inside, the one with the Templar cross created by human bone, the one with a bloody shine to it, the one that holds souls in pain, that one I gave to Alicia.

Enric had said in his letter that the ring was for the person I thought most deserved it. And that included myself. "It must be someone very strong of spirit," it said in his note, "because that ring has a life and will of its own." At that moment I didn't give much importance to that warning, but gradually I've learned all about what that ring entails. It scares me. Alicia is the one who deserves it. More than anyone else I know. She deserves to be the grand master of the neo-Templars. She achieved that position without the ring and now she has the historic symbol of her rank. Besides, she knows, better than anyone, what she'll have to contend with.

She smiled at me when I gave it to her. She didn't say thank you then, or any silly formalities like, "No, please, Enric gave it to you, keep it, it's yours." She just slid it on her finger. As if it had always belonged to her. She gave me a hug and two kisses. I'm sure that Alicia has dreamed of herself many times as an ancient Templar. Riding high on a steed, clad in a steel helmet and chain-mail doublet, on her way to the battlefield.

"Thank you," she said after looking at the ring on her hand for a while.

And that's how the mysterious ring, which had led me to the most wonderful time I've ever had, left my hand.

And now, I'm on my way back to New York to continue, one case at a time, my rise on the ladder of success as a lawyer. My parents said they would be waiting for me at the airport and . . . surprise! Mike will be there too, ring in hand, ready to forgive me and take me back, happy that I've gotten over that bad patch. That's how things are.

* * *

The treasure had been found. Arnau had been buried in the very same church of Santa Anna. The days of crazy happiness had come to an end. It was time to be sensible and plan my future.

Come, I said to him. Stay, he said to me. I have a successful career in New York, I told him. I have a job in Barcelona, he replied. What you have here you could find anywhere, I responded, I'm sure you'll find something better in America. A medieval researcher in New York? He laughed without much enthusiasm. But you could be a brilliant lawyer in Barcelona, he added. I argued that the firm where I worked has the best lawyers in the world, that there's no other place where I could learn so much, and go so far. Come, please. Dare to be your woman's man, come on, don't be sexist, I begged him, I never expected that of you.

He answered with tears in his eyes. That's not it, Cristina. You have wings, I have roots. I belong here. This is my culture, my life. I can't leave. Stay, and go as far as you can, with me, in Barcelona.

He came to say good-bye at the airport and we had one last session of trying to convince each other. But it all ended with, "Good-bye, Oriol. We'll see each other soon," I lied, and I still don't know why. "I wish you all the happiness in the world."

"Good-bye, my love. Fly. Catch your dreams," he said.

I spent most of the flight crying. I used up all my tissues, and the ones in the bathroom.

Now I'm walking through a corridor at JFK International Airport. There, beyond immigration and customs, my parents and Mike are waiting, eager to see their lost little sheep return to the fold.

And what could never be stayed behind. A great love. Not a fling. *Love.* Oriol was the first and, if my family had stayed in Barcelona, I'm almost positive he'd also have been the last. But I have to be reasonable. I have to be practical.

Reasonable. Practical. Why?

Why can't I give myself a second chance at that parallel life? My heart wanted to return, my head refused to give up my career in New York. Then I thought that maybe I could succeed professionally in Barcelona. Why not give it a try? Could I live the rest of my life with the doubt, with the grief?

Carpe diem. Hadn't I learned anything? I had lost when negotiating with Oriol. But, okay, sometimes accepting a defeat in time can lead to a victory. I had to try.

And that's why I turned around, went to the counter, and bought a ticket for the next flight to Barcelona.

"Mr. Oriol is not home," replied the maid. I had called as soon as we landed.

"Do you know when he'll be back?" I asked nervously.

"No, I don't, but I can tell you it won't be today, or tomorrow. He's left on a trip without saying when he'll return."

I felt the earth move under my feet and I wished the whole damn airport would collapse on top of me.

Oriol had certainly gotten over my leaving pretty quickly! A trip. With some little girlfriend? Maybe that sexy siren from the beach? And I had come to surprise him, offer him my life, give him everything, my career, my love . . . everything. How stupid. I felt a knot in my throat. I couldn't talk.

"I think he went to New York," added the woman when I didn't say anything.

With a tiny, thin voice I thanked her and hung up.

New York, my God. New York, I said to myself while I looked for a bench to sit down on. I could feel my legs going weak again. He too wanted to give up everything for me.

I looked at my ringless hands for a few moments. With a deep sigh, I closed my eyes and, leaning my head back in my seat, I felt my lips part in a blissful smile.

I saw the image of our ship leaving the port of Ithaca, white sails swollen with wind, to live life's adventure together and face the tests and challenges that the gods put us through. The poems of Kavafis and the music of Llach sounded in my ears. I saw the blue sea at midday on the Costa Brava, and the schools of fish, their gold and silver scales gleaming in the sun, against the green Posidonia grass and the white sands of Tabarca. I tasted the salt in my mouth and I remembered my first kiss, and the storm. I remembered him, my first love. And my last.

But an ill-timed inner voice chimed in: "Maybe . . ."

THE ✠
RING

JORGE MOLIST

An Atria Books Readers Club Guide

SUMMARY

On her twenty-seventh birthday, Cristina Wilson, a promising New York lawyer, receives two rings. The first is a diamond engagement ring from her boyfriend, Mike, a wealthy stockbroker whom Cristina has been dating for the past year. The second, delivered by a strange messenger, is an ancient ruby set in a piece of human bone—a posthumous gift from her godfather, Enric, who died a few years ago. The arrival of the ruby marks the beginning of a life-changing series of events for Cristina, who finds herself assaulted by unsettling visions of the past and enmeshed in a modern blood feud over ancient treasure. With the help of her childhood friends Luis and Oriol, Cristina must follow the clues left behind by Enric to discover the true nature of their inheritance protecting against dangerous rivalries and mysteries resurrected from the past. The three live out an odyssey that reminds them of their childhood adventures together— and the attraction that bound Cristina to Oriol in her adolescent years is rekindled with unstoppable force.

DISCUSSION POINTS

1. This novel carries the epigraph "Hidden in his papal ring, there lives a demon." What does this mean in relation to the novel?

2. Cristina wears two rings. Compare and contrast these pieces of jewelry. What do they each represent? How are they at odds?

3. Cristina sees herself as someone for whom catastrophic events cause a kind of impulsiveness, even arousal. What significant events in the novel have this effect on Cristina, and what does she do as a result? Objects, scents, and sounds often trigger memories. What triggers memories for Cristina, and what does she remember?

4. Were your suspicions aroused when Artur Boix first appeared sitting next to Cristina on the plane? Why or why not? What did you think he was up to?

5. Cristina says that, as a lawyer, she is well trained to pay close attention to detail. Do you agree with this assessment of her? Why or why not?

6. As Alicia examines the Templar ring, she explains that rubies come as male and female, Mars and Venus, and that the temperament of each is different accordingly. Discuss

the many ways in which male and female roles and sexism come into play in this novel.

7. Alicia Núñez is one of the most complicated, mysterious characters in the book. Luis calls her a witch, Cristina's mother doesn't trust her, but the neo-Templars follow her, and Oriol encourages Cristina to share her visions with her. What do you think of Alicia? Did your opinion of her change at various points in the story? Why or why not?

8. When Maria, Cristina's mother, finally reveals her secret, are you surprised? Did you sympathize with her? Explain your opinion. What would you have done in her shoes?

9. The history of celebrating the solstice is an ancient one on the European continent, rich with symbolism and meaning. What effect does the seaside, almost-pagan celebration have on Cristina? How does it change her?

10. What does Brother Arnau mean on page 333 when he tells Cristina that the danger is in Barcelona and that "the Saracens are coming back"?

11. Why do you think Cristina tells her mother that she plans to break off her engagement to Mike, even though she is returning to New York? What, ultimately, was she looking for in Barcelona? Did she find it?

12. There are several serious issues and themes just touched upon in this fast-paced thriller, such as loyalty, marital roles, AIDS and homosexuality, promiscuity, religious devotion, and violence in the name of God. Why do you think the author wove these kinds of questions into the background? What effect do they have on your reading experience?

13. What do you make of the ending? Were you satisfied by the first and final outcomes of the treasure hunt? What has changed for Cristina by the time her grand adventure in Barcelona is over?

ENHANCE YOUR BOOK CLUB EXPERIENCE

The city of Barcelona and islands along the coast of Spain provide a rich backdrop to this historical, romantic, and suspenseful story. Read through a traveler's guide or visit www.spain.info in order to map out the locations visited by Cristina and her companions.

Much has been written about the Poor Knights of Christ, popularly known as the Knights Templar. Do a little research on the members of the Order and see how the historical information available lends credence to (or contradicts) the fictional accounts given in *The Ring*. You can start with *The Templar Revelation,* by Lynn Picknett and Clive Prince, or visit www.templarhistory.com.

Gothic and medieval artwork plays an important role in the novel and in the treasure hunt. Using the internet or art books, choose a selection of religious works from the 13th and 14th centuries portraying Jesus and Mary or the saints, particularly those with relationships to the Templars—Saint George and Saint John the Baptist—and bring copies to share with the members of your book club.

AUTHOR Q&A

You were born in Barcelona. What do you most hope readers will glean from your descriptions of your home city?

Many people consider Barcelona to be one of the most charming cities in the world. I myself live in a different city, but I permanently feel a sweet nostalgia for it. I am hoping that my readers feel Barcelona's charm and that they are able to imagine its lights and shadows, the mystery of its medieval buildings, and its explosion of nineteenth-century creativity, and that they enjoy the Mediterranean vibration of the people, the streets, and the local scenes. In short, I invite my readers to discover and enjoy the magical spirit hidden in this city full of light, which lies between green mountains and blue sea.

You have a successful career as a businessman in the entertainment field. Is writing a novel something you've always wanted to do? What was it that led to your writing _The Ring_ at this particular point in your life?

Writing was my passion when I was a child. But my family did not have the economic means for me to devote my life to literature. So I was persuaded to look for a professional activity that would provide me with a solid financial base. But after graduating with a top engineering degree in Spain, and after working in a nuclear power plant, I realized that I was not happy. I then studied for an MBA and joined a very prestigious USA consumer goods company and, after several years, moved into another great USA company, this one in the entertainment field. I did enjoy my job but I was still not completely happy. So in the spirit of New Year's Day, I wrote the first line of my first novel on the first of January 1996. *The Ring* is my third novel, and it achieved great success in Spain and then in the twenty-five other countries where it was subsequently published.

The history of the Knights Templar and other secretive religious orders of the medieval period have become very popular of late. What attracted you to their story?

The Templar Knights share with Marilyn Monroe, James Dean, and the Titanic a romantic and dramatic aura possessed by those that, at the peak of their beauty and power, suddenly disappear in a tragic way. Not unlike my readers, I too was attracted to the history of the Templars because of its legend. But when I studied it, I discovered that many exaggerations, lies, and pure speculations about them are taken as proven facts. The real story of the Templars is fascinating enough, and there is no need for inventions. The historical part of my novel is as it really happened.

The Ring **delivers as much historical information as it does thrills. What kind of research did you do in preparation for writing this novel?**

I completed very serious research not only into the history of the Templars but into other medieval mysteries as well. I made two fascinating discoveries: the first was about the Christian belief in and use of rings, and the second was finding the original location of the Santa Anna church in Barcelona, which was not previously known. I published my findings in different historical and archaeological magazines, and these articles can be found at jorge@jorgemolist.com.

You are a man, yet you chose to create a narrator who is a woman. What prompted this decision? What challenges did you face writing with a female voice?

As a man I've always been fascinated by the differences between the ways men and women think and behave. It was always a challenge for me to guess the next move of my female counterpart. I do believe that the female thought process is more complex and sophisticated, and this does not always work in women's favor. This is why I enjoyed the challenge of writing with a female voice. Then, of course, I had female friends criticizing my work. So it could not reach the kind of sophistication that my male brain was capable of, but I am very happy with the result. Do I have a better understanding of how women think after this exercise? Maybe. Then again, maybe not. Many times the female thinking process still confuses me.

In the novel, Enric writes to Cristina, Oriol, and Luis that they must enjoy the journey, that their time solving the mystery together as they did when they were children will be the true treasure. Is this philosophy something you believe in as well?

Yes, definitively. I spent part of my life fighting and working very hard for things that I believed would bring me happiness. And in most cases, once I had achieved my aims I realized that I was the same person, not any better, not any happier.

You ask yourself, why all that suffering? And then you realize that life is what happens when you were busy trying to accomplish these supposedly important goals. The really important thing is life itself, and I believe that many times we could achieve the same aims if we stopped to enjoy life and were aware that happiness only happens in the present.

Cristina's ruby ring sounds both beautiful and frightening. Was there a real piece of jewelry that inspired you to create this cross-projecting, dream-inducing bauble?

Yes, there was. At the start of the novel you read that King Philip IV of France, the executioner of the Templars, accused Pope Boniface VIII of having a ruby ring in which he held a demon as prisoner. King Philip was not the only one to have made this accusation. Cardinal Pietro Colonna said that he had heard the pope talking with the demon of his ring, at times assuming the voice of a child or of an old and terrible man.

The ring in my novel is a literary time machine that allows me to have historical characters interacting with present ones. But there exists a lot of literature on the subject of objects that keep feelings and images of the past and persons with special gifts of clairvoyance who experience the power of these objects.

Partly due to the success of *The Da Vinci Code*, the Knights Templar have enjoyed a revival of interest. Why do you think people find the time of the Crusades and its religious orders so fascinating?

I feel that people nowadays are looking for spirituality, because of a questioning of traditional religion, and the era of the Middle Ages was a very spiritual time. It is also a time that fascinates us because history became legend and legend history.

Enric set up elaborate treasure hunts with clues for his three favorite children. Have you ever participated in a treasure hunt? Do you enjoy such mystery games?

I did play this game as a kid, where I would hide fake maps in very old furniture and tell my brother that the document was found accidentally. Then we would start a treasure hunt. It was great!

Some readers may be disappointed to find that the treasures they imagined—chests of gold and precious jewels—are long gone by the time Oriol and Cristina uncover the location of the Templar legacy. Why did you choose to depict the remaining treasure as gruesome religious artifacts rather than gleaming riches?

I find it very enlightening to learn the relative value of things. For the Templars, the saint's relics had the greatest material value, while gold would be merely a means to achieving their highest aim of keeping the Holy Land Christian. The value of things is very relative. If you were in the middle of the desert, you would prefer to be carrying water rather than gold.

Cristina has fond memories of seaside summers spent with her childhood friends, whose families were also friends several generations back. Did you have a similar experience as a child in Barcelona?

Unfortunately this was not my case, because my family did not have the means that Cristina's had. But some of my friends enjoyed these long summer vacations and I listened with some envy to their wonderful memories.

The question of Oriol's sexual preference seems to carry a lot of importance, and not just because it could interfere with Cristina's hopes for a romantic reunion. How has nontraditional sexual expression manifested in Spanish culture over your lifetime? Have you seen significant changes? How do you think the "scene" in Barcelona compares to that of similar big cities in America, such as Cristina's New York?

The novel is dedicated, in memoriam, to Enric Caum. He was a friend that lived and died in the same way that Enric, Oriol's father, did in the novel, and that character is partially inspired by him. He belonged to a generation in which being gay in certain social groups was a shameful thing. The real Enric chose to hide his sexual preferences from his parents.

Today the situation has changed a lot. There are those who may still choose to hide their homosexuality, but in Spain it is usually not only displayed publicly but also celebrated. There are gay districts, gay magazines, gay parades, and gay everything. I think that this is a very similar situation to that of large U.S. cities.

Ultimately, Cristina learns that enjoying every moment of the journey is the only thing that is important. What was the journey of writing this novel like for you?

Writing this novel from the ground research to the creation and publication of it was a great journey, which I fully enjoyed. Then all of a sudden it started to run out of stock in stores and to climb the bestseller charts. Can you imagine? And then it started to be published in such exotic languages that I couldn't even recognize my name on the cover of the book! It has been an unforgettable experience.

After immersing yourself in the history of the Knights Templar, you must have formed an opinion about its legendary treasures. What do you think: Is there a Templar treasure still to be discovered? Why or why not?

The destinies of the Knights Templar were very different, depending on the country they lived in. In France, they were taken by surprise and accused of treason by the king, and on the same day at the same hour all Templar strongholds in the entire country were assaulted and taken. The knights had no time to hide. In other places such as Portugal, they were under the king's protection, so they changed names and kept their possessions. In Castile, now part of Spain, they surrendered to the king without a fight. I think they could have hidden something.

But definitely in the part of Spain where my novel happens (Catalonia-Aragon, then a separate kingdom), they knew what was coming and got ready for it. So if they had time to prepare the castles to resist the siege of the king for a full year, wouldn't they have had the time to hide the riches that they knew the king was looking for? Of course they did. And there are documents showing the disappointment of King James II when at the surrender of the Templar castles almost nothing of value was found. I do not know if there is any Templar treasure still left to be discovered, but it is very probable. And I would be thrilled to have the map.